# BLUETHROAT MORNING

# BLUETHROAT MORNING

## JACQUI LOFTHOUSE

BLOOMSBURY

First published in Great Britain 2000

Copyright © 2000 by Jacqui Lofthouse

Permissions:
T.S. Eliot, *The Hollow Men* from *Collected Poems 1909–1962*, Faber & Faber.

I am indebted, also, to the following books:
*Cley*, Peter Brooks, Poppyland 1984.
*Cley Marsh and Its Birds*, Billy Bishop, Bernard Bishop (eds), Hill House 1996.
*Dover Beach*, Matthew Arnold, 1867
*Notes on the Birds of Cley, Norfolk*, Henry Nash Pashley, C. Frost 1992.
*Remember*, Christina G. Rossetti, 1862

The moral right of the author has been asserted

Bloomsbury Publishing Plc, 38 Soho Square, London W1V 5DF

A CIP catalogue record is available from the British Library

ISBN 0 7475 4834 X

10 9 8 7 6 5 4 3 2 1

Typeset by Hewer Text Ltd, Edinburgh.
Printed in Great Britain by Clays Ltd, St Ives plc

## ACKNOWLEDGMENTS

I am extremely grateful to all those who have commented on earlier drafts of this novel: my agent, Caroline Dawnay; my editor, Alexandra Pringle; Marian McCarthy; Helen Castle; Stephanie Hale; my mother, Iris Lofthouse. My thanks, also, to Dr Paula Johnson, David C. Winston, forensic pathologist and James Peries for the discussions we have shared about this book.

Most of all, again, to David Lewis, for his critical insights, his patience and love.

*for David*

Last night, I saw her smile again. I saw her, laid out like a stunned angel, pale and cold. From the door-way, where I stood, I could almost believe that she was sleeping; merely holding her breath. Only she was shrouded, of course. She lay on the high, white table, draped in a winding sheet, her head and her bare feet protruding. Before I approached, I could not discern her expression; I merely noticed her pallor. And something else – her hair had grown. Her wiry dark locks became more unruly each time I visited her. It was unnatural. Her hair spilled out across the table: a final act of defiance.

Each night it seems that hours pass before I find her. I know she is withdrawing. Before long she'll elude me altogether and I'll give up the search and let her vanish peacefully. Only not yet. Not when she smiles like that. I have to grasp the meaning of it and only then will I let her slip away; allow the image to dissolve.

It always begins like this: I am lost. I wander along empty corridors with high, white walls. The place is a maze and she is encased at the heart of it in a white, windowless room. All sounds are absorbed as if I am not there at all, my presence an illusion. Only the sight of my hot breath on the air convinces me it isn't so. I am strangely calm because I know that I always find her. Eventually I will enter the room where she is waiting.

Last night, I was astonished by her perfection. It was as if death had distilled her; taken her essence and refined it. It was more than physical, but it was reflected in her physical being. The bare soles of her feet faced me; not a corn nor a callus remained. They were unblemished. Too delicate now to walk the earth.

Then I came closer. I noticed the soft folds of cloth across her breasts, her shoulders. Her throat was still, her face impenetrable. Now I could see: there was nothing corpse-like about it. It was as if

I

she were suspended between life and death. Her skin, bleached by the light, was thin and fragile. Her closed eyes did not flicker. There was no colour in her cheeks. They were bloodless, as were her lips. Almost as if she were a figure of her own imagining. She might lack the usual charms of life and lust, flesh and blood, but what matter? Here she was immortalised. She did not contemplate her own imperfections. At last she had achieved her aim and so at last she smiled.

I leant across her, the first time that I have dared to come so close. I realised I cast no shadow. I hesitated. I had wanted to kiss her but something about her seemed to forbid it. That smile. So slight, yet it illuminated the face, creating a superiority, a transcendence. It unnerved me because it made her unknowable. I had known her, once, but that was over. She had moved into a separate sphere and I could not follow her; we would remain divided.

# 1

'C OME ON, HARRY. WHEN was the last time you got yourself
laid?'

'None of your damn business.'

'You're a handsome man. It's a waste.'

'I'm fine. I do have a social life. Give it a rest, won't you?'

It was nearing the end of the summer term. We were drinking at
the White Swan, a quiet pub, for the City, tucked away in a side
street, the perfect antidote to a day at the school. We sat outside on
wooden benches, glad to be in the shade on such an evening,
sheltered from the sun by the tall buildings that surrounded us. The
air was thick and smoggy but there was no traffic here, and though,
as usual, we were skirting around the issues that really mattered, it
was always good to have a beer with Richard, especially now, when
everything seemed so precarious, when I was putting off decisions
for as long as I could.

'I mean it's no life, is it?' he said. 'All this fending for yourself.'

'I have friends. Really. I'm quite all right. Anyway – why the
sudden concern?'

'Friends aren't the same thing. You need a woman. Alison – well,
she wouldn't have wanted you to pine.'

'It didn't look that way to me.'

He paused. We didn't normally talk about Alison. Perhaps he
wished he'd kept quiet.

'All right. But you shouldn't still be suffering. It's over six years.
Don't you think you should give yourself a break?'

I hardly knew what to reply. Richard and I had been pals for
years, but though I'd always sensed he understood me, we seldom
talked intimately and this frankness surprised me. I suppose he must
have known that things were about to change because he said
things that had clearly been on his mind for some time.

I was fifty-eight years old, but I'd decided, at last, to take early retirement from King Edward's. I felt it was time to get away. I had vague ideas about travelling but, as yet, nothing was planned. The future was a blank.

I emptied my glass. Normally Richard would be getting home now, back to Richmond. Frances, his wife, would be expecting him. But that night he offered me another and I wasn't about to refuse.

When he returned from the bar, he got straight to the point.

'There's somebody you should meet. A friend of Frances's. Why don't you come for dinner?'

I grimaced. This wasn't like him.

'Come off it, Richard.'

Since Alison, I hadn't met a single woman who moved me. The last thing I wanted was for someone else to do the choosing. And besides, I didn't want this. Richard continued regardless. The woman was called Madeleine. She was devastatingly attractive, he said, and very bright. A widow.

'You are kidding?'

'A young widow. Early forties. Used to be married to a business analyst, so you'll be a breath of fresh air. She's a freelance journalist,' he said, 'does a lot of work for *Vogue*. She's perfect for you. Well read. Very classy.'

'Richard . . .'

'No objections. You'll adore her.'

I knew that he meant no harm. Yet his words unsettled me. It was not something that I could rationalise but, given my hatred of the press, his suggestion that I meet a journalist was naïve and hardly tactful. Doubtless this woman was only in it for the story.

'I can't meet a journalist. Especially not a fashion journalist.'

'Paranoia, Harry. You haven't met the woman. Anyway, she doesn't write about fashion. Trust me, won't you?'

'I can't do it. I'm sorry. Anyway – she doesn't sound my type.'

'Rubbish.' Then he softened. 'Come on. She's dying to meet you. Nervous as hell, actually. Think of your reputation.'

'Why so keen?'

'Women are intrigued by you. You know that.'

'They're only interested because of Alison.'

'What does it matter?'

'I'm not trading on Alison's reputation to get myself laid.'

4

He smiled wearily.

'Look – the thing is, Maddy's a nice woman. And it would be good to have you over.'

In the end, I let myself be persuaded, though I knew it was a mistake. Did I guess, even then, that this dinner should be avoided at all costs? I agreed because it seemed important to Richard. In all the years that I'd known him, I'd never visited his home. This was a gesture of friendship; his way of saying he didn't want us to grow apart once I left.

'It'll be a bit obvious,' I told him, 'if you've no other guests.'

'What?'

'Your match-making.'

'Maddy's all for it. It's fine.'

Of course she was. A perfect scoop. I was determined to give her nothing.

If the invitation had come from anyone other than Richard, I would have turned it down. But I valued his friendship too much. In the years since Alison's death, he'd been the only person at work that I'd been able to trust. The others professed their sympathy but it was hollow posturing. It was easier to believe the press than the words of the man accused.

I'd been teaching at the school – King Edward VII in the City of London – for fourteen years. Perhaps I should have expected more from my colleagues. It's amazing what one grows accustomed to, over time. At first, naturally, they had been sympathetic. I had a month's leave and several of my fellow teachers sent me flowers and cards. But after I returned, I detected a certain hostility; false smiles, and awkward silences whenever I walked into the staff-room. They couldn't relax in my presence, and though their attitude eventually softened, things were never the same after that.

Richard's friendship made the whole thing bearable. Richard and, in a strange way, the boys. For them, I acquired a certain status. I saw well-thumbed copies of Alison's novel sticking out of their school-bags and sometimes I'd catch them reading it, before they had a chance to hide it away. I had become a mysterious figure with hidden dimensions. They weren't at ease with me, but they listened harder too. If I recited poetry in class, my voice embraced a

5

silence, hitherto unknown. I had gained a new respect, undeserved and oddly comforting.

But of the staff, only Richard took my side. We were the school hypocrites, claiming to deplore private education, but unable to leave the place. Before Alison's death, we'd even gone out a few times – Alison and I, Richard and Frances. Frances had seemed rather insecure in Alison's presence, but Alison worked hard to convince her that she was no different from anyone else, that her fame, her looks, were unimportant. Afterwards, I felt closer to Richard, though it wasn't something we discussed. He seemed indifferent to my public image, and though I never bared my soul to him, I knew he understood. He didn't treat me with kid gloves either. He knew how to make me laugh.

From the beginning, Richard and I clicked. He was an art master, an eccentric figure, tolerated because he produced results. He was often to be seen wandering the corridors, sleeves rolled up, revealing his bony, pale arms, lightly spattered with paint. He towered above the groups of boys who followed him like sheep, while he was lively, forever pointing things out – a high lead window, a pile of rubbish beneath the stairs. He had only to give the word and they'd be cramming themselves into small spaces with their huge sketch pads, drawing furiously and freely as he had taught them, their grubby hands clutching 3B pencils, their arms sweeping broadly across the page, inevitably smudging their efforts.

What impressed me about Richard was his ability to get away with things. Since Alison's death, I felt that I was being watched, that people were waiting for me to make a mistake. Only in my teaching could I afford to be a little daring, to stretch the boys' minds. Outside the classroom, I conformed to the image they expected: gruff, distant, moody. It was easiest like that.

For Richard, it was different. People were fonder of him, as if they knew that without him the school would turn stagnant. Perhaps it was simply Richard's manner; his nonchalance, his blasé approach. Even his voice charmed them. It was high-pitched, but his enunciation was crisp, his tone distracted. The truth is, Richard affected such innocence that the Head, who had one set of rules for the rest of the staff, made another for him and treated him indulgently. Richard *gave* the boys something, I think, opened new doors. I tried, also, to show them new possibilities, but sometimes I struggled to convey my meaning. Even in the drama classes, I felt certain that they never saw beyond the stage and the proscenium arch. Their imaginations never took flight and I knew that I must accept some blame for that.

At lunch-times, I often walked in the churchyard adjacent to the school, not an expression of my excessive morbidity (though it was perceived as such), but because it gave me space to think. Occasionally I saw Richard with his sixth-formers. He'd be squatting beside them, as they sketched the tombstones and the undergrowth. Richard didn't want them to miss anything, and when I peered over their shoulders often I saw things differently too. I noticed things which I had completely missed: the complex patina of mould on the stones, the bright flecks of blue on a caterpillar's back. Once, in Richard's absence, I came across a newly dug plot and was shocked when I saw two of his boys entrenched there, grinning up from the open grave.

'We have to view the world from new angles, Sir,' they explained.

And I stayed, watching them, as they drew the trees that loomed above them, and the distorted lines of a crumbling angel.

On the night of the dinner, a Saturday, I anticipated the worst, yet couldn't bring myself to cancel. I left home early, perhaps desiring to get it over with, but when I got close to Richmond, I decided to delay my arrival for as long as possible. I took a detour around the Green and pulled up in a vacant space. It was a fine, hot evening. Young people had gathered on the grass to drink and smoke. It looked inviting and I decided to stay for a while. I bought a beer in the pub and sat on a bench. A group of foreign students were sitting close by and one of them picked up a guitar and began to sing. It was an unfamiliar song, but it reminded me of the folk-songs I'd heard a long time ago in Andalucia with Alison. We had been staying in a mountain village, high up, apart from the world. We hadn't known each other long. She was still thin, wasted, recovering from her illness. She had wanted to go somewhere where she might not be recognised, where we might get to know each other in peace.

I remembered her now, in the guitar-bar, watching, listening, her expression rapt. The man playing was silver-haired, tanned, dressed in white. His face was creased in laughter as he sung. We were a little drunk perhaps. I had feasted on paella, sucking the meat from crab-claws, encouraging Alison to do the same. But she ate little that evening. Her pleasure came from the air, the music. 'He knows how to live,' she had whispered.

The boy with the guitar had the same easy abandonment. He threw the instrument down when some friends arrived and leapt up to greet the girls with hugs, kisses. I couldn't stay to watch. Instead I took a walk along the pavement, past the theatre, the library, then back, in a full circle, until I reached the red-brick town houses that seemed to characterise this place. Inside, lamps were being lit, curtains drawn. A middle-aged couple emerged from one, the man in black-tie, the woman in a ball-gown that revealed her stringy neck. She fiddled with her pearls and I knew it was time to go.

I drove along the leafy streets with a sinking feeling inside. I could never live in a place like this. It was too ordered, too cosy, with the great Victorian houses set back from the road behind hedges, willow-trees, high walls. When I arrived, on time, I was told that 'Maddy' was running late. The atmosphere seemed stilted. Richard didn't seem himself and Frances was flushed and anxious. I could barely believe it. Everything, from the linen-swathed table to the smouldering church candles, made me feel I was about to take part in some elaborate ceremony, not have dinner with friends. The plates and napkins were brilliant white; the cutlery and the glasses shone. In the centre, a vase of Madonna-lilies seemed to expose themselves. Ill-chosen, their scent was at once sensual and funereal.

In fact, I had not anticipated the ostentation of Richard's lifestyle. The first duet from *Lakmé* was playing, which added to the general air of opulence. Though I was impressed, I was also shocked. I'd been living pretty humbly myself, which made the grandeur seem all the more incongruous. I had always admired Richard, yet now, oddly, I pitied him. It didn't suit him, being here.

'Are these yours?' I asked. I indicated the paintings on the dining-room wall.

He nodded. 'I did them about twenty years ago. When Frances was pregnant with Helen.'

The pictures were unexpected, seemed unrepresentative of the Richard I knew. As we talked – about the end of term, my retirement, about Madeleine and how I was bound to like her – I was distracted by what I saw. The walls of the dining room were painted pale primrose, and the paintings formed a bold contrast. They were interesting: huge flowers, like O'Keefe, only more vibrant; gorgeous yellows, intense blues. Yet I felt dissatisfied. I'd always assumed that Richard's work would be more daring. These images seemed controlled in their extravagance and an unkind thought crossed my mind. Was our school eccentric quite what we believed him? Was he not, rather, as conservative as the next man? Did he simply like to play the bohemian?

At once I dismissed such an idea. Richard had always been honest about his wealth: 'I'm a kept man, Harry, Frances is loaded.' Yet somehow I had imagined a scruffy house, desks spilling books, shelves crammed with artefacts. I'd imagined he'd have an eye for peculiar antiquities, but home for Richard was more like something from *House & Garden*. The room was designed to please the eye – nothing was out of place. I looked at my friend through fresh eyes and wondered, was he happy, living like this? I thought of his manner with the boys, his enthusiasms, his passions. Were they not being strangled here? Did these possessions not weigh him down?

When the doorbell rang, I was almost relieved. All I could think of was the need to be civil. As she entered the room, my immediate thought was that she was not as I had imagined her. She was much smaller than I had expected: small-boned, small-breasted and thin, with painfully white skin and jet-black bobbed hair. Her narrow lips were painted red and her eyes had a look of uncertainty, a saving grace. Still, in her plain black dress, I thought she had the air of a diminutive witch.

She held out her hand and gave a light but firm handshake. Her fingers were ice-cold.

'Pleased to meet you,' she said. Such control, even in the voice. I wondered what Richard was thinking when he had imagined us together.

As the conversation began, as yellow wine trickled into long-stemmed glasses, I watched Madeleine, attempting to discover her motives. I had no energy for small-talk, no desire to impress, yet I knew that even if I revealed nothing I would reveal something. Though I tried, I could not get my knowledge of her profession out of my head. Her presence forced me to think of Alison, because I knew that Alison was on her mind. And what would she make of me? If I were moody it would confirm my reputation. If I made jokes, she might write that I was callous. My hands clenched the base of my chair and only the earnest look on Richard's face prevented me from leaving. I felt a vague terror begin to grip me but I knew I must mask it.

'Richard tells me you're planning to leave the school . . .' she said, as Frances placed the starters before us, small slices of white mousse, studded with pink. 'This smells wonderful, Frances – what is it?'

'Smoked salmon terrine. My mother's recipe.'

'Mmm.'

'Yes,' I said. 'A week to go.'

'Will you miss it?'

'I'll miss Richard,' I said. I swallowed the first mouthful of mousse: frothy and pungent. 'And the boys.'

'And he'll be missed,' Richard said. 'It'll be a great loss.'

Of course, Madeleine knew better than to ask about Alison. But her style of conversation was interrogative; she revealed little about herself. *Paranoia, Harry*. I remembered Richard's words. Still, I felt exposed. I didn't want to answer questions. Perhaps, somewhere inside myself, I was aware of my own vanity, the foolishness of my distrust. In every question, I could see a trap but Richard and Frances were blind to it. Furious at myself for agreeing to this, I felt I was betraying Alison. Though I made an effort to give nothing away, I constantly wanted to bite my tongue, regretting even the smallest detail I revealed. The questions were becoming more blatant.

'Is it true that you're planning to write a novel?'

'Where on earth did you get that idea?'

'I'm sorry. I didn't mean to offend you. You know how it is. People talk.'

'They talk rubbish,' I said. 'It's not true. Categorically not true.'

Perhaps Richard realised then his mistake. There was no flirting here, just a furtive battle. Frances stood up and removed our plates.

'That was lovely,' Madeleine said, though her voice was subdued. I helped myself to wine, a Chardonnay which I didn't much care for, but I kept downing it all the same. I was reluctant to speak.

Then Richard said, 'Harry's planning a trip to India, isn't that right?'

It was painful to hear him try so hard.

'Yes, at least I think so. In October.'

Richard refilled Madeleine's glass. Then Frances returned with the main course – tiny poussins trussed up with string, nestling beside baby vegetables on a large white platter. The sight made me feel faintly sick. I wasn't in the mood for dissection.

I must have had quite a lot to drink because what I remember most about that part of the evening is the difficulty I had wrestling with the miniature bones, the inadequacy of my knife and fork. There was some chat between the women about Madeleine's latest assignment, but I was barely listening. I was thinking – it's all so frivolous, so fucking frivolous. Why doesn't that woman just come out and say what she's thinking? But then I must have lost track of the conversation, because suddenly I realised I'd been asked a question. I looked up blankly.

'Sorry?'

I cursed myself for being drunk.

'You used to have a garden, didn't you?' Madeleine said.

A garden? No. Alison's garden. Alison had a garden. They seemed to take my anger for confusion.

In an attempt to help me out, Frances said, 'Maddy's very keen on gardening. She's just bought a house here, a few streets away.'

But I was no longer listening. Another memory took hold. The tiny plot of land at the back of our house in Clapham, overhung by trees, a dank, wet place, with a pond smothered by a tangle of waterlilies. Even in the drier areas, towards the back, the monotony of grey stone was broken only by foliage and the occasional white bloom: roses, a foxglove or two, clematis that strayed over the fence. She used to sit out there in the evening – when her head was too full of words, she said, and she couldn't write another thing. She'd sit by the water's edge on the wooden bench – I could see her from the kitchen window. She'd close her eyes and tilt her face to the sky, seeming so distant, so self-contained. Once I asked her what she thought about out there. I thought it might be her past, troubling her. But she said it was nothing; that she was listening to the leaves.

Now I couldn't talk any more. I watched the candle-wax fall on the table-cloth. Like Alison I closed my eyes, wishing that the world would melt away. I can't do this, I thought. I can't talk to these people. The colours of Richard's paintings were imprinted on my eyelids and I imagined them dripping from the canvas. The flowers began to blur. I opened my eyes. Still they waited for a reply.

And then I was saved. In the door-way, a girl appeared. She stood a little hesitantly; an uninvited guest. I turned to look at her. She was very tall and thin, rather boyish. She wore jeans and a loose white shirt with a blue sweater slung around her hips. Her pale, blonde hair was tied back from her face. And I nearly didn't believe in her. Her face seemed so familiar to me, I was convinced I had imagined her.

# 2

T O MAKE CLEAR THE significance of this apparition (for that's what she seemed), I must return, of course, to Alison. It will prove difficult, this attempt to unravel the past, but I am certain it is necessary. The story has been told too many times by people who are strangers to me. If I fail to set it down, there's no doubt the truth will wither.

So I begin with the facts that define my story. They are so well known I need hardly repeat them here, but do because it helps, I find, to pare down a story to the bare bones, to see it for what it is. It happened over six years ago. Six years since my life was irreversibly changed by the suicide of my wife.

She took her life on a cold and unforgiving January morning in a small village, Glaven, on the North Norfolk coast. My wife, Alison Bliss, the novelist and former fashion model, whom everyone claimed as their own. Her first book was published in a blaze of publicity, but more than that, it was good. Her work blew the lid off the industry that had made her name. She was only thirty-two years old; one might have thought she had everything to live for. But on that morning she went to the beach alone, removed her clothes and waded into the icy water. Her body was discovered a few days later, on sand-dunes several miles away. Within hours the story had reached the press.

For several weeks after her death, I was beset with requests for interview. One journalist, Gordon Hake, was particularly persistent. I knew him of old and I refused him, as I refused them all. I could barely speak to friends, let alone the press. They were dark days; days best forgotten. But what I failed to understand was the effect of my silence. I had not realised that while I mourned, a myth was growing which encompassed not only Alison, but myself as well. It has plagued me ever since.

No doubt I should have seen it coming. I shouldn't have dared hope that they would tire of the story. Some might say that in marrying Alison Oakley, I relinquished my right to privacy. But I can't see it like that. When we first got together, I told her, over and again – it doesn't have to be like this. You don't belong to them. I believed, perhaps naïvely, that we could control their game. I was wrong, of course.

Alison had always been the media's darling. How could she not be? She was one of 'ours', a British girl who had made it big. Since her reluctant discovery in a student bar at the end of the seventies, to the height of her career on the international modelling scene, Alison had always been public property. By the mid-eighties, she could not wear a dress without a full press post-mortem on the subject. She could not be left by a lover without the nation commiserating. So it was hardly surprising that later, when everything went wrong for her, the press were at her heels. It happened several months before I met her. First there were the rumours. It was easy to ignore of course: models are supposed to be skinny. But when, quite suddenly, she dropped out of sight, cancelled all her engagements, it could no longer be denied. Alison had been admitted to hospital, suffering from anorexia. But even there, she could not be left in peace. Hake was on the scene, naturally, and a pack of others, crowding at the gates, inventing excuses to get inside. She retreated to her room, and there, alone, she broke down. There were whole days, she said, where she remembers nothing but sobbing and being sedated when it all became too much. She told me about the pain of eating, how the nurse would bend over her with a spoon and how she gagged when the broth touched her tongue, how she could not swallow it. The process of recovery was slow, but it was there, in the small, white room of the hospital, that Alison picked up her pen at last.

When I met her, she was still emaciated. She had not returned to work. There have been countless theories as to why a woman like her might have been attracted to Harry Bliss and it will serve no purpose to add my own to the list. When I first saw her, I did not even recognise her, though what difference that made, I can't say. In her former life, I am sure our paths would never have crossed, but Alison's doctors had suggested she take some time out to pursue what mattered to her. So it was that she visited the National Gallery and it was there that I found her, standing, amazed, before a Piero.

Alison had always been a difficult character to pin down, but the last place one might expect to meet a famous model is before a Renaissance painting. In fact, it had never been easy for the press to couple her fame with her intelligence. Yet before her career began, she'd embarked on a degree in English. She had never finished it. Somehow, the modelling thing had caught her and she hadn't known how to escape. Only her illness, in the end, forced her to fall back on her first love, a love of words.

When she published her novel, *Sweet Susan*, Alison had desired, merely, that she be taken seriously, that her story be heard and recognised. But it was not so simple. After her silence, following our marriage, the press had nothing to go on, no story remaining. She had been, in effect, taken from them and they didn't bear that lightly. Later, the novel made her public again, relaunched her, which caused her enormous distress. That summer, her photograph was everywhere. She was the cover-girl feminist, the palatable voice of dissent. Nobody had expected her novel to be good and the critical acclaim took the gutter press by surprise. Her novel broke rank. True, there was nothing new in her revelations: everybody knew about the drug-taking, the anorexics. But *Sweet Susan*, with its painful honesty, the intimacy of its language, did more than most novels can ever hope to achieve. It changed attitudes.

Her later suicide made no sense. The note she left for me, at her rented cottage, explained nothing. *I'm so sorry, Harry. Forgive me. I can see no other way*. It was discovered by the police, shortly after her body was found. They were tipped off as to her identity by a group of students on holiday. They had witnessed her arrival at the beach several days earlier, just as they were departing, after a night of frivolity. They had recognised her, of course, and had thought her behaviour strange. At the cottage, the police found the note immediately. They must have had a cursory look about the place, but they were satisfied with what they found and left shortly afterwards. There was a delay of several hours before they contacted me. Alison's words offered no consolation.

That one who had argued so passionately for life, should take her own, left everybody reeling. Had it not been for Gordon Hake, however, my own role in this might have been less explosive. Hake, a journalist with a grudge I did not, at the time, understand, took it upon himself to blame me for her death. This was, in any case, a shock story, but it also provided a ripe topic for debate: the self destruction of the female artist. Like every good story, it was not complete without a villain. And who better (oh, familiar tale) than the silent husband to fill that role?

Looking back, I suppose I might have acted differently. Had I spoken to the press at the beginning, they might have found some sympathy for me. Hake's version of events might have been rewritten; some other truth might have emerged. But for Hake, my silence was a perfect opportunity to slaughter me in prose. After a couple of weeks, his story gained weight, solidified. I ought to have sued, but at the time it was the last thing on my mind. Backed up by opinions from one-time 'friends', Alison and I were cast in our roles. There was one person, of course, whom they failed to find, but this didn't deter them. Apparently an American woman had been seen with Alison in Glaven, but nobody knew who she was and nobody, not even Hake, could track her down. For me, this was a source of tremendous frustration. I could not help but hypothesise what this woman might reveal about Alison's state of mind when she killed herself. I often wondered, if this woman were found, might my innocence at last be established? But it was a futile fantasy. While Alison herself achieved near-iconic status, I remained the one who had destroyed her, the bitter, thwarted husband who quashed her creativity.

The situation was not helped by the discovery of the manuscript. A fortnight before her death, Alison had left our home in Clapham to do some writing and research. She was working on a second novel, set in Glaven. The new book had proved difficult to begin with, but now it was flowing and she appeared happy when she left. The day following the discovery of her body, Alison's landlady cleared her property from the cottage and found the remains of a manuscript – the unfinished novel – lying in the grate. Overlooked by the police, most of it was burnt to cinders. Only a few pages had escaped.

Naturally the landlady jumped to the inevitable conclusion: that Alison had burnt the manuscript before committing suicide; destroyed it, just as she had destroyed herself. For the press, however, this self-effacement was unsatisfactory. They began to flock to Norfolk in ever-increasing numbers and it didn't take much for an alternative version to be conceived – that I, her husband, had done this deed. It was Hake who first suggested this. Naturally, he didn't exactly allege that I was guilty, but he made it clear that I had been seen in Glaven before the landlady discovered the manuscript and confirmed the fact that the cottage had not been locked. I had visited Glaven, that evening, to collect Alison's belongings, but according to Hake, I might also have found time to obliterate the last traces of her work.

All this was merely the beginning. I comforted myself with the thought that this, at least, would soon be over, that before long they would lose interest in Alison. It was a foolish hope. As the weeks passed, the stories proliferated. A few grains of truth were scattered about, but mostly what was written was pure fantasy. I had never harboured an artistic ambition, but I was portrayed as a frustrated writer, consumed by jealousy. While I had supported my wife financially – they wrote – I had made her pay by constant criticisms of her work; she always looked to me for approval but I never gave it. And when she left for the rented cottage on the Norfolk coast, apparently I had known she was suicidal, but I let her go.

It was Hake, of course, who spearheaded this campaign. His was a presence that had haunted us throughout our marriage, though to me he never seemed so sinister as he appeared in the days following her death. My refusal to be interviewed was assumed to be a tacit admission of guilt, but in fact my distress made explanations impossible. I wanted to keep the real Alison to myself. The private words that passed between us, the tenderness, the elaborate map of her anguish – these were all that I had left.

All the rest, they took. There were days when I could barely remember her face and yet her face, once again, was omnipresent, in every newspaper I opened, the endless catwalk shots, the spoils of the paparazzi. Oddly, these images troubled me the least. I barely recognised Alison Oakley, the model. It was the images of Alison Bliss, the novelist, that disturbed me. There were three photographs which the press obtained fairly swiftly, used to illustrate more serious articles about my wife. Yet even these, of a woman I should have recognised, somehow alienated me from her memory. The images became almost emblematic – this was the author of *Sweet Susan*, not the woman I had married. They were frozen images, repeated obsessively, and the more I saw them, the harder it became to conjure the real thing; her infinite, subtle variations of expression.

But in truth I cannot forget her. I have my own photographs and in these she is familiar and expected: the Alison I knew, not the manufactured woman, the publisher's dream. Still, in these others, the triptych I call them, she will remain, always, unknown.

The first photograph – the one they printed next to her obituaries – is the one I like the least. In this she is brooding, her dark hair loose about her shoulders. It is the 'official' photograph, from the dust-jacket of *Sweet Susan*. Here she is serious, intense, gorgeous. Her mouth is closed (concealing that famous smile) and her brown eyes smoulder. Objectively she is most beautiful like this: air-brushed; mysterious. But I am not objective.

The second is more like Alison but I dislike it because it is posed, not *her*. Again it is a professional image from her publisher's portfolio. She sits at a typewriter. Her hair is tied back. She wears horn-rimmed glasses and squints at the page, biting on a pencil. This one is used for articles that proclaim her feminist credentials. It is the serious image that validates their claims, and though I dislike it, it moves me more than the first. I can imagine a moment afterwards when she swivels in her chair and breaks into a smile as I enter the room, interrupting her work. Not that it was always so. Often I was banned from her study and any interruption would infuriate her. Generally I knew when to stay away.

The last photograph is used most frequently. It hurts me most because it was taken on our honeymoon in Greece. This one is used to show her vivacity, to emphasise the tragedy. Alison is sitting in a taverna, tanned and laughing, throwing her head back with pleasure. Her hair is dishevelled. The thin straps of her dress reveal her bony shoulders. I used to love that photograph but now I can't. It's been appropriated. I used to look at it and remember our morning in bed; how I ached still from the intensity of our love-making. I remembered the taste of ouzo on her tongue and the funny story she was telling me. But now these memories are tainted. This is a universal loss, the photograph seems to say, a common loss. I have no special claim on it.

There is another photograph, however, that the press have failed to discover. It is not a photograph of Alison, yet it lies at the heart of my story. It is an old family photograph. I remember the evening when Alison discovered it.

It was October, three months before her death, and winter was creeping in. Alison had been between novels for over a year and the strain was beginning to show. When she had finished *Sweet Susan*, she had been exhausted. After such intense work, she had found it difficult to begin writing again. She was afraid because she had no ideas and though I told her to take a break, let it come naturally, she was unable to do so. Instead she spent her days leafing through old books, jotting in notepads, searching for inspiration. But there was none. And yes – she was hard to live with at that time. I found it difficult to understand her. Even the success of her first novel failed to make an impact. She said that she didn't deserve it. That the critics were wrong and swayed by her fame. What did it matter anyway, she said, if she couldn't produce another?

That day in mid-October, I returned from school with only a couple of hours to spare. It was Parents' Evening so I wasn't in the best of moods myself. I walked into the sitting room, hoping she might be a little better, but I was disappointed. Alison was curled up on the sofa, hugging herself, crying silently, all her grief poured inwards. I put my arms around her.

'What's the matter, love – what is it?'

I stroked her hair, dried her tears. She looked at me, couldn't bring herself at first to speak. But eventually she told me.

'I'm quitting, Harry.'

'What?'

'Writing. I've had enough.'

'Allie – we've talked about this . . .'

'I know. I know I said it was what I wanted. But I was wrong, OK? I'm not up to this. Maybe I was happier before.'

'What? As a model? Allie, you ended up in hospital . . .'

'OK. OK, but at least I was good at what I did.'

'Good at starving yourself! At flashing a smile you didn't feel.'

'I was successful.'

'You've just found success as a writer.'

'Yes. Because I was once Alison Oakley.'

'Because what you write is good.'

'No. It's not. Right now I can't do it at all.'

'You will. What you write has value, Allie.'

She hesitated. I knew that she wanted to be a writer and I felt the need to guide her back, to remind her why she wrote. I sensed there

19

was something deeper troubling her, but I couldn't guess what it might be. We had been talking, the previous evening, about money. Was this at the root of her distress? I still refused to pay off the mortgage with her modelling money. It was an old argument, but one we constantly returned to. I couldn't face the idea of living in a house that had been paid for by her suffering. I wondered, now, if I had been too harsh.

'When you were writing *Sweet Susan*,' I said, 'you said you'd never been happier.'

She paused, remembering.

'But that was then. Right now, I don't know if I even *want* to write any more.'

Her lips trembled. It all felt rather unreal: the cold, grey afternoon; the steady hiss of the gas-fire.

'I'll make some tea,' I said.

When I returned, with the steaming mugs, she had recovered a little and ventured an unconvincing smile. She had changed recently. She wore no make-up and her face looked drawn again. Her eyes were bloodshot and her skin dull. Her hair hadn't been washed for days. She hadn't been out of the house for a while either. The idea of being photographed worried her. And I remember being very afraid. I had thought that I could make her happy, but suddenly I felt I was losing the battle. The idea of therapy crossed my mind. She seemed quietly intent on self-hatred.

'You know, you couldn't stop writing if you tried,' I told her.

'Yes I could. I don't *need* it. It's a bloody disease.'

'Exactly. You can't get rid of a disease just like that.'

'I can cut out the diseased bit. I'd be normal then, wouldn't I?'

'Allie, love, do you *want* to be normal?'

'Yes,' (and again she was almost crying) 'I do.'

'Really? I can't see you living a mediocre life.'

'Because it's no longer possible. They won't let me.'

'Try to remember what we have.'

'But I'm all dried up, Harry.'

'If you'd just rest.'

She shook her head in disgust and gave me a look of such hatred that it was all I could do not to cry myself. She was so self-obsessed. I couldn't bear to see her destroying herself like this. Little beads of sweat appeared on her forehead and I wanted to wipe them away. I had to talk to her. Repeating the same lines, like incantations.

'You're an artist. It's what you've always wanted.'

'I don't want it now.'

'You want to be like me? To get to my age and have nothing to show for it?'

'You've got so much to show for it.'

'Like what? Nothing. I've created nothing. No books, no paintings.'

'No children.'

Again an attack on herself. She'd had two miscarriages earlier in our marriage and couldn't face the idea of trying again.

'I never said I wanted children.'

'It would have been nice though, wouldn't it?' she said.

Like her, I could not forget. When Alison first told me she was pregnant, the whole world had seemed to expand, to ripen. We saw a different future then. It was astonishing how many dreams could be built in a couple of weeks. They were common dreams but no less fragile for that. A large house full of children, dogs and cats. Only two weeks later, everything changed. I awoke, early, to hear her retching in the bathroom. She was dressed in a blood-stained silk nightdress, one hand clutching her stomach, the other the toilet-seat. Her small body was convulsed and I stood at her shoulder, uttering useless words of comfort.

She blamed herself, her past, even now.

'Fucking anorexia,' she said. 'I'd rather be you, Harry. Think of all those kids who'll remember you.'

'Everything I do is second-hand. You're doing something that matters. You mustn't quit.'

'And if another whole year passes and I still haven't written anything worthwhile, will you say the same thing then?'

'It won't happen,' I said, though the thought had begun to trouble me.

That night I didn't want to leave her. At that stage I wasn't sure what to make of her depression. I had visions of coming home to find her unconscious on the bed, a bottle of sleeping pills by her side. But I dismissed these thoughts as stupid. Allie was down, but her breakdown was in the past. I told myself – her worries are natural, everything will change once she gets an idea. I'm still not sure how convinced I was. Sometimes it was difficult to remember how she used to be. When we met, she had been so interested in things. She had hungered for knowledge.

Later, I helped set up the school hall for Parents' Evening. Richard was there too. We were shifting furniture, but he sensed my mood and we didn't speak much. I remember being irritated by the squeaking of table legs against the parquet and by the smell of the place – that odd combination of polish and the vague tang of fried cabbage lingering. The hall, without the boys, seemed vast and full of echoes – like a deserted church. I peopled it in my imagination, could almost hear the mournful voices of the boys singing hymns. But now it was empty and I wanted to be home with Alison.

I always hated these occasions: the fraternising with uptight mothers and fathers with a bee in their bonnet about discipline. The fathers never seemed to like me. I knew it from the way they looked at me, could read their thoughts. 'Who does he think he is, this Bliss chap? Does he think he's something special, just because he married Alison Oakley?' They all wore grey business suits – I couldn't tell them apart. Or else they had changed after work into smart trousers and thick-knit jumpers.

Myself, I have the look of a shabby academic. My clothes look forlorn, my jacket crumpled. The women liked me a little better. I have a cynical look that some find attractive, though no doubt the Alison thing affected their view of me also. And I think they liked the idea of a man who reads poetry. But not the fathers.

Whenever I had a moment to myself, my mind strayed back home. There were no easy answers. If Alison were to stop writing, she would be unhappy. But equally, her work caused her distress. What she needed was some great injection of confidence, but if the recent prizes and reviews hadn't done the trick, what would? Though her modelling career had near destroyed her, she could not change the impact it had made. She was so used to being watched, I thought, that she felt a failure when she was alone. She needed the literary equivalent of the camera's gaze.

I watched the women who milled about the hall, such ordinary women by comparison, behaving as if they owned the place. What was it about the upper classes that they must speak at such a volume? The shrill tones of these women, the arrogant grunting of

22

the men. I thought of Alison. I had always been drawn to her. It was her seriousness, her sensitivity, her impatience with trivialities. She had no time for people who were not serious. Perhaps it was the excess of frivolity of her former life. Frivolity appalled her. Now she gained pleasure from words, from ideas, from art, from music. The world of fashion had not suited her and she knew she could not go back to it.

The lights were out when I returned. It surprised me because it was only ten; she never went to bed so early. I had already convinced myself that something was wrong but tried to stay calm as I walked quietly upstairs. I opened the bedroom door and there she was in half-light. She had left the curtains open. The room was cold, condensation on the windows. As I entered she murmured, 'Harry?' But then she was asleep again. I moved to her side. There were no pills on the cabinet; her breath was even. She never slept easily, was always the insomniac, and it gave me pleasure to see her rest. I had overreacted. Her eyelids flickered, the rhythm of her dream. I kissed her forehead and left the room.

In the kitchen, the fluorescent light stuttered. I lit the gas to boil some water. The click of the cat-flap was followed by a mewing at my ankles. The cat was always greedy.

'All right,' I said and took some milk from the fridge. I couldn't stand the sight nor the smell of cat food. That was Alison's job. 'All right.'

I took my tea into the front room and sat down on the sofa. Alison had been smoking; she'd hidden the ashtray but I could smell it, though she had left the window open. On the coffee table was a book of verse, Christina Rossetti, and I was about to pick it up when something else caught my eye which made me smile. On the desk in the corner was a huge cardboard box. I hadn't seen it in years: a box of photographs, once my father's. My mother had given it to me after his death.

Now the box was falling apart. I was reminded of a grey Sunday, shortly after we were married, when Alison had asked to see the photographs and we'd spent hours looking at them. She hadn't wanted to stop. The photographs spanned about sixty years, from my great-grandparents' time to my own childhood. Alison had been fascinated by the oldest ones and asked a whole series of questions to which I had no answers. Although I enjoyed looking at the pictures, I had never taken a great interest in my ancestors. The Victorian images had blended together in my mind. I couldn't differentiate between them. I preferred the sepia photographs of my parents when they were young, and the black and whites of their friends that I remembered from my childhood. There were several of my father, clearly drunk, with his arms wrapped around the shoulders of his drinking partners. I remembered a picture of my mother before her hair turned grey, when it was still a vibrant red and she was bedecked in a lurid green evening dress that plunged to reveal her enormous bosom. It surprised me that these images returned to me so vividly. For years I had not given these photographs a second thought.

But now I was curious about Alison. What had inspired her to look at them again? I didn't even know where she'd found them. Switching on the lamp, I realised that she had left one photograph out, a Victorian photograph, one of several encased in silver frames. No wonder that the box was falling apart. It couldn't take the weight.

The photograph stood in a pool of light and I bent down to examine it. It was a delicate thing, the frame elaborately moulded, a honeysuckle pattern around the edge. Dust had settled in the crevices, but Alison had wiped the glass clean and I looked at the image as if for the first time. It depicted a man in formal dress, standing in a garden. Quite apart from him, a little way back, by a gateway, was a younger woman, his wife I guessed, and a boy, their son. The garden was in flower – hollyhocks and lupins – and the man seemed out of place there. He held a top hat and was wearing a dark suit with a white cravat. The woman wore a pale, tight-fitting dress that emphasised her slimness. She stood at a slight angle; you could make out the curve of her bustle.

There were several of this type, small, framed family groupings, but I realised immediately why Alison had chosen this one. It was strange that I had never noticed it before, perhaps because five years ago it was not so plain. Now it was clear that the man resembled me. Like me, he was tall, though less broad across the shoulders. Our faces were remarkably similar, but perhaps his mouth was different, his lips thinner. When I looked at his eyes however, I might have been looking at myself. They were dark as mine with the

24

same heavy brows, the same frown lines between them. His great beard made him seem a caricature of myself, his heavy jaw an exaggeration of my own.

I felt uneasy, seeing this former version of myself. Already I suspected his identity. It was cold and I reached up to close the window, but the wind caught it and I ended up slamming it, with more force than I had intended. I listened to see if Alison stirred but heard no movement.

I sat on the sofa holding the photograph. I felt humbled looking at it, stripped of my uniqueness. To see this Victorian so like me – I felt I was nothing but an amalgamation of genes, a repetition of what had been before.

Still I wondered why Alison had sought out this photograph. It didn't fit with her earlier despondency. Unless – and then it was clear – unless she was looking for inspiration. Had I ever truly believed that she would quit? I was confused and examined the photograph again. This time I tried to see it as Alison might. But the more I looked, it seemed, the less I saw. I wanted it to have a meaning, even as I realised it might have none.

I settled back into the sofa and the cat leapt up beside me; I stroked her absent-mindedly. I was probably being ridiculous but I wondered if there were something obvious that I was missing. The first thing I noticed was the great disparity in age between the man and the woman. He was clearly in his fifties, yet she, perhaps, no more than twenty. Why then had I assumed her to be the boy's mother and not his sister? There were twenty years between Alison and myself; perhaps that explained it. The woman in the photograph was tall and thin, with pale hair. Her face was a perfect oval. Although she appeared uneasy, she looked directly at the camera. There was a stiffness to her pose, indeed to all their poses, typical of the Victorians, but something about the woman's character transcended that. The way she stood suggested deference to the man, yet there was defiance in her expression.

As I looked closer, it struck me how arrogant the man appeared. He was smiling, but I was convinced it was ironic. There was a smugness and a secrecy about him that I did not like. Though I had a good idea of his identity, I could not relate to him. It was just a hunch, but I was sure that I was right. This must surely be my great-grandfather, and the boy, his son, the grandfather that I never knew. It should have affected me more perhaps, but I felt removed from them. I told myself – that boy – your father's father – but it seemed unreal, impossible. I looked at him as one looks at a stranger and I looked at the man and could only wonder why he was standing so apart from his family. I felt no real connection. I was curious, but that was all.

Eventually, I'd had enough and I replaced the photograph. It was impenetrable – simple as that. It's possible that I even fell asleep as I sat there; I don't remember. But it was a half hour later when the cat disturbed me, digging her claws into my shins. I shook her off and went upstairs, wanting to speak to Alison but without the heart to wake her.

# 3

T HE NEXT MORNING, SATURDAY, I awoke alone. It was 8am. Too much sunlight already. I could hear music downstairs, some kind of innocent folksy wailing. I turned over and went back to sleep.

An hour later I heard the door open and Alison came in. I'd just about opened my eyes when she kissed me, smelling of shampoo and perfume. She hadn't been so tender in weeks.

'Hello, Harry,' she said.

'Hello.'

I'd seen such changes in her before and I was always cautious. Still, I was glad. Her skin was glowing, her hair glossy. She'd put on a little mascara and a dusky lipstick. In spite of the cold, she wore the blue silk dress that I'd bought her the previous Christmas.

She's back, I thought. But for how long?

'I've been awful, haven't I?' she said. I had to smile. It was always like that. 'D'you want some breakfast?'

I nodded.

'Come on then!'

She pulled the bedclothes away, laughing.

'All right,' I said. 'All right. What time did you get up?'

'About six.'

'Six!'

I remembered other mornings when she'd been up at six, brooding. But this was different.

Downstairs, I realised Alison was serious about being better. On the table was a vase of daisies, a newspaper and a pot of fresh coffee. There were chocolate croissants in the oven and she was taking orange juice and little tubs of yoghurt from a carrier bag. For the moment, I accepted it. It was what she wanted. I let her play the good wife because it pleased her. It pleased me too. She was taking such delight in everything that I didn't want to question it. At least not yet.

'You're looking gorgeous,' I told her.

I had almost forgotten that she could be so beautiful. For months she had taken no trouble over her appearance, but now she was bright and alive. I wanted to kiss her, to make love to her, only I knew it wouldn't be right. There would be time for it, later. So I sat at the table, unable to take my eyes from her as she took the milk from the fridge, poured the coffee. Such simple things, but she was flirting with me, surely? There was a fluidity to her movements. The dress clung to her legs and I watched the swing of her hair and the way she smiled secretively, her lips closed. It seemed impossible that this was the same woman who only yesterday I had seen crying, her face swollen and blotchy.

She took the croissants from the oven and sat down, cradling her coffee, watching me eat. We were silent for a while, didn't know what to say. I began to flick through the paper, but I couldn't concentrate.

'I know it's been hard for you,' she said.

I couldn't think how to reply. She struggled with her words.

'I know I've been selfish.' Again a pause. 'And self-obsessed.'

'Don't be too hard on yourself.'

'I don't know how you've put up with me.'

I took her hand.

'I'll always put up with you.' It was true. Even when things were really bleak, I had never considered walking out. 'But it's no good for *you*, the way you've been. You have to get out of it.'

'I know. I know. But I couldn't help it. I couldn't *see* a way out.'

'But you can now?'

She considered.

'I've got an idea.'

'Anything to do with an old photograph?'

She seemed relieved.

'You saw it?'

'You left it out for me, didn't you?'

'Not really. Just for myself.'

She spooned some sugar into her coffee, stirred it as she spoke. I was already worried. I couldn't see how a photograph could change her mood like this. I was convinced she would be disappointed.

28

'I'm not sure I can explain it. Last night, after you went out – I was in the kitchen, cooking some pasta. I was really tired, you know?' I nodded. 'I don't know why I thought of it but I remembered that photograph.'

'You've seen it before?'

'Years ago – you remember.'

'I don't remember that one.'

'But the man looks so like you – that's why I noticed it.'

'It made an impression? All that time ago?'

'Mmm.'

Now she was preoccupied with her croissant. Crumbs were falling from her lips. She laughed. I liked to watch her eat; it was a good sign.

'But you don't know why it came to mind?'

She shook her head and wiped her lips with the back of her hand.

'I suppose I must have been thinking of you. You've become so like him.'

'I never saw it. Not before.'

'But it's so obvious, Harry!'

I shrugged.

'Now,' I said, 'are you going to tell me about your idea?'

I wanted to know what she was thinking, but she took my question at face value and seemed to weigh it up. Then she shook her head.

'I can't. It'll spoil it.'

'Not even a clue? You're not writing about me, are you?'

I didn't want to be flippant. Something serious was at stake here. It was painful that we were so light. These words meant nothing. I wanted to be certain that she was all right. Was it for real, this transformation, or was she merely fooling herself or play-acting? How else might the change come so suddenly? If it were inspiration, how could she be sure of it? Surely an idea isn't enough? I could foresee trouble. What if she could find no form for that idea? What if the idea died on the page?

'No. I'm not writing about you.'

Yet I felt implicated.

'It's the woman. It was the man I thought of, when I went looking for it, but when I saw it again – there was something about her.' She paused. 'But I don't really want to talk about it.'

I was used to her secrecy. It was pointless to push it. Her state of mind was delicate and it wasn't worth the risk. There was nothing new about this. During the first four years of our marriage, when she was writing *Sweet Susan*, she never spoke to me about the work. She wanted me to wait until it was finished. It was a difficult subject. I knew that she was writing about anorexia. So much of her past was being uncovered but, strangely, she had remained cheerful with me, almost as if she were able to cut herself off from the pain that I later witnessed in the writing.

But I, also, had often felt cut off. Though I could not put my finger on it, I sensed that she was hiding from me. No matter how good it felt to be with her, no matter how happy she seemed, I wasn't seeing the whole of her. There was a secret part of her that I hadn't been able to reach. Once I got furious and we had a great row about it. It came to nothing in the end. It was just a lot of ranting (on my part) and crying (on hers). But afterwards, she tried to explain it.

'It's got nothing to do with our relationship. It's the work. The work is affected if I speak about it.'

Still I felt isolated. Already she was different from the woman I had met by the Piero. In the early days, she had craved my approval for everything. Now she had the confidence to work alone. She was deeply involved in her writing and I was left outside. Occasionally I wondered if I knew her at all. But I had listened to her arguments, and I tried to understand.

'It's all so fragile. My ideas only grow because they're grown in confinement. D'you see? If I spoke about them, you'd want to make some comment.' Even if I countered her, she would never give in. 'If I talk, it loses something – its intensity, urgency. When I'm writing, it's like . . .' She paused, searching to find words that would express the truth. 'Like something unfurling, something that's been cooped up in darkness, seeing light of day for the first time. That's what makes it fresh. It's the first telling of the story, the words are unrehearsed. It's rawer, purer like that.'

And I knew this was a part of her. Didn't I enjoy it, after all – being married to a writer? At least, the idea of it. I had to take the rough with the smooth.

All this I remembered as Alison told me, once again, that she'd rather not talk. Still, there was a conflict within her – the wife versus the artist. It pained her. She had the artist's selfishness, but she had a desire to conform as well. Always, since the early days, she would interrupt her writing day to make sure the house was clean when I returned from work. I told her it wasn't necessary. I would have been content living in a pigsty, if only she were happy. But she insisted on these stupid rituals. As a teenager, it had been her responsibility to keep the house in order. After the years living in luxury, not lifting a finger, she seemed to enjoy returning to these household tasks. No doubt it was her mother's influence.

Alison's mother had died of breast cancer when Alison was ten years old. She, also, had been a writer, a minor poet, but she had given up writing after her daughter was born and devoted herself to the family. After her death, Alison's father, a successful banker, had gone to pieces. They lived in a rather isolated spot, out in Suffolk, and for a year or two Alison was looked after by a series of nannies, while the house began to deteriorate and her father became increasingly reclusive – managing to hold on to his job, but only just. He tried to be a father to her, but he never recovered from the death of his wife and he simply did not know how to relate to his daughter.

I only met her father twice. He came to our wedding and to Alison's funeral. He was a peculiar character – tall and gaunt; rather wasted-looking but well dressed and terribly polite. Yet he never looked directly at me. His eyes shifted nervously about the room. There was an immense sadness about him, I thought, as if some great emotion were welling beneath that well-groomed surface. It seemed that there was something important he wanted to say. But somehow he could not bring himself to say it. He had been silent for too long perhaps.

I never told Alison how I pitied her father because she could not forgive him for failing her. It was hardly surprising. Often she had conjured images for me and these partly explained her sense of isolation. I could imagine how it was for her after her mother's death. In the evenings, she would feel herself alone in the house, yet her father was in his study, a cold and mildewed room, poring over books of poetry as if he might find something there that he had lost. She barely knew him really, though by the time she was fourteen the nannies had left and it was Alison who cared for the house and cooked. They were, the two of them, still in mourning. But they could not bring themselves to mourn together.

I never had any doubt of the effect on Alison of her mother's death. Her mother was well-regarded as a poet, though she had not produced sufficient work to merit any great status. But Alison idolised her mother and regarded her as a thwarted genius. Sometimes she blamed herself for her mother's failure to rise to her full potential. She had seen the dates on the final poems – December 1959. Her best work, written in the days leading up to Alison's birth. Alison was no fool. Her birth had stopped her mother's pen and she faced this fact with a certain defiance. A part of her reacted against her mother's retreat into domesticity and child-rearing, determined she would not follow in her footsteps. But I also suspected she felt inferior. She told me that before she began her modelling career, she had already written several stories, but she had destroyed them, certain that her prose could never match the power of her mother's. Perhaps that explains why she was so easily side-tracked. She avoided what she most loved for fear that she might fail.

It wasn't until I married Alison, however, that I understood the full implications of her upbringing; the oddities of her behaviour. I had never known, before then, the true meaning of the word ambition. In all those years when she was idolised wherever she went, inside she felt a fraud. She was too intelligent to believe that she deserved the adulation she received. She knew it was an accident of genetics and nothing more. Her only real desire was to write something she might be proud of. She wanted to live up to her mother's promise but, more than that, she harboured a secret ambition: to write something that would out-live her.

Alison's early success had a quite devastating impact. After that, it seemed, she couldn't bear to fail in any aspect of her life. It was invisible to others, who saw only her social self: how bright she was, how beautiful, how interesting. Yet few realised that this social ease was no more than a carefully constructed façade, made necessary by the desire to be loved. Her social life was one aspect of her all-consuming perfectionism. It extended to her work, her marriage, her friendships. She was so desperate to make up for the time that she had lost that she would make reading lists for herself and work through them methodically. At times it seemed there was nothing that was not a chore for Alison. Even 'pleasure' and 'relaxation' had their allotted places in her carefully scheduled timetables.

But on that day, after she had discovered the photograph, she was a picture of contentment. I remember her, licking chocolate from her fingers, appearing totally carefree. I had decided not to push her about the photograph, though I was irritated to be left out. The woman who so fascinated her might have been my great-grand-mother or, at the very least, my great-aunt. But she seemed happy and I didn't want to upset her.

'So,' I said. 'What are your plans for the day?'

I expected her to say that she was writing.

'I thought we might go out.'

I couldn't believe it. When was the last time we'd simply 'gone out' on a whim?

'Where did you have in mind?'

'Maybe the Tate? The Pre-Raphaelites perhaps? I haven't seen them in over a year. Are you up for it?'

'Of course.'

It was all very bizarre. She acted as if her behaviour were completely normal and I treated it as such. But I was astonished. She had no idea, the effect it had on me to see her like this – interested in a world beyond her own imagination.

Outside, the raw autumn light dazzled us. Alison still wore the silk dress, but with an old cashmere jumper and her long black coat and boots. She had a purple velvet scarf about her neck and she walked slowly, a slight smile on her lips, her skin blanched by the sunlight, her nose reddening at the tip. We didn't speak but the silence was not uneasy. We crossed Clapham Common. There was a frost underfoot and a vast blue sky above us. The frost had somehow stilled everything. The voices of children seemed distant, the sound of traffic far away. I remember now the balding trees and the high, bright sun. Alison walked a little ahead of me, she thrust her hands deep into her pockets, and I thought – she looks as if she's stepped from the pages of a Russian novel. Sometimes, now, I think she knew it. I think she was playing a role; she saw herself as the tragic heroine. Perhaps I'm being ridiculous when I imagine that all along she courted death, she was preparing for it. When I remember her, how she looked that morning, I tell myself – wasn't it clear it couldn't last? Didn't you see it, Harry? She was brittle, so fragile, so unreal. Yes, like a character from a fiction. I could never imagine her growing old. By taking her life she has crystallised herself, cheated somehow on mortality.

We took the tube to Stockwell and changed to the Victoria Line. It was crowded and we stood close together, uncomfortable in the heat. People were watching her, of course. They always did. But she made sure she caught no-one's eye and she clung to the overhead handle as the train rumbled between stations. When it stopped, a man stumbled and she was pressed closer to me. She laughed and I circled my arm about her waist. Then she moved her face closer to mine and whispered.

'There's something I want to tell you. When we get there.'

I nodded and kissed her forehead. At last, I thought. She's going to talk.

Outside, the wind was bitter. We walked along Millbank and Alison was quiet, looking out across the river. I was grateful when we were inside, descending the stone staircase into the basement cafeteria.

We bought cakes and warmed our hands on the coffee cups.

'So?' I said.

'So what?' she teased.

'You wanted to tell me something.'

'Oh yes. That.'

'Well?'

'You know how I hate talking about my work.'

'You don't have to, Allie.'

The light was dim. All around us, the chatter of voices, but I focused on hers. She unwound her scarf revealing her pale neck, a bluish-white. There were moments, like this, when I wondered, once more, what she was doing with me. When I became aware of the anomaly of our marriage.

'No – I want to tell you what I've found out.'

'What do you mean?'

'I spoke to your mother last night. She told me a couple of things. She said you didn't know.'

'Know what? Why have you been speaking to my mother?'

I knew I shouldn't be defensive, but I couldn't help myself. Why did she speak to my mother, but not me?

'I wanted to ask her about the photograph. Do you know who they are – those people?'

'I have an idea.'

She hesitated.

'You're being very mysterious, Allie.'

'I want to write about them, but I wasn't sure what you'd think.'

It was getting crowded in the café – everywhere the sound of clinking crockery and the buzz of conversation. A group of teenage girls were giggling close by and one approached and asked for Alison's autograph. She shook her head impatiently and the girl scuttled away, embarrassed. Alison leant across the table. Her voice was low.

'Well?' she said.

'What's this all about, Alison? How can I say it's all right when I don't know what you're talking about?'

'Last night, when I found it, the photo was just as I remembered. Only the man looked even more like you than before. It made me feel nervous.'

'Why?'

'You'll laugh – but I just had a feeling about it. I knew it would lead to something.'

'A novel, right?'

'Mmmm.'

She nodded.

'Go on.'

She pushed her cake aside, reached in her bag for a packet of cigarettes.

'Do you mind, Harry?'

I shook my head. Alison always felt guilty about smoking. But she lit up anyway, frowning as she inhaled.

'I was trying to figure it out,' she said. 'I mean – I kept looking at that girl – and there was something wrong. It was as if she wanted to say something. There was a story there – I was sure. When I closed my eyes, I could hear her voice, but I couldn't make out the words. I know you'll think I'm talking crap, Harry, but that's how it was. And the man looked so like you – I thought perhaps he was your great-grandfather.'

35

'I thought so too,' I said. 'But I'm not sure.'

'It is him. Your mother told me.'

I felt uneasy. I was glad to know I had been right, but anxious about Alison's plans. I wasn't sure that I wanted her to write about my ancestors. I wasn't sure that they were safe with her.

'And you want to write about the woman?' I said. 'My great-grandmother?'

'No. She's not your great-grandmother.'

'So who?'

'I hope you don't mind. I opened the frame.'

Actually, I did mind. Though I had never taken an interest in my ancestors, Alison's interest fuelled a new possessiveness. But I held back. I knew what would happen if I even hinted at my irritation. She'd falter, get upset. The story would go by the wayside, and we'd be talking about 'us', analysing what made us squabble. Alison couldn't take even the *idea* that I might disapprove of her. So generally I took the easy way out and kept quiet or simply lied.

'Of course not,' I said. 'So?'

'I couldn't stop myself – I had to find out. I had this idea that the photograph might not have been touched since it was first put there. When I opened it, there was an inscription.'

She paused. Perhaps it was genuine emotion that stopped her, or perhaps she was more of an actress than I gave her credit for. She wanted me to ask the question. She stubbed out her cigarette and a waitress whipped the cups from beneath our hands. Our cakes were untouched. We moved apart, embarrassed by our intimacy. Maybe we were lingering too long. There were people hunting for tables. But I looked back at Alison, leaned towards her again.

'What did it say, love?'

'I guessed it was there – you know? Before I opened it. It was faint but I could make it out. It said, "Charles Bliss, his new bride Arabella, and George. Hope Cottage, Glaven. May Day. 1889." '

I hadn't expected to be affected by this, but it was moving. To hear the name – George. My grandfather's name. He died before I was born. My father refused to talk about his family, but I knew from my grandmother that George Bliss had survived the Somme but had died shortly after the war. Perhaps he was distracted by his memories. He was knocked down by an omnibus and died from his injuries. He survived the trenches but was defeated by modern transport.

36

'Harry?'

'My grandfather. That small boy.'

'But the woman. Arabella. His second wife. Not your great-grandmother at all.'

I was ashamed – I'd missed her point.

'Don't you see?'

'I'm sorry, love. It's stuffy in here, isn't it?'

I couldn't concentrate. I didn't know what she meant.

'It was their wedding day! Can you believe it from the way they look? The way he's standing so apart from her?'

'No. It does seem odd.'

I remembered the pale flowers in the woman's hand and the unlikely formality of their clothes. But my reaction was false. I still couldn't see what she was getting excited about.

'He looked so self-important, didn't he? And she just seemed unhappy.'

I knew she was disappointed by my reaction. She wanted me to feel as she did but I felt nothing. I was preoccupied, wondering *why* she identified with this woman. I wasn't sure that I liked the idea of it. Why did it intrigue her after all? Charles Bliss seemed a reflection of me – was that the reason? But I had nothing in common with that man except my genes, and it was foolish to pursue it. There was, after all, something she hadn't explained.

'Why did you call my mother?' I asked. 'You said there was something I should know.'

'I found another photo of Arabella. It was loose in the box. It said, "Arabella Bliss. 1870–1901."'

'She died young.'

'That's why I called your mother. I wondered whether she knew anything.'

'And?'

'She seemed a bit edgy.'

'Why?'

'Something about your father . . .'

'But she did talk?'

'After a bit of cajoling, yes.'

'So?'

'She didn't know much.'

'But she knew something?'

'Yes. Your grandmother had told her about it apparently,' she said. 'You know she brought up your father pretty much on her own?'

I nodded.

'She was a strange one,' I said. 'I do remember her. A tiny, quiet thing. Dad always used to say that his father married beneath himself. I always thought that pretty odd, considering how proud he said he was, to be a working man.'

'I wish I'd known him,' Alison said. 'Despite everything you say.'

'Believe me. You wouldn't have liked him.'

She shrugged.

'So come on!' I said. 'What did my mother tell you?'

Her expression changed then. Her smile faded.

'It was about Arabella. According to your grandmother, George was traumatised by what happened to her. He always spoke about it. He never forgot it.'

'What? What didn't he forget?'

'Apparently Arabella killed herself. One night she just walked down to the edge of the beach and took off her clothes. Can you believe it? She left her whalebone corsets on the beach and walked into the sea.'

Alison looked at me then but her eyes flickered nervously. I took her hand, kissed her fingers. But I'd long ago given up trying to discover my father's secrets. I felt removed from all that had happened in the past, and though it was an intriguing story, I couldn't understand the intensity of Alison's reaction.

'Come on,' I said. 'Let's go and see some paintings.'

She nodded, picked up her scarf and bag and stood up. We would not talk of this again.

Only later did the image of Arabella come to haunt me. Knowing that my wife had followed in her footsteps gave that face a meaning that it never possessed, for me, in her lifetime. I often wondered, if I looked closely enough, might I find in that photograph an answer to my questions?

But on that day, as we ascended the stairs to the gallery, its significance remained obscure.

# 4

T HE GIRL STOOD IN the doorway. Pale, blonde hair; the face so familiar to me. And for a moment I thought I was hallucinating. It was as if I'd been waiting for it. Every day since Alison's death – every vague and insubstantial day, like living underwater – it had been leading to this. I can't help but give it this significance. Sometimes I imagine that the whole damn story spun into being the instant that I saw her. Before we even exchanged a word.

I realise now how odd my behaviour might have seemed. Madeleine and Frances must have given up expecting an answer to their question. But however it seemed to them (perhaps they interpreted it as lechery), I was in a state of confusion. I thought she was a vision, a projection of my imagination. I truly did not think that she was real.

I can't say how long my delusion lasted. For as long as she was complicit perhaps. A second or two, no more, when she stood very still, watching me. I was aware of her before the others, and I stared back. She was flesh and blood, but briefly I lost confidence in the concrete world. She looked at me, frankly, entirely without artifice. Despite her modern clothing, it was Arabella's face. Then she looked away and walked into the room, and I saw her face was not the same at all. There were many similarities – the pale hair and skin, the shape of her face, her eyes – but she was not identical. I had invented her to fit my desire.

The girl approached Richard.

'Can I have a drink, Dad?'

It was like a slap in the face. 'Dad.' Richard had spoken about his daughter. She was nineteen. A first-year drama student.

'Oh, I think so. Why don't you join us, Hels? Get yourself a glass. Madeleine, you've met Helen before, haven't you? But not Harry. Harry, this is my daughter, Helen.'

39

'Hello Helen,' I said.

'Hello.'

She glanced at me as she poured the wine. Clearly she knew who I was. I often get such a reaction from young women – a kind of guarded interest. I watched her also, still shaken. There was indeed something of Arabella about her, not just the shape of her face and her colouring, but her body too – the androgyny of those long limbs, her slight lankiness. But then I looked for the points of difference. Her hairstyle, naturally – tied back, her fringe across her eyes. Like Arabella, she had a small, bird-like face, but Helen's nose was sharper and her lips were generous where Arabella's were small and prim. The resemblance could not be called uncanny, but neither could it be denied.

'It's nice to meet you at last,' I said.

'You too,' she replied and continued to stare at me. I was disarmed. It seemed more than the usual curiosity. She raised her glass, but didn't look away. And in embarrassment, I looked down at my hands. They looked so old suddenly: the raised veins; the coarseness of my skin. 'Has Dad been boring you about his painting?' she asked.

'Not at all!' I smiled. Something about this girl had moved me. I was a touch drunk.

'No,' Frances said. 'Harry was going to tell us about the garden he used to have.'

'Oh.'

She pulled a face.

'Exactly,' I said. I wanted to intrigue Helen, to make her take notice of me. 'And anyhow, that garden's out of bounds.'

'Out of bounds?' Madeleine said.

'I don't like talking about it.'

I was irritating her with these dead-end answers. Madeleine glimpsed at Frances, who in turn gave me a look, half apology, half vitriol. I didn't care. My mind was elsewhere. After Alison's death, I had tried to forget the photograph. But Arabella's face appeared to me in dreams. Perhaps it was not surprising that I saw it now. Perhaps I had been looking for it.

I found myself divided. There was a part of me, present, in the dining room, aware of Frances and her embarrassment. But all that seemed very distant. I focused on Richard's daughter. I was already in awe of her. She had an easy grace, seemed possessed of qualities that the rest of us had lost. She was differentiated from us, not only by her youth, but by something more subtle. Even the way she walked, it was unselfconscious. She didn't track herself like we did.

I watched her furtively. I couldn't help but make comparisons. The faces of the other women were dredged in make-up. Madeleine, her skin dry and powdery, perfect but unreal. And Frances, she wore make-up like grease-paint – her red cheeks bloomed right through it. Even as I thought it, I could hear Alison's voice. 'Christ, do you *have* to always judge women by their appearance? You can be so bloody sexist.' But I can't help it, Alison – I thought – you should know that. I can see it your way, if you like. 'There's a particular beauty in maturity' (the feminist text is raging in my head). I can see it that way. It doesn't stop her skin from being so white. Like yours was. So fresh and so unflawed.

The others attempted to ignore my behaviour. They were talking about the play that Helen had just performed in, a Pirandello. But I heard only Helen's voice. It was not affected like her mother's. A clean sound, a certain lightness. She glanced at me, as if willing me to speak. And Madeleine, a credit to her profession, had noticed. A false smile played on her lips and her expression was condescending. I tried to avoid her eyes, because every time I looked at her, I imagined her wanting to question me, to invade my thoughts. I was remembering Gordon Hake, the days following Alison's death and the terror of those early-morning hours. Waking in sudden panic, seeing the empty space beside me. Then watching the telephone, taking it off the hook even, but knowing that he would reach me soon, by some means, any means, reminding me, again and again, that she was gone.

Now I looked at Helen and instantly I felt calmer. I didn't want to take my eyes from her face, for fear that my darker thoughts might return, but the longer I looked, the more I knew I was being observed. Madeleine must have seen me, and I imagine she raced to the inevitable conclusion. I considered explaining myself, but I was cautious. I had told nobody about Arabella Bliss. The press were ignorant of the connections between her death and Alison's and I wanted to keep it that way. So I would be taking a risk, if I mentioned the photograph.

Or would I? There was no need to reveal its significance. And what of the alternative? If I didn't explain myself, who knows what the others might think. Helen sat opposite me and I leant towards her.

'You know,' I said, 'it's odd.' She looked interested. All eyes were upon us. 'If I've been looking at you strangely, you must forgive me. When I first saw you – you reminded me of someone.'

She laughed in a self-deprecating way.

'Really?' said Frances. 'Who?'

'Sounds very mysterious,' said Richard. 'Don't tell me – some old flame?'

'Oh shut up,' Frances said. She was always embarrassed when Richard talked like this. She thought I would take offence. Madeleine was silent. Her cool stare rested on me.

'It's nothing,' I said, already regretting it. 'I don't know why I mentioned it.'

'But now you *have* . . .' said Frances.

'It's just a similarity.'

'Who to?' Helen said.

'Somebody in an old photograph. A family heirloom.'

Helen looked confused and I realised how stupid I had been. It would be impossible to explain the significance of this. But I continued.

'It's a photograph of my great-grandfather with his wife.' I tried to laugh it off. 'You look a little like her, Helen. A small coincidence.'

Helen gave me a certain look. She was trying to appear cynical, but something betrayed her, a slight trembling of her hand about the glass. I could tell that she didn't want to like me. Perhaps Richard sensed her unease because he guffawed loudly, an unnatural reaction, a split-second too late.

'Your great-grandmother?' he said. 'I don't think she'll thank you for that!'

'No – not my great-grandmother.'

Without warning, Madeleine stood up. She pushed her chair back abruptly, made a gesture to excuse herself and left the room. It surprised me. There was an interesting situation building here. Surely she would not want to miss it? Frances said 'oh dear', and followed her.

I was thrown by this. Was it my fault? At least, so far, Alison had not been mentioned. That alone was a blessing. Richard did his best to lighten things up.

'So then. What is all this, Harry? You are joking?'

'No. But it's not important.'

'Who was she then?' Helen said.

'My great-grandfather's second wife.'

'Even better!' Richard said, but Helen threw him a look which silenced him.

To be honest, I didn't care, at that moment, what Richard thought. He was edgy, but I don't think even he knew quite why. Perhaps only Madeleine had read the situation accurately.

'Can I see the photograph?' Helen asked.

'I don't have it on me,' I said, mocking her a little.

'No. But you'll show it to me?'

'Of course. If you like.'

Then Frances reappeared, and Madeleine behind her, wearing a raincoat.

'I'm off, I'm afraid,' she said. 'Cab's on its way.' Her lips were pursed; she was trying to hold off a frown. 'I've a busy day tomorrow.'

I was surprised by her reaction. It didn't fit with her earlier behaviour. But I smiled and waved.

'What's the matter?' I asked Frances when she had gone.

'Oh . . . it's nothing.'

'It didn't seem like nothing. She didn't even stop for coffee.'

'Well.' She paused. 'To be frank – you were so obviously uninterested in her. She was humiliated.'

'Humiliated?'

'Yes. She was a bit tearful in the kitchen. She did try very hard, you know.'

I realised at once what I had done. I hadn't, for a single moment, even considered that she might be genuine. A genuine lonely heart. Not with all that guile and make-up, the designer dress, the vampire smile.

'You're not serious?'

'Of course I'm serious.'

Her irritation put me on edge. Frances was accusing me. I imagined the work that had gone into the evening: stuffing the poussins; arranging the flowers. All to fix Madeleine up. I had proved a disappointment. Instead of flattering Frances's friend I had focused my attentions on her daughter. I glanced at Richard.

'I don't suppose Harry can help it, darling, if he didn't find her attractive.'

43

She seemed to relent, though I knew it was simply good manners.

'I'm sorry. I just thought . . . oh, I shouldn't be so rude, but you did seem offhand. She was rather terrified of you, you know.'

'She's a journalist,' I said.

But for the first time, the response seemed inadequate. I thought of the small, strained Madeleine in the back of a cab, going home to an empty house.

'Journalists are people too,' Frances ventured gently.

'Yes. Perhaps some of them are,' I replied.

For a moment I saw myself quite differently. As others must see me. What happened to Alison, it had distorted me in some way.

'Well, if you ask me, he had a lucky escape!'

Helen's irreverence broke the gloom.

'Honestly!' her father said.

'If you will try and fix him up with *Maddy*.'

'What's wrong with Maddy?' her mother asked.

'She's foul. And neurotic.'

'You don't know her,' said Frances.

'I don't have to know her. Just look at her.'

'Helen, you really must learn to look beyond the surface. Just because she's not a supermodel, you know, doesn't mean she isn't suitable for Harry.' She grimaced, no doubt regretting her words. 'Harry, I didn't mean . . .'

'It's OK,' I said.

'Pay no attention to my daughter,' Richard said. But I could tell he was vaguely amused.

We changed the subject over coffee, espresso from tiny white cups with handles barely large enough to hold my index finger. Outside, a soft rain began to fall. We sat quietly at first, watching the candles as they sputtered out. I was aware of Helen's presence but did not look at her. Richard was uneasy. It was too much for him, this peace.

'So,' he said. 'How does it feel? To be finishing at King Edward's?'

I shook my head. The question came as a surprise.

'Actually I'm beginning to regret it. I can't even say why I'm going. Just weary of London, I suppose. But I'm a bit old to go globe-trotting, aren't I?'

'Was Madeleine right? *Are* you planning to write?'

In truth, I didn't know what lay ahead. I'd had vague fantasies about travelling, about writing, but until that evening thoughts of the future – the idea of so many blank, interminable days – had filled me with dread. Suddenly I didn't feel that any more.

'Yes,' I said to Richard. 'I may write. But I'm keeping my options open. Don't you think that's best?'

We finished coffee and I knew it was time to go. Frances made it clear enough.

'How are you getting home, Harry?' she asked.

'Oh – I'll drive. It won't take long at this time.'

'That's hardly wise, is it?'

'I'm fine.'

'Why don't you stay?' Richard said. 'We could go out for brunch tomorrow.'

Helen smiled but Frances's lips tightened.

'Dad's right,' Helen said, 'you shouldn't drive.'

I felt a rush of adrenaline, but I merely smiled politely at Frances.

'I don't want to get in your way.'

'Not at all,' she said.

I knew she was lying. She wanted to call a cab. But she couldn't get out of it. The spare bed was already made up, she said, with clean sheets, and there were blankets if it should turn cold.

We said goodnight. Helen was polite but cagey. Her glances were possibly more intimate than she realised. I followed Frances upstairs and she left me waiting outside the bathroom while she fetched some things. The adjacent door was open and I glanced inside. Helen's room. What I saw took me by surprise, but though I was somewhat shocked, I remained silent. I didn't want to attract Frances's attention. Perhaps it was not unusual. Helen was nineteen after all. Such obsessions are not uncommon. There, at the far end of the room, above the desk, was a collection of images, forming a kind of collage. They were stuck to the wall, at least twenty cuttings, photographs of my wife. Oddly, I felt no anger. There was a strange symmetry to this which I could not ignore. All of the important images were there, the triptych, alongside a number of catwalk shots and a copy of the novel jacket. There was one that had been taken shortly before Alison was hospitalised. Helen would

45

only have been six years old when that was taken and twelve when Alison killed herself. I should have been used to it by now, but Alison's posthumous fame continued to astonish me.

Frances emerged from the bathroom, muttering to herself.

'A towel, toothbrush, pyjamas, bathrobe. There, Harry, I think that's it.'

But even as she spoke my name, she realised what I had seen and hastily pulled Helen's door shut.

'I'm sorry.' She paused. 'You know what young girls are like . . .'

I nodded and she hurried along the corridor. I followed her to the spare room and smiled to myself as she placed down the items she had collected. I wondered what Alison would have made of such things. When we had last-minute guests, we used to put them up on a camp-bed and give them an old T-shirt to wear and a hot-water bottle.

'Sleep well,' Frances said. She pulled the creamy curtains across the bay.

But I had no inclination to sleep. I sat on the edge of the bed, took off my shoes and socks. The room was cool and airy – painted white, with stripped floorboards. I undressed and put on the bathrobe.

This room wasn't grand like the dining room. Yet I wasn't comfortable. The room was self-conscious; studied in its simplicity. Sitting there, on the edge of the bed, I found myself thinking about the house where I grew up.

It was a rather dilapidated place, an end-of-terrace in the north-east suburbs of London. I remembered my home as claustrophobic, which was due, perhaps, to the omnipresence of my father. He had suffered a shattered thigh in the war, and now spent his days hobbling about the house on his shortened leg and crutches, making himself conspicuous, imposing his demands on my mother. Before I was born he had been a sheet-metal worker. In those days, my mother told me, he was wittier, brighter, but by all accounts he had never been an easy man. It was hardly surprising. His father's absence during the Great War – followed shortly afterwards by his death – must have marked my father in ways I could not begin to understand. When I considered, now, the photograph of the young George Bliss, I could hardly believe that he was my grandfather. It was such a genteel portrait and gentility was markedly absent from my own upbringing. I remembered my father, most of all, as a

46

cynical, hard-done-by invalid. He fluttered his spare pennies on the horses or at the card table, a habit which my mother subsidised with her work at the local bingo hall.

Sometimes I can barely understand how I became the man I am. I wonder what inspired me to read books that my father had never heard of and imagine a life so different from the one that seemed to await me. Was it the sheer dullness of the place? The sound of my father's coughing, the stink of cigarette smoke, the tap of his crutch against the kitchen floor or the repetitive nature of his conversation. Perhaps it was the dark wallpaper of my bedroom or the bleakness of the streets, the dull red brick of the houses or the persistent greyness of the skies.

Or else, it was in my blood. I had not considered it, until that day at Richard's. Though as a boy I knew nothing about my ancestors, I wondered now, was my desire for an education perhaps inherent? I had always wanted to be better than my parents. I read books because they did not; I valued good manners because they did not. Most of all, and to my shame, I studied the accent that would disguise my upbringing, so that, when I arrived at Oxford in the late fifties, I appeared to slot in. I lay low for a while, watching and learning, so that I would make no mistakes. I thought that you could disguise anything if you were clever enough. And though I was awed by the place, besotted by the streets that I wandered, the libraries I frequented and the formality of college suppers, I did not reveal my sentiments. I worked further on my vowels and learned to twist the truth. I discovered that it was possible to make friends by appearing knowledgeable and I cultivated the air of an intellectual. Before long I believed that I belonged.

It is difficult, now, for me to sympathise with that young man who so distanced himself from his family, who was ashamed of his mother's unruly red hair and coarse humour, of his father's vicious banality. I used to dread going home for the vacations.

At the time, I never saw the damage that I caused. If my father had a chip on his shoulder before, his son's new 'hoity-toity' ways were enough to destroy his pride completely. Now I questioned myself for the first time. When my father saw me, I wondered, was he reminded of his own father? Was there something cyclical about this, after all? Did he hate my manners because they reminded him of something he had lost? I could not tell. But I knew my mother, also, was hurt by my behaviour, though she always made a joke of my new ways. To make matters worse, my efforts at college were in vain. Later, I understood that accent and affectations were not enough. I did not have the cash to live as my friends did, and though they constantly bailed me out, I would always be essentially different from these people. There was something deeper that I could not change.

The undergraduate that I had been seemed a remote creature now. Now I rejected the values that I had so eagerly embraced at Oxford. I was uneasy with shows of wealth. I despised good manners. While I had never fully lost my affected accent, there was always a part of me that wanted to rebel; the part of me that during the dinner had wanted to ask for a proper leg of chicken; had wanted to smash the neat white plates. Sometimes I wanted to shout – what's the point of this? Who do you think you're kidding? Do you think you're infallible because you're serving salmon mousse? I would remember my father and the strain on his face with each step that he took.

Now I suppressed such thoughts. There was no purpose, I knew, in dwelling on such matters. I had long ago understood that I belonged nowhere, neither to my father's world, nor Richard's. Instead I took a look about. One thing, at least, made me warm to the room. A number of canvases were piled in the corner beside a folded easel. I became aware of a faint whiff of resin in the air, softened only by the scent of sandalwood – a bowl of potpourri on the dressing table.

I paced the room, picking things up, examining them: clay pots, sea-shells, papier-mâché boxes. I rifled through a few papers but they were of no interest: theatre programmes; invitations to gallery openings. I scanned the shelves, sniffed a book or two. There was a row of children's books and I pulled out an edition of *Alice* with the Tenniel illustrations. I flicked through it, the familiar image as Alice falls, endlessly, down the rabbit hole. I went to close it, but some writing on the inside cover caught my eye: *Helen Cregar, Form 3C. 1989.* She would have been ten years old in '89. Jesus.

I approached the canvases. I was too curious to stop and pulled a couple out. I particularly liked a large self-portrait, and examined it for some time. It was restrained, in grey tones and muted blues, perhaps unfinished. Richard stood by his easel, and stared directly out. His skin was near transparent – you could see the under-

48

painting, the lines of the window behind. But it captured something about him – as in life his skin was pale and his long face rather ghostly. There was an ambiguous quality to the painting. At first I thought his expression suggestive of despair. Then I saw a blatant arrogance. I stepped back and immediately I understood it: this duality was his intention. The artist's face seemed to flicker between two moods, like a plastic gimmick in a cereal packet, an image that changes as you twist it from side to side. But then I doubted even this. Surely the face was simply blank. It was the blankness that confused me. The directness of the artist's stare was a challenge to the observer. In his pale face, we see only a reflection of our own wavering souls – terror, egotism, panic, self-love. Richard at once implored me and chastised me. I slid the canvas back among the others and wondered what I was doing here.

I switched out the light, took off the robe, and lay down, pulling the sheets about me. The moon shone through thin curtains and I stared at the ceiling, tracing the shadows of trees. I began to think of Alison.

I remembered her as she was in the last weeks that I knew her. She was working long hours but I believed that she was happy. When she emerged from her room, late, she would be glowing. She always wanted to talk. Though she never discussed the subject matter of her writing, she liked to express the feelings it engendered in her. She had never cared so much about a piece of work. I used to wait for her. I always wanted her when she was inspired. There was an energy about her, almost tangible. Just over a fortnight before she killed herself, we made love. It was early afternoon. She had finished work sooner than usual. After the months of near-celibacy, now she was easily excited. It was as if we explored one another's bodies for the first time. Yet there was the intimacy of the familiar. Outside, beyond the gauze curtains, it was snowing. The gas fire was burning, but the light on her skin was the stark, white brilliance that reflected from the garden. Afterwards, we stood together, naked, at the window. She seemed unreal; too perfect that day to begin to comprehend. We looked out, past the bare rose-stems towards the pond, where dark, indigo irises were blooming still. The snow was settling now, and we watched it, as it clothed the black trees in its brilliance.

Even now, in the pale, calm room, I failed to understand it: the transition from living flesh to corpse. I could not understand that she willed it. She was beautiful. Her story was flowing. For the first time in over a year she was inspired. I was there for her, whatever the journalists and the critics wrote, and she knew it. I was more *present* than I had ever been. I had felt that our relationship was deepening; redefining itself. That final fortnight, when she was in Norfolk, we didn't speak, but it was on her ruling – no telephone calls to break the flow. She wanted to immerse herself in her work.

Since her death there had been no other women. It was inevitable. What she did – it left too deep an impression. I couldn't look at others without comparing them to Alison. I couldn't think of Alison without thinking about her death. Nobody could compete after that. How do you compete with a suicide? What happened left me untouchable.

Until now. Helen Cregar was nineteen years old. I could surely not act on my feelings. Yet the resemblance between her and Arabella had sparked something. The photographs on her wall, far from distancing her from me, had added to her allure. Because I remembered Alison's desk. In the weeks before she killed herself, she was obsessed with the photograph of Arabella's face. She had enlarged it and photocopied it several times, then pasted it to form a collage, the grainy face, almost surreal, repeating itself.

I had been celibate for too long. Once or twice, I'd brought women back to the flat but I always ended up apologising. I simply didn't want them. Even the thought of kissing someone else had repulsed me, let alone undressing them, making love to them. Now my desire was real and urgent. There was a part of me (call it my sanity) that warned me off. 'She's your friend's daughter – does that mean anything? What are you? A bloody paedophile?' But the knowledge that nothing could come of this, that nothing *should* come of this, did not prevent me from wanting it.

An hour had passed since I switched out the light but it felt much longer. I was sweating and dying for a pee. Eventually I summoned the energy to get up. I put on the robe and went out into the hallway.

I remember standing in the Cregars' bathroom, poised over the china bowl, unable to pee at all. I was too excited – the air in that house prickled my skin. Afterwards, in the hallway, I realised I wouldn't sleep at all that night. I parted the curtains of a window that had a view across the garden. It had stopped raining. Long shadows fell across the lawn, the leaves of the beech tree were quivering. The window was open and the garden seemed to exhale. The rain had intensified the odours: grass and night-scented blooms. I wanted to be outside; far away from this house. I felt suddenly homesick.

In summer, plagued by doubt, Alison would wake up in the night and go outside, wearing only her satin dressing-gown and mules. Sometimes, if she was away too long, I would follow her. I remember once, I found her lying on the lawn, staring up at a thin moon, chilled by the wind, immobile. That night, in the garden, a world away, I touched her, and she did not seem to recognise me. So I lay by her side and breathed the night air. At first I was a little impatient, but with time, it seemed the night revealed itself. I remember the scents of earth and roses, the fine, blue shadows thrown by the moon. It was a humid night and the hot air seemed to cling to us as, above, the huge and generous night unfolded. Behind us, the solid, dense walls of the house, but overhead no such solidity, only space beyond space, diaphanous cloud and the infinite unreachable stars. Even now, I do not know how long we lay there, silent and quite separate. But I know that when I touched her, she hardly seemed to recognise me and I had to coax her inside as if she were a child. The next day she behaved as if nothing had happened. We never talked about it.

Now, I decided, I must go outside. I went downstairs, treading carefully, but the kitchen door was locked. I started looking in drawers and pots for the key. Then I heard footsteps. I'd woken somebody. I turned, expecting Richard or Frances, and was startled to see Helen, wearing a thin, blue gingham robe, her hair loose and untidy. I tried not to be affected by the sight of her.

'I'm sorry,' I said. 'I didn't mean to wake anybody.'

She smiled.

'I couldn't sleep. I thought it must be you. Mum and Dad sleep like logs.'

'I was about to make some more coffee,' I said (thinking, how stupid, hardly a remedy for sleeplessness). 'Do you want some?'

I was worried that Richard might hear us, but Helen didn't seem concerned and nodded. She was taking out mugs, milk, spoons.

'I heard you outside my room,' she said.

'Yes,' I said. 'I was looking at the garden.'

I still don't know if she believed me.

I find myself in a small lounge with Helen, an intimate room, painted dark red with elaborately carved mahogany furniture, Moroccan prints on the walls. I've forgotten the urge to go outside.

Helen has opened the curtains over the French windows and she lights a couple of candles. It's bright enough like that, but not right, I'm thinking, to be alone with her. Underneath the robe, I'm naked. I sit in the armchair, my legs close together, praying that my erection won't get any bigger.

'I never sleep well,' she says. 'I don't know why.'

The softness of her voice is uncalculated. She could not know how she affects me.

'No. I don't either,' I reply.

She's in the corner of the sofa, quite close to me, her legs tucked beneath her. She seems a little nervous.

'Why do you think that is? That we can't sleep?'

'Some people can't rest,' I say.

'Like Lady Macbeth,' she says, but doesn't smile.

'I hope not.'

We were silent then. She held her coffee-mug close to her lips. I can still see it: the muted light, the dim shapes of trees beyond the windows. I was edgy, but also astonished that this was happening. I wanted to prolong it.

'You're not what I imagined,' she said.

'Ah,' I said. 'What did you expect? An ogre?'

'Give me a bit more credit than that.'

I imagined that she was putting up barriers, reminding herself I was not to be liked.

'What then?'

'I don't know.'

'But you've read about me?' I said.

'Just about everything there is to read.'

I didn't fool myself into thinking it was me that interested her. I knew, of course, that it was Alison.

'And do you believe what you read?'

'I did believe it.'

'You can't have changed your mind – not just in an hour or so of knowing me.'

'No. I suppose not.'

She held my gaze. I had to tell myself – she doesn't know what she's doing. I mustn't misread the signs. She's just a girl. I looked away.

'I'm sorry,' she said. 'I've embarrassed you, haven't I?'

'No.'

'Yes I have.'

'Helen – if you want to believe what they write in the newspapers – go ahead. But surely your father's spoken about me?'

'I know that he likes you. But he won't tell me anything else.'

'Have you asked?'

'Hundreds of times. He wants to keep you to himself.'

'What do you ask him?'

'All sorts.'

'For example?'

'The stuff that everybody must ask.'

'Ah – the money?'

She said nothing and I knew that I'd hit upon something. I couldn't help but be defensive. I could guess what was going through her mind and I wanted to diffuse it. A recent article by Gordon Hake had hinted at my hypocrisy. Having once claimed that I would not spend Alison's money, it was now clear that I intended to retire early on the proceeds of her work. A film of *Sweet Susan* was already in production and the royalties from the novel were pouring in.

'People can change, Helen, that's all I can say. I still won't touch her modelling money. But yes, the film has been very lucrative. And it looks as if it will be a lousy film – which doesn't please me by the way. The thing is, Alison wouldn't have wanted me to stay on at the school if I weren't happy.'

She considered this.

'But doesn't it bother you?' she said.

'You think I should give it to charity?'

'I didn't mean . . .'

'They forgot to balance the scales, Helen. They forgot to weigh grief against gain,' I said, though I didn't know if she'd understand me. But when she spoke, it was in a different tone.

'My dad's really protective of you, you know? He really admires you.'

Had she forgiven me so easily?

'I should go to bed,' I said.

'I thought you weren't tired.'

'What would your parents think – if they found me here with you?'

I sounded so pompous.

'Their room's at the other side of the house. They never wake up.'

'Even so – I should go.'

'Why? Are you planning to seduce me?'

She laughed. She thought it a joke.

'Of course not.'

'Well that's all right then, isn't it?'

'Yes.'

I realised I was still rather drunk and wondered whether she was too.

'Did you make it up,' she asked suddenly, 'about that photograph?'

'No,' I said. 'I didn't make it up.'

'It's a coincidence, isn't it?'

'Yes.'

'Can I ask you a question?'

She was more subdued now. I nodded.

'Did you love Alison?'

I was shocked at her audacity. I couldn't keep the sting from my voice.

'Of course I loved her.' But I regretted my tone instantly. Perhaps it was simply naïvety that made her ask. 'Look – I can't talk about this.'

'I'm sorry. I'm really sorry. It was really stupid of me.'

'It's OK. Honestly.'

'I've lost count of how many times I've read her book,' she said.

Alison and her book had become so inseparable. People thought that they might find her there, if not in the words themselves, then somewhere between the lines. A myth had grown up about Alison and more often than not people swallowed it – not just the flesh of her story, but the stone as well, the indigestible lies. These days there wasn't a feminist group in the country that hadn't held a seminar on *Sweet Susan* and its author. Everyone, it seemed, had a claim on her. They analysed her prose – smooth and easy, yet acerbic where it mattered, so witty, so biting. Yet she was not afraid to reveal her vulnerability. Poor Alison, they'd say – how impossible it was for her to live in the world.

But for me, she was more than just the author of that book.

'I thought I'd hate you,' Helen said. 'But I don't.'

'Perhaps because you guess the truth is more complex than you imagined it?'

'Maybe. And she married you, didn't she?'

'What's that supposed to mean?'

'I can't help it if I'm curious about you.'

'I see.'

'What's the matter?' she asked.

'Nothing.'

'Yes, there is. I can tell.'

She was perceptive. And insistent too.

'Do you always speak with your father's friends like this?' I tried to deflect her, but she laughed, mocking me. She didn't think my question worthy of a reply. 'Well? Do you?' I decided this was for the best. I wanted to remind her of my age, to speak to her as I ought.

'I don't often sit up talking with my dad's friends in the middle of the night – if that's what you mean,' she said.

'No – I wasn't suggesting . . .'

And she started to giggle.

'What? What is it?'

'You're so *serious*,' she said. 'You're really worried about this, aren't you?'

'Yes, actually.' I was embarrassed. She thought me old and stuffy.

'Mum and Dad wouldn't care about us talking.'

'Perhaps you don't know them as well as you think you do.'

'Oh, forget them, can't you?'

There was a brief silence. I felt self-conscious – aware of my bare legs and feet, the hairs on my chest that protruded from my dressing gown.

'Will you tell me more about Alison?' she said.

She looked me in the eye. Perhaps this was sheer deviousness but I couldn't refuse her.

'I'll tell you something. The photograph I mentioned. It was important to her. She had it pinned above her desk.'

She hesitated, seemed to retreat into herself. She uncurled her legs, leant forwards and placed her mug on the table. A little triangle of flesh was exposed above her breasts. It was nothing. I looked away. How could I stop her noticing what was happening? I leant forwards also, crossing my arms about my groin.

'That's why I was taken aback when I saw you. Alison was writing a novel about it. She was obsessed by this woman – Arabella – my great-grandfather's wife.'

'That's amazing.'

'Don't get me wrong. Please. It was my imagination – that's all. The resemblance isn't exact.'

'No. I know. You said.'

But I could tell she was secretly pleased. And seeing her pleasure was too much for me.

'I ought to go to bed,' I said.

I wanted to lean towards her, to press myself against her. I wanted to fuck her. Oh God, I wanted to fuck her. It was more urgent than my need to speak.

'You can't go now. We've just started talking.'

'I'm suddenly very tired. I'm sorry.'

Anything to get away.

'Can I meet you again?' she asked. 'You said you'd show me the photograph.'

'Yes. Of course.'

'Tomorrow?'

Her eagerness threw me.

'No. I have to stay home. I've got work to do.'

'Monday then? Can I come and see you?'

'I don't know.'

I thought of saying, 'look Helen, we should meet in a bar or something,' but I didn't. I *wanted* her to come to my place.

'All right.' I picked up a pen and paper from the coffee table. 'Here's my address and number. But give me a call first, OK?'

'Thanks.' She wore a smug smile, as if she'd scored a victory. She stood up. Perhaps she knew what I was hiding from her. She blew the candles out. 'See you at breakfast then.' And she left me in the darkness to contemplate what I had started.

I was awake till dawn. I sat in the armchair, dazed, unable to grasp quite what was going on. For years I had been unable to feel. How was it possible that the desire I now experienced could be so strong? There was a violence to the emotion that worried me, even as it excited me. I despised myself for my thoughts but I could not stop them. She was nineteen years old. The daughter of my friend. But I wanted to make love to her. And I had a terrible fear that she would let me, that she wanted it too. There was only one way to avoid it. I talked myself through the phone-call that I'd receive.

'Yes, I'm sorry,' I'd say. 'I know I said you should come. But I was a bit drunk. The photograph? It doesn't exist. Just the whisky talking. There's no reason for you to come. I'm very busy this evening. I've promised to see a friend.'

Yet the more I thought of this course of action, the more ludicrous it seemed. The realisation shocked me. Normally I was a rational man but now I was persuaded by the most flimsy arguments. I was fascinated by what was happening. I convinced myself that her appearance, the photographs above her desk, had some significance. Though the consequences of seeing her again might prove disastrous, I wanted to see her all the same. In fact I wanted it more than I had wanted anything in the last six years. But I knew that it was madness. In the real world, it was impossible.

Outside the window, birds began to sing. It was shortly before daybreak. Everything was still and silent except for their cries, and that reminder of the new day disturbed a dream, though I'd never actually slept. Slowly a soft, blue light penetrated the room. Indistinguishable forms became concrete. By daylight I'd have to face Richard and smile politely at Helen.

I stood up and opened the window. A chill, fresh air against my face. I was wide awake. A squirrel ran across the lawn. I knew I couldn't stay in that house any longer, I had to get out. Richard told me, months later, that he had woken to the sound of my engine starting up, and he had looked from the window to watch me go. He wondered what possessed me to leave like that, without warning. He rather envied me, he said. It was a clear, bright, morning – the streets would be empty. No doubt he thought of me, driving about at dawn, while he returned to his wife, in bed, and kissed her on the nape of the neck.

# 5

I HAD BELIEVED THAT I was simply heading home. I drove along the empty roads, desiring nothing so much as forgetfulness. Something about the emptiness outside, I thought, would soothe me now, if only I might focus on it. I hoped my mind, also, might be hollowed by the sight; the glare of headlights on silver tarmac, preparing me for sleep. When I reached Piccadilly, however, I turned right, along the Haymarket. I didn't question this wrong turn at first. I suppose I must have known where I was going.

Trafalgar Square, at dawn, was near-deserted. I stopped the car, illegally, and got out. The sun had just risen above the buildings to the east and long, blue shadows stretched out towards me as I headed down the west steps, pausing briefly to question the empty plinth that stood there. I crossed the square and now, glancing up at the sinking moon, I approached the plane tree, where I had first stood thirteen years ago. Once again I stood beneath it. I closed my eyes, to hold the memory closer.

I saw her, first, before the Piero. It was in the west wing of the gallery and I had been heading for the Bellinis, though I never actually reached them. It was late autumn, one of those grim, grey days when the rain drives one indoors and the east wing of the gallery, where the Impressionists were housed, was packed pretty full. I had come in on a whim, after lunching with a friend in the Crypt at St Martin's. Before lunch, there had been no sign of rain, but as we emerged from the restaurant, the sky bore down on us and the clouds were yellow-edged and heavy.

My friend, an archivist, had to get back to work and he headed off, before the rain began. It was half term and I had no plans, so I wandered down into the square, hoping that the weather would hold a little longer. I suppose, at the time, I was enjoying my freedom, having recently split with a woman, a fellow teacher who had grown tired of waiting for a proposal. I felt relieved at the whole thing. Something about being single again made me feel carefree. I wanted to make the most of the city in which I lived.

I walked beneath Nelson's Column, watching the pigeons scatter at my feet. It was then that the skies opened. There was nobody else about, none fool enough to risk the downpour, so I retraced my steps, took refuge, alone under the plane tree. I remember feeling happy, quite indescribably happy as I breathed the fresh, damp air and watched the rain drip from the leaves above and from the noses of the great stone lions.

About me, above the pavements, black umbrellas blossomed. I knew I could not stay out for long and the gallery looked more than inviting. During a brief lull, I made a dash for it. I crossed the road, being nearly run down by a black cab, and headed towards my future.

I noticed her as soon as I entered the room. She was the only one before that particular painting, *The Baptism of Christ*. I remember halting, briefly, when I saw her. I did not recognise her, but rather, what impressed me, was her apparent communion with the painting. Not just her eyes, but her whole face, even her body seemed affected by what she saw, as if the whole of her attention was focused on the image before her. It was most remarkable. She lacked the distraction of ordinary people.

Oddly, I remember thinking that she was beautiful and that I wanted to get to know her. I said to myself, 'It's not the kind of beauty that most people would like, it's a strange, surreal beauty.' Of course, if I had guessed, at first, that it was Alison Oakley, I would never have approached her. But I didn't see it. True, she had height and poise, but she had not fully recovered from her illness and she was far too thin. She was dressed in jeans and a loose sweater, which swamped her. Her hair was dishevelled and she wore no make-up. What attracted me, most of all, was her expression. She was captivated, almost as if she had never seen anything quite like that before. I didn't want to break the spell, so I simply stood beside her and we looked together. I told myself this was ridiculous, a mere fantasy. I was aware of all the clichés surrounding such a meeting and I didn't know how to avoid them. Instead, I allowed my attention to be drawn upwards, to the painting itself. And when I looked at the Christ-figure, so still and serene, I felt myself inadequate. I wanted to enter the painting, as she did, but I felt myself excluded.

In the end, it was her that spoke.

'Is he famous, this della Francesca?'

I laughed, relieved. I had assumed she was an art critic or scholar.

'Yes,' I said. 'Very.'

'I thought so.'

'What do you make of it?' I asked.

She hesitated, looking at me a little strangely. Then she smiled, that huge, broad film-star smile that was instantly recognisable, despite her drawn face. Why had I not seen it before? I started, felt rather terrified, but somehow guessed that she didn't want me to know who she was. In any case, it wasn't Alison Oakley the model that I was interested in. It was the woman I had first seen before of the painting.

'It's beautiful,' she said at last. 'But I can't say why I like it.'

'Try.'

'The purity of it, I suppose. Oh, I don't know much about art.'

'You don't have to know to enjoy.'

'I remember we came here when I was in the sixth form. I haven't been since. It makes me feel a bit ignorant. I suppose you know all about this stuff.'

Again, I laughed.

'I know a little,' I said.

'So tell me some more about this guy.'

I couldn't believe that this was happening.

'Well,' I said, 'he was a Florentine artist. But what really marked him out was that he was a mathematician and he used his knowledge of geometry and perspective in his work. Perhaps that's one reason why this painting has such a sense of harmony. Look at how symmetrical the body of Christ is and the dove, above him. You can divide the painting up into segments, like this.' I gestured to illustrate my meaning. 'It makes the structure of the painting clearer.'

'I suppose it's obvious, once you know that.'

'He's known for his use of colour too. Most of his paintings have a certain stillness about them, so that colour and form are heightened. There's kind of luminous quality, don't you think?'

'Yes. There is. I've got a lot to learn, I guess.'

'No,' I said. 'I think you know a lot already.'

She shook her head.

'I haven't read an art book since I was at school.'

'I think you understand this picture better than I do.'

'No, I don't.'

'What did you feel,' I said, 'just now, before I arrived?'

She hesitated, looked directly at me. Her gaze disarmed me.

'Why? What does it matter?'

'It matters a great deal.'

Already, I felt a fraud. I'd fed her a few fragments of information that I'd gleaned from books and she was impressed, but wrongly. In her look, I had seen more authenticity of reaction than I had ever felt myself, towards any painting.

'I suppose I was just blown away by it,' she said. 'I wanted to leap in and be part of it. Like that figure in the background, pulling his shirt over his head. I wanted to be next.'

'To be baptised?'

'Not literally. But I've been through such shit lately. I suppose I wanted to be . . .' Her voice trailed off. She seemed suddenly embarrassed. 'I'm sorry,' she said. 'I don't really think any of this is relevant to the painting. I wish I knew the stuff you knew. Look, I shouldn't keep you any longer. I mean I'd like to know more, but you must be busy.'

'No,' I said, bemused. 'I'm not busy at all.'

The rain had stopped at last. The pavements were still drenched, great puddles at the kerb-sides, as we walked up Charing Cross Road. It was my first experience of being watched. Alison seemed not to notice the eyes that were upon her, but I was aware of it and it chilled me, even then.

She wanted to stop and browse in the second-hand bookshops. She knew by now that I was an English teacher, and she wanted my advice on who to read, the best contemporary fiction, the classics that I most admired.

'I'd love to have read as much as you,' she said. 'I feel like there's a fucking great hole, up here, where my brain should be.'

'You mustn't underestimate yourself. You're intelligent. Perceptive. That matters. Not just book-learning.'

We had not yet touched upon the fact of who she was and in a way it seemed rather unimportant. Perhaps it was her illness, but I still couldn't see Alison as a conventional beauty. She looked so different from the woman that I'd seen in newspapers and on television. But I did find her beautiful. Something about the way she looked at me, and her voice, the slight sharpness of it, the earnestness, the desire to be understood. It wasn't until later, when she started gaining weight, that her physical beauty manifested itself once more. Later, when her hair became glossy again, her breasts fuller, her hips more fleshy.

'I didn't know who you were,' I said, 'when I saw you, earlier.'

'No. I know. It's just as well, really. Nobody knows who I am, actually. They just think they do.'

'Nobody?'

She shrugged.

'A few friends, I guess.'

'No family?'

'No.' She hesitated. 'There's my father. But I don't see him any more.'

There was a part of me, a small voice in my head, that kept whispering her name, insisting on the absurdity of receiving her confidences. But already I felt extremely protective of her, aware somehow that she did not want to be reminded of her identity. She kept talking about her time at university, her failure to finish her course. And I knew, instinctively, that she wanted to find the person that she once had been.

Oddly, watching her, I too was reminded of my youth. Something about the way she held the books, sniffed them even, ran her hands along the shelves. She seemed to revere the books, to treasure them, and it was wonderful to watch. She was clearly in no hurry and that too was refreshing. We spent half an hour in the first shop and she left with a brown paper bag containing three volumes: Orwell, Edith Wharton and *The New Poetry*, edited by Alvarez.

We wandered towards Soho. She seemed relaxed; easy; excited even.

'I really can't wait to read these,' she said. 'I read *The Age of Innocence* years ago and it was wonderful. I remember being totally swept away by it.'

'I hope you enjoy this one,' I said. She had bought *The House of Mirth*. Was it too bleak, I wondered.

'I'm sure I will.'

Already I sensed a certain pleasure when she spoke to me. She grinned, wrinkled her nose. It wasn't an expression I'd ever seen, in a photograph. But it didn't last for long. As we reached the corner of Old Compton Street, a man stepped out, into her path, and took her photo.

'Oh God,' she half shrieked.

'Alison!' the man said.

'Look, fuck off! Why don't you just fuck off!'

'Oh, come on – you've been avoiding me . . .'

My first reaction was fury: that he had robbed her smile, so easily. I could see that she was terrified of this man. His voice was rich and plummy, very public-school. He was tall, broad-shoul-dered; fit.

'Look. You heard what she said,' I began.

The man raised his camera and photographed me, also. There was something weirdly cherubic about his face: fat, hamster-like cheeks; fair curls flopping across his forehead. He wore small steel-rimmed glasses, disguising a slight squint.

'And who the hell are you?' he said.

'I'm . . .'

'Have you followed me, Gordon?' Alison asked. 'Can't you just leave me alone for one day?'

'Why should I leave you alone? If you'd just co-operate . . .'

I knew I had to do something. But what? Alison instinctively clutched my hand and already I felt drawn into this. I was not an observer. I was a part of it. We continued to walk. The man stood in our way and I pushed him aside. He stumbled slightly, then recovered.

'Look,' he said, slightly hysterically I thought. 'Keep out of this, OK? You know nothing about this.'

'Don't I? I can see what you're doing plain enough. You're in our way.'

Again, he raised his camera, captured my anger. I couldn't stop myself. I swiped the camera from him and it went flying across the pavement, shattering the lens.

'You bastard!' he said. 'Fucking bastard! Keep her. Keep her.'

He bent down to gather the pieces of his camera.

'Come on,' I said to Alison. 'Let's get out of here.'

I was surprised, myself, at my reaction. Something about Alison, I think, made me behave in that way. Since the man's appearance, her whole demeanour had changed. Her confidence evaporated.

I suggested we try the Patisserie Valerie. It wasn't ideal, too public, but we needed to sit down, to calm ourselves.

'It must be hellish,' I said, as we entered.

'To say the least,' she replied.

I ordered us tea and pastries at the counter. It was fairly crowded and people stared as we squeezed between tables to find a place in the corner where we might avoid their glances. We sat down. She was trembling.

'Who is he?' I said.

'His name's Gordon Hake.'

I shrugged.

'I guess if you don't read the tabloids . . .' Her voice trailed off.

'OK. So clearly he's a journalist. I just thought there was something more. You seem . . .'

'I know. He freaks me out.' She paused. 'Look – thanks.'

'I didn't do anything.'

'Yes. You did. If I'd been on my own . . . It's just him, you know? I can cope with the others.'

Her face crumpled and she was fighting back tears. I didn't know what to do. I simply took her hand again, held it tight.

'Do you want to tell me about it?'

For a moment, I thought she wouldn't be able to. She seemed on the point of losing control. But somehow she gathered strength and spoke.

'It's not the fact of his hounding me,' she said. 'I've been turning it over and over in my mind. I thought it would be OK. I really did. I've spoken to all the shrinks, but it doesn't seem to do much good.'

'What is it about him?'

She hesitated, watching me, as if deciding how much trust she might place in me.

'I thought I could deal with it at first. I let him have things his way. But now, I don't know . . .'

'So tell me.'

'He writes a lot of stories about me. I guess I'm his main source of income.' She laughed, a vacant laughter. 'Even recently, when I came out of hospital, he was there, waiting on the pavement. I was supposed to be better, but I didn't feel better, seeing him. I felt so weak.' She paused, looked into my eyes, held my gaze for just a moment too long. 'You don't need to hear this,' she said.

'Yes. I do. I think I've heard about your illness. Anorexia, right?'

'Damn cliché, huh? Anorexia. Breakdown. All in a day's work.'

'And are you over it now?'

'Over the worst. I'm starting again, I suppose. From where I left off, before all this crap began.'

Our pastries arrived then, and tea in small china cups. I saw the way she looked at the food and knew that she wasn't going to touch it.

'Do you really want to hear this?' she said.

My hand now rested upon hers. I lifted it to my lips, kissed it lightly. She smiled, briefly, and it thrilled me.

'Yes.'

'The first time I met him, I liked him. I mean, he wasn't like most tabloid journalists. Nothing seedy about him, at least not to look at. I guess I thought he was pretty good-looking, you know?'

I nodded.

'I met him in Paris at a party.' She laughed suddenly, as if she found herself rather ridiculous. Her eyes caught mine again, seemed to light up. 'I can be pretty dumb, I guess. Anyhow, we talked about literature. He said he didn't want to be a journalist, not really. He was writing a novel.'

'A novel?'

'Well, you can imagine. It was music to my ears. All the wankers from the fashion industry swanning about and fawning on me, and here's this guy who's wearing preppy glasses and is writing a novel.'

'And you got it together?'

She looked away, embarrassed. She lowered her eyelids, took a sip of tea – no milk. She nodded.

'I was young. Well, twenty. But already I was so tired of the people I'd begun to meet in the industry. I'd got used to people making passes at me, but I thought that Gordon was different. We slipped away from the party and went for a walk over the Pont Neuf, then down by the Seine. He seemed interested in me, as a person. How was I to know any differently? He was romantic, I suppose. It was high tide and the banks of the river were flooding. February and freezing cold. He wrapped me up in his coat. He kissed me.'

'I can't believe it's the same man.'

'No.' She shook her head. 'Neither can I.'

'It was madness really. I should have known not to trust him. I really believed that he wouldn't write about me. I mean, we didn't even go to bed together that first time. He walked me back to the hotel and said goodnight. I thought he was very sweet.'

'But he wasn't?'

'I was so used to all the clichés: champagne; caviar; roses. And Gordon operated differently. He took me to Les Deux Magots and talked about de Beauvoir and Sartre.'

'But . . .'

'Yes. Clichés too. But I didn't know that. It was all new to me. I went back to his hotel that second evening. I slept with him. But it wasn't . . . God, I shouldn't be burdening you with this.'

'It's no burden. But don't tell me, if you feel uncomfortable.'

'It wasn't how I thought it would be, Harry. I can't explain it. I mean, even as he began to undress me, I just sensed something was wrong. He didn't seem engaged. How can I describe it? The way he smiled to himself, a kind of quiet triumph. I just knew all at once that I'd misjudged him, that I shouldn't be doing this. But I didn't stop him. That was the worst thing. I hated myself for going through with it, but I didn't say no. I even did things that he asked me to do. I don't want to remember it. I hated every minute. And when it was over, he lay beside me, talking about himself. I just wanted to go. To get out of there. Only I didn't know how. I felt so small. So useless.'

'And then?'

'I must have been exhausted. Somehow I fell asleep. But the next morning, when I awoke, I said I was going to the bathroom. Only I didn't. I just gathered my things and walked out. Well, that was the beginning of it. He wouldn't leave me alone. His ego couldn't take it. At first it was OK, I thought it would stop. But it didn't. And the more he was on my back, the more I couldn't erase the memory of that night we spent together. That's the worst part of it. Not just that he's hounded me for so long. I can't describe it.'

'Has it never relented. How long has this been going on?'

66

'I don't know. Around five years I guess. But he has an excuse, you see. His job. He's made it his job to follow me, to be wherever I am. I'm public property and it's supposed to be all right. Shortly after that night together, he began turning up at my home, early, before I was even awake. He was there, outside, when I drew my curtains, or else he'd call me in the middle of the night, when I wasn't with it.'

'Couldn't you have called the police?'

She shook her head.

'Maybe. I mean it got pretty bad. They might have stopped him calling me in the night. But it wasn't long before . . .'

She looked at me then, an expression of such pain on her face that it was difficult to watch her. It was odd. All around us were students and media types, chatting happily. And opposite me, this woman that I hardly knew, telling me her most intimate secrets.

'Before?'

'Only a month or so after I dumped him, he called me and told me something new. He said he had some photographs of me. Photos he took when we spent the night together.'

'Were you aware of this?'

'No. I don't remember it. But I believe him. I mean it would have been easy, wouldn't it, to have hidden a camera somewhere.'

'But that's outrageous . . . how could he do such a thing? Is he blackmailing you?'

'No. He says he just wants to keep them. That's it. He still has them. They're his little hook, if you like.'

'So he doesn't threaten to print them?'

'No. He's been very careful. He's just made it clear that he owns them. But at first I was really afraid. I mean, I thought my career would be ruined if something like that came out. So I complied with him. I began to talk to him again, gave him interviews, exclusives, until . . .'

'Yes?'

'I shouldn't have let it go on for so long. I don't know why I'm so afraid of him. It's not just the photos. It's like he has some hold over me, like I don't even know how to get rid of him any more. Even if I didn't talk to him and let him print the bloody things, he wouldn't go away. He'd find ways to make my life hell. He couldn't get into the hospital. But now I'm out . . .' She looked at me, an urgent plea.

'I have to get him off my back, Harry. I have to find a way out of this.'

She came back to my place, candidly, unwilling to play games, her growing attachment to me already clear. My room, that night, had never seemed so inhabited. Other women had slept beside me in the selfsame bed, but none had made me feel at home there; I had always felt a stranger in my own environment.

She loved my room, said she loved it as she had never loved a room since she was a child. I was not afraid of the admission. We closed the door, undressed one another in the dim light. I felt, mostly, a kind of deep relief, as if, always, I had been waiting for something, and now at last she was here. Already my awareness of her public persona was slipping away. I saw no perfection in these wasted limbs, the bony face, nor even the marvellous smile, for it was too sad a smile to cause my arousal. I said her name to myself. Alison Oakley. Alison Oakley. But it meant nothing. Nothing at all. The meaning was condensed in the places where our bodies touched. It was as if we each traced the pattern of our separate pasts upon the body of the other. It began in intimacy, in a knowledge of the safety of this, the inevitability of our togetherness. I too felt the presence of the room, the low, crumpled bed, the shelves surrounding us, crammed with books; books on tables, on floors, in boxes. There was a single lamp, a light drape across the window, an electric fire humming. As I kissed her, I did not think of the other men that had lain beside her, the numerous beaux that I might have seen by her side, had I ever taken an interest in such things. Nor did I think about the difference in our ages, for what was twenty years but an idea of difference? Rather, I felt the need to extinguish her pain and my own, the years of not belonging, the failure to connect. When I had first seen her, it was the communion with the painting that had drawn me. Now, for the first time, I began to understand such a communion, for it was here, between us; we each drew life from the other. What began slowly, intensely, built into a sweet, unravelling dance, where nothing was forbidden, no secrets were withheld. We sucked the very essence from each other, so that by the morning there was hardly a space between us. The dull solidity of my life seemed to have dissolved at last into a fine, white mist of being. Such nights come rarely. Such a night I remember.

In the days that followed, before school began again, she stayed in my flat, going home only to collect clothes, toiletries, papers. Neither of us questioned her presence there. There was a near-tangible joy about her at that time, a kind of quiet excitement within her that drew me. We took long walks each day across Wandsworth Common, feeding bread to the geese, watching the cormorants, high in the trees, and the children playing in the deep carpet of fallen leaves. Afterwards, we sat in the cafés of Bellevue Road, talking about books and paintings, about her writing, my teaching.

Already, in the course of a few days, I could see the change in her. She talked about wanting to go to Florence, to see the Baptistery doors before the Duomo. She asked me about Ghiberti, Brunelleschi, Donatello. She said, would I take a look at her writing, and tell her, honestly, if there was anything worth pursuing. On the third day, she brought a few pages of her work and as we sat outside the café, I began to read. I had taken a chance and ordered buttered toast with her coffee. When I had finished reading, amazed, I told her that I was impressed. She smiled, radiant. She began to eat the toast.

The call came on Sunday morning. We were in bed, wrapped in the duvet, our heads touching, she engrossed in Orwell's 'down and out' phase, I with the newspaper. Reluctantly, I picked up the telephone.

'Hello?'

'Is that Harold Bliss?'

'Yes. Who's speaking?'

'I wondered if you might like to comment on your new relationship?'

'What is this? Who are you?'

But already, I knew.

'It's Gordon Hake. I'm working for the . . .'

I hung up.

'How the hell did he get my number?'

'I don't know,' she said. 'I don't know, Harry.'

She looked pretty terrified. I didn't know, then, that my anger made things worse for her. The phone rang again.

'Ignore it,' she said. But it kept on ringing. 'Pick it up, then hang up.'

I lifted the receiver.

'Mr Bliss. A few moments of your time is all I ask . . .'

'Right,' I said. 'Say what you have to say.'

'Can you confirm that you are having a relationship with Alison Oakley?'

I remained silent.

'Perhaps you might like to comment on her illness. Is it true that she's cancelled every one of her scheduled appearances?'

'I'll say this,' I said. 'It seems to me, Mr Hake, that your persistent hounding of Miss Oakley amounts to a gross intrusion of privacy. All she requires, right now, is to be left alone. If you continue to call, I won't hesitate to make a formal complaint.'

'Is it true that she hasn't fully recovered from her breakdown?'

'Did you not hear what I said?'

'I heard, Mr Bliss. I've heard it all before.'

'Get off the line,' I said, and hung up again.

Within minutes he was on the doorstep. I lived then in a basement flat, with the bedroom at the front. We could hear him, outside the window. The doorbell rang, again and again. Alison was trembling.

'Do you think that's him? I didn't think he'd find us here. Not so soon. Why does he have to spoil everything?'

'He can't spoil this,' I said.

I got up, dressed, and went to the door. Hake smiled, held out his hand. I couldn't believe his audacity: as if he expected me to forget our last encounter and start again.

'Hake,' he said.

'I think we've met!'

I could not stop myself imagining him with Alison. What he had done to her appalled me. I wanted to wipe the grin from his face.

'Perhaps you should ask Alison if she wants to talk to me?'

'She doesn't.'

'Really? That's not like her. She and I go back a long way.'

As he spoke, a second man appeared at the top of the steps, with a camera about his neck. He'd photographed me before I had time to protest.

'Have you got the shots of the flat, Mike?' Hake said.

'You can't print pictures of my home,' I said.

Hake shrugged.

'Look,' he said. 'I just want to know when she'll be back to work. Our readers care about her. They're concerned.'

'Sure.'

The photographer continued to work and I hardly knew what to do. All this was entirely new to me. I was winging it.

'She's inside, right?' Hake said.

He was pushing forwards, wanting to cross the threshold, trying to provoke a reaction. I steeled myself, willing myself not to react, knowing that any violence on my part would be duly photographed and reported. I stood firm, in the doorway.

'For Christ's sake, Bliss. All I want is to talk to her.'

'No chance.'

But as I spoke, I heard a movement behind me. I turned and Alison, having dressed herself, had appeared in the hallway. I couldn't understand it. When I was protecting her, why did she come forward like this? I began to realise, then, that I didn't yet understand the depths of her involvement with this man. The photographs in Hake's possession were more than a mere image he might one day choose to print. For her, they symbolised something more, a sense that she no longer belonged to herself, she no longer possessed a private self. I could not stop her. She approached the door.

'Is this what you want, Gordon?' she said. 'Proof? Another photograph? Well, you've got it. You've got your story. Now piss off.'

'You're not looking too good, Alison.'

'I've been ill.'

'Too bad. We can't have you on the catwalk looking like that . . .'

'Fine,' she said. 'Just fine. You want another story? I'm not coming back, OK? Tell that to your readers. This shit is finished with. I'm gonna have a normal life.'

Hake appeared, briefly, disconcerted, but covered his expression with a disbelieving whistle.

'Good luck to you sweetheart,' he said. 'Come on, Mike. Let's get out of here.'

In Trafalgar Square, a wind had risen. I was sitting on the brink of a fountain and now the spray caught my back, disturbing my thoughts. I shifted slightly, pulled my jacket across my shoulders. Goose-pimples rose on my arms as the wind wrapped itself about me. A distinct chill in the air, the shadows shrinking, the hum of traffic getting louder. Why the hell had I come here, I wondered, allowing these spectres to rise up again? That wind, caught in the confines of the square, seemed to have nowhere else to go. It was a crazy wind, a manic wind, teasing me, parading my memories, pressing them close. Until, at once, it was gone. It passed me by. And now, the great stone lions felt it. That wind ruffled their manes and I knew that if I stayed much longer, I would witness their fury. Soon, so soon, they would wake, shiver and rise up to shake their stony necks and roar, after a long night of cold and dreamless sleep.

# 6

THE PHONE RANG, WAKING me, and I reached across, half-asleep, to answer it.

'Yes?'

'What happened to you?'

It was Richard. I glanced at the clock. It was nearly midday. I didn't want to talk to him.

'What?'

'We missed you at breakfast. Went to a lovely café in Kew. Brilliant bagels.' He paused. 'You are all right, Harry?'

'Yes.'

But my tone was abrupt.

'No you're not. What's up?'

'Nothing. Honestly.'

'Couldn't sleep?'

'I just woke early. Fancied a drive.'

'You weren't offended, were you? Did Frances say anything to upset you?'

'Of course not.'

'You're sure?'

'I fell asleep when I got home. You woke me. Just a bit phased, that's all.'

'Oh – sorry.'

That much at least was true. My mouth was furred, my eyes clogged with sleep. I was thirsty, wanted to get off the phone. But I knew what he'd be thinking. He wanted an explanation.

'The thing is, I had a bad dream last night,' I lied. 'About Alison. Nothing to worry about. But I needed to get home, have some time on my own.'

'Gosh. Poor Harry.'

'I'm fine now. Just sorry I missed the bagels.'

'Right.'

I could hear his relief. He didn't want to talk about Alison.

'It's a good place,' he said. 'Great coffee too.'

'We'll go some other time then?' I said.

'Definitely.' And again he paused. 'You know, Helen seems quite sweet on you.'

It took me by surprise. I didn't know how to take it without seeing his face, but I couldn't believe that it was innocent. So he knew. This whole conversation had been a façade.

'God knows why,' he said. 'Although come to think of it, she's always asked questions about you.'

'What do you mean – always?'

'You know how young girls are. You should be flattered.'

'Why?'

'I would be.'

I had been wrong. He knew nothing. He was too relaxed about this.

'You put her right then? About me?'

'Oh yes.'

'What sort of questions anyway?'

'I thought you were half-asleep.'

'You've woken me now. What sort of questions?'

'Just what you'd expect really. If I thought it was true about – you know.'

'No. I don't.'

'Come on. It's not a good idea to talk about this.'

I guessed that he was talking about the manuscript. Was it true that I burnt it?

'All right. But stop taking the piss. Sweet on me! Christ, what next?'

'It's true. She had that faraway look this morning. She's smitten.'

'I doubt it.'

'Well, hands off, anyhow.'

'What do you take me for?'

'I'm kidding!'

'Yes. Of course.'

'She still wants to see that photograph you mentioned. Is that OK?'

'Fine.'

'I'll tell her she'll have to pop round to your place. I don't want to put you out. She's awfully unreliable anyway. I doubt she'll turn up, not knowing you and all.'

It was strange. We had it all planned, but now Helen had spoken to her father. She hadn't told him about last night, but she wanted him to know that she was coming here.

'Anyhow – sorry to wake you. You take care, eh?'

'Sure. Look – thanks for last night.' I was good at this, the banalities of polite conversation. 'It was lovely to see Frances again. I'm sorry about Maddy. I was probably over-sensitive. But I enjoyed myself. Very much.'

'Right. Well, see you tomorrow.'

'Yes. See you tomorrow.'

I put the phone down with a sense of foreboding. The final week of term. Suddenly I didn't want to go through with it. I didn't want to see Richard. How could I remain infatuated with his daughter when I had to face him each day at school? I realised, then, that I didn't want to see sense. I wanted to lie down again, pull the duvet about my shoulders. Once again, memories were unfolding – they had not been so clear nor so insistent for years. The fact of Alison's death seemed suddenly as raw and painful as if it had happened yesterday. It was Helen who had done this. Helen had opened doors inside me, doors better left closed perhaps, but I had no choice now but to look inside. It was the only way ahead, the route out of this darkness. I allowed myself to remember.

Later, I tried to behave as if nothing had changed. By early evening I was at my desk contemplating a pile of essays. Each one spouted the same uninspired sentiments; not a single spark of brilliance to lighten my mood.

Outside, the City was quiet. I lived then in the Barbican complex, at the top of the Milton Tower. When I first moved there, shortly after Alison's death, everyone told me how noisy it would be. They said I wouldn't be able to bear it. But it's not true. When you live so high, the noise of the City seems distant. It's a vague hum far away, another world. You hear the closer noises – the scufflings of other people, the whir of the lift – but you get used to these, even find some peace in them.

At the time, friends said I was self-destructive. 'You're punishing yourself. You shouldn't make such rash decisions.' They guessed that Alison's money was somehow involved, but my reasons were more subtle than that, hardly discernible even to myself. I remember leaving the Clapham house, packing our belongings, wondering what the hell I was doing. Opening her wardrobe for the first time since her suicide, and how the sight of it shook me. Knowing I'd have to reach out and touch her clothes, still neatly racked on wooden hangers. I did it in a kind of trance, trying not to catch the scent from her dresses, wrapping each one in tissue before packing it in a trunk. I didn't know what to do with them, so I kept them as a kind of gift for myself. When I had finished, I knelt on the wooden floor beside the window that overlooked the garden. The silver birch was in bud and the white magnolia beyond the wall. A cruel spring light fell on my face and I turned away, sunk to my knees.

My thoughts were interrupted by the buzz of the intercom. I was surprised. It was rare that anyone called on me, unless it was my pal Will Langley, turning up drunk again.

'Yes?'

'It's Helen.'

I was silent; unprepared.

'Can I come in?'

'Yes. Yes, of course.'

She wasn't due until tomorrow. She was supposed to call first.

I had a few minutes before she arrived on the doorstep. I hadn't washed that morning. I dashed to the bathroom, wiped my forehead, brushed my teeth. When I looked at myself, I wanted to laugh out loud at the very idea that she might find me attractive.

She stood in the corridor, looking nervous. It was a warm evening; she wore a white linen dress and a denim jacket. Her hair was up, her throat bare. She smiled, nervously. She held a letter in her hand.

'Hi,' she said.

'Hello. You've caught me unawares, I'm afraid.'

'I'm sorry – I shouldn't have come. It was stupid of me. You're busy, aren't you?'

'No.'

'Honestly. I'll go.' She turned, then seemed to remember something. 'Oh – this is for you.' She handed me the letter. 'I saw it in your pigeon-hole.'

'Thanks. Look – don't go. I'm glad you're here.'

'You're sure?'

'Positive.'

I invited her in and she followed me to the lounge. I dropped the letter on the coffee table and began clearing magazines from the sofa. Helen approached the window and looked out at St Paul's. I followed her.

'It's a brilliant view,' she said.

'Yes. Isn't it.'

I could smell her perfume: a sharp, citrus scent.

'Are you sure it's OK? Me being here?'

'I've said so.'

'You're probably just being polite.'

'Yes, probably,' I said, mocking her.

She grinned, then took a deep breath, as if composing herself.

'Do you like it here?' she asked.

'Yes. Very much.'

'Mmm.' She turned around. 'It's a nice flat. I wanted to get a flat this year. I can't stand living at home.'

'Why not?'

'I'm sick of being with my parents, I suppose. I want to live in a real place.'

'Real?'

'I'm sick of Richmond. My parents are just so bourgeois.'

Her words were a reminder of how young she was. I knew that in reality her life and mine had no common threads. Helen was discovering things for the first time, she had none of my pent-up bitterness, my guilt. I was self-contained, a tight spring, but she was open and vulnerable and interested. I never said a word that was not guarded. She uttered banalities, not realising or caring even if what she said was unoriginal. To her the experience was new. It charmed me.

'It looks strange from up here, doesn't it?' she said.

'What do you mean – strange?'

'Kind of unimportant.'

I smiled. I knew exactly what she meant. I liked living here. Up high, immune. I liked the anonymity I felt when I crossed the walkways beneath, losing myself among the theatre-goers, the art-lovers, the cinephiles. 'A concrete jungle' my mother had called it, when she first visited. 'I don't know how you can bear it, Harry.' She didn't see the beauty of the place, how it had risen from a wasteland, the ruins of the Blitz. I was entranced by it still. The concept of living in the cultural heart of the City appealed to me. True, in the maze-like walkways, one often felt dwarfed, like a character from Kafka, but this too had its comforts.

'Would you like a drink?' I said.

She nodded. Her eyes were flickering, wouldn't fix on one thing.

'Why don't you sit down?' I said. 'What can I get you?'

'Thanks. A beer?'

It threw me. I didn't keep beer in the flat. I had plenty of wine, but I hesitated to offer it. Perhaps it was too *bourgeois*.

'Sorry. I'm out. Will whisky do?'

She looked surprised, but laughed.

'Great.'

I poured us each a large measure.

'Won't be a moment. I'll just get some ice.'

I took the opportunity of going to the bathroom. I washed my arm-pits, applied deodorant. When I returned, with ice, I stopped just outside the door. I watched her.

She was standing at my desk. She'd taken off her jacket while I was out. Underneath, the thin white dress revealed her long arms and the slight curve of her breasts. She'd picked up a photo of Alison, taken on a holiday in the Peaks. If it had been anyone else, I would have been furious, but not with Helen. I simply watched, a little awed by her presence. I took her in. I knew it was a rare moment and I enjoyed it. Her beauty seemed improbable. Her head was tilted and her hair fell across her face.

'Do you like it?'

She put it down as I spoke; was nervous again.

'I'm sorry. I shouldn't have touched it.'

'It's OK.'

I knew, of course, why she was here. It wasn't just me. It was Alison. I had to remind myself of that. I knew, if I was to interest her, I'd need to be subtle. The sooner I revealed myself to her, the sooner she might lose interest. I had to tease her, to keep parts of myself, and Alison, hidden.

'Why don't you sit down?' I said. 'I'll dig out the photograph of Arabella. That's the one you came to see, isn't it?'

The photographs were kept in a folder in the bottom drawer of my desk. I'd been tempted to find them earlier that day but I'd held back, perhaps because I still harboured a fantasy: that Helen and Arabella were indeed identical. I wanted some explanation for my feelings towards Helen. For these events to have a neatness that in reality they lacked.

I sat down beside Helen. She seemed tense so I decided to get it over with. I opened the folder and took out the photographs. There was Arabella, bearing – yes – some resemblance to Helen, but she was, without doubt, a woman in her own right. I thought of Alison and asked myself, once again, what it was about this woman that had so moved her.

I handed the photographs to Helen. She looked at Arabella and clearly saw my meaning. Certain physical similarities were plain. Helen's face, however, was bolder, her features sharper, more defined. Helen's face spoke volumes whereas Arabella's, delicate and neat, was closed. All her spirit was in her eyes.

'She is like me, isn't she?'

'Yes. Quite like you.'

I tried to shrug it off. But Helen was serious.

'Why are these pictures important?'

'Who said they were important?'

'You did. Last night. You said she was writing a novel . . .'

'Ah.'

'Well?'

I shook my head and she hastily put the photographs back in the folder. Then, no doubt despairing of me, she picked up her glass and took a large swig of Scotch. Soon, I knew, I would have to speak about Alison, find words for thoughts I had never dared articulate.

'You'll have to tell me what this is all about, Harry,' Helen said.

It was the first time she had used my name.

'I don't know where to begin.'

I felt almost resentful. That she had imposed herself on me. That she had so little tact.

'Tell me about the photograph.'

'What do you want to know?'

'Why was it important to her?'

'Your guess is as good as mine.'

She didn't like my evasiveness.

'You must know something.'

'A little. Yes.'

'Well?'

'Give me time for Christ's sake.' I regretted my outburst immediately, but I couldn't stop myself. 'Look – you're asking me to tell you things I've never told anybody. Do you think I've got it all off pat? Why all the bloody questions?'

'I'm sorry.'

It surprised me to see that her lip was trembling. She was afraid of me.

'You must understand,' I said. 'This isn't easy.'

'I shouldn't be so nosy.'

'No. It's my fault.'

'I can't believe I'm really here, you know?'

'What do you mean?'

'I mean with you. It's like being closer to her. I've always felt as if I knew her, ever since I read her book. But everyone says that, don't they? It doesn't mean anything.'

'Yes. I suppose it's a common thing.'

I was irritated. She had stated what I already knew to be true. She wasn't here for me. But even so, my answer had cut her. Her brow was knitted and she had wrapped her arms about herself. She wouldn't look at me. I could tell that she was close to tears but she didn't want me to know. For a few minutes she was silent and I did not help her. I waited until she was ready to speak.

Then she simply said, 'Is it OK to have a cigarette?'

'Of course.'

I fetched her an ash-tray then went to the window and opened it wide. It was a warm night, a wonderful sky, heavy with cloud. I could hear laughter from way below. And I stood, listening for a while, breathing the fresh air, bracing myself.

It seemed an age before I turned again, though only a few minutes had passed. The light in the room seemed dim, shadows stretched across the floor. She had slipped off her shoes, the smoke from her cigarette coiled across her face. I could see her eyes were reddened.

80

And I leant back against the window-sill, sensing that she didn't want me close. When she spoke, her voice was tight and constrained.

'The novel about Arabella. That was the book you burnt, right?'

So that was it.

'No. I didn't burn it.'

'And I'm supposed to believe that?'

'You can believe what you like.'

There was a muffled hysteria in her voice but my own was calm. I wasn't hurt by her accusation. I had heard it so many times, it couldn't touch me. Instead I felt a kind of elation. The strength of her emotion was unexpected and I realised that I had a hold over her. So long as I could keep her guessing, I wouldn't lose her.

She took another drag, held the smoke inside her, then blew it out as if reluctant to let it go. She crushed out the stub.

A little stab of pity touched me, but I ignored it.

'How am I supposed to trust you,' she asked, 'when everything I've ever read about you is bad?'

'You have to learn to judge people for yourself.'

'So they're all lying?'

'First it's one story, then another. Can't you see, they despise me for what I did. For marrying Alison.'

'What do you mean?'

'Before I married her, she was public property. Her face was everywhere. It sold newspapers. Afterwards, there was no story. She stopped going to glitzy parties. She stayed home and wrote her novel.'

'They say you stopped her from going out.'

'And you believe that?'

She said nothing, merely shrugged.

'She hated those parties, but she couldn't imagine a life without them. It was a huge relief to her, staying home, doing ordinary things. But the press didn't like that. Gordon Hake certainly didn't. It was only the beginning of their hatred, but it's been going on ever since. There's a biography about to be printed. And the film, of course. Christ knows why I allowed that to go ahead. More excuses to open up the whole can of worms. Only recently, another article, Hake again, implying I should have recognised the symptoms of depression. I closed my eyes to her illness. It's utter crap. The people who were close to Alison – myself, her real friends, even her father – we've all kept quiet. Why is that, do you think? We don't want to get involved in their stupid games.'

'But if they tell lies, you should put them right.'

'Do you think they'd believe me? They've made up their minds. And all the "facts" they relate about her suicide are pure fiction. A few ill-gathered stories from the villagers of Glaven. And the testimony of a handful of so-called friends. They've even failed to track down the American woman – it's pure incompetence. The press can find no reason for Alison's suicide, so they invent a reason and call it Harold Bliss.'

I could tell she wasn't convinced.

'I won't speak about this in public, Helen. My innocence is plain, to anyone who has eyes to see. When I arrived in Glaven, I went directly to the mill. The burnt manuscript was discovered before I even went near that cottage. If people wish to draw conclusions from my silence, then let them.'

'But if you didn't burn it – who did?'

'Alison did. Alison.'

'Can you prove that?'

'No. But I can tell you things that might help you to believe me.'

'Go on then.'

I paused. My motives were hardly pure.

'It would take weeks.'

She picked up her glass. She seemed to be weighing something up.

'I'm still trying to take this in. That manuscript – I've read so much about it. And now I find out that she was writing about me.'

'Hardly.'

'OK – not literally. But Arabella does look like me.'

'A slight resemblance. That's all.'

I was worried about her then. But I didn't stop her.

'I know. But when you first saw me . . .'

'A trick of the light. Nothing more.'

'I want to know everything. I've got weeks, if that's what it takes. Term's over. I've got nothing planned.'

'I don't know.'

My hesitation was genuine. If I said yes, I couldn't account for what would happen. For myself, I didn't care. But Helen was young and impressionable. She had a fixation about Alison and it would be kinder to let her go. She would have to accept it; she could get on with a normal life.

'What's the problem?'

'There are questions I haven't yet asked,' I said. 'I'm not sure I want to know the answers.'

'I don't believe you.'

'Some things are best left alone.'

'Do you know why she killed herself?'

'No.'

'Don't you want to know?' she asked.

'I can't say.'

I began to wonder who was leading who here. We were both of us caught up in it. I tried to think about Richard. I remembered his voice, only that morning. *Hands off* he'd said. His tone was jokey, but I was thinking of a different Richard now, as he appeared in the portrait – that immobile face, staring at me. But it wasn't enough to stop me. The more I looked at her, the more his face faded. The room seemed darker now, the last light fading from the sky.

She approached me at last. Then, barely knowing what I was doing, I was kissing her and she was responding. All the time, my hands were working, sliding the dress from her shoulders, marvelling briefly at the flesh that was exposed, then wanting more, finding her zip, working it loose. There was no thought. I did nothing that was not necessary for both of us. Her complicity astonished me. Her long arms twined about me, unbuttoning my shirt, my trousers. So long since I'd made love, it was like the first time – the scent of almonds in her hair; the way the dress slipped across her narrow hips; the small, private probings of her tongue about mine.

I kicked off my shoes and we stumbled through to the lounge, each circling the other. I stepped on her dress as I unhooked her bra and turned her about, long and white like a boy, her breasts so slight. She was gasping and afraid, as I was.

'Are you all right?'

She nodded and pulled me to her, on the floor, against the edge of the sofa where she finished undressing me. There was an unreality about it. She was lithe, unflawed, and I wanted her, I put my fingers inside her and watched as she closed her eyes and gave herself to it; the little thrustings of her hips, the way my fingers slid so easily back and forth, and I let my palm play against her too – it all came back to me, as if six years hadn't passed.

Her excitement took me by surprise. I had no idea that I could do this to a woman – let alone a girl. I bent to kiss her again and as I did so, she came, with unexpected suddenness and fury. It frightened me, this lack of control. But I couldn't think about it. I turned her over before she could rest. She lay with her arms above her head, breathing, waiting. I wondered whether she was on the pill; perhaps I should have thought of condoms – wasn't that what you were supposed to do, these days?

I told myself, then, this was more than just sex. I convinced myself there was some meaning to it.

'You look ravishing,' I said.

It was the sweetest thing. So simple, this taking of her flesh, letting six years slide away. I pulled her buttocks up towards me and she let me do it like that, not seeing her face, and I adored her for it. I believed I fell in love with her as I watched her hair uncoil across her back.

## 7

T HE FOLLOWING MORNING I awoke, before dawn, barely
believing what had happened to me. Yet I turned and there
she was, beside me in the darkness, sleeping quite peacefully. I
watched her, astonished: her pale face against the pillow, her mouth
parted, exhaling softly.

I knew, when I saw her, that everything had changed. I could
surely not go to school that day, nor face Richard after this? The
previous evening, Helen had called her mother and a friend as alibi.
So Richard knew nothing. Yet the idea of lying to him was nearly as
bad as the sin I had already committed. I got up and walked through
to the lounge, wondering to myself where I might go from here.

We had left a lamp on, the curtains were drawn, and the room
stank of stale tobacco and alcohol. Helen's clothes remained
scattered across the floor. I picked them up, arranged them on a
chair and, as I did so, the letter on the table caught my eye. I laughed
to myself, remembering how Helen had stood there so nervously,
holding it. I imagined her, rifling through my pigeon-hole. I hadn't
checked on Saturday. The letter must have arrived then, a couple of
days ago.

Now I examined it. The handwriting was unfamiliar; the envelope was full. My address was written in black ink in a distinctive,
self-conscious style. I looked to the postmark for some clue. York. It
meant nothing. I sat down on the sofa and tore it open. It contained
not only a letter, but also a newspaper cutting dated the previous
Friday. I glimpsed at it. Jesus. So, Hake had gone upmarket. He was
writing for the broadsheets now. It was a double spread, headed
with the following words:

### A NEW VIEW ON THE BLISS SUICIDE
#### A SECOND BIOGRAPHY COMMISSIONED

My first reaction was the usual one, the deep, biting anger that I ought to have learned to live with. Hake was the last thing I wanted to think about this morning, while Helen lay sleeping in my bed. I wanted to go to the kitchen, make coffee for her, wake her. But it was too early, so I settled in the sofa to contemplate this news.

I was aware, already, of the first biography of Alison, which was going ahead unauthorised. I had spoken to the publisher and refused to allow any of Alison's work to be reproduced there. It would be a farce of a book, yet it could still be damaging. A second biography, however, was news. I could not believe that this article had appeared without my knowledge, that nobody had told me about it. Had Richard seen it, I wondered? Had Helen? As the implications of the headline began to sink in, I turned to the letter for an explanation. It was hand-written on smart, headed note-paper. It came from Professor Judith Frazer, a name I had not heard before. I began to read.

*Dear Harold Bliss,*

*I'm writing in relation to the enclosed article, which you are no doubt aware of. If you have read it – and God knows I wouldn't blame you for not reading Hake – you'll know that it addresses the difficulties faced by your late wife's biographer, Paul Vinton. You will also have seen me named as a second biographer, though in fact I haven't yet begun work on such a book.*

*I have to say, first off, I had no involvement in the publication of this article. It is a grossly defamatory piece of work, and how this man retains his credibility is anybody's guess. In any case, the article has prompted me to write. I ought to apologise, I know, for not having contacted you sooner. We met briefly, at your late wife's funeral, but of course you won't remember me. I got to know Alison during her stay in Glaven. I was holidaying there and we shared several memorable evenings. Our friendship was short-lived but intense. I found your wife very witty and bright, but I also thought she was rather disturbed. I won't forget some of the things she said to me.*

*As you know, I've never spoken to the press. I've taken a real interest in the speculation surrounding her death and indeed my own identity but it has not been difficult to shun publicity. You will have identified me by now as the 'American woman' some-*

times mentioned in reports – a tag which truly amuses me, considering I've been an honorary Brit for fifteen years. I went by a different name at the time I visited Glaven and moved to York shortly after the funeral. I thought, at first, that my identity would come out, but thankfully the people of Glaven have kept quiet.

I'll come to the point. I'm currently lecturing at the university here, in the English department. My short friendship with your wife and the calamity of her death led me in recent years to begin a study of suicide and the female artist. I have now completed this work and would be grateful for your permission to quote several passages from Sweet Susan. Hardly professional, I know, to have delayed so long but I guess I was nervous of the infamous Harold Bliss. Perhaps we can discuss? With regard to my planned biography of your wife, I have not yet begun work. My publisher, unfortunately, has not exactly been the soul of discretion. I had intended to approach you shortly and am dismayed that my identity should first be revealed to you by this frankly second-rate article which surely did not merit publication.

It goes without saying, I'm hopeful that you may permit me to write an authorised biography. I wonder if we might meet? At least, I ought to tell you what I know about your wife's suicide: the confidences she shared with me. I can't claim to fully understand Alison's motives, but I can reveal the identity of one who might. His name is Ern Higham and he got to know Alison in the final weeks of her life. He's an old man – in his late-nineties, I believe. The people of Glaven have protected his identity also. If he could be persuaded to speak, however, I feel sure we would be closer to understanding what motivated Alison to act as she did.

I imagine you'll have some questions. Doubtless you wonder why I haven't contacted you sooner. I'm sure, however, that we do share certain concerns. Paul Vinton's planned biography for example: Sweet Alison. The title alone is cause enough for despair, but frankly the flimsy credentials of the man have left me reeling. I do feel that it is time a more balanced view of events is made available. It won't be possible to beat Mr Vinton to the book-stands. Still, I'd like to write a biography that will provide a broader context for Alison's story as well as giving a more detailed, truthful and intelligent account of her life, work and

87

*suicide. My intention would also be to examine the campaign the press has waged against you, singling out Gordon Hake, naturally. I want to investigate his role in this business, as well as the injustices inherent in his version of events. I do so hope, Mr Bliss, that you'll agree to meet and talk? With your co-operation I'm convinced we will be able to move towards a fuller understanding of what happened to Alison and the blame might finally be lifted from your shoulders.*

*With all best wishes.*

*Yours sincerely,*

*Professor Judith Frazer*

It is not easy to describe how this letter affected me. I looked again at the cutting and noticed the photograph of Professor Frazer: a striking woman, though not exactly attractive. She appeared to be in her mid-forties, with dark, cropped hair framing a large-boned face. Her nose was very prominent but balanced by a generous mouth and heavy-lidded eyes. She had a fierce, disconcerting look. I put the cutting down. There would be time enough, later, to read it.

I leaned back in the sofa, shaken. So – the infamous American. A professor. But weren't they all Professors, these American academics? Did the title mean anything at all? Still, I was stunned. For so long, I had been waiting for this, never believing it would happen. The timing was uncanny, as if my past was now unravelling. All that I had struggled to contain was spilling out, and though I did not believe in fate, only in accident, there seemed to be some pattern to these events. I had wanted to move forward, to lay these ghosts to rest, but now I realised it would not be possible.

I knew, of course, the tricks these people played. This Professor Frazer might pretend sympathy, but was she really so different? I felt myself divided: that the American woman should turn up at last, but in the guise of a biographer; that the person I hoped might save me might instead undo me further. Already, I felt my anger rising. For over six years this woman had kept silent and her silence had condemned me. If she knew something that might have spared me the years of vilification, why did she not speak earlier? The answer was plain. Now the time was ripe. Alison's fame would peak when the film of *Sweet Susan* was released. Frazer's book, like Vinton's, would be nothing more than merchandise.

Still – I could not help it – there was a part of me that wanted to trust her, wanted to find some reason for her failure to speak. But I could think of none. I asked myself, if Judith Frazer was Alison's friend, was that not some recommendation? No. Alison had no friends in Norfolk. If she'd had friends, surely she would not have killed herself. This woman was simply a casual acquaintance who had leapt on the merry-go-round like everyone else.

Why then, did her words disturb me? And this Ern Higham – why had I never heard of him? Was it possible that an old man might know the answers I had been vainly seeking for over six years? That he had been Alison's friend? I wanted to dismiss it, to tell Professor Judith Frazer to go screw herself. But my fury was tempered by desperation – I needed to know the truth. When Alison took her life, she permanently altered mine. I had no choice but to find out why.

On the table, I caught sight of Helen's cigarettes. I picked them up. Much as I despised the habit, I was a hypocrite in a crisis. I lit up, inhaled – it had been a couple of years but it felt good. I stood and paced the room. I peeked into the bedroom. Helen had not moved. It was clear now, I would not return to school.

There were several things that did not seem right about this letter. I was worried about the description of Alison as 'rather disturbed'. It corroborated the press view of events and sat uneasily with the story I told myself: that when she left for Norfolk, she had recovered from her depression. It forced me to go over the fundamental problem I had with her suicide. There were two possibilities. Either I had been blind and the press were right: I had, in some inconceivable way, contributed to her suicide by my own neglect. I should not have let her go. Was that more likely than the other scenario? That something had happened to her, later, in Norfolk, that I knew nothing about. Was it possible she had been unbalanced by a person or an event of which I was ignorant? And if so, did Judith Frazer or this Ern Higham have the answers?

I sat down at my desk. Something else was bugging me. I did remember Judith Frazer. There were several people present at Alison's funeral whom I did not recognise, but took to be the token guests from her publishing house. I couldn't believe that I had never made the connection. A strong-looking woman in an expensive black suit. I took her to be an editor. She was not tall but she was large-boned and trim. She had longer hair at the time, which explained why I had not recognised her from the photograph. Like Alison's father, she had not attended the reception, but she had shaken my hand before she left the church-yard. 'I'm so sorry. Truly.' The banality of the words, but the accent had struck me and the way she looked directly at me. Barely anyone had looked at me that day. As if they wanted to protect themselves from my grief.

Now I picked up Hake's article and read it through. I wondered why he didn't simply make an effigy of me and stick pins in it, then be done. There was nothing terribly original about this latest piece. No connection was made between the professor and the American woman. Only the news of the biography marked it out. What also astonished me was that Vinton's work was apparently complete. That it was written so quickly suggested a shoddiness which worried me as much as the event of the book itself. I had always ignored Vinton's letters but now I half regretted it. I knew one thing. His biography would pander to the demands of Alison's ever-hungry public. I was beginning to think that nothing would satisfy them. They wanted a spectacle; as if to read about her despair, to imagine her cold, humiliating plunge into the sea would somehow purge them of their own inadequacies.

I replaced Hake's article on the table. I could remember a time, before the publication of *Sweet Susan*, when I believed that I had finally headed him off. In those years – when Alison avoided the public arena, recovered from her illness, wrote her novel – Hake appeared to vanish from our lives. He continued to be successful, pursuing the stories of countless other bright young things, but it seemed his interest in Alison had died at last.

Alison, however, could never forget Hake. I made an effort not to mention his name but my silence had little effect. Sometimes, in the night, she would wake in a cold sweat, her eyes wide and full of panic. I would stir, yawn guiltily for sleeping so well, and find her like that. She would tell me her dreams; she had a need to exorcise them.

'I was on the catwalk, Harry, and everybody thought I was fine. I mean, I looked no different from the other models, but I knew that I *was* different. They were wearing only clothes, but I wore clothes and a false skin too. Underneath the skin was my real body which was nothing but a skeleton. It would have been OK. I would have got away with it, except that Hake was there, in the audience. Just as I got to the front of the stage, he leapt up and started laughing. He was clawing at me, pulling off my skin. "Look at this," he was saying. "She's a fake. She's made of latex!" Only, as he pulled at the skin, I realised that we had both been wrong. It was my real skin, after all. I was screaming out but he didn't listen. He was tearing me to shreds . . .'

At times like that, I felt myself pretty powerless, and furious too. Hake still had a hold on her. Perhaps it was because she knew him, she knew he too would not forget. When she retreated from public life, I believed that would be the end of it. In the early days of our relationship, he continued to follow us, to make stories from the fact of our relationship and her new, rather hermit-like existence. But eventually, after several months, such stories became old news. Once Alison's life became less glamorous, the public no longer hungered for her and there was nothing left for Hake to write. I told Alison that it was over; she could finally put him behind her. I could not have been more wrong.

It was five years from the date of our first meeting that Alison's novel was bought by an English publisher. The foreign rights, the film rights, were sold soon afterwards. When I thought of Hake, during this period, it was like remembering a person from a past life. He was never present for me, as he was for Alison. True, I knew that the publication of her novel would bring her, once more, into the public arena, but I thought that Hake, by then, would have moved on. I had failed to understand the nature of his obsession.

On the day that the deal was struck, the telephone didn't stop ringing. Even then, Alison insisted that I field the calls for her. She must have known that it was coming. When I heard his voice, however, I was struck cold.

'Gordon Hake, Harry. Good to speak with you again.'

For the first time, I believe I understood Alison's fear. I told myself, he's just a man. Just a man, doing his job. But I knew that it was more than that. Perhaps her terror had struck something within me. I can't say.

'What do you want, Hake?'

I could hardly understand my own feelings. Was it the knowledge of the photograph in his possession, or was it simply that I had been worn down by so many disturbed nights, with him the phantom that prevented my wife from sleeping? It is possible that in that moment when I heard his voice again – the arrogant, upper-class, velvet-smooth insincerity – I understood that Alison's nightmares had been justified. Did I suspect, even then, that she was right? That he had never been absent from our lives. He had been horribly present, all along.

'I want to speak to Alison.'

'She's not available.'

'Sure. Look, I'll be straight with you. I'm looking for an exclusive on this book, OK? Very simple. If you have other offers, let me know. We can top them.'

'She won't do business with you.'

'I'd like to hear that from her.'

'Why don't you fucking leave her alone, Hake. Haven't you done enough damage?'

'No,' he said. 'I don't think so.' He paused, perhaps realising what he'd said. 'It's a good offer, Harry. Nobody can lose.'

'You're wrong there,' I told him. 'It's your turn to be the loser.'

Now, at last, seven years after that conversation, I was forced to confront the fact that Hake had never lost. Perhaps it had been my fault. My own silence had allowed him a certain freedom. I picked up the article again.

Judith Frazer, at least, had been true to her word. She had refused to comment on her forthcoming book, yet I remained cynical about that woman's motives. How could she comment, when to do so might reveal her own identity? At present, her connection with Alison had not been revealed, and I imagined that she was keeping quiet, so that her own writing, when it appeared, might make a greater impact. The thought of it infuriated me.

The only other 'exclusive' contained in this article was yet another interview with two of the students who had seen Alison, as she approached Glaven beach for the final time. As usual, the students were encouraged to wax lyrical. It was superstitious twaddle. They said how ethereal Alison had seemed, as if, in those final moments of her life, she had already crossed to the other side.

The piece continued with a contribution from Vinton himself. He had made a pilgrimage to Glaven and described the cottage where

Alison had stayed. In a crass attempt at originality, he described his walk along the beach shortly before dawn. He imagined Alison there. He fictionalised her last moments, her thoughts and feelings – what could have driven her to this? He reminded us of her glittering past, her literary prizes and her promise; attempted, audaciously, to enter her mind. He romanticised my wife's despair.

Surprisingly, it did not hurt me to read his words. I have imagined that scene too many times myself, with a clarity of vision far greater than this hack could achieve. Rather, I was angry. I was tired of the lamentations of strangers. They mourned her loss and the loss to modern literature but they knew nothing about her. These 'facts' don't make a life. The source of their fascination is not pure. They want to distil the essence of the Suicide, to turn the base metal of her life into gold. Indeed she contributed to this alchemy. When she stopped her life, she also fixed it. She will never write bad books. She will never grow old. Alison will always be young and vibrant, always the tortured soul. And I'm caught up in that too. In the eyes of the world, I remain in the past with Alison, the husband who did not understand her: the scapegoat. Now I find I have lost possession of my own life. My life has been ransacked by thieves.

Some people report that what I did, that summer with Helen, makes me no different from the others who wrote about Alison. Like them, I've heard it said, I wanted to recreate the past when I should have let it lie. But I can't agree with that verdict. Was it so wrong to want to understand my wife's suicide? What were Hake's motives? Obsession; resentment; greed. He rendered me two-dimensional, a character in a bad fiction. I had no sympathy for him, just as he had none for me.

What happened with Helen was different. True, it was Alison's story that attracted her to me and I knew that she would only stay so long as my words had power to enchant her. It wasn't me that she was after but the experience I offered. Yet what happened that summer was so complex, so inconceivable even, that anyone who so much as caught a glimpse of it, would have reeled at its brightness. It was a bright web that we wove about ourselves, brilliant in detail, marvellous in execution. And – I know – to unravel such a thing might prove disastrous yet I am determined to unravel it. I'll see no way forward until the thing is done.

# 8

AT LAST, I HEARD A stirring in the bedroom. It was still early, around seven. Though it was light outside, I could not bring myself to draw the curtains, to allow the morning in. I wanted our time together to be a continuation of the previous evening, did not want the real world to intrude.

I made coffee and brought it through to Helen.

She sat up, nervously, the sheet wrapped across her breasts.

'Thanks.'

As she drank, the sheet kept slipping and I realised she was coy about her nakedness.

'Have you got a dressing gown?' she asked. 'I'm a bit cold.'

I paused. I didn't actually possess a dressing gown of my own. But I approached the chest in the corner of the room, bent down and opened it. The scent hit me and I was overwhelmed, but I tried to ignore my reaction. I rifled through the clothes and soon found it. Alison's dressing gown – cream satin with a faded rose-bud design.

I held it up.

'Here.'

She hesitated.

'Are you sure?'

I nodded and averted my eyes as she wrapped it about herself. Then she got up and sat at the edge of the bed. I was in shock, rather, at the sight of her.

'Do you mind if I get a cigarette?' she said.

I shook my head and followed her through to the lounge. Something heady, sensuous even, about the atmosphere there: the dim light; the empty glasses on the table.

'I think I'll join you,' I said and she offered me the packet.

'I thought you didn't.'

'I don't.'

We lit up, but I didn't know what to say. We were silent for a while. I wanted to tell her about the letter. Then I realised that something wasn't right. Something about Helen's expression.

'Hey – what's the matter?'

'Nothing.'

I couldn't understand it. Why hadn't I noticed sooner? She was on the verge of tears.

'What is it?'

'Really – nothing.'

'Please. Tell me.'

'It's just . . .'

'Yes?'

'I suppose you won't want to know me, after last night.'

'What are you talking about?'

'Now we've – you know. I might not see you again.'

'What on earth gave you that idea?'

I couldn't help but laugh.

'It's happened before. I've slept with someone on the first date, then I don't see him again. I can be so stupid.'

'Helen – I'm not one of your usual young men. I'm beyond one-night stands, believe me. I do want to see you again. I want . . .' But I couldn't say, exactly, what I wanted.

Over breakfast, I made an effort to lighten things up. I had found an old bottle of champagne and I poured us a couple of glasses. We curled up on the sofa, drinking and eating toast. I didn't like to see Helen so tense and the alcohol did the trick. Before long, she was laughing. I tried to steer the subject away from anything too meaningful. I mentioned my desire to go to India and it turned out that she had been there, the previous autumn – touring in a play. It had been her first professional role. I remembered Richard telling me about this: what a marvellous opportunity it had been for his daughter. Some entrepreneur had been touring the drama schools looking for fresh talent, unwilling to pay full Equity rates.

I drew her out. She drank another glass and before long it was as if our first conversation of the morning had never happened. I tried not to think about Richard, about school, as Helen told me crazy stories about rickshaw drivers with no sense of direction; theatres that had black-outs half-way through the play; cockroaches and geckos in the dressing rooms. I warmed to her as she told these stories, even as I wondered what she had really made of it. I wondered how she had reacted to the beggars, the architecture, the caste system. I thought of Alison. She could not have visited a country like India without being deeply affected by it.

'What's the matter?' Helen said.

'I'm sorry. It's Alison . . .'

'Oh.'

Perhaps we had no choice but to return to this.

'We never laughed much, you know?'

I stroked her hair, to reassure her.

'I couldn't be like her,' Helen said.

'You wouldn't want to be.'

'What do you mean?'

'Often I wonder where all the pain in Alison came from. I'm not saying she was always sad, but sadness could descend on her, quite suddenly. As if she had an aptitude for it. And yet . . .'

'What?'

'Most of the time, she was incredibly bright and enthusiastic. It made her depressions all the more unfathomable.'

'I can't imagine what it must have been like for her. I only know . . .'

'Yes?'

'When I read her book – she has this power, doesn't she, to make you feel things?'

'She wrote well.'

I was beginning to feel uneasy. It didn't come naturally, to talk about Alison. Whilst a part of me was ready for it, another part resisted. It was not easy, to articulate this, when for so long I had kept silent.

'But more than that,' Helen said. 'There's this sense that life was so precious to her. Reading her novel – it reaffirms life, doesn't it? It's not nihilistic.'

'I know what you mean. It was like that being with her. Even when she was sad. Something about her.'

It was not difficult to find the right words, yet I did not want to speak. I felt the strain of it.

'What was she like?'

Quite suddenly I'd had enough. I snapped.

96

'I'm sure you've read all about her. What can I tell you that you don't already know?'

'Please.'

'Let me clear this stuff away,' I said.

I removed the empty glasses from the table and went to the kitchen to wash up. But Helen followed me. She circled her arms about my waist, lay her head on my back.

'You smell good,' she said.

'Do I?'

'Tell me about her.'

'What's the point? What's the bloody point?'

Even her closeness could not soothe me. She moved away.

'Why are you suddenly so angry?' she asked.

Why indeed? I had only to look at her.

'I'm tired of how public my life has become. And it's all lies.'

'So tell me the truth.'

'Why should you believe me?'

'Because I want to believe you.'

'There's still so much I don't know,' I said. I dried my hands. 'Come on – let's sit down.'

I knew I could hold back no longer.

'Look,' I said. 'There's something I should tell you about. This letter . . .'

I picked up the envelope. She looked embarrassed.

'I shouldn't have been so nosy, looking in your pigeon-hole.'

'It's not that. Only, I thought it might interest you.'

'What is it?'

'It's from a woman who knew Alison in Glaven. The "American woman". She's finally come forward.'

'That's incredible!'

'Yes. I hadn't expected it. The thing is, she wants to speak to me. I thought you'd be interested.'

'I am. But why do you want me to see it?'

I realised she did not understand, even now.

'Because I like you, Helen.'

Again – a short silence.

'What do you mean?'

'I thought it was obvious.'

97

'It's not "obvious". The way you were, in the kitchen just now . . .'

I took a deep breath.

'I'm sorry. That was . . .'

The excitement that I felt seemed wrong, which only fuelled it. Was it then, as I spoke, that the idea occurred to me, that my plan was conceived?

'It's not wise you know. To get involved with me.'

'I know.'

'Your father would be furious.'

'Forget him.'

'He's my friend.'

'But it's none of his business.'

'I think you're wrong there.'

'Look, will you show me this letter?'

I handed it to her. She read in silence, with immense concentration.

'I can't believe it,' she said, when she had finished reading.

'I don't know what to think,' I said. 'I've been waiting for this, you see. For years, hoping she might come forward. But now it turns out she's writing a biography. And she wants me to authorise it. Christ Almighty, the woman has a lot to learn!'

'Are you going to meet her?' Helen said.

'I just don't know. The idea of meeting a biographer . . .'

'You must.'

I fell silent then.

Helen came closer, rested her head on my chest.

'You know,' I said, 'the things that happen to us – there's no pattern. Everything is random.'

'Why do you say that?'

'Because it seems right now there *are* patterns. It's deceptive.'

'What sort of patterns?'

'Meeting you for a start. The way you remind me of Arabella.'

'And the man in the photograph – he looked like you, didn't he? Like seeing ourselves there.'

'He was my great-grandfather, of course. But then this woman – the American. Her coming forward like this – the timing of it.' I held back then, wondering if she was ready for what I was about to say. 'You said you wanted to know more. You didn't care if it took weeks.'

Her face lit up and she nodded.

'You're still on for it?'

'For what?' she said.

'I want us to go away together.'

'Away?'

She seemed excited, uncertain.

'Yes. To Glaven.'

She was clearly stunned, said nothing.

'I'll tell you what I know, the whole story – which isn't much. But what I don't know – well, let's do our own investigations, shall we? Why leave it to the scavengers? We'll find this Ern Higham – see what he can tell us and take it from there?'

'Are you serious?'

'Perfectly.'

'It would be painful for you.'

'I should have done it a long time ago.'

'But you've been to Glaven before.'

'Yes. Shortly after her death. It was a mistake. Hake was there with a photographer. He took that famous photo of me, as I arrived at the mill. They started the ball rolling, all over again. I was in a daze, Helen. I barely remember it.'

'So Gordon Hake was the only journalist there? After her suicide?'

'He was the first. It wasn't long before the place was crawling. I got out pretty swiftly.'

'It must have been really hurtful. The stuff they wrote around that time?'

'How do you know about that? You couldn't have been much more than a kid?'

'I was twelve. I remember Dad was in a rage about it. He kept ranting on about how it wasn't true. I knew who Alison was then, but only because Dad talked about her. He wouldn't let me read her book, said I was too young. But I remember reading the newspaper articles.'

'Do you? Do you remember it? Hake wrote that I was *composed*. Can you believe that? Perhaps it seemed that way to him. I'd just come from the mortuary where I identified her body. I did every-thing that I was required to do. I had to collect her things – which meant going to Glaven. That man, Hake – he saw only the surface.

99

"Harold Bliss." You know all about *him*. This sombre face . . .' I gave her a look and she laughed, then stopped herself. 'Expressionless. He invented its meaning. But you know – that man in the photograph, he was nothing but a façade. My body was simply a shell – the shape of a man. Do you see what I mean?'

'I think so.'

'Only beneath the shell – are you with me?'

'Yes.'

'I experienced a collapse. How can I describe it? As if my flesh had lost its form and purpose. I kept it together – on the outside – but inside I was nothing but a mass of organs. Internal bleeding – you see? But no scars. I was unscathed – or so it appeared.'

'I can't imagine it.'

'Hake's side-kick took that photo on that first night. I'd arrived, late. I parked by the windmill where I'd booked a room. It was pitch black. I remember stepping out of the car, fumbling with my keys, trying to make out the path. Quite suddenly, there was this great flash. It startled me. Then I saw them, approaching. I locked my car and began walking and Hake started asking me questions. *How are you feeling, Harry? Do you know what caused Alison to do this? Had she been suffering from depression again? Why was she alone up here?* I kept walking. I wanted to spit and scream at him. Worse. You see, earlier . . .' I stopped myself. She didn't need to know everything. Not yet. 'There was a moment,' I said, 'just before I reached the door, when I heard the cry of a bird and for some reason I thought – I'm not going to make this. But I did. I rang the bell and the proprietor let me in. Hake slunk away into the shadows.'

Throughout my speech, Helen had leant towards me, listening intently. I had not planned this. I had not wanted to reveal myself in this way. Yet there was something about her presence, the dim light, the sense of being removed from my usual life. The words I'd spoken had been in my mind for too long. No doubt I was ripe for it. I wondered if I'd scared her off.

When she was sure that I had finished, Helen slipped from the sofa to the floor. She took my hands and pressed her lips to them. I had not experienced such tenderness in years. She looked up at me, searched my face as if to find my sorrow in the lines that were etched there. Then again, she stroked my hands, the hair on the backs of my palms, my square fingertips. I eased the robe from her shoulders, still awed by the whiteness and softness of her flesh. She moved from my hands to my waist, untied my robe and began to caress my prick. For a moment I wanted to protest but she moved her mouth to it and already I was hard again. She began to lick at me, as if it were somehow necessary for her. The satin robe was about her hips and she was between my legs, drinking me up. I gave in to her. I watched the movements of her tongue, the way I filled her mouth. Then she raised herself and sat on me.

'It'll be all right,' she whispered. 'Don't worry. I'll come with you. To Glaven.'

Then I remember nothing except the sex itself, the movements of her legs about my waist, her breasts against my chest: my own relentless journey to the heart of her.

# 9

Now, it seemed, there would be no turning back. I had only three days remaining to serve at the school – the term was due to end on Wednesday – yet still I could not return. Helen agreed. She wanted to go immediately, said it would be easier, slipping away without a fuss. People would disapprove, she said, however we did it. And though I was aware that we did wrong, I also felt that I had little to lose. I knew it would end and I knew it would end unpleasantly. But I was sure of two things. I had to understand Alison's death and I had to be with Helen, for as long as she wanted it.

Before we left, Helen persuaded me to call Judith Frazer. I was having second thoughts. I wondered if I were not using this woman's letter as bait to ensnare Helen. I feared that I was acting too rashly. But how could I stop myself? Though I reminded myself, silently, that Judith Frazer, like all the others, wanted my story, nothing more, there was a small part of me that clung to my old hope: that this professor would have answers to my every question. Now Helen watched as I dialled.

I expected an answer-phone but instead I was greeted by a voice, cold and uninviting.

'Hello?'

The accent was not so strong as I expected, but I knew that it was her.

'Is that Professor Frazer?'

'Yes.'

'This is Harold Bliss.'

'Oh.' She paused. 'Yes.' I thought I detected a slight uneasiness. Certainly the tone of her voice changed – a warmth crept into it, though I wasn't convinced that it was genuine. 'Mr Bliss. You have my letter?'

'Yes. I thought that we should talk.'

'Good. We have a lot to talk *about*. We could meet perhaps?'

'It might be difficult.'

'I'll come to London, of course. It's no problem.'

It seemed unreal, that this was her voice, at last. There was a smoothness to it that I distrusted. Her accent was anglicised and I remembered that she'd been living in this country for some years.

'I'm afraid it won't be quite so easy.' I paused. 'Actually, I'm planning to go to Glaven.'

'Glaven?'

'Yes. I'd appreciate your confidence . . .'

'Sure. It goes without saying. When are you off?'

'Today.'

'Might I ask why?'

'It's time I made some enquiries. I've delayed too long.'

'You'll be speaking to Ern Higham, I guess?'

'Yes. Possibly.'

'I wish you luck. But perhaps we should meet first.'

'It really can't wait.'

'Well, my term's over. I could drive to Glaven – tomorrow, say?'

'Just one moment.'

I turned to Helen, covered the mouthpiece.

'She wants to come to Glaven. What do you think?'

'Say yes.'

'All right,' I said. I felt distinctly uneasy at the prospect. 'But I'm making no promises. About your biography – you mustn't as- sume . . .'

'I'm assuming nothing. Have you an address in Glaven?'

'Not yet. I'll call this evening – to let you know.'

'Good. I'll look forward to it.'

We wanted to leave at once, but there were problems. I packed a case for myself but Helen had come unprepared. She could not go home because she couldn't face her mother. We debated the idea of buying all she needed, but Helen was looking at me in a certain way and I knew what she was thinking. She had seen the open trunk in the bedroom. It was full of Alison's clothes. She shook her head. I didn't need to say it.

'I'm not sure I like it,' she said.

But I guessed she liked the idea very much.

'It's just good sense,' I said. 'What use are they otherwise?'

'They might not fit.'

We both knew that wasn't true.

'They'll be fine.'

After that, she didn't protest. We were, after all, entering into something that we barely understood. We knew that for her to literally step into Alison's shoes was in some way immoral, but it was what we wanted. We kidded ourselves into thinking that it was a purely practical move, but we both knew it was more than that. We were on dangerous ground.

For the journey, Helen chose a dress, the blue silk one that Alison had worn that day at the Tate.

'What do you think?' she said, twirling before me.

It struck me as auspicious but I said nothing. I simply kissed her. And I swear that I could still smell Alison, as if she had remained there, in the fibres of the silk. I know that I used such coincidences to justify my actions. If I had allowed myself to be objective, I could not have acted as I did.

When I think, now, of the journey we made, I remember the sense of relief I felt as we left London behind. Perhaps, somewhere deep inside, I knew that I was journeying towards something far darker than I cared to admit. But if this were true, that knowledge was so buried that I did not recognise it. After all, this was new territory. When I had travelled to Norwich, after the suicide, I'd taken the train and hired a car to go to Glaven the following day. So these roads were unsullied. No memories were attached to them. Helen held the map and we ceased talking about Alison. Neither of us was ready to face up to what we were doing, nor what lay ahead.

There was an ideal quality about that day. For the first time in years I was acting irresponsibly. I realised how stifled I had been and for how long. In Helen, I had found a catalyst that released me. I appreciated the pleasure that comes from breaking rules, from acting out of character. By walking out on the school, by refusing to wait for their false farewells, I felt that I had triumphed. Here was I, Harry Bliss, driving out towards Thetford Forest, with a girl of nineteen by my side, the beautiful daughter of a friend, stolen away.

'For she had eyes,' I said aloud. 'And chose me.'

'Ah, the wicked Moor,' she said.

'Something like that,' I replied.
And she smiled.

We had intended to stop in Norwich for a late lunch, but we got lost in the centre. Eventually, we came across the railway station and the river, and immediately a blind panic struck me, a thousand awful memories crowded my mind of the afternoon when I saw Alison in the city mortuary. Helen, naturally, was concerned, but I brushed her off. I suggested that she get some sandwiches and drinks for us – we'd have a picnic later. She agreed and I pulled into a road rather aptly named Tombland.

I watched Helen as she left the car, distracted momentarily by the way the dress played about her legs, the slight sway of her hips. She moved with a certain ease, seemed strangely relaxed, like a person in possession of some grand secret. I allowed myself to imagine that she was Alison, that Alison had never left. But then I remembered – the image of her body, beginning to decompose. Now I wanted to get away, though I realised that I had nowhere to run to. The place we were travelling towards held terrors far greater than those I sensed here. Even so, I wanted to move on. I found this city oppressive. The sheer Englishness of it incensed me. It was so quaint, with its cathedral spire worthy of a Constable painting, its cobbled streets, full of aimless pedestrians, and its little 'hopper' buses. These things were my idea of hell.

Very soon, we were out of it.

'What's the matter?' Helen asked, when the silence had continued for too long.

'Don't worry,' I said. 'It will pass.'

As we approached the open fields, my gloom did indeed lift. The sun had burnt through clouds, and there was a sweet, sticky smell in the car, as the plastic seats began to bake. Helen opened her window wide and lit up and I joined her.

'Don't you get hot, with that beard?' she said.

She had reverted to her former lightness. Perhaps she guessed it was the only way to get through to me.

'You want me to shave it off?'

'No. I like it.'

'Well stop complaining then.'

'I'm not!' she screamed.

I laughed. She could not have known what it meant to me, to laugh like that.

Now the country unfurled before us. This part of the journey was in a way familiar. I had travelled these roads in darkness, in a state of distress, when I first journeyed to Glaven to collect Alison's things, the day after her body was discovered. It was a tribute to Helen that these memories did not immediately trouble me, that I was, for a while, able to distance myself from them. We were taking the same roads, travelling to the same place. But it was difficult to believe there could be any link between the blackness of that evening and the unforgiving light that now illumined the fields about us. It seeped into every crevice, leaving nothing unrevealed, a sharp definition of objects only possible where the land is flat and there are so few shadows.

'What is it, Harry?'

We had been silent for several minutes. Helen lobbed her cigarette from the window. I did not reply.

'What's the matter?'

'It's not what you imagine. Do you mind if we stop the car?'

She shook her head.

'Shall we eat?' she said. 'I'm starving.'

I pulled over. She smiled coyly and I leant over and kissed her. She was so warm and I could smell the sunlight on her skin. I felt as if I knew her.

We left the car and clambered over a stile into a field, saying nothing, overcome; everything was different here. It was the silence that struck me first, or rather the lack of human sound. Across this vast, flat earth, birds were swooping. Their cries seemed almost haunted. At first I couldn't figure why, but then I realised – there were no echoes in these fields. The air swallowed sound.

'It's amazing, isn't it?' Helen said.

I nodded and squeezed her hand.

'Look at that sky. Have you ever seen anything like it?'

It was true. We had been living so long in the city that we had forgotten there were other possibilities. We were surrounded now by huge fields that stretched uninterrupted to a distant horizon. The earth was so flat that the cloudless sky seemed to engulf us; the sky was everywhere.

'You know,' I said. 'There's nowhere to hide here.'

She smiled but said nothing. I was thinking about London. How the sky there is so erratic. It skims above the city but is never seen. It's simply not part of the landscape. The thought worried me; that I had been living so high above the city, yet had never looked anywhere but down.

We ate lunch slowly beneath the shade of a large horse chestnut tree. I had been expecting sandwiches – something simple – ham and cheese. But Helen had bought marinated black olives, slices of quiche with asparagus, vine-ripe tomatoes, focaccia bread and strawberries. She looked at me as I unwrapped the luxuries, to see if they pleased me. I was touched, unused to being cared for.

We talked in a light-hearted way and afterwards, when we were gorged, we were quiet for a while. The sun was lower in the sky and the shadows that had previously been absent now began to stretch across the fields. Helen lay back, smiling lazily.

'Tell me a story, Harry,' she said.

I leant over and kissed her.

'It's about to begin,' I whispered.

Perhaps my answer did not satisfy her. I couldn't tell. She fell silent again and I let her be, wanting to give her space. For me, the enormity of our act was beginning to sink in. I imagined that Helen might be thinking about her parents and I, also, thought of Richard. I knew that my actions were unforgivable. And I guessed that there was worse to come. How long, I wondered, before Hake was on to us? What a field day he'd have, when he discovered this.

Yet I refused to solidify Helen's doubts by expressing my own. Any weakness that I displayed would only disturb her. If I failed to be positive, she might falter and I would lose her. I understood that my seduction had only just begun; I would have to work to make her certain that this was not madness we were indulging in.

She lay with her back towards me now. I leant over and traced my finger along her spine. She turned, expectantly, and smiled but I was not convinced.

'What's wrong? Are you having regrets?'

She shook her head, then laughed.

'Just a few.'

'Do you want to tell me about it?'

'It just seems – a bit crazy, that's all.'

'Would you like to go back? It's not too late. Nobody would ever know.'

'Is that what you want?'

'No. But I'm concerned about you.'

'And about Dad, right?'

I hesitated.

'It won't be easy to placate him. But we've gone some way together. I'm not entirely sure that we *could* go back. Unless you really wanted to.'

'I don't.'

'Don't be afraid to say what you think.'

'You want me to be honest?'

'Yes.'

'OK. I am a bit scared. I don't even know you. And I don't know how I'll feel when we get to Glaven. I mean – what if we don't find out anything? This Ern Higham guy – how can we be sure he'll even talk to us?'

'We can't be sure of anything. But as I said, you're free to change your mind, if you like.'

But Helen didn't want to change her mind. Something spurred her on. Still, there had been a change in the atmosphere between us; as if we were affected by the thought of what lay ahead.

I drove in silence. We were each absorbed by our own private imaginings. There was something I had failed to tell Helen, the previous evening, when I spoke about my first visit to Glaven. Hake's appearance at the mill had taken me by surprise, yet it was not entirely unexpected. The day before my arrival in Glaven, the same day that Alison's body was discovered, I had been in good spirits. There was another week before school began, and I knew that Alison would soon be home. I worked in the garden to surprise her, planting bare-root roses, preparing the earth for spring. It was late afternoon when the telephone rang. I was in the shower and I leapt out to answer it. I hoped it might be her, letting me know when to expect her.

'Harry.'

It was Hake. His voice a grim monotone. I was enraged. We had a new telephone number, which he ought not to have known.

'Jesus,' I said. 'What do you want?'

'I wondered if you wanted to make a comment – about Alison.'

'What about her?' I was taken aback by the strangeness, the generality, of his request. Again, the flatness of his voice struck me, the dullness. Not like Hake at all. I stood, naked, water dripping down my back. 'What? Something about the book? The nomination?' A silence at the end of the line. Then he hung up. Odd, I thought. Odd.

But then I knew. Some instinct kicked in, a sudden, gut-wrenching certainty. I felt the world close in on me. I closed my eyes, drew my grief inwards, and before I could let it out again, the howl that lay in wait, there was a knock at the door. I stumbled to the bathroom, grabbed a towel to wrap about my middle. Two policemen on the doorstep. 'Yes,' I said. 'Come in.'

We were coming closer to Glaven now, and I realised that these roads were indeed familiar. Something about the rhythm of them, or the way the trees hung above us – no more than a hunch, but it was enough. I forgot that Helen was at my side. I forgot the present. Overwhelmed by a sense of loss, I barely knew where I was heading or why. It was as if the years had not passed and I was again driving these roads on that starless evening, with only my headlamps to light the way. I remembered being hunched over the wheel, salt-tears dripping on my fingertips, my reason abandoned. I saw spectres in the trees. So many shadows, containing unknown terrors, so that I frequently swerved the car, half fleeing my fears, half hoping I might career into a ditch and be done with it.

It was a more than literal darkness that surrounded me that evening; a darkness that has remained. Why I had chosen to make the journey in such a state of agitation, I can only guess. Perhaps it was the need to act; the feeling that so long as I was moving, I might avoid the worst of the terror – which would come with contemplation. How could I have lain awake another night in the chintzy bedroom of the b & b by the river, staring at the floral wallpaper, huddling beneath the feather duvet?

But movement did not help me to forget. It was impossible to delete what I had seen that afternoon. Nothing could have prepared me for it and I wish to God I had never seen it.

Alison's body lay in the mortuary in Norwich. Her dental records had been obtained and her identity established. I did not need to identify her, but I wanted to see her. I knew, if I did not, I would not accept that she was gone.

It took some strength of purpose to convince the mortuary staff of my intention. I came up against a balding, pink-faced administrator, with large ears and an expression of permanent surprise. He had the wrong face for the job, yet his manner was perfect. His expression was unmoving, his voice unfeeling. These attributes lent him a weird authority. Yet I was insistent. There was no reasoning behind my request to see her. Had I thought it through, perhaps I would have realised that it was unwise. Yet I was possessed by a need that I could not articulate.

'I must see my wife,' I told the man, after we had talked for some minutes.

'I'm simply pointing out what you should expect,' he said. 'I understand your situation. But perhaps you should give the matter further consideration?'

'There's nothing to consider. I wish to see my wife's body.'

'Of course. But it's my responsibility to advise you that what you'll see is likely to be disturbing.'

There could not have been a greater contrast between us. I was furious; full of pent-up bitterness and rage. He spoke from a sense of duty. I guessed he didn't really care whether I saw my wife or not.

'If I regret it, that's my problem.'

'Your wife was in the sea for several days before her body was washed up.'

'Yes. I get the picture.'

'Fine,' he said, despairing perhaps of my sanity. 'I'll arrange it.'

Eventually I was allowed to see her. A plump, blonde woman escorted me down a cheerless corridor. Her manner was brisk but I preferred her to her colleague. Foolishly, I had imagined that Alison would be in the morgue, stored in a drawer beside countless others. Instead I was led to a small, brightly lit room and I hesitated in the doorway. It was sparsely furnished with a couple of chairs. A small cross hung at the far end. Beneath it lay Alison's body, raised on a kind of hospital trolley and covered by a white sheet. I tried to remain composed, but it wasn't easy. An unpleasant odour permeated the room which reminded me of the chemistry labs at school.

As we approached Alison's body, the woman glimpsed at me. Though she was young, she would have seen hundreds of corpses in her time, whereas I had only seen one – my father's. I looked back, reluctant to let her see how I was affected. But I was close to tears. My legs threatened to buckle.

'You can change your mind,' she said.

I remained silent. We stood by the side of the trolley above the shrouded figure. I was steeling myself. I shook my head.

'Show me,' I said.

She hesitated, averted her eyes, then peeled back the sheet to reveal the face of my wife. Only it was not the face of my wife at all. The face was bloated out, half eaten away. It was the fish, I later discovered. They had eaten her eyes and picked at her flesh. A few days in the water had left her so deformed that she was, indeed, barely recognisable. Half her hair was gone and her lips were rotten. I had intended to kiss her. I could not believe that I had been so naïve.

But now I understood. I saw that Alison was no longer Alison. Yet I also knew, quite instinctively, she could not have known it would come to this. This was no sea-change that she had suffered. She was not, like Millais' Ophelia, to be transformed by her death, left lovely and ethereal. When I think of that image, the beautiful drowning Ophelia, her arms in open surrender; when I think of her hair twining about her body, of the lush green river-bank, the wild-flowers released from her hands, I cannot help but wonder – did Alison think it would be like that? Did I?

I turned from the stink, from the face that I had cradled and kissed and called mine. I had to flee. I stumbled blindly from the room, vaguely aware of the woman who followed me, strangely aloof from my grief. One thought plagued me: Alison had done this to herself.

'Is there anyone I should call? A relative?'

The woman's voice behind me was an irritation. I remember the bright lights, the endless corridor.

'Can I get you a taxi?'

'You can get me nothing,' I bellowed, as we reached the reception area. 'Please. Leave me.'

Outside, I leant against the wall, retching. When it had passed, I stumbled to my hire-car and slammed the door. I did not know where I was going; why I was alone here; how I would live beyond that day. It was January and dusk was falling. I drove back to the b & b and threw my belongings in a case. With the image of her face before me, I started out for Glaven.

# 10

W E APPROACHED GLAVEN FROM the east, crossing the salt-marshes that bordered the sea. Helen, who till then had seemed ill-at-ease, suddenly brightened and I wound down my window as she stared past me, across the shifting reeds. There was something about the place that afternoon that seemed to move her. We remained silent as we left Salthouse behind and drove along the coastal road, but it was a different silence now; we were both struck with a certain awe, mesmerised by the brooding landscape. Cloud was gathering above the marshes and gulls dived low, crying out against the wind. The marshes stretched for miles, and though the sea still eluded us, we could hear it, sense it. Most of all, it was the monotony of the scene that astonished me. I had not known it was possible to be moved by such things: the hissing of the sea-grasses; the absence of humanity.

Now I felt certain of my purpose. For the first time in an hour, Helen touched me, placed her hand on my thigh. From the beginning, the spirit of Glaven seeped into our pores. I am not superstitious, but if I say we were possessed, I'm speaking of a natural process. Isn't this what *déjà vu* is about? Not the suggestion that this has happened before, but that a moment in time or a place so perfectly accords with one's dreams and one's desires – the rhythms of the soul – that it seems a repetition. Something in the emptiness, in the wild sky, that I would never forget. In the distance I could see the windmill where I had stayed on my previous visit. But even the knowledge of the tragedy that was stored here did not sway my conviction that I had somehow come home.

As we drove into the village, however, I became less certain. It was different there, the narrow streets peopled by ageing locals and a handful of tourists clambering into their cars at the end of a day's outing. It's a pretty place: little flint cottages huddled together; the famous pub, 'The Ship', where the ornithologists gather; the Pottery on the high street; the second-hand book shops; the tea-rooms.

'I didn't think it would be like this,' Helen said.

I wondered if she were disappointed.

'How did you imagine it?'

I was looking for a place to park and turned off along a side road.

'I don't know. I liked it better out there – on the marshes. Where are we going to stay?'

'Don't worry,' I said. 'We'll find somewhere outside the main village. It is rather cramped here.'

We were now driving along a quiet lane where the cottages were set back from the road, seeming lost in their huge gardens. I realised at once where I was. It startled me because I was convinced it was accidental, though now I question whether there wasn't a part of me that had intended to find this place all along. This was the lane where Alison had lived and we were fast approaching the cottage she had rented. I slowed to a halt.

'Come on,' I said.

I took her hand and led her up the lane but she was reluctant to follow.

'Isn't the village that way?'

I hesitated, stopped walking and looked at her.

'Maybe it's too soon,' I said. 'But just up here is where Alison lived. I wanted to see it. But if you'd rather wait.'

'No!' she said – a little too eagerly. 'I want to see it.'

In the light of late afternoon, this lane seemed far removed from the village. The fields glowed amber. Small clouds of mosquitoes gathered and the scratching of crickets droned in our ears.

We walked in silence. The air was dry and still, the ground parched. The rough path that we trod had been baked hard; cracks spread out beneath our feet. And I was struck by the contrast between the warmth that now permeated my body and the dreadful coldness I had experienced the last time I was here. Then, the trees were bare and black, the ground sodden. Alison had never liked the English climate: dark skies could drain her spirit. I imagined her walking this lane, muffled in thick jumpers and scarves, wearing jeans, her boots plunging into the mud, her hair rain-sodden. Was it possible that we were in the same place? That two such scenes could coexist in time?

We walked around a bend in the lane. I still don't know what I expected to see or feel. It seems, in retrospect, like an artful game played by the gods. Such things don't happen in real life. At least, I didn't used to think so. Now I'm resigned to the nature of chance. I know that months and years can pass when one feels that life is an aimless series of unconnected events. But I also know that there can be times when every event appears significant, as if everything that has ever happened to you has its place in a strange yet almost imperceptible pattern whose greater purpose remains unclear.

I saw the sign almost immediately. It was large and red and it stood out against the scorched landscape. TO LET.

'It's that one,' I said, almost nonchalantly. 'The one with the "To Let" sign.'

She dropped my hand and stopped in her tracks.

'You're not serious?'

I nodded. 'Perfectly serious.'

From here we could not see the cottage. It was set back, down a small hill. The garden was bordered by a dry-stone wall in which rock geraniums were flourishing. We paused at the gate.

'Have you seen it before?' Helen asked.

'Only in pictures,' I said. 'In the papers.'

It was true. When I came before, six years previously, I had stopped the car where we stood, but could not bring myself to approach the cottage.

'It must have been really lonely here,' Helen said.

'That's what she wanted. It's the writer's lot.'

The cottage had a pleasing simplicity. It was not the stuff of fairy-tales but a small, flint, workman's cottage. It was the garden that made it stand out. Though it was not well tended, it had been planted so densely that there was barely room for weeds. Some of the roses had run to seed long ago, but many were still flourishing, pale blooms and lethal stems, rambling up arches, trespassing across paths. Where weeds should have been, wildflowers were growing. Huge red poppies meandered among white foxgloves and hollyhocks. Alison would have liked this, yet she never saw it. The only flowers she might have seen here would be a few snowdrops, a Christmas rose if she was lucky.

'Was she happy being a writer?' Helen asked.

I shrugged. 'She had no alternative.'

We walked down the stone path to the cottage. I held a thorny branch out of Helen's way and she lifted her dress above her knees to avoid tearing it. I was divided then, between the lust I felt on seeing her bare limbs, and the knowledge that we were here, by Alison's cottage.

'It's pretty dirty in there.'

Helen had overtaken me and was peering through a window.

'Christ!' I said. 'What makes them think anyone would move into this?'

We were looking into the kitchen which was very basic, to say the least. In the centre was a large, bare table and chairs. There was a pot of dried-up flowers on the sill and a couple of faded prints on the wall. It was clear the place hadn't been occupied for some time.

'I'm going to take a look around the back.'

Helen was gone before I could stop her. She was excited, but for me it was too much. It struck me that Helen might never be more than a mere sightseer here. What she felt for Alison was infatuation. Despite her protestations, she undoubtedly saw Alison as the tragic heroine. I couldn't blame her. She was young and knew only Alison's image, her words and the spirit that they expressed. Such words, almost prophetic, returned to me now. Words from *Sweet Susan*:

*He looks on me and sees something more than what I am. I am skin and bone but he fleshes me out. I am fading. My lips, already yellow, but he paints them red. My hair turns to dust, my fingernails crumble. What does he see beyond this body? Does he think that when it's gone, I'll still be here? He should see the truth. I'm leaving nothing behind me. He has loved a worthless thing whose brightness was a joke he failed to laugh at.*

Were those words addressed to me? Should I have realised them as a warning? The difference between Helen and me was this: I knew more than words. I knew the woman. I could see her sitting at that table before her writing-stand, her legs tucked under the chair, a look of intense concentration on her face. When the work was going well, she needed nothing else. She had shed her past, had lost the need for adulation. On such days she would barely have noticed the dark clouds outside or the stillness of the house. The story would burn in her and later she would sleep undisturbed. My absence then would have no meaning. She needed me only when she suffered: when the walls of that kitchen hemmed her in, the sky weighed down on her and her pen had no life.

'Harry! Why don't you come round!'

I followed her to the back of the cottage. I noticed paint peeling from the shutters.

'Look!'

I craned my neck to the spot which Helen had polished and looked into a cosy, low-ceilinged room with an inglenook fireplace surrounded by low settees and a staircase at the rear. The place had charm. It was easy to imagine it as Alison might have seen it, spruced up for a new tenant. Again, I imagined her, with candles burning and the fire catching; curled up with a volume of poetry – George Barker perhaps or Yeats. I liked to think there had been good times here. When she was happy, she was never timid. I remember one night when we were holidaying in the Peaks. After dinner she said she wanted to take a walk, to see the stars. I told her I'd get my coat, but she said, 'Actually, sweet – I'd like to go on my own.'

'You can't, Allie. It's not safe.'

'What do you mean – *not safe*?'

'Come on – you know what I mean.'

'You mean that women shouldn't walk alone at night.'

'I didn't say that.'

'I don't want to argue,' she said. 'Just let me go. Do you really think there's some madman hanging around outside on the vague off-chance that some woman might be crazy enough to take a walk at this hour?'

'No, but . . .'

'I'll be fine.'

She had her way. After she had gone, I fixed myself a Scotch but soon I regretted letting her go. Quickly I donned my boots and stepped outside into the lane. There was no moon and the stars were meagre. The darkness had swallowed her; I called her name. Was it possible she was already out of ear-shot? I called again. No reply. I wanted to be with her; her desire to be apart irked me. Where was the romance in that? For her, there was a greater romance out there, which she could only find alone. She needed me when she was afraid; when the outside world seemed too large and unfathomable. But when she was strong, she wanted raw experience; to be touched by the world.

'Harry? What are you looking at?'
Helen touched the small of my back.
'I'm sorry.'
'That's OK.'
She looked awkward. We knew what was next but neither of us was willing to say it.
'We'd better find a telephone,' I said.
'Yes.'
'And then, I suppose we should look for somewhere to stay.'
'Mmmm.'
'Not like you to be so quiet.'
'What do you want me to say?' she replied.
'Say what you're thinking.'
'Why should I? You're not.'
'Ah,' I joked. 'But I'm very old. And very inhibited.'
But she wasn't amused.
'You're not being fair.'
'All right,' I said. I started back towards the car and she joined me. I hoped to hell I'd read her accurately. 'You're wondering whether we should stay here.'
She paused, as if unwilling to admit it.
'I don't know. It doesn't seem right, does it?'
'We might be too late,' I said.
'It might have gone, you mean?'
'Yes.'
We both knew this was highly unlikely.
'But what do you think?' she said. 'Is it a good idea?'
'Probably not. But we haven't exactly been sensible so far. Why start now?'

'We'll do it then?'

'I think so. Don't you?'

The estate agent didn't recognise me. She was a young woman with fair, lacquered hair and brilliant pink lipstick. She spoke with a strong Norfolk accent – seemed very happy to chat. I sensed she was amused at the difference in age between Helen and me. She kept glancing at my wedding ring.

'Aren't you wanting to have a look about the place, 'fore you go ahead?' she said. 'I could arrange a viewing this evening?'

'No,' I said. 'We're quite sure. It's exactly what we're looking for.'

'We won't be able to refund your deposit, see, if you decide you don't like it.'

'I'm sure it will be perfect.'

'It's in a nice area. Right pretty. You'll like that.'

'Good.'

'I've just moved here myself, from Norwich. Got hitched to a local about six months ago.'

'Oh,' I said, relieved somehow that she was not from the village. 'Congratulations. How do you find the place?'

'Dead quiet, but you get used to it. And I've got a little one on the way, so I'm hardly going to be out clubbing now. I can't wait for him to be born.'

I hadn't noticed the girl was pregnant – her belly was hidden behind the desk. I enjoyed hearing her speak.

'When's it due?' I asked.

'Not till December. It'll be a Christmas baby.'

'Well – good luck with it.'

'Thanks. Now then, I must stop gossiping. How long will you be wanting the cottage for? A short let?'

'That's right. A few weeks, perhaps?'

I looked at Helen. She nodded.

'How long has the cottage been empty?' I asked.

'Oh, well that I wouldn't know.' She paused, as if weighing something up. 'You're not superstitious though?'

'What do you mean?' Helen said.

The girl giggled.

'I shouldn't have said that. I don't reckon my manager would be pleased – to know I'd been blabbing.'

'You haven't told us anything,' I said. 'But I'd like to know. Is there a ghost?'

'Oh no – not a ghost. Well, not as far as I know.'

'What then?'

The girl leant forwards. 'Well, I don't know the full story, but according to my husband, there was an authoress lived there – some years ago. She was a bit strange, you know? Kept herself to herself. Anyway, there were rumours . . .' She hesitated. 'You're not from the press, are you?' I shook my head. 'No – 'course not. It's none of their business, my hubby says.'

'It sounds fascinating,' I said. I was suddenly aware that at some point I would have to give my name but decided to take the risk. 'You mentioned rumours?'

'She was friendly with an old man, Ern Higham, who lives over Blakeney way. They say he's a weird one too. A right old misery guts. Should be dead by now, he's that old. Anyway – apparently no-one could understand why they got so acquainted. He was a real hermit until she came along.'

'So what happened?' Helen asked.

'She went and topped herself, didn't she? Can you believe it? Threw herself into the sea.'

'No!' I said. 'Do you know why?'

'Not really. They say her husband was a bit rotten. But that don't seem enough reason, does it? She was probably mad. Oh dear, I hope I haven't put you off.'

'Not at all,' I said. 'It's an interesting story. Now then, do you know when we can move in?'

'I don't have the keys here. The owner wanted to get a cleaner in. It's right filthy in there – needs a bit of polish. Perhaps you could stay at the mill for a couple of days? It's lovely there. But I'll need a deposit. And your details.'

'Of course. But I'd rather not stay at the mill. Couldn't we get into the cottage straight away? We've fallen in love with it, you see.'

'Can't think why!' she said, suggestively.

I looked at her, stony-faced. She opened her mouth to speak again, but was distracted by the sound of the bell, which rang whenever someone entered the premises. I turned, also. A young lad, around Helen's age, had come in. He was tall, rather lanky, and he raised his hand in a casual greeting.

'Oh,' the estate agent said. 'Perfect timing. It's Phil. Phil, these people are interested in your mother's cottage.'

'Oh, great,' he said. 'Pleased to meet you.'

He came forward to greet us, holding out his hand. His eyes had been drawn by Helen. He beamed on seeing her. But now he looked at me and started. His hand dropped to his side. He faltered.

'Yes,' I said. 'We'd very much like to let the cottage.'

'Right,' he said. 'Right.'

Phil was clearly disconcerted. He was a handsome lad, with soulful, brown eyes and a large, sensuous mouth. But there was something of the privileged layabout in his manner. He didn't know where to look, it seemed. His eyes flickered from me to Helen and back again. Clearly he knew who I was.

'When can we get in?' I asked.

'I don't know,' he said, vaguely. 'I'm not sure it's still available.'

'Oh,' said the estate agent. 'We haven't had anyone else in –'

'No.' Phil cut her off. 'But there's a possibility . . . I'll have to check with Mum.'

'We'd like to get in tonight,' I said.

'It's a beautiful cottage, isn't it?' Helen said. 'I hope it's not taken.'

At her voice, he seemed to soften. He smiled.

'I'll see what I can do.'

I should not have been surprised to be recognised. But something about the boy's attitude worried me. The question of who owned the cottage had not, until then, crossed my mind. Now I remembered Alison's landlady. Was this boy her son? If so, and the cottage remained in her possession, it was no wonder he felt uneasy. Yes, I remembered his mother. How could I forget her?

'Do you think it'll be OK?' Helen said, as soon as we were outside.

'I'm sure it will,' I said. 'Don't worry. If it doesn't work out, it won't be hard to find a place for tonight.'

We had been told to return to the office at six-thirty. If the cottage was available, the keys would be there.

'Wasn't that woman awful?' Helen said.

'Really? You think so?'

I had rather liked her. Her reaction to Alison's story and her eagerness to talk made me think there was a lot these villagers knew which they had never revealed. There was clearly a conspiracy of silence here, else surely the press would have heard of Ern Higham. I was lucky. This relative outsider knew little. She had not flinched when I mentioned my name.

Helen wanted to call her parents alone, but first we discussed how best she might break the news. I concealed my own anxiety. I did not regret my actions but wished, simply, I might have fallen for somebody else's daughter. Richard had never been anything but decent and this was a betrayal of the highest order.

In the end, Helen decided to tell it straight. There was no need for the sordid details, but they had to know she was with me. She'd say we were here to find out the truth about Alison's death. I knew that telling them where we were meant risking a confrontation. Frances might leap into her car and be on the M11 in no time. But it was unlikely. Richard was clever; he'd persuade his wife to do things his way. I couldn't predict what tactics he would use. I simply imagined they would be subtle.

I told Helen I'd go for a walk in the churchyard and she agreed to meet me there. I kissed her hard to give her courage. She was near to tears and I told her again, 'It's not too late. If you've changed your mind, just tell me. I can get you home tonight.' I think I wanted to give her a get-out clause. I didn't want her to blame me, later.

But she shook her head and turned towards the phone-box.

'I'm going to tell them. I want to stay.'

# 11

T HE CHURCH WAS SET back from the road, at the top of a small hill, in a quiet part of the village, surrounded by fields. It was a huge, Gothic construction with a tower, dating from the fourteenth century I guessed, the kind of church, with its decorated stone porch, its heraldry, that would sit well in a large old English town, but was out of place in such a sleepy village. It was a giant that did not belong in this arid field, beneath this hot sun; it did not seem easy here.

It was not the church itself, however, that really interested me. It was the idea that my ancestors might lie here. Their bones might nourish the wildflowers which clambered between the graves and about the fading monuments. Such thoughts served as a distraction. I did not want to think of Helen and her parents, nor of the words that passed between them now. Instead I wandered among the gravestones reading the inscriptions, where they had not been eaten away – the dates and names and lines of poetry that I supposed gave comfort once. The yard was huge. It would take me half a day to check all of these stones and discover, for sure, whether the Bliss family was buried here. Now I simply soaked up the atmosphere. I was alone in a place of ghosts and I relished it. In this church, no doubt, my great-grandparents, and possibly my grandparents, were married. I had been told nothing, so I invented memories. At first I could see only the empty graveyard, the unpeopled church. But then I imagined I could hear the church bells ringing. I half closed my eyes. The yard was thronging with people and colour and voices. I saw the bride Arabella, as she emerged from the porch with Charles at her side. The air was strewn with rose-petals. They walked towards me, their figures thin as air and pierced by sunlight. They were conjured from more than simply dust. Yet they had no substance. Even so, very briefly, they lived for me as they must have lived for Alison.

The air was still again; the sun low. The shadow of the church tower advanced across the field. I caught a movement at the corner of my eye and, as I turned, my expression must have changed as I saw Helen coming towards me. She was crying. I hurried forwards, took her in my arms. She was childlike now and I could almost imagine myself her father and not her lover. I knew what I would say if she had run from *my* house with a man who purported to be *my* friend. I knew what I would think of him and that I would do anything to get her back.

But when she looked up at me, I remembered myself. Her face was reddened, her eyes wet and – Christ, why does this always happen at the worst of times? – I found myself hardening against her and, strangely, she was encouraging me. She removed her hands from my chest, found my buttocks and pulled me to her. She lifted her face, swallowing back her tears. My tongue was in her mouth and everything, everything was forgotten as our legs gave way. I thought she would stop then, but she didn't. My back crossed one of the tombstones but she climbed on top of me. She grazed her knee on a stone and a trickle of blood coloured her leg. I thought of the cold bones beneath me; the earth. If she would not stop it, I must. But what I saw – the strap slipping from her shoulder, her white flesh – was stronger than imagination. Or was it the contrast that turned me on? Was it the conviction that I should take her flesh to prove we were alive? We were alone. Nobody could see us. The blue silk dress; the blood; the hardness of the stone on my back; the sky above, so vast and unblemished. It was over in minutes. We had committed ourselves. Whatever her parents had said, there would be no going back. She looked down with an expression that said nothing at all. And I wondered where the hell this would lead us.

Afterwards we lay on the grass between the stones. She showed no desire to move and I, also, felt the need to stay. It would have been easy to feel shame but I wanted to feel something more. By staying put, I wanted to confirm our innocence. The churchyard was peaceful at this hour. It was marvellous, simply to be here, alive. For a long while we said nothing. My senses were acute. I wanted to remember everything and I found myself thinking of Richard and how he taught the boys to see. Now it came naturally. I noticed the texture of the long grass, the precise movements of an ant. When I looked up at the trees, it was as if I could discern the movements of individual leaves. And when my eyes came to rest on Helen's face, I saw a scattering of freckles, so small I had never noticed them. My eyes traced the line of her brow; pigmentation of individual hairs, colours of straw, snow and honey.

'What did they say?' I asked.

It was time that I found out. She turned.

'I spoke to Dad. He couldn't take it in.'

'I don't see.'

'Like he thought he must have misunderstood me. He kept saying, "Harry? Harry who?" "Your friend, Harry," I said. "Harry Bliss." "And *where* are you?" he said. But I'd already told him twice.'

'And then what?'

'He asked me what in God's name was I doing with you? And whether I'd be back tomorrow. He didn't get it. I had to spell it out. That I wasn't coming back for a while. And then he swore at me.'

'Tell me.'

'He said . . .'

She faltered. Briefly she had been calm but now the words of her father were welling inside her.

'He said what the fuck did Harry think he was doing taking me away from home? "What the fuck is going on?" he said. Dad just doesn't use that language.'

'He does now,' I said, wryly, then regretted my flippancy.

'The worse thing is, he still hadn't put two and two together. He kept asking what we were trying to find out? I'd told him about Judith Frazer, so he thought maybe it was just to do with Alison. But then suddenly he saw it. I could tell. He just went quiet. I thought maybe he'd hung up. I kept saying, "Dad, Dad are you there? What's the matter?" I knew he was there, but he didn't say anything. Then I started crying, and he said, "Helen – what have you done?" But I couldn't speak.'

'And that was it?'

She nodded.

'He knew. He definitely knew.'

'Did you give him the address of the cottage?'

'No. I was too upset.'

'So what did you say?'

'I told him I'd be in touch again and he didn't reply, so I put the phone down. It's awful. I feel like he really hates me.'

'He's in shock. He doesn't hate you. He hates me.'

She paused, seemed about to stand up. But then she said, 'Harry – can I ask you something?'

'Of course. What is it?'

'What do you feel for me?'

It had been so long since I'd been with a woman that I'd forgotten how often such questions were asked; I'd forgotten that need – to have feelings defined. Helen was asking prematurely. How could I know what I was feeling? I barely understood it myself. How could I put it into words for her, so the words would not sound empty?

'You don't have to answer,' she said.

'I want to be with you. Doesn't that tell you something? You're the first woman I've made love to since Alison died. I don't do such things lightly.'

She nodded, disappointed perhaps, but satisfied for now. I couldn't give her the words she wanted: the flattery; hollow protestations of love. Perhaps she expected me to ask the same question in return. But I did not want an explanation. Instead, I said, 'Come on – we've got to find out about this cottage.'

She smiled as she stood up. I think she wanted to make me laugh again.

'You're a wicked man, Harold Bliss,' she teased. 'Stealing this young virgin from her father's home.'

I faltered.

'Well – he probably *thinks* I was a virgin,' she said. And she held out her hand to pull me from the grass, and when I was up, she ran ahead.

'I'll race you,' she shouted. It must have been false bravado but I followed her down to the road where, out of puff and laughing, I took her hand.

# 12

THE ESTATE AGENT HANDED us the keys shortly after seven. The owner, we were told, had been difficult. But finally she had surrendered the keys, saying she had left a few groceries at the cottage, together with cleaning materials and fresh bedding. It was curious, that she should be suddenly so accommodating.

'Mrs Bobbin said she'd pop in this evening – about eight, if that's all right? To check you've settled in and to sort out a few particulars.'

'Yes. Of course.'

It unsettled me to hear the name. I had met Mrs Bobbin on my previous visit to Glaven. She was hardly so sweet as the name might suggest.

'I'll tell her you'll be expecting her then.'

Helen and I stood in the porch, trying to figure out which keys to use. I felt immense trepidation. I wondered who had lived in this cottage since it had been Alison's. Was it possible there would be traces of her here? I thought of the charred pages that were found in the grate. Alison's belongings had been cleared by Mrs Bobbin and brought to me at the mill. I did not like to remember the occasion. Yet I had often regretted not seeing the place where Alison had lived. In the early days, I had been unable to face it.

The first thing I noticed on entering was the smell: a musty odour, with a sour edge of dampness. It was clear the place had been uninhabited for some time, but I wasn't put off by this and I hoped that Helen wasn't either. She followed me into the living room.

'Perhaps this was a mistake,' I said.

'You're joking aren't you? This is fantastic.'

'It's filthy.'

The fireplace had spewed soot across the tiled floor; strands of dust hung from the ceiling, attached by threads of cobwebs that the spiders had long ago deserted. I had been foolish to take the place without a viewing. Nobody in their right mind would pay good money to live here.

'Why are you so grumpy, Harry? Come and look at this!'

She was opening an intricate wooden dresser, removing a number of glasses, holding them up to the light.

'Aren't they beautiful?'

The glasses were attractive enough. They were small sherry glasses in shades of blue and green and mauve. They had elaborate twisted stems which caught the late sun and sparked off light, so that when Helen twirled a few together she created a kaleidoscope of colour on the wall.

She reminded me of myself when I was ten years old, unwrapping the Christmas baubles, marvelling at the glitter and spangle of them. These glasses were mere trinkets and I smiled at the thought of Helen's home, where the glasses were all made of crystal. Gaudy specimens like these would never had got past the front door.

We took our time discovering the cottage. I didn't want to rush it. I opened the windows wide, a struggle because they were terribly stiff, but already my mood was altering. We didn't speak about Alison, but I'm sure that Helen, too, was thinking about her. Whatever we touched, whether it was the dried-up roses on the kitchen table or the blue-rimmed china dinner-service, we couldn't help but ask ourselves – were these hers? Did she pick these flowers once? Eat from these plates? Drink from these cups? I wondered whether I was not violating something precious here; encroaching on a territory that was not mine.

After a while, I fell silent, and Helen did not object. I believe she knew what this meant to me. Each door that I opened seemed more than physical. I was not simply exploring a cottage. My own heart was flapping open. I entered the bathroom. It was not the austerity of it that shocked me, not the stains on the bath, nor the bare stone floor, the fraying curtains, but rather that I could see her there, alone in winter, the room ice-cold, the water steaming about her nakedness. I could almost see her looking at me. Or looking through me. She didn't see me; couldn't see the future. But perhaps she was wondering why I was not there to wrap her in warm towels and rub her dry.

It was the same wherever I trod. I placed my hand on the banister and I saw her, walking before me. I knew it was madness. Other people would have lived here in the meantime. But as I ascended the stairs, wiping the dust from my fingertips, I wanted to believe that this dust had been building ever since she had left, that the cottage had been unoccupied since her death; waiting for my arrival.

At the top of the stairs, there was a small hallway with two doors leading from it. The first room was small and spartan. Both the walls and the carpet were a sickly pink colour. There were no curtains and the only furniture was a bare double bed and a chest of drawers. I guessed this had not been Alison's room so I opened the second door. This time I could imagine her there.

The room was painted white and the floor was covered with a tatty greyish carpet. The furniture however was more pleasing. The bed was cast-iron, Victorian, and there was an oak chest of drawers and dressing table. Above the chest, a gilded mirror, and an armchair by the bed, covered in a faded blue William Morris design, echoed in the thinning curtains and the cushions in the window seat which over-looked the garden. Then I turned and saw something else.

Above the bed was a painting. It was a wide canvas that stretched the length of the bed-head: a depiction of the sea. There was nothing welcoming about the image. The oils were thickly applied; some-thing indifferent about it, as if the artist cared not a jot for an audience. Yet it was truthful. It made me think of the poem by Arnold, 'Dover Beach'. I often taught it at school and whenever I did, the lads listened knowingly as if to say, 'we know why you've chosen this one, Sir'. What did they care about the Victorians' crisis of faith and the implications of Darwinism, when they could read their schoolmaster's personal anguish in every line? I had always believed them mistaken but now I realised that they were right. It was personal. The poem's description of the sea seemed contained within this painting, the grating roar of pebbles as the waves withdrew, their relentlessness. Now I recalled the poem's conclud-ing lines:

> . . . for the world, which seems
> To lie before us like a land of dreams,
> So various, so beautiful, so new
> Hath really neither joy, nor love, nor light,
> Nor certitude, nor peace, nor help for pain;
> And we are here as on a darkling plain . . .

'What's that, Harry?'

I had been speaking aloud. I was grateful for Helen's interruption.

'Don't I recognise that?' she asked.

'You probably did it at school. Everybody does.'

'It sounded a bit grim.'

'More than a bit.' I smiled.

She looked confused and I pitied her. We'd had enough morbidity for one day.

'Is this what I get for running off with an English teacher?'

'Ah, but you might get some rewards as well. Who knows, I might start quoting Shakespeare's sonnets later.'

'Fantastic,' she said, sarcastically.

But despite the jokes, her eyes returned to the painting. She appeared uncomfortable.

'Come on,' I said. 'Let's go downstairs. We'll see if we can get a kettle to work in this place. I noticed that our landlady has left some milk. You wouldn't get that kind of service back home.'

'Mmm. I'm dying for a cup of tea.'

But she seemed preoccupied.

'Anything the matter?' I said.

'Just . . . Well, you have noticed, haven't you?'

'What?'

'The signature.'

I didn't know what she was talking about so I leaned forwards to take a closer look. Now I understood.

'Well,' I said, trying to play down my reaction. 'The plot thickens.'

The signature on the painting was clear. *Charles Bliss. 1901.*

'I thought you'd seen it,' Helen said.

'No.'

'What do you think? I mean – how did that painting get here?'

I couldn't think clearly.

'I didn't even know he could paint,' I said. 'And it's the same year that Arabella . . .'

I paused. I hadn't told her.

'Go on.'

'I should have mentioned it before. Arabella drowned herself. Here, in Glaven.'

'What?'

She paused, taking it in.

'I'm sorry I didn't tell you before. I thought I had.'

'Shit, Harry!'

She turned away, hesitated, then left the room. I followed. She stopped on the stairway and sat beneath the landing window, shaking her head.

'Budge up,' I said.

But she wasn't in the mood to be placated.

'Why didn't you tell me?'

'I have told you. Now. I've barely had a chance. What difference does it make?'

'I don't know.' She paused. 'You are telling me the truth?'

'Of course.'

She appeared distracted but moved aside and I sat down beside her.

'This whole thing is so weird,' she said.

'I know.'

'So Alison copied Arabella. But this isn't public knowledge, right?'

'No. The press have missed it. Arabella has never been mentioned in print.'

'But what's the connection? I mean, why did Arabella commit suicide?'

She was being drawn in; I sensed a quiet excitement building.

'I haven't a clue.'

'But Alison must have known why, right?'

'It's possible,' I said. 'She didn't talk much about her work. But I'm pretty sure she didn't know the reason before she left London. My guess is that she came to find out.'

'Didn't she begin the novel before she came to Glaven? She must have known something.'

'I can't say. My impression is that the book was as much about herself as Arabella.'

'But when she got here and spoke to Ern Higham – he must know what happened, is that what you're saying?'

'I hope so. But even if we discover why Arabella killed herself, it may tell us nothing about Alison.'

'Except that she was a copy-cat.'

'Exactly.'

'What about Professor Frazer? Does she know any of this?'

'I'm not sure. We'll find out soon, no doubt.'

'And the painting . . . Do you think it belonged to Alison?'

I shook my head. I was about to speculate when there was a knock at the door.

'That'll be our Mrs Bobbin,' I said. I was rather dreading the encounter but I stood up and brushed myself down. I was determined to remain calm.

At first, I hardly recognised her. I had construed her face differently in memory and the reality surprised me. It was a waxen face, an almost yellowish complexion. Her black hair was strewn with grey and her smile was tight and imperious. She was the type of person who gave the impression of being taller than she really was.

'Mr Bliss?'

'Yes. Mrs Bobbin.'

I was momentarily distracted by the sight of her Land-rover which she'd driven down to the cottage.

'May I come in?'

She was already inside.

'Of course. Of course. Oh, and this is my . . . friend,' (the hesitation was slight but she caught it) 'Helen Cregar.'

'Pleased to meet you, Miss Cregar.'

Helen smiled uneasily and was wise enough not to attempt a handshake.

'Please, sit down.' I indicated a kitchen chair. It did not come naturally to be polite to her, yet I was oddly bound by convention. Mrs Bobbin glanced at the chair.

'We haven't had a chance to clean up yet,' Helen said. She picked up a cloth and began dusting the chair down. I wanted to say, 'for Christ's sake don't be intimidated by this harridan,' but the truth was, I was intimidated myself. I could not forget our previous meeting.

I had first seen her on a cold January morning, the first I had spent in Glaven. She had arrived at the mill, announcing that her car was full of Alison's possessions, and – I had her greatest sympathy of course – if it *were* possible I could take these things away, she would be most grateful. From the beginning, her coldness had struck me. Her expression, her apparent contempt, made a deep impact. I was fragile then, true, but was I wrong to think she took pleasure in her actions? I had come to Glaven to collect Alison's belongings, had intended to contact the landlady later that day. But something about her haste disturbed me. She observed me, as I unloaded my wife's possessions from the boot of her car into my own. Though she was middle-aged, there was a youthfulness about her eyes; a sharpness. I had the impression that she was waiting for me to make a mistake.

Afterwards, I rationalised these feelings. I told myself it was natural to feel victimised. Now, as she watched Helen dust the chair, I wondered whether my impressions had been so inaccurate after all. The woman was doing her utmost to make us uncomfortable. This time, however, I was determined not to be cowed.

'Mr Bliss,' she said. 'I must apologise for the state of the cottage. I hadn't expected to find a tenant for immediate occupancy.'

'It's not a problem,' I said.

Her voice was calm, detached. I detected a Norfolk accent but it was submerged beneath a more polished, rather clipped tone. She was one of those brisk, no-nonsense, country types. Like so many women of her class, she dressed in an understated way, in trousers and a light anorak. Now, as before, I mistrusted her. Her whole demeanour seemed designed to conceal something.

'Well, I can organise a cleaner in the next day or so.'

'I'm sure that won't be necessary,' I said.

'As you like.' She paused. 'Of course, the agency will fill you in on the details of the tenancy.'

She raised her fingertips to meet beneath her chin – a brief prayer perhaps? – then said what she had come to say.

'We've met before, of course.'

'Yes.'

'It was a surprise, when Phil mentioned your name, especially in relation to this cottage. The girl at the agency is a little slow, I must say. She's not from these parts.'

'Clearly my fame is waning,' I said.

'Your late wife seems as popular as ever.'

There was derision in her voice.

'What do you mean?'

I should not have been drawn into conversation but I was curious.

'Oh, we still get the day-trippers. More than ever in fact. These days it seems that the fans of Alison Bliss outnumber the ornithologists.'

Helen glanced at me. I knew that she was angry but she said nothing. Neither could I suppress my own agitation.

'Does that bother you?'

She shrugged, non-committal. Then changed her mind and said, 'Of course, we'll have an added attraction now.'

'What are you implying?'

She laughed; waved her hand in the air as if to brush my questions aside.

'Mr Bliss, this is really none of my business.'

It was a wonderful trick, the oldest in the book. The lightness of her tone; the flippancy. But I fell for it. For some reason, I began to justify my visit.

'I was simply looking for a place to stay. I don't want publicity.'

'Neither do I,' she said.

'Good.'

'But people have a habit of talking.'

'Are you saying you don't want me here?'

'As far as I'm concerned, this is purely a business contract.'

'As it should be,' I said.

'Quite.'

There was a brief silence. Then Helen spoke.

'There's a painting upstairs, on the bedroom wall,' she said. 'We were wondering, is it yours?'

'I should think so. Who else would it belong to? The one of the sea, is that the one?'

Helen nodded. I wished she hadn't mentioned it.

'Where did you get it from?'

'I have no idea. It's been there for as long as I can remember. Why do you ask?'

'I just liked it.'

'Ah. Well. You'll feel at home then. Good.'

I sensed that she too was curious, that she wanted to know why we were here, what our plans were. I was torn between my intense dislike of the woman and my need to ask questions.

'How long has this place been empty?' I asked.

'Almost a year. Before that I had other tenants. A very polite

young man and his wife. They only used the place occasionally –
mainly at weekends.'

'And you've had no luck in renting it since?'

'Strangely not. There's been a great deal of interest. People
wandering about the garden, peering in through the windows, that
kind of thing. You'll probably find that. It's difficult to keep people
away. They can't help but be –' she paused, 'fascinated.'

'I'm sure we'll deal with that,' I said. 'Was there anything else?'

'I don't think so. I'll leave my telephone number, in case you
should have any questions. And regarding the cleaner?'

'We'll do it ourselves.'

It was Helen who answered. It surprised me, but I agreed with her
decision. I didn't want anybody hanging around. I stood up. Mrs
Bobbin took the hint and followed me to the door. When I reached
to open it however, she stood in my way. She fixed her eyes on me. I
remembered the look from the first time we met, an ice-blue,
predatory stare. I said nothing, returned her gaze.

'Mr Bliss,' she said eventually. 'I do hope you will not be
bothering my grandfather.'

Her words seemed nonsensical. I could not imagine a grandfather
of hers could still be living. And besides, if such a man did exist, I
had not a clue who he was. Yet there was a threat in her voice which
troubled me.

'Your grandfather?'

But even as I spoke, I worked it out. Still, I decided to play
ignorant.

'I don't know what you're talking about. Is this some kind of a
joke?'

'No. Not a joke. I'll be off now. I wish you a pleasant summer.'

She turned and left. Helen closed the door, and as soon as it was
shut, she pulled a face, sticking out her tongue. I laughed.

'Come here,' I said. 'Kiss me!'

She smiled as I embraced her. Then we sat down again at the
table.

'Wasn't she gross?' Helen said.

'Not a nice lady.'

'She's off her trolley if you ask me.'

'Why do you say that?' To me, Mrs Bobbin seemed frighteningly
sane.

'What was all that stuff about her grandfather?'

'Ah. Haven't you guessed?'

She shook her head.

'Ern Higham, I imagine.'

Helen hesitated.

'What makes you so sure?'

'What other old man are we planning to "bother" around here?'

'Shit.'

'You're not frightened of her, are you?'

She shook her head. 'Why should I be?'

'No reason.'

But her laughter had subsided. Like me, she was quiet, trying to piece it all together. This house was a museum full of exhibits that I could make no sense of. Without Alison's manuscript, nothing yielded meaning. If it were true that Mrs Bobbin was Ern Higham's granddaughter, then was it possible that she knew more than I? If she did, she had kept her secrets well. The press had questioned her often enough. No doubt it was she who revealed the existence of the burnt manuscript to Hake. But beyond this, and since, her comments were always to the effect that she knew nothing. Why then did she seem to despise me?

'You look tired,' Helen said. 'Why don't you sit down in the next room? I'll make the tea.'

'I can do it.'

'No. Really. Haven't we got some biscuits left in the car? You could get them.'

I looked at the clock. Eight-thirty and we hadn't eaten since lunch. I felt terribly responsible suddenly.

'Should we try to find somewhere to eat?' I asked.

I thought perhaps the pub might serve food, though I was hardly keen to go there. Helen shook her head.

'I'm too tired.'

'I'd suggest we dial-a-pizza, but I don't suppose they have such things out here in the wilds.'

'I think we'll survive without pizza,' Helen said.

In the sitting room, the light was diminishing. I lit a lamp and began to pull the curtains, bringing down a light rain of dust on my face. Outside, the sky was paling and the sun, now concealed behind a strip of cloud, threw its last rays across the dim fields. I realised that I was exhausted. The day had brought so many changes. I had woken with a young woman in my bed and the knowledge that I desired to run away with her. But wasn't it simply that, a desire? Didn't old men always have such thoughts when goaded by the promise of young flesh? Flesh and more flesh – wasn't that what this was about? When I closed my eyes, I could still taste her, smell her. Had I taken my fantasy too far? What was I was trying to do here – to forget Alison or resurrect her? I had abandoned everything: my job, my equilibrium, my reputation (what was left of it – or might I say instead, I had confirmed it?). I had lost a friend, and for what? I could not tell whether I was resolving something or simply plunging myself back into a past that was at once dangerous and irresistible.

Yet this was not the past. When I had lain beside Alison, there had been an affinity between our bodies. Mine was older, more weathered, but Alison's body too had marks upon it to show that she had lived. She had a birthmark on her shoulder that I used to tease her about. I said it looked exactly like a little mouse. She had a jagged scar on her left knee which had been stitched after she fell once when we were climbing Helvelyn. I remembered Alison's slightly rounded belly, a symbol of her recovery, or, as the press would have it, a political statement, a two-fingered salute to the industry that nearly destroyed her. It was a body that had lived, but also one that had been lived in. Her womb, too empty always, had none the less twice been home to the seed of a child. Yet Helen was still a child herself. The whiteness of her skin, the lack of blemishes – these were her marks. When I lay beside her, I was acutely aware of my age, my imperfections. Our two bodies formed too great a contrast. My large and loose old limbs did not fit against hers; the skin was too dark, the flesh irregular. It was as if she was not yet ripe and I was already rotting and being eaten by wasps.

I closed the curtains and turned back to the room. Helen had brought tea. We sat together in the lamplight, which reflected in the windows of the dusty glass cabinets. If this was unnatural, I thought, if I had indeed beguiled her, I could not, as yet, regret it. Helen's eyes fixed on mine and I read uncertainty there. I knew that she missed her parents, that I was a stranger to her and this was simply a romantic dream that, being realised, might quickly lose its lustre. Above all, I knew I must not weaken, nor must I forget that she was vulnerable and I could damage her unwittingly. I moved to her side and placed my arm about her shoulder. I had fooled myself. Because she was unblemished, it did not mean she had no depth.

'It's good tea,' I said, and she smiled.

# 13

WHEN I THINK, NOW, of those early days in Glaven, I remember a sense of being hurried; of everything moving far too quickly. I had not intended it to be like that. I had expected to find a stillness out there, away from the city, where I might find courage to shed the skins I had accumulated over the years. I wanted to slough the façades one by one – the false bravado, the irony, the defensive chitchat, the unconvincing smiles. What lay beneath was anybody's guess. Perhaps I suspected I might find a man: what was left of Harry Bliss, the man who once married a woman called Alison, believing, no matter how naïvely, that he could make her happy.

But if I had wanted stillness, I should not have come to Glaven. I should have found some other wilderness, anywhere but this Norfolk village where my ghosts had not yet been laid to rest. Not that Helen would have followed me – that too is part of the equation – but having chosen Glaven, I should have known that I would find no peace.

So it was that, contrary to my expectations of a quiet morning, our first awakening in Glaven was a sudden one. We had decided to spend the night in the second bedroom, too tired to deal with the implications of sleeping in Alison's bed. I had planned to go out early to buy things for breakfast. I'd wanted to treat Helen to a huge fry-up, but I slept for longer than I had intended.

My dreams that night were vague and incoherent, yet I remember this: I was in the classroom, drawing on the blackboard – a diagram of the female genitals. I did not consider this an unusual thing for an English master to be sharing, yet when I turned to face the class it was empty, except for one desk where a man sat scribbling furiously with a lump of charcoal. It was Richard. He looked up: the same blank stare that I had first seen in his self-portrait. I wanted to run but I knew the classroom door was locked. I turned to the window in the hope I might escape that way but the window was crowded with faces. Every boy in my class was there and they began knocking furiously. They wanted to share the secret. 'Calm down,' I said as my own panic mounted. 'You'll be in here soon enough.' But this only served to make them madder.

Then came the moment when dreams and awakening blur. I was awake but the boys were still knocking. Helen turned towards me.

'There's someone at the door.'

'What?'

'The door.'

'At this time? Oh God, it'll be that wretched woman.'

'Mrs Bobbin?'

'Perhaps she'll go away.'

But it resumed again, and I got up reluctantly, put on my robe and went downstairs. It was not Mrs Bobbin, however, who greeted me. There was no mistaking the face of Professor Judith Frazer.

'Hi,' she said. 'I'm early, right? Have I got you out of bed?'

It was so unexpected, so completely absurd that she should be there, that I barely knew what to say. The heaviness of sleep was upon me and my mood was still unsettled. I had not called her the previous night as I had promised. It had slipped my mind. I had no idea how she had found me.

'Professor Frazer,' I said. 'Come in.'

'Call me Judith,' she replied, and smiled, displaying far more teeth than I considered decent at that time of day.

Frankly, I felt a wreck. My mouth was dry and foul-tasting. She was intruding on my first morning here with Helen. Had I not been weak from lack of food and ill-tempered, I might have created more of a scene, demanded more answers. What did she think she was doing, turning up like this, without an appointment? As it was, I stepped aside and she entered the cottage.

I was embarrassed to be seen in this state. I was not a pretty sight in the mornings. My hair would be dishevelled, my eyes heavy. Professor Frazer appeared bright and polished. It wasn't just her teeth that gleamed. Her cropped hair was tinted a shade of deep burgundy and shone as if she'd just emerged from the salon. Even her glasses looked brand-new. Oval and silver-rimmed, they perched on her commanding nose: exactly the type of specs that a trendy academic *would* wear. To complete the image, Professor Frazer wore a dark linen trouser suit with a flimsy white T-shirt, revealing the slightness of her breasts and her rather scrawny neck.

'Take a seat,' I said, affecting no doubt the 'Harry Bliss' she might have imagined – the gruff and uncommunicative type. 'I'll put the kettle on.'

Instead of sitting, however, Professor Frazer took the bag from her shoulder and placed it on the kitchen table.

'I've brought an offering,' she said. 'A few croissants from the local bakery.'

Though mightily cheered by the prospect of food, I didn't see why I should be overly grateful. Already I'd gathered enough strength to regret letting her in so easily.

'Thank you.'

'You're wondering what I'm doing here, right?'

'I hadn't expected you quite so early.' I glimpsed at my watch. It was already 10am. 'I didn't telephone last night. How did you find us?'

'Us?'

'I'm here with a friend. She'll be down shortly. I don't suppose she'd say no to a croissant.'

Professor Frazer grimaced.

'The more the merrier,' she said.

I began making coffee and there was a brief silence. Professor Frazer broke it.

'I hope I'm not intruding.'

She paused but I did not reply.

'I'm keen to get going, aren't you? There's so much to talk about.'

I could not take this seriously. This was insane. Professor Frazer had waited over six years before contacting me. Why the sudden urgency? She was less guarded than I'd expected, yet my own suspicion had not abated.

'Actually I didn't wait for your call,' she said. 'I figured it was a pretty small village, so I set off yesterday afternoon. I stayed over at the mill. I thought it would be easy enough to find you out, but it was easier than I expected. I ran into your landlady this morning.'

One thing I hadn't expected about Professor Frazer was her slight nervousness in my presence. There was a surface confidence – the slick image, smooth voice and daunting smile – but she also seemed uncomfortable.

'You know Mrs Bobbin?'

'I've met her a few times. I wouldn't exactly say we were friends.'

'So you've been to Glaven more than once?'

'I keep a low profile.'

'Not *so* low evidently.'

'Let me explain. Mrs Bobbin is *not* the type to go blabbing. She doesn't want publicity. She's terrified of it, in fact. If the press were to find out about her grandfather's involvement with your wife –'

'Her grandfather – Ern Higham – yes?'

'Exactly.'

I was intrigued.

'Let me get this clear. First of all, what *is* this "involvement" you talk about? And second, if Mrs Bobbin doesn't want publicity, why does she tolerate the likes of you and me?'

The Professor shrugged. I had the feeling she was holding something back.

'Well?' I said.

'I can't say. Can't put my finger on it exactly. But there is something . . .'

'Yes?'

As I spoke, I heard footsteps on the stairs and looked round.

'Good morning,' I said.

Helen was wearing Alison's floral blouse and loose white skirt, which hung low on her hips revealing her navel. I'd bought the blouse as a birthday present, shortly after Alison finished *Sweet Susan*.

'Morning.' Helen seemed on good form. 'You're Professor Frazer?' she said.

'Judith. Call me Judith.'

The women eyed each other; they shook hands.

'Pleased to meet you,' Helen said.

'You too.'

She was looking at Helen with some disbelief.

'I'll get the croissants,' I said and busied myself while they exchanged small-talk. Once I was seated again, I was about to repeat my earlier question, but Professor Frazer spoke first.

'Tell me,' she said, 'you have seen, I suppose, the photograph of Arabella Bliss.'

'Of course,' I said. I was taken aback. 'Yes.'

'Then you are aware –'

She glimpsed at Helen and her meaning was clear enough.

'Of Helen's resemblance – yes.'

She seemed relieved. But I was astonished. That she had seen the photograph.

'It's been a while since I saw it. But I remember it well enough.' She turned to Helen. 'I'm sorry. I've been staring. But it's uncanny.'

'It's OK,' Helen said. 'I've been through all this with Harry.'

Professor Frazer smiled. Something about the way Helen said 'Harry' had made our intimacy clear. 'I'll say one thing,' she said. 'You guys look like you haven't been fed for a week.'

'We skipped dinner last night. Listen – why don't I get ready and go out for some more food. D'you fancy bacon and eggs, Helen?'

'God, yes,' she said. She was flirtatious and territorial and I was flattered. I wanted to please her, though there was a part of me that wanted to stay here, to hear what the Professor had to say about Arabella.

'I have another idea,' Professor Frazer said. 'Why don't you two relax and I'll fetch groceries.'

'There's no need,' I said. 'We're perfectly capable.'

'It's the least I can do. I'll bring you some provisions then let you settle in. We could meet up this afternoon?'

I looked at Helen. She shrugged.

'All right,' I said. 'Why not?'


In Professor Frazer's absence, I began to feel uneasy about her arrival in Glaven. I realised that I knew nothing about her and I turned questions over in my head, irrelevant questions perhaps, but I wanted to know the answers all the same. Was she single, I wondered, or attached? Why had she come to England in the first place and why had she remained here? Did she have children? I doubted it. Who were her friends? And where did it stem from, this interest in my wife? Was it purely academic? Financial? Why, if she had a choice, did she study suicide of all things?

She returned, briefly, true to her word, with two bulging carrier bags. I did not detain her, and when she had gone I cooked a full breakfast, attempting to push thoughts of her from my mind. Afterwards, Helen and I made a start on the cottage. I hadn't imagined that Helen was the type to want to get her hands dirty but she went about the task with enormous zeal. We worked hard and built up a sweat. We opened the doors wide.

Now I knew for sure that Alison had not been the last inhabitant, I felt less hesitant about cleaning. The place was no longer untouchable. We scoured and polished; we collected flowers from the garden and stuffed vases with roses and poppies. Helen found a plum tree and filled a bowl for the table. Then she stood on a chair and took down the curtains. As I scrubbed the stove, she began washing them. I remained puzzled by her enthusiasm. I couldn't imagine her lifting a finger at her parents' house. Then I understood.

I realised that this was the first time she'd had a place of her own. It was a chastening thought. This small cottage would be our home and she wanted to inhabit it, to make it hers. I cast my mind back to my Oxford days, when I, like Helen, wanted to forge my place in the world. There was something about that memory: myself as a gangling, would-be spiff, a veritable class-traitor complete with phoney accent, second-hand tweeds and the obligatory secret stash of port. It shocked me. Was it possible that Helen, also, was simply playing at being adult? That she was naïve as I had been? I wondered, was our time together nothing more than a dress-rehearsal for her real life? It occurred to me that Helen, like myself all those years ago, was merely practising. This was a preamble; a beginning. Whatever her future, she would look back and say – that was where it started, when I met Harry Bliss. That was the turning point and he the catalyst. Now we were engaged in the same tasks, yet their significance, for each of us, would be different. For me this was a gathering of threads, an attempt to clarify the past. But Helen had no threads to gather. She was throwing them out, experimenting with possible futures. She might think there was a togetherness in this, that the flowers on the table, the plums in the bowl, might symbolise some kind of union. She might think we had a life ahead of us, whereas I knew that my life lay behind me and this late blossoming of love (for want of a better word) was merely illusory. How else, I asked myself, might I explain it?

# 14

'ARE YOU UP FOR a walk on the beach?'
The suggestion was Judith Frazer's. She had arrived promptly, dressed in jeans and a thick cotton jumper. She wasn't wearing her specs and I imagined that she was trying to look more friendly, almost wholesome. It bothered me immensely.

'I thought the fresh air might be good for us. That is, if you feel . . .'

'If I feel I could *cope* with it?'

'That's not exactly . . .'

'No. You wouldn't have used those words exactly.'

'Mr Bliss . . .'

'I think it's a good idea. I haven't seen the beach yet. I have to face it sometime.'

No doubt Judith Frazer was not exactly charmed by my manner but then I was hardly charmed by her. She was doing her best to organise our lives here and, while I agreed that a walk might be beneficial, I still resented her. For a start, she held more cards than I. She knew more about what had happened here than I did and I believed she was milking the situation. I wanted to ask her more about Mrs Bobbin. What was it that she hadn't told me? But right now I couldn't bring myself to question it. I was certain that, whatever motivated her, it was not love of Alison. Perhaps she did sympathise with my views. She claimed to enjoy her work, to have some involvement in Alison's story, but the fact remained that she stood to profit. And it was not mere financial advantage. Judith Frazer would gain a reputation, be lauded by her colleagues and bask in reflected glory.

I knew I had to face the beach at some point, but I was not looking forward to the event. No sooner had I agreed to go than I was cursing this woman for making me confront such a thing in company. I was tracing the steps of my wife on the last morning that she lived and I should have walked alone. Instead I was engaged in conversation, arguing trivialities with this flashy academic. I might revisit the beach a second or a third or a fourth time, but the first would always be sullied.

Helen clutched my hand as we walked. I wanted to shake it free but was not so cruel as to follow the impulse. A dark band of cloud hung on the horizon and it seemed impossible that only yesterday we had picnicked in open fields. I felt angry and put upon; not in the mood for conversation. But Professor Frazer was determined to talk.

'It's vital you understand that I'm on your side, Mr Bliss. I can imagine what you've been through and it's not surprising that you're suspicious. I'm not expecting instant decisions.'

'But you'll write the book whether I co-operate or not.'

'I can't answer that yet.'

'I'll take that as a "yes".'

'You can believe that if you like.'

'The book's commissioned, isn't it? I don't imagine you'll be paying back your advance.'

She shrugged and I let my irritation get the better of me.

'I think what you fail to understand is this: I have no time for biographers.'

'You didn't say as much on the phone,' she said.

'I said I'd talk to you. I promised nothing more.'

I realised, as I spoke, that things were moving too quickly. I should have waited for this. After all, I was still hungry for information. And it was unfair on Helen. She clearly felt left out. Yet the conversation had begun and I could only continue. Throughout, Professor Frazer played her role perfectly. She never once lost her cool. There was something about her demeanour that suggested a certain superiority – anyone with a nose like that couldn't help but appear to be looking down it – yet she spoke bluntly and her words betrayed more intelligence than I had anticipated.

'The way I see it,' she said, barely flinching at my refusal to work with her, 'biography has an important role to play in our understanding of writers.'

'Rubbish. It's pure titillation.'

'You can't deny that a writer's life has an impact on their work?'

'Not at all. Simply that we should be able to judge the writer on her work alone.'

'But if it's the work alone that matters,' Professor Frazer said, '– I don't know how to say this without you taking offence . . .'

'Just say it.'

It seemed absurd that such a conversation should take place here, out of doors, and so soon; it didn't seem appropriate somehow.

'If it's just the work – Alison Bliss would not be considered an important writer. A few prizes for a single novel – it's not enough.'

I caught the look on Helen's face but she said nothing. It surprised me that Professor Frazer would express such a view, especially to me. I admired her frankness but I was also confused by her statement. After all, didn't her whole enterprise rely on the idea of Alison as thwarted genius?

'You're saying you don't admire her work?' I said. 'That what matters is her former career, that she was a model?'

'Not exactly.'

'Oh come on,' I said. 'I've heard it all before. You're interested in her cultural significance?' I could not keep the irony from my voice.

'To an extent, yes. I'm not saying that her work isn't good. But that her status now depends on more than literary talent. Her past, yes. But what fascinates me most is the connection between her vocation, as novelist, and her despair.'

'You're making the assumption it was her writing that depressed her? Have you forgotten that she had a breakdown when she was a model?'

'No. And anyway, these things aren't just cause and effect. It's more complicated. I mean, for example – are certain personality types more likely to be drawn to an artistic life? She always wanted to be a writer, didn't she? Even when she was modelling? It's the link between the art and the misery that interests me. Why *have* so many writers taken their own lives? Why so many women? My book won't just be a biography of Alison. I want to examine the broader issues, taking Alison's life as a particular case.'

'Haven't you written that book already – didn't you say as much in your letter?'

'My first book was very general. What I want to do here is

different. I want to write about the link between a particular female poetic sensibility and the act of suicide . . .'

'Oh God – the female poetic sensibility – what next?'

'Mr Bliss . . .'

'Hasn't it been done before?'

'*Everything* has been done before. I'm sure you're aware of that. But I'm writing the book purely in relation to what Alison's story can teach us.'

'A *moral* book.'

'Oh come on – stop analysing every word I say.'

'But isn't that what you academics like – close analysis?'

'Of *text*, Mr Bliss. Of text.'

'Oh, for heaven's sake – all this "Mr Bliss" rubbish is getting on my nerves.'

She smiled, as if she'd won a small victory.

'So I may call you Harry?'

'Yes, yes.'

'Think of it this way, Harry. A person lives her life, but she can't see what lies ahead. It's impossible to know. She walks blindly if you like. We all do.'

'I'm sorry?'

'Every life has a pattern, OK? When we're only half-way through we can't see it because it's not complete. Only at the end of a life is it visible and that's where biography comes in. The biographer can be objective. She tries to make sense of the pattern.'

'And I always thought the biographer was just a sycophant. Thank you for enlightening me.'

'Harry!' Helen chastised me; the first words she'd spoken. 'Why don't you two stop arguing? I mean, aren't we all trying to do the same thing? To understand why Alison killed herself?'

'The same task,' I said, 'but we have different motivations.'

I said nothing more. I had reason to be hostile to Judith Frazer, but, much to my chagrin, I could not afford to drive her away. I realised, if I wanted to hear her story, I would have to win her over.

We approached the edge of the village where the marshes began. Sunlight glinted across the reeds but beyond them, towards the sea, a shadow had fallen. We took the road that crossed the marshes. There was a chill, salt breeze and I felt the loneliness of the place.

Even now, in midsummer, in company, it struck me: a sense of my own insignificance. The strangely darkening sky loomed above me and the cars seemed pathetic ants that crawled across an alien landscape. In winter, and alone, this place would be unbearable.

Shortly after first light, my wife had walked this path. She had been seen by a group of holidaying students, on their way back from the beach after a pre-dawn dip. They had described her, often, to interested journalists who seemed to take some ghoulish pleasure in the reconstruction.

Now it was my turn. As the cloud gathered overhead, I imagined this place stripped of light and warmth and humanity. I could see the students as they must have appeared to her: two boys, three girls, soaking wet, their hair still dripping, but laughing still. They walked towards her out of the darkness. She could not have expected to meet anyone at that hour. They must have seemed almost otherworldly, creatures of a dream or portents come to mock her. How could they laugh, she must have thought. What was there to laugh about? Perhaps if they had stopped, spoken to her, even shared the joke, her death might have been averted. Instead, they were in awe of her. They recognised her, but could hardly believe that it *could* be her. Alison Bliss. The novelist. She too, ghost-like, had seemed to appear from nowhere. Several days later, when they heard a body had been found, they knew, instinctively, it was hers. Thanks to their statements, Alison's identity was quickly established.

I remembered the recent newspaper interview with the two lads, a feeble report but it allowed me to picture her. Her hair was about her face; she wore the black coat that reached nearly to her ankles. She didn't acknowledge the students; they weren't even sure that she had seen them. However she had justified this act, whatever had led her to it, she would have been afraid. If I had been there, I might have prevented it.

'Are you up for the climb?' Professor Frazer asked.

We were approaching the beach car park, where twenty or so vehicles stood. A steep bank of pebbles rose above us and stretched for at least a mile to left and right. To reach the sea, which was out of sight, we had to clamber up the pebbles. They shifted constantly beneath our feet so that for each step we took, we slipped back half a step. I could hear the sea beyond – its harsh, unflinching roar – and I tried not to think of Alison, making this climb in near-darkness. Once I stumbled and Helen helped me up. Judith Frazer had already reached the summit, and as we approached, I noticed a few ornithologists, perched at the top of the bank, scribbling in their notebooks or gazing out to sea through their binoculars.

I scrambled up the last few feet on all fours. I stood up, breathless, and what I saw astonished me. Neither the photographs in the colour supplements, nor the painting by Charles Bliss could do this sea any justice. It was so huge and furious and unforgiving. It thrust itself upon me and I looked down on it, almost unbalanced by its grey-green virulence and the curdling and spitting of its spume.

Beneath my feet, the pebbles sloped steeply to the water's edge. There, the waves lurched forwards, claimed the pebbles and hurled them back.

'Isn't it amazing?' Helen said.

I nodded and walked ahead of her. I turned my head.

'Do you mind if I have a few minutes to myself?'

She agreed, though I suspect she was rather hurt. She sat down beside Judith on the pebbles and I walked quickly away. I approached the water's edge, then walked alongside it. When I turned again, I realised that I had now descended so far that I could not see beyond the pebble bank. There was no-one ahead of me and the further I progressed, the more alone I felt myself to be. Only the scavenging birds kept me company with their obscure and violent squawking. I was isolated between two horizons, engulfed by pebbles, sea and threatening sky. I felt myself not on the shore of England but at the very edge of a vast, flat world.

I had no desire to turn back. Some instinct propelled me. The wind was strong and harsh on my ears. The incline hampered my progress, the pebbles sliding at my feet. I was out of breath, panting like a dog. I pulled my light coat about myself and walked faster. Now my eyes were stinging. It could have been the wind, of course, or the salt air. My legs were weak and I sank down and faced the sea. I knew this bank was man-made, the pebbles forced to such a height by bulldozers. Yet the scene had the air of a place that had not changed for millions of years. It seemed both primeval and apocalyptic. I might have been the first man or the last.

So Alison must have felt. Now fine shafts of sunlight broke the cloud, but the sun had been absent for Alison. A listless moon hung above her, its cold, unflinching stare the sole witness to this waste. An hour or so before her, the students would have been here, racing across the pebbles, laughing. There is a particular night-time phenomenon that attracts the youngsters to Glaven. In the darkness, if one stamps on the pebbles, they will spark, being made of flint. Occasionally a group of students will arrive after midnight, clutching bottles of wine, for the sheer pleasure of running in the darkness and watching the beach catch light beneath their shoes. Dazed by alcohol, bolstered by laughter and the brash confidence of youth, they aren't ready to feel belittled by anything. They might feel themselves invincible, blind to the fact that the sea and the wind could crush them. They could be licked up in an instant and the landscape wouldn't mourn them.

But Alison would have been only too aware of her own smallness. They found her clothes later, blown by the wind on to the marshes. She walked naked into the sea. Was it possible to imagine such a thing? I tried to remember her body, the delicate feet, square knees, voluptuous thighs. I remembered her smooth hips, her navel, full breasts. In the years we were together, she lost the emaciated look. The contours of her body became real, nourished, true. Now I remembered her face – and I felt myself begin to tremble, to break. The body alone meant nothing. It was the whole of her I had lost.

'Alison . . .'

A wave broke across my legs and soaked my trousers. I leapt up, cursing.

'Harry? Are you all right?'

Helen approached me from behind. Somewhere within me was the urge to howl and rage and scream. But some reflex cut in.

'No. I'm soaked.'

'Is that all?'

It was difficult to make ourselves heard; the wind was so strong.

'I'm fine. Where's our friend the Professor?'

'She's back there. I hope you don't mind me coming down.'

I shook my head to reassure her. I turned and saw Professor Frazer, in the distance, a small black silhouette against the stones.

'I didn't realise I'd come so far.'

Helen said nothing.

'What do you think of her?' I asked.

'Of Judith?'

Our voices sounded exaggerated as we did battle against the wind.

'Judith,' I said – trying out the name for the first time. 'Yes. Of Judith.'

'She thinks a lot of herself.'

I wasn't sure that she was right, but I didn't disagree.

'So you don't like her?'

'I don't know. She's trying to be really friendly, but I know she's impatient. She wants to speak to you. She thinks I'm just a kid, you know? And I can't believe what she says about Alison's book – I mean, how can she not see the quality of the writing?'

'It upsets you, doesn't it?'

'Yes. Doesn't it you?'

I shook my head.

'She may be right,' I said.

'What!'

I had been about to express my own doubts about Alison's genius, but I held back. I didn't want to hurt Helen. She would think it a betrayal of Alison and an insult to her own perceptions.

'What I mean is – it's difficult for me to be objective about Alison's work. I can't be critical. Only an outsider could judge.'

Helen smiled coolly. I could tell she did not believe me.

'That's what they say in the papers – that you didn't like her work.'

'It's more complex than that.'

'Maybe you liked it, but not enough.'

'What are you trying to say?' I asked.

'Nothing.'

'Please.'

'Maybe if you'd seen what I see in her work. Maybe it would have helped.'

'And what do you see?'

She shrugged. 'If you *can't* see it . . .'

I wanted her to argue her case but she was either reluctant or incapable. It was attractive in a way, this inexpressible passion that she professed. I remained charmed by her naïvety. She was not yet old enough to be embarrassed at her inarticulacy. She thought that a few emotive phrases would suffice to prove her point.

I fell silent. I was thinking of Judith Frazer. I was apprehensive of her motives, yet I was certain of one thing: her views on Alison's work had validity. I had loved my wife. I had supported her writing. But I had often felt that the posthumous praise heaped upon her was unjustified. Once I had been fool enough to speak my mind and my views were seized upon as some kind of evidence. My words were taken out of context. It was suggested that I thought her work empty, that I had no regard for it. But my true opinion was quite different.

I had always valued Alison's work. From the beginning, when we used to sit in the cafés of Bellevue Road, she reading Wharton, I the very beginnings of *Sweet Susan*, I was convinced of her talent. I knew that what she was writing about would have popular appeal, but more than that, I was impressed by the honesty of the work. True, I sometimes found the prose rather purple, but there were also moments of sheer inventiveness, when her language was so complex and playful that it seemed to leap out and grab me by the throat.

But Alison always had doubts about her work. Perhaps it was because she knew it would be seized upon, printed because of who she was, whether it was good or not. It took her five years to complete *Sweet Susan*, but during that time, she seemed possessed of a vibrancy that seemed to fade when the book was finished.

It wasn't until the novel was nearly complete that Alison allowed me to read it, at last. In the very early days, I had ventured to give some constructive criticism, but she hadn't liked it. It had hurt her to think that a single word might be out of place and after that, she decided it would be best to wait, until she herself was satisfied. As a result, when I eventually read the manuscript, I wasn't honest enough. I believed that with careful editing, the novel might be rather remarkable, but I would not be that editor. Yet if it came from a professional? I knew that it would sting her, but she would not see me as the cause of her hurt. Instead, I might be the one to suck it out.

As it happened, the editor who bought Alison's work was bowled over by it. She didn't change a word. 'You know,' she told her, 'this reads like a sixth or seventh novel, not a first.' But Alison was not so easily flattered. Nor did the good reviews and the prizes make a difference. I understood, later, that Alison was quite aware of the novel's faults. After her death, I found a proof copy of *Sweet Susan*, scrawled over in Alison's hand. Sometimes individual words were changed. Sometimes it was sentences, paragraphs or whole pages. The margins were covered in notes and the comments were often brutal and unforgiving. Mostly she savaged herself but occasionally her criticisms were sharp and brilliant and I saw glimpses of the writer she might have become.

Finding this copy of the novel was an immense blow because it showed not only how she could despise herself, but also proved that she could have been great. The novel, in a further draft, would have been altogether different. The weaknesses would have been erased. A new voice was forming. It was for this reason, more than any other, that I regretted the loss of her last manuscript: the Arabella novel. I longed to see that work because I knew instinctively that this would have proved her talent. As it was, Alison took her life and found an easier path to fame.

When I found the edited copy of *Sweet Susan*, I toyed with the idea of handing it over. But I thought better of it. By then the novel had gained its reputation. There was not a soul who dared say a word against it. I preferred to keep my secret. Keeping it was a way of keeping a part of Alison for myself, a part of her that nobody else could touch.

Now, walking the beach with Helen, I wondered what Judith Frazer might make of the altered manuscript? I wasn't planning to show it to her, yet a small temptation lingered. Judith Frazer, in spite of everything, had spoken the truth. She had said the forbidden words that I had not been brave enough to say. That Alison Bliss had not been a genius: she was merely human. I wondered whether the time would come when such an idea might be accepted. That Alison Bliss had faults. And that it was for her faults, as well as for her brilliance, that I had loved her.

# 15

A S WE MADE OUR way along the beach, the small black silhouette that was Judith Frazer came into focus and she turned and waved at us from the top of the pebble-bank where she sat beside the bird-watchers. The dark clouds on the horizon had taken hold of the sky and were gathering above us. The sea-spray spattered our faces as we walked.

'How are you feeling?' I asked Helen. We hadn't spoken for a few minutes. I had been catching my breath. Helen shrugged. I leant forward and kissed her, closed my eyes and felt her warmth as the wind beat about us.

'Better now,' she said.

'Good.'

'I've been thinking about my parents. They must be going berserk. Mum'll be on the sherry by now and Dad'll be running around like a headless chicken. Or else he'll lock himself away in his studio and leave her to get on with it.'

'Do you think they might come here?'

'I don't know,' she said. 'I really don't know.'

'Do you want to go home?'

'No. Of course not.'

Judith Frazer stood up as we approached and smiled, that broad, unnerving smile. The wind had reddened her face and she looked strangely at home here.

'Good walk?' she asked.

'Yes thanks,' I said, surprising myself with the friendliness of my tone. 'I had to face a few ghosts, you know?'

'I know exactly what you mean,' she said. 'I remember the first time I came here after – after it happened. It's not easy.'

'No.'

I was immediately irritated again. How could she possibly compare her experience to mine? But I vowed to hold back, at least for the moment.

'That's some wind, isn't it?'

I nodded.

'Shall we get some tea?' she asked. 'Or would you prefer to stay here a while?'

'No. It's getting cold. I could do with a cuppa.'

I glanced once more at the sea before we made our way down the bank towards the emptying car park. At its side, next to the toilet cubicles, was a small café serving tea, hot-dogs and pasties. It wasn't much, but I was chilly and hungry and the smell was inviting.

'Do you want to stop here?' I asked.

'Sure,' Judith said.

'Great,' said Helen.

I got the distinct impression that Helen didn't want to eat here, yet I also guessed that she thought it was somehow 'cool'. It was like a reversal of my own snobbery at that age. She'd told me already about the greasy-diners that she frequented with her drama-school friends, as if she were proud of going to such places. But they didn't really suit her any more than swigging port in a fellow's rooms at Oxford had suited me.

Behind the counter, a gangling and bespectacled youth was serving. I glimpsed the sandwiches, beginning to curl, and the limp cheese salads.

'What can I do you for?' the boy asked.

The hot food looked more promising. Judith chose a sausage roll, Helen a baked potato and I had a hot-dog. There was tea all round and Judith and I had jam doughnuts.

We sat outside on wooden benches and tucked in. I was still shaken but the food soothed me: the juicy sausage in a doughy roll, the thick oozing ketchup, the crispy onions. We drank our tea from chipped cups. It was over-stewed, but I didn't care. It kept my hands warm and the taste comforted me, reminded me of childhood tea-times, when my aunts would come and sit around the table exchanging gossip, while mother kept topping up the pot, in between offerings of pease-pudding sandwiches and malt-loaf.

At first we said little. There was so much I wanted to know. I wanted the story from the very beginning but I was reluctant to ask. Why should I make myself so vulnerable? In any case, we were hungry and it hardly seemed appropriate to talk about Alison as we licked our lips between bites of sugared doughnuts. Helen was perhaps a touch contemptuous of our appetites. On one occasion, a dollop of jam spurted out as I took a bite and she looked almost offended. I wiped my mouth on a serviette and Judith got some more teas in. It was cold now, but we were shielded from the wind by the pebble-bank and the walls of the café.

'So,' I said to Judith, concerned that by sharing a smile or two and a snack, I might have given too much ground. 'You said in your letter that you had things you wanted to tell me.'

'That's right. Yes. There's a lot to discuss.'

'Tit for tat, is it?' I said.

I couldn't help myself.

'I'm sorry?'

'You scratch my back, I'll scratch yours.'

'I'm not sure what you're implying.'

'If you're to talk, you want something from me too – an agreement to authorise your book.'

'No. Really, you misunderstand me. Sure, I want you to help me – but that's not the only reason I'm here. I just thought it was time we talked.'

'I see.'

'I understand your suspicions. It's natural.'

'Why now?' I said. 'Why wait till now?'

'For a long time I've wanted to forget about this.'

'By writing books about suicides?'

'I thought I could exorcise it like that. But I couldn't. I've realised now I need to face up to what happened here.'

She made it sound as if she were affected personally by Alison's death, but how was that possible? She could hardly have known her.

'And now you want to talk?'

'Yes.'

'Well,' I said, knowing that if I wanted information, I had no choice but to give her the benefit of the doubt, 'why don't you start? Tell me what happened here – what you know.'

Judith glimpsed at Helen.

'You're not making this easy for me.'

'No. Perhaps not.'

She turned to Helen. 'I don't want to bore you, Helen.'

'I'm not bored,' Helen said. 'I'm not just tagging along with Harry, you know. I care about what happened to Alison too.'

'Oh?' Judith looked surprised. 'Did you know her?'

She shook her head, embarrassed.

'My parents knew her – through Harry. But I never met her.' She hesitated. 'Sometimes I feel as if I knew her, though.'

'Through her work, right?'

Helen nodded. 'I know that *you* don't like it,' she said, 'but whenever I read her book, I feel really close to her. She writes about things that I've felt myself.'

Judith nodded smugly, as if to say – of course, you're young and easily influenced.

'What do *you* make of it then – the fact that Alison committed suicide?'

'How do you mean?' Helen said.

I was thinking: come on, stop wasting time – tell me what you know.

'Do you think it has an impact on the way you read her work?'

'Knowing what comes after, you mean?' Helen said.

'That's right.'

'I s'pose so. I mean you can't help but think about it.'

'Do you ever wonder whether you'd have thought so much of her, if she hadn't killed herself?'

'Oh – come on,' I said.

'You think I only read her because she killed herself?'

'I didn't say that,' Judith said. 'But if she hadn't – you probably wouldn't have read the book.'

'I would have read it. Because Dad knows Harry.'

'But if that weren't the case?'

'Maybe. Maybe not. But if I'd happened to pick up the book and I'd read it – I still would have thought it was amazing.'

'I hope so.'

Judith was clearly cynical and Helen didn't like it. There was a tremor in her voice. She was holding back her frustration.

'Judith,' I said – the first time I had used her name, 'this is out of order.'

It wasn't her opinion that angered me but the fact she was upsetting Helen. In any case, it wasn't her opinion that I wanted. I wanted her story.

Judith nodded. 'You're right.'

It was clear she had more to say on the subject. Perhaps she realised that if she wanted to discuss this, she'd have to stop involving Helen.

'Too many women writers have taken their own lives,' she said. 'When is it going to stop? When will they find other ways to express themselves?'

'Self-expression,' I said, '– is that what you call it?'

'What comes first,' Judith said, answering a question with a question, '– are unhappy women attracted to writing or does writing make women unhappy?'

'Seems to me you're making huge generalisations.'

'Why do we take more notice of the anguished women? The ones who write about their own tragedies, then prove they're serious by committing suicide?'

'There are plenty of women writers out there,' I said, 'leading fulfilled lives and enjoying fine reputations.'

'You're right, of course.'

'And if anything, it's people like you who are fuelling people's fascination with Alison.'

'Touché, Harry.'

'You admit it then?'

'From time to time I ask myself if that's so. But I'm not Paul Vinton. I'm not Hake. All they're doing is spreading rumours: stoking the fire, if you like. You can't put us in the same category. I'm trying to find a pattern – to reveal a pattern, and to condemn it. I don't see myself as part of the Alison Bliss industry, if that's what you mean.'

'Not cashing in?'

'You may find that difficult to believe.'

'You're right. I do.'

We were getting nowhere. These theories were all very well but I was no nearer to understanding Alison. I wanted more specifics: to know how Judith had perceived her state of mind; to understand Ern Higham's involvement and the importance of Arabella. I refused to believe that Alison's death was simply part of some greater pattern: that she killed herself because Woolf did, because Plath did, or because Sappho once leapt to her death from a rock. Surely my wife had possessed a will of her own.

It was a bleak afternoon and I felt suddenly frustrated and impatient. I turned away and looked out to see a couple of cows grazing on reclaimed marshland. We were the only customers left outside the café. We'd finished the tea and it was too cold to stay here. Only one car remained in the car park: a battered Golf. Its owner was now descending the pebble-bank. The sky seemed increasingly gloomy and rain threatened. It couldn't have rained here for weeks. It was as if, in the middle of summer, a winter's day had descended, to remind me how it had been for Alison.

The owner of the Golf spotted us and came over.

'Are you chaps on foot?' he asked.

'Unfortunately, yes,' I said.

He was a young man with thinning blond hair and small pale eyes. I took him for a city-dweller. He looked up at the clouds, low and yellow-edged.

'You'd better have a lift, unless you fancy getting soaked?'

It turned out that he was staying at the mill. I was reluctant to revisit it but it seemed only logical that we should return to Judith's room. The man didn't say much about himself; talked mainly about his latest sighting – a white-winged black tern, which had appeared after the other ornithologists had left the beach. It was double Dutch to me: it might just as well have been a black-winged white ostrich for all I cared. But apparently it was a rare sight and it pleased him, at least. He ought to report it, he told us, to the warden of the marsh, but he was reluctant to do so. 'I'd like to keep it to myself,' he said. Somehow he had guessed that we weren't here for the birds, and his secret was safe with us.

As we crossed the marshes, the skies opened. The wipers swept across the windscreen, flinging the rain aside. It was only a few minutes' drive, but I couldn't wait to get out. Yet when we reached the mill, I felt an urge to turn back. The rain had flattened the reeds and made a dull, thudding sound as it hit the boggy ground. My memory of the night I spent here was undiminished and I half expected Hake and his photographer to appear from the gloom. I remembered my face in the photograph: pale, bleached by the flash. I wore the startled look of a fleeing criminal.

We crossed the small car park and the bridge at the front of the mill. We got pretty wet and were glad once we were inside, climbing the stairs to Judith's room. It was circular, recently renovated, far more pleasant than the cramped and grubby side-room that I had occupied six years previously. Judith fetched towels and handed them round. Then, sensing our mood, she lit small lamps and candles – though it was still only four in the afternoon – and fetched a bottle of brandy from her suitcase.

'We'll feel better after this,' she said.

As Judith poured, Helen loosed her hair. It hung dishevelled about her face and she leant over and rubbed it dry. She tugged her fingers through the fine white tangled strands. Something about her concentration moved me.

'Cheers,' Judith said. She sat down opposite us in a large, chintzy armchair.

'Cheers.'

It was a fine room and romantic in this light. Outside, the immense darkness of the afternoon hovered and the rain beat on the window panes all around us, as if jealous of the warmth and the flickering candles. I tried not to remember the night that I had spent here, when the rain had kept me awake and I had never in my life been so alone. I was glad to be in company, to drink brandy, to attempt to block out that memory.

'I heard something once,' Judith said, 'about the clouds in Glaven.'

'What's that?' I asked, raising the glass to my lips, feeling my mouth and then my throat begin to burn.

'It's all a nonsense, but kind of eerie all the same.'

'Tell me.'

'Ern Higham said it.'

'You've met him?' I asked.

'Don't sound so surprised.'

'Well?'

She smiled, making us wait. 'I only met him once. And that's plenty. I think he was trying to frighten me off.'

So many questions brimmed on my tongue but I was restrained. 'So what did he say? About the clouds?' I asked.

'He said,' and here she lowered her voice and spoke in an odd accent, that might have been amusing, had the words not grabbed my attention, ' "You ain't got a chance here, Missy. You're out of your depth." '

'What did he mean?'

She didn't reply. Only continued with Ern's words.

' "See that sky," he said. "It'll devour the likes of you. That's our sky. You won't see clouds like that anywhere else." Of course I smiled, I humoured him. It was a bad move. "You might laugh," he said, "but you'll be gone by the week's end, see? It'll get too much for you. The clouds will weigh you down. They drive you mad, those clouds. Infect you." It was almost medieval. I could hardly believe that I was listening to him. "It takes generations," he said, "to come immune to our clouds. You need a hard skin. Thick as flint. You people are too soft. The clouds will get to you. Seep through your skin." '

Judith paused, as if affected by the memory. I, also, was silenced. Judith was right: it was nonsense. Yet was I not already somewhat infected by the spirit of this place? Didn't I feel – what were his words? – weighed down? Though I was drawn to Glaven, I also longed to flee it.

At first, none of us spoke. We waited, cradling our glasses, listening to the rain. Back in London, I thought, boys would be spilling from the school gates; buses would be rumbling through the streets; black umbrellas would be jostling above the pavements. It should have been my penultimate day at the school. Perhaps there would have been another drink with Richard, the two of us sharing a pint in the White Swan. Instead – where was he? I didn't like to think about it. Nor did I like to dwell on other goings-on in London. I knew I had been foolish, to have taken off like that. If I'd waited only three days, I might have caused less fuss. By now the other staff would know what had happened. For six and a half years I'd worked to prove that I was not the cad I was supposed to be. Now I'd undone it all.

Helen roused me from my musing. She placed her hand on my knee and when I looked at her, her face bathed in yellow light, I could regret nothing.

That was how it began – the unravelling of Alison's tale – with the three of us together in that circular room, sipping brandy and watching the candles burn low as the rain outside beat grimly down, indifferent to the stories that were gathering here. Whatever I thought of Judith Frazer, I knew that I had to befriend her. Our mutual need was undeniable. We were each of us assembling a incomplete jigsaw. We each held parts that the other coveted and now a subtle bartering would begin.

And there was something else, a thing I barely understood. Before I even met Ern Higham, his presence hung over me. Now I could barely separate the idea of him from the elements outside, as if he and his clouds were somehow haunting me. Though I could not articulate it at the time, I believe the three of us were drawn together by our dread of that man and that place. But we had a need, also, to find out what he knew. It seemed we had a simple choice. To be put off by the bleakness of Glaven, to do as Ern might expect and get the hell out of there, back to the metropolis where we belonged. Or else we could fight it. Alone, I wouldn't have lasted longer than a day. The place held too much tragedy – I couldn't be immune. But in that room, we banished the gloom about us and clung to our sanity. Something was beginning and I knew that I was ready for it.

# 16

A T FIRST, JUDITH FRAZER was cautious. I remember how she
appeared to me that afternoon – no longer as the brash, semi-
American that I had at first classed her, but rather as a woman
uncertain of her purpose, torn between her professional imperative
and her personal doubts. She maintained, throughout our conversation, a certain briskness, a hard-edged perceptiveness and a definite
air of superiority whenever she felt threatened, yet I sensed that she
was uneasy with her role and suspicious of me as I was of her.

Yet in spite of this, as she spoke, I began to recognise something
of myself in Judith Frazer. It was all conjecture but I found myself
wondering whether she, like me, felt trapped beneath a façade that
did not suit her. I had grown tired in recent years of being Alison
Bliss's husband, yet I had also grown into the role and taken it on. I
had not always been reluctant and mistrustful, hostile and solitary.
Now I was doing battle against that man.

Being with Judith made me question whether one could help one's
own manner. Her face made me profoundly uncomfortable. Her smile,
unnaturally broad, did not seem genuine. Her large nose and heavy-
lidded eyes imparted a regal look. She seemed to wear a permanent
sneer. Then there was the voice – the unlikely, honeyed ease of it. She
might have looked less forbidding if she didn't crop her hair, but it went
deeper than that. That afternoon I began to think that she, like I, was
somehow imprisoned; that the true woman was out of sight. I realised
that if I focused not on the impression she created, but rather on her
words, curiously, against my will, I was starting to like her.

But to return to the beginning. She leant back in her chair. She
didn't rush to talk. It was as if she were trying to find the right way
into this maze and perhaps, also, she was trying to please and to
intrigue. If her manner was unrepresentative of her self, still I

believe that she exploited that manner. She was aware of the power of her presence.

I prompted her with a question.

'Why don't you tell me how you met Alison,' I said. 'Maybe that would be a good place to start?'

She agreed.

'I could do with a cigarette first,' she said.

'Me too,' said Helen. 'I've left mine at the cottage, else I'd offer you one.'

'No problem. I've given up anyhow.'

I was impatient.

'Well?'

She raised her eyebrow, as if she enjoyed keeping me in suspense.

'It's not terribly romantic, I'm afraid.'

'I'm not asking for romance.'

'OK. I met her in that little tea-shop on the main street. Do you know the one? It's very quaint. They do home-made cakes to die for.'

'Alison? In a tea-shop?'

'Is that so weird? There's not much to do in this place – in case you haven't noticed.'

I shrugged. 'Go on.'

'It was kind of deserted in there. She was the only other customer, so I had to notice her. Well, I would have noticed her anyway. She looked different from the image I remember from the early eighties. But I'd seen recent photos too. I'd read a lot about her, when *Sweet Susan* came out, what was it, six months before?'

I nodded.

'She was in one of the window seats. The window was steamed up; it was raining. She had a small notebook in front of her and didn't seem to notice me at all. Most of the time she seemed to be staring into space, but sometimes something would occur to her and she'd jot it down in her book. Naturally I was intrigued. I didn't want to miss this opportunity to meet her.'

'How did she look?' Helen asked.

'Oh – you know – pretty damn gorgeous. More so in the flesh than in the photos. And interesting too. She was wearing a fantastic brown mohair sweater – I was envious of it – and her hair was pulled back from her face. She was wearing glasses and the tip of her nose was red. I wondered what she was writing in that notebook. I felt pretty starved of good company, though of course I didn't know then whether I'd like her. I'd come here to be alone, but it's amazing how quickly the novelty wears off.'

'Did she notice you?' I asked.

'Not at all. She was too caught up in her own thoughts.'

'So how did you get to speak to her?'

'I almost didn't. She seemed so preoccupied, I couldn't interrupt. I gave my order and read my book, glancing at her occasionally, in the vague hope that we might make eye-contact – but no such luck.' Judith smiled in a self-deprecating way and took another swig of brandy. 'When she left, she gathered her things, put on her coat and a little black hat and gloves. She picked up her bag and umbrella. She glanced in my direction. Then she walked out.'

'So you didn't speak?' I said.

'Not immediately. But as soon as she'd gone, I saw that she'd forgotten something. She'd left her scarf hanging over the back of the chair. It was a great scarf – a kind of velvet patchwork.'

'Yes. I remember it.'

'So I went after her. I caught her as she was about to go into the bookshop.'

'And then?'

'We got talking. She was awfully grateful. We were sheltering from the rain together, and I suppose we just gelled. Actually, her manner surprised me. I'd imagined she'd be aloof, but not so. I asked her if she was here to write and she told me that she was, that she was really excited about her latest project. I told her I was an academic, but confessed I hadn't read *Sweet Susan*. She seemed kind of relieved. Said I shouldn't really bother – it wasn't all it was cracked up to be. Well, that was refreshing. I'd been spending so much time with academics around that time, too many egos for my liking, and the fact that she didn't come from that environment really appealed to me. I hadn't expected that someone so beautiful, so recently successful, could be so humble. I was impressed. I wanted to get to know her. We were in Glaven for different reasons, but I sensed that we were both keen to have some decent company.'

'Why *were* you in Glaven?' I asked. 'You never said.'

She simply looked at me, and I decided not to push it. Instead I let her carry on with her story. Already I was hooked. For years there had been a large blank in my mind and now it was beginning to be filled.

This period of time – between Alison's leaving for Glaven and her appearance on the mortuary trolley – had haunted me. It was as if she had ceased to exist for those two weeks. Despite newspaper reconstructions, I had never been able to think about Alison's absence in concrete terms. I had thought that forgetting was easier but now I understood that I would not forget. I needed to hear Judith's story.

'I'm sorry,' I said. 'Go on.'

'I suggested that we meet the following evening. We agreed on a pub in Blakeney and that was that. She went into the bookshop and I came back here and spent the afternoon curled up with a novel.'

'And she seemed fine on that first meeting?' I asked.

'I didn't notice anything out of the ordinary.'

'In your letter you weren't so sure,' I said. 'You called her "disturbed", if I remember rightly. You said you wouldn't forget some of the things that she told you.'

'Yes. I think she *was* disturbed. But I didn't realise that until later. At first I was taken in. She wanted to appear really together; she was playing a role.'

'From the beginning?'

'Yes. I think so. Though I think her state of mind deteriorated. She was affected by being here. Things were getting to her. A couple of times, later, I suggested that she should go home – that maybe this novel wasn't good for her. But she reacted quite violently against that suggestion. I was kind of shocked, in fact, at the strength of her feelings. But I'm getting ahead of myself.'

'No matter,' I said. I wasn't sure I had the patience right then to hear every detail of the story. Eventually I would want to fill the gaps, but for the moment I wanted to hear the broad sweep. 'Tell me about that first evening. What did she tell you?'

'She told me a little about her new novel. But just the bare bones, no more than that. She showed me the photograph of Arabella, but I couldn't make out why she was so fascinated. *I* thought the whole thing sounded kind of gruesome. And I was confused. Alison told me how little she knew about the story but also said she'd written around thirty thousand words. I didn't understand how that was possible.'

'Neither did I. Before she left London, I knew that she'd written a fair amount but it didn't make sense to me either.'

'So you never read the manuscript?' Judith asked. I couldn't tell whether this were a genuine question or an accusation, but I decided to let it go.

'She didn't like me to read her work, though I was curious. I wondered what the hell she could be writing about.'

'It wasn't just about Arabella. I know that much. That's clear, in any case, from the fragment that survived. But I'm not even sure that you could call what she was writing a novel. She told me there was an autobiographical element to it again. She was writing about her own obsessions, about the nature of story-telling, the discovery of narratives. And about her mother, of course. It's a real pity we don't have that manuscript . . .'

She paused, pointedly, and looked me in the eye as if she might discover the truth there. I wasn't offended. I half expected it. There was something about her look that suggested she didn't expect to see my guilt, rather that she was testing my nerves. But Helen jumped to my defence.

'Look, you're not suggesting that Harry . . .'

'I'm not suggesting anything.'

There was silence all the same. Outside the rain began to abate. I stood up and walked to the window. The small canal that ran past the mill was close to overflowing. The landscape was grey, an infinite greyness. I could imagine Alison alone in this place. It must have been easy to forget other days, other possibilities.

I turned again to the room. I bent and kissed Helen's forehead, then sat down again.

'Were you interested?' I asked Judith. 'In Alison's ideas?'

'I liked them but I wasn't convinced that they would translate into a book. I thought it would depend on the nature of the true story, on whether that held an intrinsic interest. What did intrigue me was Ern Higham. She talked about him from the beginning.'

I helped myself to more brandy. 'So tell me, what's the connection?'

'You have to understand – until she mentioned him, I hadn't thought there was anything unusual going on. My impressions of Alison were straightforward. Despite her fame, she seemed good-humoured, intelligent – together. But I sensed that she was holding something back.'

'What?'

'On the surface, here we were, two women sharing a drink in a pub. Just the kind of pub I like actually – low-beamed ceilings, the fire roaring in the grate. Only we were out of place. The locals kept looking at us, especially the men. But I guessed, somehow, it wasn't because they recognised Alison. I mean, they were hardly the type to read the literary press, and though they might have remembered Alison Oakley, they wouldn't have expected to see her there, in their local.'

'But surely,' said Helen, 'anyone would recognise her.'

'No. Not then. In those years, when she was with Harry –'

'She kept out of the public eye,' I interrupted.

'Anyway,' Judith continued. 'I tried not to be affected by these guys. I was more interested in Alison. But the more she spoke, the more I began to think that there was something she wasn't telling me.'

'And was there?'

'It came to a head when an old guy started pointing at us, from the other end of the bar. I asked Alison – 'Do you still get recognised?' – and she said it wasn't that. She said she'd spent a lot of time here, in Blakeney. She'd been meeting with an old man – a recluse. It had aroused suspicions.'

'What kind of suspicions?' Helen asked.

'I don't know. She said she had been lucky. By chance she had heard about the old man's existence, and that he knew Arabella's story. Mrs Bobbin had let it slip out – against her will it seemed. Alison had asked if she might meet the old man, but Mrs Bobbin told her it wouldn't be possible. He saw nobody, except herself, that is.'

The mention of Mrs Bobbin once again aroused my curiosity. What was that woman so afraid of? Why was she so protective of her grandfather?

'But Alison did see him?' Helen said.

'It hadn't taken much to find out where he lived. She simply turned up on his doorstep.'

'And he let her in?'

'He was reluctant at first. He was an impossible character, she said: bad-tempered; manipulative. But when he discovered why she was there, he relented. After that, she spent each morning with him. He began telling her Arabella's story and she was working it into her novel.'

'This is astonishing. So what exactly was his connection with all this?'

Even as I was drawn in, a part of me resisted. How was it that this woman who had known Alison for less than two weeks, could know so much more than me?

'I don't know. Alison was cagey. What I do know is how being with him affected her.'

'Which was?' Helen asked.

'Ern Higham is a difficult man. I don't have much experience of him, but I know that he's revered here. It's as if people fear him, though he has to be harmless. Children are terrified of him, apparently. They don't dare go near his cottage. When you see it, you'll understand. It's like something out of a fairy-tale: over-grown garden, ivy-clad walls. And so isolated.'

'But what's he like? You said you met him.'

She laughed.

'Pretty terrifying, if you ask me. But he and Alison clearly had some kind of bond; something intense between them. He had no time for me. I got the cold shoulder.'

'What is it about him?' I asked. 'Is he really harmless?'

'He's in his late nineties, Harry!'

'He must be on his death-bed.'

'Not when I saw him. He seemed in extraordinary shape. He's over six foot tall but he barely stoops. There's a strength about him.'

'You said that he affected Alison. Do you mean that he was responsible . . .'

'For her suicide? I don't think so. I can't believe that anybody can have that much power over another person.'

'I don't know. Alison was extremely vulnerable. He might have influenced her.'

'To kill herself?'

I shrugged. 'Look. I have to know what went on between them. I can't believe that so many years have passed and it's only now that I'm finding out about this. Why the hell didn't you tell me this sooner, Judith? I mean, you were right, keeping the press in the dark. But I should have known. Jesus, I should have known. What about Vinton? He doesn't know?'

'I haven't seen Vinton's book. I doubt he knows much. As for me – for a long time I just haven't felt it was right to pry further. I wanted to let it rest. Even now, when I meet the likes of Mrs Bobbin . . .'

'Yes?'

She shook her head, still reluctant. Her explanations weren't good enough.

'Come on . . .' I urged.

'When I met her this morning – honestly, I almost felt like backing off, like I didn't want to enter into this.'

'Into what exactly?'

'Oh, I'm not easily scared off. It doesn't really bother me.'

'What?' I asked, agitated. 'What are you talking about?'

'She seems to hold some great hatred within her – don't you think? I can't really fathom it. But it makes me uneasy. She seemed really shocked to see me again. Literally, she turned pale. Then she seemed to recover. She told me straight out you were her new tenant. As if she got some kick from it. But all the time she was staring weirdly at me. Then she said something kind of peculiar. Like something her grandfather might say.'

'Yes?'

' "You people can dig up the past all you like," she said. "You won't get to the bottom of it. Do you think I care what you do any more?" '

'What *is* her problem?' Helen said. 'What have we ever done to her?'

'Well, she's worried about her grandfather, I imagine. But there must be something more to it than that. "Just ask yourself where it will end," she said. "Who'll suffer in the end?" Do you think that was a threat?'

'Who can tell,' I said.

I was surprised that Judith was affected by such talk. Surely she could rise above it. Perhaps I was also disappointed. I had wanted to know more about Mrs Bobbin, but she remained elusive. If there was some great secret that she was guarding, then Judith was no closer to it than I. I couldn't figure it out. It was as if she had reason to fear us, not vice-versa. But why?

'Was that all she said?' I asked.

'I didn't stick around to hear more. Her face – you should have seen it – like a great mask of hatred. Such stillness in that face. Fucking English reserve.'

'She didn't sound very reserved,' Helen said.

'Not the words themselves. But the mask. Like she couldn't express anything with her features. It was all compressed in her voice. Turned inwards. It spooks me.'

'You're not really afraid of her, are you?' I asked.

'No. I said not. I have to write this book. The likes of her won't stop me. You see I tried, with my last book, to free myself from thoughts of Alison, but it didn't work. Too many unanswered questions, I guess. The constant coverage doesn't help. So many lies. Before long the film will be out and then the whole damn circus will begin again.'

'And your book will be part of that circus,' I said. 'Just think, if you can publish in time, you'll make a fortune.'

I had gone too far. Judith fell silent and her expression froze. Helen appeared nervous.

'You really believe that, don't you? That I'm only here to make money. Jesus, I can see how you got your reputation.'

'What are you talking about?'

'You're so fucking self-obsessed. Poor Harold Bliss. It's no wonder the press have it in for you. You don't make it easy for people to like you, Harry. It's time you stopped shifting your own guilt on to other people. Time you stopped feeling sorry for yourself.'

'You know nothing about this.'

'No, of course not. How could I? Maybe it's time you faced up to the truth. If Ern Higham is guilty, then so am I. So are you. Don't pretend you've never blamed yourself because I won't believe it. But there's nothing that you or I can do to bring Alison back. We can't change the past. So we either have to forget about her or to try and understand what happened to her. I've tried forgetting. It's not easy for me so it must be a damn sight worse for you. But can't you, just for once, accept that somebody might be on your side? Can't you trust somebody for once?'

I hesitated, looked at Helen, but she would not look at me. Judith's words had touched a nerve but my instinct was to fight back. To tell her to get the hell out of my life. Yet without her, Helen and I would be getting nowhere fast. Beyond the window, the sky hung heavy, the clouds like bruises. I relented.

'I can try,' I said and smiled wryly. 'Will that do?'

'Sure,' Judith replied, though there was no hint of forgiveness in her expression. 'For now, that will do.'

# 17

W E MIGHT HAVE TALKED for longer but after Judith's outburst, I sensed it might be better for us all to get some rest.
One glimpse at Helen convinced me it was time to leave. She had
doubtless hoped for some kind of romance here in Glaven and so
far I had provided no such thing. The previous day's love-making
hardly counted. It had been memorable – that desperate coupling
amongst the gravestones – but was a far cry from the comfort that
Helen clearly needed. I guessed that she was thinking of her parents.
My squabbling with Judith could hardly help matters. We needed
time alone.

Judith drove us back to the cottage and was tactful enough to
suggest that we should meet in a couple of days' time. She had a
friend in Norwich whom she'd be visiting the following afternoon.
Helen and I should get settled, she said. There was no hurry, after
all.

When we reached the cottage, however, Helen's mood intensified. Immediately we were alone, she fell silent. As we entered the
kitchen I made a few banal comments which she ignored. Then,
when I asked a direct question, she simply said, 'Please, Harry. Get
off my back.'

Her tone was distinctly chilly and she would not look at me. I
realised, quite suddenly, how fragile was the ground on which my
current happiness was built. If Helen should back out now, I could
not think what I would do. It was not enough simply to be here, to
be on the point of discovering the truth about my wife. If Helen
should go – and now she left the room, I heard her tread on the
stairs – then I would be forced to recognise that all this had been
simply a fantasy. That there was no underlying pattern, no God-
ordained scheme. I would be forced to confront my own foolishness
in ever believing I might keep her. I would look on what I had

discarded – the shreds of a reputation; a friend; self-respect – and I might once again despise myself.

I leant back against the sink to steady myself. The events of the afternoon had unsettled me, but I gathered my resolve. If Helen saw my points of weakness, she might unconsciously exploit them. Rather than following her, I decided to bide my time. I discarded thoughts of her leaving and sat down at the kitchen table, intending to write, but my pencil faltered. It hovered above the paper, then fell again, drawing small, light circles, unable to form words that would express my confusion. Only one person could tell me what I needed to know and that was Ern Higham. But he was an old man, a recluse. He might refuse to speak. And then what? There would be no way forward. If he remained silent, I would never know what had driven my wife to her death. His silence would condemn me.

It was an hour later when Helen descended the stairs. For want of anything else to do, I was frying some steak and boiling vegetables. The steak wasn't yet done, the blood still running in the pan. I handed her a glass of wine.

'Smells good,' Helen said.

She had applied lipstick and changed her shirt.

'Very simple stuff, I'm afraid,' I said. 'Not what you're used to.'

'No, it looks great. My mother won't touch red meat but I love it. You were lucky to get poussin when you came to dinner. Normally it's some veggie concoction.'

She smiled and I wondered if it were genuine. I wondered whether we should discuss her parents but decided against it. She'd talk when she was ready. In the meantime, I raised my glass.

'Cheers!'

'Cheers.'

She put the glass to her lips, leaving a red stain on the rim. I was reminded of Alison, an image of her, lying stretched across the sofa wearing that shirt, stroking the cat. It was a summer evening and the light from the garden streamed into the room. She had been pregnant at the time. We'd known for a week. She hadn't yet started to bleed. In those early days of our marriage, I had been buoyed up by my love for her. We'd just bought the house and I felt, for the first time, fully myself. Something of her honesty, her authenticity, had touched me. Being with her, it was like coming home. The cat purred between us.

I opened my eyes. What was I doing here? Helen could never *be* Alison, no matter how much I might desire it. Yet she was beautiful – the image that Alison had dreamed of, the image that led her to Glaven, to the sea.

'Turn your head a little,' I said. I knew it was wrong. I knew what I was doing to myself.

'What?'

'Just to the left.'

She did as I asked.

'There. Now – stop smiling. Close your lips.'

'Harry!' she said. But she obliged. 'What's this about?'

'Just humour me. Let me look at you.'

I think she guessed what was going on. I was thinking of Arabella now, as she appeared in the photograph with Charles Bliss and George in the garden. Was I missing something? Was there some answer in the photograph itself?

'My God!'

'What?'

It was suddenly so obvious.

'What is it?'

'I'm not sure. Perhaps it's nothing. Wait here. I want to get something.'

Upstairs, I fumbled in my suitcase. I couldn't find it. I was about to unzip another bag, when I caught sight of the painting above the bed. That sea seemed familiar now. The painting yielded meaning: the violence of the brush strokes, the depth of the palette; inky green; indigo. I remembered Judith's words. 'Don't pretend you've never blamed yourself, because I won't believe it.'

Now I found the photograph, wrapped in tissue, which I removed. I had not been mistaken. I heard a noise behind me and realised that Helen had followed me.

'What is it?' she said.

I could hardly believe it myself.

'Look at this.'

I gave her the photograph. At first she was simply confused but then she saw it.

'Shit.'

174

'Exactly.'

'It's this cottage, isn't it? *Hope Cottage.*'

I nodded grimly. Why had I been so slow? The newspaper photographs of the place had all been taken from the front, so I had never made the connection. But it was unmistakable.

For a few minutes, neither of us spoke. Helen wound her arms about my waist and leant her head against my shoulder. She was shaking. Clearly she read something into this. I tried to fight such an impulse. Though I was being drawn in, I wanted to stand back. It made sense that Alison should have rented this cottage. It was logical. The room we now occupied had once belonged to Charles and Arabella. I knew what was going through Helen's mind. They were like shadows of ourselves.

'I should have realised,' I said eventually.

'Why? I don't see how.'

'That painting – it's always hung here. Charles Bliss himself would have hung it.'

'I'm scared, Harry.'

'Don't be.'

'I can't help it. I feel I'm being drawn into something.'

'No.' I had to fight it. 'There's nothing out of the ordinary here.'

'There is. I only have to look in the mirror. I feel as if . . . No, you'll think I'm . . .'

She paused.

'I won't. Go on.'

'It's as if I've been waiting for this, all my life. Like it was fated, you know?'

In spite of myself, I snapped at her.

'You don't believe in all that rubbish, do you?'

'I told you. I don't know why I bothered to say it.'

'I'm sorry.'

'Ever since we've met there have been coincidences. You can't say you don't believe in fate.'

'You think we're living in a Hardy novel. Is that what you mean?'

'It's not so far-fetched.'

I might have been seduced by it, but I could not allow myself such an indulgence.

'You have to stop thinking like that. It makes sense that Alison would have rented this cottage, doesn't it?'

She didn't reply.

'We're following Alison's trail, as she followed Arabella's. That's all. There's nothing supernatural here. These are all chance happenings. Believe in chance if you believe in anything. If there's a pattern to events, it's a random one.'

'You can't tell me what to believe.'

'I don't want to mislead you.'

We were sitting on the floor, close to the bed. She shifted to face me.

'I just have to look at you. You just have to look at me.' She picked up the photograph and handed it back. 'Then look at this. We were meant to be here.'

'No.'

'Yes.'

She leant forwards and kissed me. I tasted salt on her tongue. I didn't want to give in, but her lips parted mine and I was weak. Perhaps this was simply an elaborate game; a kind of play-acting. How could I not take part? Had I not initiated it by bringing her here? I was seduced by her fantasy. As I kissed her, I was drawn down with her; such warmth and depth. Truly, I could not now leave it alone. I left the rational man behind. My clothes unravelled and I glimpsed the painting: deep indigo, sea-green, pearl-grey. I allowed myself this luxury – a dissolution – losing track of the boundaries of my self. I dreamt I made love not to a woman but a kind of merwoman or sea-creature. She lifted me on to the bed. Her hair was loose, her limbs encircling mine. I closed my eyes and thought of Charles Bliss taking Arabella. His blood had become mine. He had lost her, but now she returned to his bed. It was delight beyond words: a sea-change after all. This pale, white flesh had not suffered for going down. It was all the softer for it.

'Harry!'

I ignored her. I didn't want to be Harry.

'You're hurting me.'

I opened my eyes.

'Oh God – I'm sorry.'

Already I was losing it; such fantasy was futile. I shifted a little, tried to thrust deeper but it was no good. I felt my prick go limp, a mollusc, slipping from its shell. To tell the truth, I barely cared. Helen lay in my arms but I could think only of Alison.

'What's the matter?'

I rolled from her. I couldn't look her in the eye.

'Harry?'

She took my shoulder, tenderly, and tried to turn me. A single thought now gripped me. Alison spent her last night in this bed. No doubt she did not sleep.

'You're crying!'

This time I couldn't hold back. It was too much. The cottage, the painting, the room, the stories.

'It's all right. It's all right.'

I didn't want her to see me like that; so naked. She held me as I wailed. I looked up at her face, her flawless skin, pale hair about her shoulders. It was not the face that I desired. I knew then that there was no returning to the past. Alison was gone and no explanation, however good, could bring her back.

# 18

THE FOLLOWING MORNING WE did not talk about what had happened. I was certain that it had affected us in some way, but Helen seemed keen to ignore this shift in the balance of our relationship. Outside, the sky was clear. The heavy clouds of the previous day had passed. We sat in the kitchen eating boiled eggs and buttered toast, drinking coffee.

'I think we should pay a visit to Ern Higham,' I said. 'I can't see any reason for delaying.'

'Shouldn't we speak with Judith first? We didn't say we'd go today.'

'You don't want her permission?'

'No. I just thought maybe we ought to know a bit more about him first. We don't want to make mistakes.'

'You could be right. But I'm not sure how much she knows. I think she likes to give the impression of being knowledgeable, whereas in fact she's pretty much in the dark. The thing is, I don't want Judith Frazer dictating our every move, do you?'

'Didn't you listen to a word she said yesterday? About trust?'

'We don't have to do everything her way. We have to grasp the bull by the horns.'

'You've made up your mind, then.'

'I don't want to hang around. I want to meet this man – find out what he knows.'

'What if he won't meet you? Or won't tell you anything?'

'He has to. I can't see that he'd turn me away.'

'I hope you're right.'

'Of course I am,' I said. 'Come on, eat up. We've got a big day ahead.'

It was around ten when we set out. I was nervous and less confident than I may have seemed, yet as we stepped into the garden I felt that there was something *right* about all this. The rain of the previous day had refreshed the landscape. The air was clearer, less stifling and, at our feet, huge dew-laden poppies tumbled across the path. Helen appeared serene. She wore the blue silk dress again. It caught the light, like the sea itself.

As we neared the gate she ran ahead and paused there, taking up the pose that Arabella had struck in the photograph. Then she laughed and I was glad that she had made a joke of it. Even so, I felt a warmth in my groin; an urgency. We left the garden and walked up the path to the lane. The sun was on my shoulders. Her light hand rested in mine and I looked at her – something impish in her expression. I felt as if I had been lifted somehow, quite removed from my former life. I relished the feeling. I had a presentiment that it would not last.

We decided to take the car to Blakeney. In more clement weather it might have been a pleasant walk, but the sun was unforgiving. As I drove, my confidence began to evaporate further. I wondered whether Helen hadn't been right – that perhaps we should be better prepared for this. I also harboured a nagging fear, a thought that ought to have occurred to me sooner, but which, in my own exuberance, I had neglected. It was over six years since Alison had known Ern Higham. He was an old man. There was a strong possibility that his memory might fail him. He might have gone ga-ga by now: a doddering, dribbling idiot with lighted rooms inside his head, but the doors completely sealed. Stubborn as ever, I said nothing. It was too late to turn back.

It wasn't difficult to find Ern Higham's place. Judith had described the location. The cottage lay outside the village in a fairly remote spot, not far from the sea. It was a small dwelling, yet visible from some distance due to the flatness of the land and the waters about it. The isolation of it struck me most of all. I could not imagine how a man in his nineties could survive here. The cottage was a couple of miles from the nearest house and as we approached, I began to wonder whether Judith had got it wrong. Already I felt extreme apprehension. I remembered Mrs Bobbin and her veiled threat. I wondered what she was so afraid of.

We drew closer and I decided to stop the car.

'Let's get out here. We don't want to arouse his suspicion.'

We stepped out and I was struck, as if for the first time, by the scope of this wilderness. The air was fresh and salty, though the sea was not visible. All about us, the boggy marshland, the estuary. Gulls complained loudly overhead and waders stalked the waters. A warm wind crossed my face and I felt myself displaced – (such a townie, I thought, I'm such a townie) – but I was overwhelmed by the noise and the spectacle.

We approached the cottage in silence, rather awed. If this were Ern Higham's home, I thought, he must be either extremely strong or extremely stubborn. It could not be an easy existence at his age. There was no shelter from rain or sun, no electricity or telephone lines, no television aerial. It was the kind of place that would indeed frighten children. The garden was unkempt and choked with weeds: bindweed scrambled up the shrubs; nettles meandered the path; ivy scaled the walls. Nothing delicate might flourish here. It was too exposed.

'Your shoulders will burn,' I said to Helen.

She shrugged.

'It feels good to be out here. I feel good, Harry.'

She paused, tilting her head to the sky, then turned back to face me. 'It seems impossible, doesn't it, thinking about London now.'

'Yes. Like another world.'

We were putting off the moment when we would walk down the path towards the door.

'Come on. We have to do it.'

'All right,' she said. 'In a minute.' She paused. 'Look, I've left my bag in the car. You go on. I'll catch up.'

I tossed her the key and let her go, turned and approached the cottage.

When I reached the door, I hesitated. There was a small flower-bed close to the wall where a row of red-hot pokers were planted, strangely flourishing. I wanted to laugh but could not. I knocked. No reply. I felt rather a fool standing there. Even if he should answer, I did not know what I planned to say. I figured that he might be slow to reach the door so I continued to wait. It seemed as if hours passed though it was no more than a minute or two. When I remember that time, it is the stillness that impresses itself on my memory and the immense heat; nothing moves or changes. Even the air is motionless.

I knock again. Again, stillness. I am disappointed and feel weak. It must be the sun; I should have worn a hat – a Panama would have done the trick, a hat so fine I might roll it up and pull it through my wedding ring. Visions then of myself in India: a different path I might have taken. I imagine the heat, the shady corridors, the mirrored halls, mosaics. I see brightly painted elephants lumbering up a hill, the vista of a garden below me.

'What are you wanting?'

I had heard nothing. I had not even seen the door open. But there was no doubt this was him. He stood before me and I looked him in the eye. At over six feet tall, Ern Higham defied the stereotypes of old age.

'What are you wanting in my garden?'

I had not expected this. His huge presence unnerved me.

'Well, lad?'

Ern's frame was like a wasted athlete's. He did not stoop, though he leaned forward a little to rest his hand on a cane. He was large-boned, but there was no meat on him. His skin hung like chicken flesh. Ern's hands were square, spade-like, with a light spattering of liver spots. His shirt was grubby, his trousers were too short. He wore tartan carpet slippers.

'I'd like to speak to you,' I said.

Ern Higham did not seem to cringe or apologise for his decrepitude. He merely stood, snowy eyebrows raised, full lips compressed. He was bald on top with a few wisps of brilliant white hair about the crown. His ancient skin was tanned and thick, the myriad creases like dried-up river beds. Everything about him was suggestive of former strength, of enormous pride. The whites of his eyes were blood-shot but the irises were dove-grey and clear.

'It's about time,' he said. 'I know you.'

The voice seemed familiar but his words threw me. I hadn't thought that he would recognise me. We stared at each other like school-boys, egging each other on. Something bothered me about his face but I couldn't put my finger on it.

'Can I come in?'

'And what if you can?'

He did not move.

'You knew my wife, I believe. Alison Bliss.'

He was silent. I realised why I recognised the voice. Judith's imitation had been accurate. It was a powerful, blunt voice with a strong Norfolk accent. There was a mockery in his tone; a superior pleasure.

'So. You be the infamous Harold Bliss?' He paused, leant closer and surveyed my face. 'What kept you so long, laddie?'

The condescension irked me, but I decided there was no point in disputing trivialities. I was almost half his age. There would be time, later, for challenging him. For now I had to keep him sweet. In a sense I was delighted at the recognition. It suggested that his memory might indeed be intact.

'What does it matter? I'm here now.'

'And you're wanting to talk to me, eh?'

There was a twinkle in his eye. I thought he was about to laugh but he did not. I found myself staring at his face. It was a magnificent construction yet entirely impenetrable. I realised then it was his teeth that had been bothering me. They were too good for a man of his age, yet too yellowish and imperfect to be false. Was it possible to reach such an age without one's teeth rotting away?

'Yes. I'd like to talk to you.'

'You're too late.'

He moved his cane to turn, as if he had resolved the matter and was about to leave me like a fool on his doorstep.

'I'm sorry?'

'Too late,' he muttered.

I began to panic.

'Please . . .'

He turned back, briefly, and as he did he seemed to look, not at me but at something behind me. His expression was nothing short of blind fear – as if he literally withered before me. I turned to see Helen approaching. I understood what had happened and knew I must turn it to my advantage. Helen came closer and took my hand. When Ern spoke it was with an unprecedented ferocity.

'What's this? Trickery?'

I shook my head.

'I'm pleased to meet you,' Helen said.

'It speaks!'

Helen glanced at me uneasily.

'This is a friend of mine, Mr Higham. Helen Cregar.'

He wasn't listening. He looked suddenly pale and skeletal. Without warning he reached out and grabbed Helen's arm. His long, spotted fingers encircled her wrist and though she flinched, to her credit she did not complain.

'Flesh and blood?'

'Yes. I'm perfectly human.'

'What are you wanting with me?' he said.

'We're here to talk about my wife. Alison Bliss. You remember her, don't you?'

'I reckon I remember her.'

'Can we come in?' Helen asked. 'It's really hot out here.'

'He can come in. You stay outside.'

She snatched her hand away.

Ern laughed. 'I know what you're at, see. You don't frighten me.'

'That's hardly our intention,' I said.

'Come here, girl. Let me see you.'

He leant forward and touched Helen's face. She recoiled as he traced his fingers, almost lovingly, across her cheek but did not pull away. Such old hands, as if the flesh had shrunk from them. They were brown and angular with yellow, square fingernails. Had he touched Alison like this? His hand lingered but Helen said nothing. She knew the delicacy of the situation. He seemed to dote on what he saw. Then, quite suddenly, he snapped out of it.

'You can't fool me with this,' he said. 'This ain't no ghost.'

'We didn't want to fool you,' I replied.

'So why are you bringing her? Send the girl away. I'll be talking to you if I must.'

I hesitated. A few minutes earlier he was ready to turn me away. Now he was willing to talk. I didn't want to alienate Helen but in the end, she made the decision for me.

'You go in. I'll wait,' she said.

'You can't wait out here.'

'All right. I'll take the car back.'

'Are you sure?'

'Yes.'

'I'll make my own way home then,' I said. 'It's not such a bad walk. You don't mind?'

'It's fine, Harry. You don't have to apologise.'

Before I could stop her, she turned and walked down the path. I thought I detected some regret in Ern's look, but he did not express it.

'You'd better come in if you're wanting to,' he said, 'before I be changing my mind.'

# 19

E RN LED THE WAY and I followed, acutely aware of the
strangeness of this. I recalled that this would have been my
last day at the school. This very morning I should have been in a
special assembly where speeches would have been given about my
dedication, my flair for my subject. Whatever they really thought of
me, the ceremony for such a long-standing member of staff would
have been the same. I would have been presented with a fountain
pen inscribed with my name and a card signed by all the staff. The
choir would have sung, with one of the sixth-formers soloing. One
of the boys might have read a sonnet. And Richard – certainly
Richard – would have spoken in my favour. I could barely believe
that I had left it all behind.

Ern walked before me. He had a slight limp and walked slowly
with some difficulty. I was reminded of my father and his war
wound. But if Ern was in pain, he was striving not to show it. There
was a stiffness to his gait as if he were struggling not to buckle under
his own weight. I had the impression that if he walked too quickly
he might literally snap.

After the sunlight, the hall seemed very dark. The only light came
from an open door at the end and it took a few seconds for my eyes
to adjust. A small stairway rose to my left but at first I was aware of
little else. There was a peculiar smell, a mouldering odour, and it
was cold here, as if the walls retained some portion of the previous
winter. As the hall came into focus I realised how bare it was. The
walls were unadorned and the paint-work flaking. There was no
carpet, just a hard stone floor. Then, as we passed the stairway, I
started.

In the dark recess was a large, glass cabinet: a display of taxidermy. I felt an involuntary heaving in my throat which I suppressed. I saw it only briefly but there must have been over fifty

stuffed birds in that case, staring out with their glassy black eyes. There were gulls suspended in full flight, ducks, little song-birds, geese, a heron. It was a depressing sight, so much death in one place. A grim spectacle for an ageing man.

We entered the room at the end of the hall. I felt apprehensive and reluctant. Everything here was alien. There is something about the clutter that old people create which irritates me immensely, but this was different. On shelves and tables and at my feet, the accumulations of a lifetime were stacked. Despite the sheer number of objects, each one was placed in a very particular way, as if Ern had some obscure filing-system for his belongings. Teapots, for example, whether dented tin or cracked china, were arranged on a shelf to my right. Eight of them were lined up above the shelf where egg-cups crowded, next to trays full of spoons. It was difficult to know where to look. My eyes alighted on various objects: a stack of weather-beaten oars beside the fireplace; baskets full of fishing nets; several shotguns leaning casually against the wall.

'You'll be wanting to sit down,' Ern said.

'Sorry?'

'A chair. You'll be wanting a chair.'

He was agitated, as if my need were an unreasonable request. 'Yes.'

There was only one chair in the room, close to the fireplace, and that was clearly meant for the old man.

'Chairs are next door,' he said. 'In the next room. I'm not having much need for them these days.'

'Right. Shall I fetch one?'

'What are you wanting to go in there for? Nosing about, eh?'

'No. Of course not.'

'I'm not an invalid, see? I'll fetch it.'

His stubbornness was evident from the beginning. He always spoke to me as if I were some kind of inferior being, an inconvenient presence. I might have fetched the chair in a quarter of the time but I did not argue. I was still in shock at meeting him. Already I realised how attractive he must have seemed to Alison. He had a certainty about him that she had always lacked. Alison was constantly doubting of herself, worrying what people thought of her, whereas Ern seemed possessed of a supreme self-confidence. He didn't give a damn about such trivialities. I watched him as he walked, painfully, from the room. His body was that of a man half in the grave, yet his mind was capricious and apparently sound.

I stood marooned at the centre of the room. I moved to the window and saw Helen getting into the car. The window was closed, the room airless and humid. There was a clattering next door and I turned but was distracted by a display of photographs on the wall. They seemed to date from before the turn of the century and my eyes scanned them: a shooting party on a rowing boat by the mill; a man with one arm, looking somehow familiar, clutching a rifle against his chest; a small boy in a bathing suit. Then I found what I was looking for. Strange, how it shocked me, even so. Arabella, of course, an image I had not seen before, quite different. It was a moment of unguarded joy which broke every convention of the Victorian portrait, a sepia snapshot. She stood on the beach, her skirts wind-ruffled, her hair loose. She appeared to be laughing, unaware of the camera. It did not seem possible that such a photograph could exist.

'What are you seeing there?'

Ern walked towards me, his cane in his right hand, a wooden chair hooked over his left elbow. He placed it down, opposite his own.

'I was looking at the photographs.'

'And what do you find?'

'This woman. Arabella Bliss. My wife was interested in her.'

Ern raised his eyebrows.

'Sit down,' he said. 'I have some questions for you.'

I did as he asked.

I watched him carefully that first morning. I had a feeling, even then, that I would have to be vigilant if I was to gain anything from this experience. As I got to know the old man, I found that he was always trying to catch me out. He wanted to reveal the inconsistencies of my behaviour. As I watched him, my fascination grew. His face was a constant enigma. It was almost aristocratic, something about the bone structure, the hook nose and prominent cheekbones. His skin stretched across his skull at these points, but elsewhere it was flimsy, like a crumpled paper bag. I had never seen skin so ancient. The sight distracted me from my intentions. I could almost not believe that the face had life in it.

Ern sat down and said nothing, seemed to forget his need to ask questions. Later I understood that there would often be times like this when he would retreat into himself, to the closed rooms inside his head. His eyes would glaze as if he saw nothing of the present and lived only for the fragments of memory that were lodged within him.

'Mr Higham. Are you all right?'

'Hmmm?'

'Are you all right?'

He jolted up.

'Ha? I'm right as rain.'

'You said you have some questions.'

'In good time.'

'I'm eager to find out what you know about my wife.'

'Your wife?' He considered this. Then he smiled. 'She's dead.' He said it quite matter of fact and I couldn't take offence.

'I've waited a long time to find out what you know.'

'My lips are sealed, boy.' He pulled them tight across his teeth.

'I don't want to play games. I'm here to find out the truth.'

'Depends on how you look at things, see? Now answer this. Do you think I'm a fool?'

'Of course not.'

'Then why are you bringing that girl to see me?'

'Helen's a friend of mine.'

'It won't make no difference. Won't help me neither to remember, nor to forget.'

'I don't follow you.'

'Like your wife, lad. Slow on the uptake.'

'So you remember Alison?'

'You do think me a fool.'

'Mr Higham . . .'

'Call me by my name. You know my name, I reckon?'

'Yes.'

'Good. Now let's get started.'

I remember, first of all, the room. When I think of the hours that I spent in his company, it is not only the words that were spoken but the place that I remember, the sense of being distanced from all that I had previously known. Nothing could have prepared me for it.

Despite my cynicism, I began to guess what it must have been like for Alison. I could imagine her being taken in by Ern, drawn into his vision.

The room was like a shrine to his life. That life as yet remained a mystery but it wasn't difficult to piece together certain details from the categories of objects that were lodged there. Birds, for example, were clearly important. Stuffed birds, of a shabbier variety than those displayed in the hallway, huddled together on several shelves. There were so many of the bedraggled creatures that I was amazed they didn't topple on to the books beneath. The books were stacked in piles on the floor and were mainly of little concern to me – volumes of ornithological interest, histories of Norfolk, Victorian gardening manuals. There was a stack of poetry books which surprised me. Palgrave's *Golden Treasury* and Everyman editions of Kipling, Longfellow, Tennyson. But they didn't keep my attention. I was distracted by other proofs of Ern's obsession: the water-colours of birds; jam-jars stuffed with brilliant coloured feathers; an oak table where at least a hundred bird skulls were arranged, labelled according to species.

I remember these, as I remember the driftwood, the shell cabinet, the boxes of pipes, the garden spades. I can still picture the walking sticks, the tea-cups, the Wellington boots, the candles. But when I think of that room, it's something else, not the objects, that strikes me: the unnatural quietness of the place. Apart from our voices and the bird-cries, I heard nothing. In the pauses between speech, when the birds were briefly silent, there was a hush that moved me. There was not even a clock pacing time. Clocks were noticeably absent in that room. And mirrors. And calendars. And newspapers. And radios. It struck me later, on my second visit – there was nothing in Ern's cottage that might remind him of the date, the time, his age. Perhaps this was how he bore the monotony of his days: not knowing how long he had borne it; banishing the proof of his longevity was perhaps the key to his continuing strength.

'You're fidgeting,' he said, that first morning. 'I can't stand fidgeting.'

'I have some questions.'

'Answer me this first – why does Charles Bliss come haunting me now?'

'What?'

'You. You might as well be him. You look like enough.'

'He was my great-grandfather.'

'I know that. I pity you.'

'Why? Do you remember Charles Bliss?'

I hadn't considered it before, but it was possible that as a boy he might have known him.

Ern laughed.

'You don't know? Your father never talked?'

This stung me. It injured my pride that Ern might know more about my family history than I did.

'My father liked his privacy.'

'Best way. There ain't many folk that are worth talking to in my opinion.'

'But you talked to my wife.'

'I got acquainted with her, aye.'

'What did you talk about?'

'That's our business.'

'What have you got to lose by talking?'

'Nothing to lose. Nothing to gain.'

'My wife took her life here – don't I have a right to ask why? You were the last person to know her. What happened, Ern? What did you tell her?'

At first he didn't reply. He closed his eyes, his fingers curled slowly into his palms, then he was still. It shocked me. His face, like that, had the appearance of death. He didn't break the illusion by moving. I decided to wait. I thought of Alison, in this room, with this man. She had wanted a story and Ern had stories to tell.

'I told her what happened,' he said. 'Don't go blaming me, boy. It was her. Her as got caught up in it.'

His lips were tight and twisted.

'I didn't mean to blame you,' I said.

'You're not the only one that's had a loss, see?'

'No.'

'She was wanting to know. For her book.'

'She was a curious woman.'

'And I was wanting the book to be written, see? We were both of us wanting it.'

'Why did it matter to you? I don't understand.'

'I know the story well enough.'

'Then tell me. For God's sake, tell me.'

'Not today. I'm tired. Come back tomorrow. Bring the girl with you. I have a fancy to see her.'

For all I knew he might be dead in the morning. I was about to argue, to use any means of persuasion to get him to talk. But he closed his eyes again. It was not possible, surely, to fall so quickly from wakefulness to sleep, but when I touched his arm, he grunted and his head fell to one side. If he were pretending, which I suspected, this was an accomplished skill. I felt I had no choice. It seemed indecent to watch him like this. Then, suddenly, he seemed too quiet, too still. I stood up, hesitated, then put my hand on his chest. His shirt was clammy. He drew breath and a small smile crossed his lips. I turned and left the room. The door clicked behind, I crossed the hall and soon I was outside, sheltering my eyes from the sun, feeling the heat on my back, walking quickly.

# 20

I T HAD NOT BEEN wise to undertake that walk in the heat of the afternoon. I arrived at the cottage feeling a profound sense of exhaustion. I was not accustomed to such extremes. Before, a certain order had made my life bearable, an ordinariness that I had clung to despite my notoriety. Here, my own smallness struck me. I was weary and hot. I had not half the stamina of Ern Higham. Yet I had escaped the ordinary, the daily repetitions. I had walked slowly, dwarfed by the earth, the sky; insect-like. It was a relief, the knowledge of my own insignificance.

Wanting nothing so much as a beer and a cool bath, I was startled to see a second car on the drive-way. I recognised it immediately as Richard's. My shirt was soaked, my forehead was dripping. I felt marooned, unable to turn back or go in. But turning back was not an option. I could hardly sit, unremarked, in the local tea-shop. In any case, that was the coward's option.

I walked into the kitchen and immediately saw my friend. He was alone at the table, staring vacantly ahead. He turned and looked at me. In all the years that I had known him, I had not seen such scorn, such sorrow cross his features. He was paler than usual and purple about the eyes. There was a hopelessness in his posture. The sight of him nearly broke me.

'Richard – I . . .'

'Shut up, Harry.'

It was all that I deserved, yet it was unbearable. How could I explain my betrayal? I thought of the Richard I had known, the trust he had bestowed on me. I thought of him with the boys, out in the graveyard, pockets full of oil-pastels, ordering them to look closer. I remembered that. Nothing is what it seems. Put anything under the microscope and its form will change unutterably. The surface is not a lie but a disguise. Magnify it, he'd say. How many hues of green in a single spot of mould?

'You've spoken to Helen, I presume?' I said. He looked me in the eye. 'I don't know what to say, Richard.'

'There's nothing to say.'

His voice was brittle.

'I didn't intend for this to happen.'

'Go to hell, Harry.'

I saw there would be no talking to him. I went through to the sitting room, which was empty, then ascended the stairs. Helen was in our room. There was a suitcase on the bed. She was crying.

'What's going on?'

Seeing me, she wept harder. She was folding the sleeves of her denim jacket – one of the few pieces of clothing that were her own – but it fell to the floor.

'Dad's asked me to come home.'

She could barely get the words out. I felt, suddenly, terribly responsible. I thought – yes, let her go, stop playing with her, let her get a life. But selfishness kicked in. I couldn't be without her now. If she went, I'd have to abandon the whole thing. I couldn't do this alone, couldn't be here alone. Nor had I forgotten Ern Higham's desire to see her. She was a part of this now; a part of me.

'So you're going?' I said.

'I don't know.'

'What have you told him?'

'That I'll stay.'

'So why this?'

I gestured the suitcase.

'He told me to think about it. He's waiting for me to change my mind.'

'And will you?'

'I don't know. He's my dad. I'm scared of losing him.'

I paused. I knew that what I said, the way I said it, would influence her. I had to get it right. I was terrified of screwing up and only knew that she must not go. Moving to her side, I took her hand, stroked her hair.

'I love you, Helen. Please don't leave.'

I held her gaze. Perhaps this was love, of a kind. I looked at her –

this strange, lithe creature that I had somehow come to possess. Her lip still trembled.

'What did Ern Higham say?' she asked.

'I didn't get much out of him but I think he will talk. He had a picture of Arabella on his wall. She looked happy, can you believe it?'

'Really?'

'I'll show it to you. Ern wants to see you.'

'Then why did he send me away?'

'The shock of it, I suppose. He wants you to come tomorrow.'

'What's Arabella to him? Why was he so freaked out by me?'

'I don't know. I think we're on the verge of finding out.'

She nodded slowly.

'Did you mean what you said, Harry? Just now.'

'Of course. I don't know what I'd do without you.'

She turned to the window; looked out at the bright fields.

'Poor dad,' she said quietly. 'He doesn't understand.'

When I entered the kitchen, Richard hadn't moved. He looked wrecked.

'Where's Helen?'

'She's staying here.'

'She can't face me, you mean? I want to hear it from her.'

'Don't put her through any more, Richard. She wants to stay. Can't you leave it at that?'

'No. She's my daughter, for Christ's sake. Do you know what that means?'

I said nothing.

'No. I don't suppose you do.'

'She's an adult. Old enough to make her own choices.'

'She's not yet twenty. You make me sick, Harry. You make me sick.'

I turned, wanted to leave, but could not. I remembered the evenings in the Swan, tried to reconcile the man before me with the one I had known. There had been a chemistry between us once, but perhaps it had been false, based on nothing more than a shared antipathy to the school, an artistic bent, a fondness for warm beer and a quiet courtyard. I remembered the intimacy of our discussions and realised how I had admired Richard. He had class, eccentricity, sharpness of wit. He was everything that I was not. My bluntness and cynicism had no doubt attracted him. But now I was confused. Our two desires were opposed and I did not see how we could move beyond this. Somewhere, inside, I imagined his fear; his dread of losing his daughter. It was as if his pain and mine were the same, but only one of us could win. There could be no easy resolution and though I knew that I was wrong, that my friend suffered, I also knew I could not let Helen go. I found myself thinking of the self-portrait. That silent mask appealed to me now. Richard's naked emotion was not easy to bear.

'I can't help what's happened,' I said. 'Don't make it harder for me. We're on the verge of understanding something. It's about Alison.'

'Alison killed herself six years ago. Put it behind you. Don't get my daughter involved in your stupid attempts at self-redemption.'

'It's not so simple.'

'You're screwed-up, Harry. Face it. You're so wrapped up in your own self-pity that you don't give a damn about fucking up my daughter's life.'

'You're wrong.'

'Am I? What have you told her? That you're in love with her, I suppose?' I didn't reply. 'She'll come running home soon enough. You're using her. Aren't you ashamed?'

'He's got nothing to be ashamed of, Dad.'

She stood in the door-way – just as I had first seen her, less than a week ago. She spoke so earnestly, yet she was wrong. How could I call this love? It was something else. Something huge, beyond my comprehension. But not love. How could love blossom in such a short acquaintance? That was the stuff of books and romance. This was a more troubling phenomenon. I was dependent on her. To contemplate losing her was to contemplate a certain void and darkness. Yet who was she? I barely knew her. Perhaps she barely knew herself. I knew only her charmed lightness, the way she adored me, our shared obsession. Was it enough? When coupled with her resemblance to Arabella, it was enough to bind me to her. After all, I had loved Alison, but at last she proved she was a stranger. So many nights in the same bed, so many conversations, so much love-making. What did it amount to? What was love, if it could not keep a soul alive? There would always be an essential separateness, a division that kept people apart. We lived alone. In our own skins. We could not cross the boundaries between us. Sex was an attempt at curing this loneliness but the merging of flesh was an illusion. What I had with Helen, it was more than I had hoped for.

'You're making a fool of yourself,' Richard said. 'Why don't you come home?'

'We've been through this, Dad. Please. Accept it.'

Richard looked at me briefly. I looked away.

'And when he's finished with you, love, what then?'

'Don't underestimate me,' I said. 'You might as well get used to this.'

'Ah – so you think this will last? Well – good luck to you.'

'Why can't you just be happy for us?' Helen said.

'Your mother isn't sleeping, Helen. She's seen the doctor. He's given her some pills.'

'Surprise, surprise.'

'What's that supposed to mean?'

'If you can't get me back by persuasion, there's nothing like emotional blackmail.'

'I'm just telling the truth.'

'She'll get over it,' Helen said.

'If you don't come back, she won't leave it at that.'

'What are you saying?'

He seemed reluctant to expand.

'I can't come back. When we've finished here . . .'

She paused, looked at me. We hadn't talked about the future. Richard was right to be cynical.

'We'll both come back to London,' I said. 'Together.'

'And?'

'You think because we've no definite answers, it invalidates our relationship,' I said. 'That's not true. We're thinking about the present because we're driven to, because what's happening to us right now is absorbing us. We can't think beyond it because we don't know where it will lead. Surely you understand that?'

'Do you hear him?' Richard said. 'He won't commit. That's what he's saying.'

'No. I don't see what the problem is, Dad. You should be glad I'm with somebody you know and trust.'

'I don't *think* so.'

'Look closer,' I said to Richard. 'Magnify it.'

'I look closer at this mess, Harry, and it just gets messier.'

'You're wrong. Something important's at stake.'

'Your libido, perhaps?'

'Dad!'

'I wish you could see it,' I said.

'There's nothing hidden here. I look closer and it's crystal clear. You're exploiting my daughter's naïvety, not to mention her obsession with Alison.'

'I see you're determined to be blind.'

But I no longer knew who was right and who was wrong. I had come so far that to return would be equal madness. I looked at my friend. A small muscle flickered above his left cheek-bone. He seemed suddenly effeminate. He couldn't take the brute reality of his daughter's sexuality. The old black ram tupping his white ewe.

'Will you come with me, Helen?' he said.

She paused. She shook her head, turned, and left the room.

# 21

THERE WAS NOTHING MORE to say. I did not want to be alone with Richard, nor did I imagine that he would want to stay. The door to the garden clicked. Helen had left the cottage. I stood up in the hope that Richard would be encouraged to leave. Instead, he hesitated. He was staring at his hands, as if he might find answers there.

'Can I get you anything? A drink?'

He shook his head, pushed his chair back from the table. He remained silent for a while, then looked at me.

'You might as well know,' he said.

'Know what?'

'You'll find out soon enough, I suppose.'

'What are you talking about?'

'I heard through Maddy. A colleague of hers let the cat out of the bag.' He looked at me, as if he thought me undeserving of the news he had to convey. But I suppose what he knew was of too great a consequence to keep to himself. 'It's about Paul Vinton. He's claiming to have a few pages from a notebook of Alison's.'

I was uneasy but not alarmed. Alison's notebooks, since her death, remained in my possession. I owned the rights to her work. I had never agreed to publication. Vinton could have nothing of any consequence – a few fragments of juvenilia perhaps.

'Thanks for letting me know. I appreciate it.'

Again he paused.

'I can't imagine your little quest with Helen will unveil anything like this,' he said. 'They're pages from a notebook she kept here, in Glaven.'

'What?'

He smiled. A small, tense, deriding smile. I couldn't believe his words. Since arriving in Glaven I had felt whole, enclosed in a world of my own making. Now that world gaped open.

'Yes. Don't ask me what's in them. I just know that they exist. That they'll be published.'

'Published?'

Even if what he said was true, Vinton couldn't publish. I had the copyright to her work. He couldn't risk it.

'In his biography,' Richard said.

'He can't publish.'

'The word is that he's going to risk it. You've never taken Hake to court, after all. Vinton's publishers will take the chance.'

'Hang on! Where do you get this information? Who is this colleague of Maddy's?'

'You know how people gossip. I only know what she told me.'

'And where is Mr Vinton supposed to have got this information?'

'I've no idea. Look – why don't you leave it alone? Leave Alison alone. And Helen. You can't relive it ad infinitum.'

'What do you suggest I do? Stand by helplessly while other people churn up the past?'

'You might do better to get away. Do what you've always wanted to do. Go to India. Anywhere. When you come back, it will be over. The film. Vinton's book. And Frazer's. I'm not just thinking of Helen, I'm thinking of you. Why can't you stop being the husband of Alison Bliss and get on with your own life? Start afresh.'

'No.'

'Then do it alone. You only have to say the word and Helen will come home.'

I shook my head. 'It's too late.'

He stood up. He pushed a hand through his hair but said nothing. Then he turned and left the cottage, and though I wanted to call him back, I couldn't. There was nothing that could change what had happened. I had lost a friend. It was quite simple, really.

The afternoon passed. Helen did not return and I had no desire to leave the cottage. So, Vinton knew more than I had imagined. I had thought that any notes of Alison's would have been destroyed with the novel. To discover this was not so troubled me. What were these notes? Real or fake? Where had Vinton obtained them? Would he really risk publishing? More important, what would these notes reveal?

Such thoughts plagued me as I attempted to go about household tasks. The cottage was a mess. Our suitcases spilled open and soiled underclothes were strewn across the bedroom like so much jetsam. I began with a frenetic energy but shortly that subsided and I worked diligently, as if there were some purpose in these tasks. I fetched polish and dusters and began on the dresser. If I glanced up occasionally, at the painting above the bed, it was to admire the way Bliss caught the breakers or to be drawn, briefly, to the brush-strokes of the storm-clouds. The painting reminded me of Turner's seascapes. There was a luminosity in Bliss's vision. I was drawn by the mood of the work and in turn to thoughts of Alison. In this room she had penned a journal, a few pages of which had fallen into the hands of Paul Vinton. If several pages had survived, it was possible there was more. It was the thing I had hoped for. That she might speak to me again.

Eventually I tired myself out. I got carried away, scrubbing window-sills, brushing up dirt. The room was in shade now and I lay down, willing sleep to overcome me. When I awoke, I felt disturbed, as if something awful had happened, but I could not recall my dream. I looked at the clock. It was early evening. I was disorientated, but I could hear noises downstairs and soon smelt the familiar odours of fried onions and garlic. The dream still eluded me. I roused myself and went to join Helen.

'Hi!' she said, as I entered the kitchen.

She was putting a brave face on.

'You look terrible,' she said.

'Thanks.'

'I saw you were sleeping – thought I'd better leave you.'

'Just as well. What's that? Rosemary?'

She nodded. 'I found it in the garden.'

'Smells good.'

'Did you have a row with Dad?'

'I think he was resigned to it. He had some news – did he tell you?'

She shook her head. 'I've got some news as well. Judith's back. I bumped into her in the village. She went to Norwich early and decided not to stay. Said she'd explain later. She wasn't exactly happy.'

'What?'

Helen looked sheepish.

'I told her that you saw Ern Higham.'

'Oh God – what did you do that for?'

'Sorry.'

'Never mind. What's her problem?'

'I don't know. She seemed really het-up. Asked if she could come over this evening.'

'And what did you tell her?'

Helen screwed up her face in embarrassment. 'I said yes. She'll be here in about an hour.'

Once the meal was prepared, Helen went upstairs to change and after a while I followed her. I found her before the mirror, in her underclothes. I sat on the bed and watched her, held back, knowing that later I could have her. She turned to me and her expression seemed familiar. At once I recalled my earlier dream.

I dreamt I was disturbed in the night. I had got up, drawn by the moon at the window, and looked out at the garden below, the cavernous sky above; huge banks of vertical black cloud, moving quickly, obscuring the stars. In the garden something caught my attention. Standing by the gate, her back towards me, was the tall figure of a woman in a long, pale dress. I pulled on a robe and left the room.

Outside the grass was wet beneath my feet. The woman was still there, and as I moved closer, she turned. Briefly I saw her face. It was the same look I had just seen. It was Helen's face – or Arabella's. I knew that I must follow her. Yet it was difficult. She slipped away and I couldn't get close. She moved effortlessly, while I felt weighed down, my limbs heavy. The ground was boggy, my bare feet covered in mud. I was almost sinking.

I was astonished now that I could have forgotten this, it was so vivid. I followed the woman into a wood. We were lost among the trees. There was a scent, a sweet, unfamiliar odour. And the striated light between the trees, like a stage-set. Still I followed though the effort was immense. And suddenly I was beyond the trees, on a long, flat pebble beach, like the beach at Glaven, only there was no bank to stop the sea. Now the woman was gone. I saw only birds. They were vultures, violently squawking as they ate. And a pair of them were mating at the water's edge.

I did not mention the dream, but it remained with me throughout the evening. I kept it to myself – enough was being shared. When Judith arrived, she was pretty tense. My visit to Ern had clearly annoyed her.

'I just thought you might have waited, Harry, OK? Till we'd had a chance to talk.'

'I couldn't wait,' I said. 'Surely you understand that?'

'It's a delicate situation. I just don't want anything to go wrong.'

'You mean you wanted to come with us.' I paused. 'Look, have a glass of wine.'

Despite her mood, and though I hadn't expected it, it was good to see Judith. I had been disgruntled at her early return, yet as the wine took effect, she softened, and I did, too. Something about the evening perhaps that brought us together, the three of us about the table. The night was hot, the door open to the garden. On the table, lighted candles, bottles of wine. I was oddly happy.

Judith explained why she was back so soon. She had heard the same rumour I had. She knew about the extract from the notebook. In fact she had always known that Alison kept a notebook here. Alison had told her. She had even wondered whether it might have survived and was now furious that this extract had fallen into Vinton's hands. We would have to tread carefully, she said. We had to keep Ern Higham sweet. She had a strong hunch that the notebook was in his possession.

'But you can't be sure?' Helen said.

She was thrilled at the idea of more words from Alison's pen. We all were. Helen, I guessed, wanted to revel in the poetry: the magic of the words alone. Judith wanted the credit of discovering them. She wanted to analyse the notebook, to tease meaning and hypothesise. I wanted what I had always wanted. To make sense of the senseless. Words couldn't do it, I knew, but I had nothing else to cling to. At the very least, the cause of my misery might be unveiled.

'It seems that what Harry's heard is true,' Judith said. 'Vinton must have had these pages for some time, but he hasn't talked. He was waiting for the right time, I guess.'

'So why now?' I said. 'And how is it suddenly common news?'

'Don't be naïve. Once these things are leaked, the word travels fast. It'll probably be in the press at the weekend. Not the extract itself. But the rumour that it exists.'

'And the timing?'

'A follow-on from last week. The stakes are rising. We have to get moving. I tell you, this place will be crawling with hacks before we know it.'

'So Vinton's publishers leaked this?' Helen asked.

'Exactly. They want to maximise sales and profits. There's talk about one of the Sundays printing the extract. I doubt they'd risk it, of course. But there's nothing stopping them from revealing the gist of her words.'

'How can I prevent them?'

'It might be better to beat them at their own game. Forget their measly extract. We could get hold of the rest of the notebook.'

'Hang on! This is no game, Judith. If – and I mean "if" – that notebook exists, publication would be out of the question.'

'You can't say that. You don't even know what's in it.'

'And you don't even know that Higham has it. What on earth gave you that idea?'

'I'm pretty sure. Vinton spoke to Ern Higham. I've been meaning to tell you. It won't be long before his name's in the public domain.'

'What? How do you know that?'

'I've seen a small extract from Vinton's book. I have a friend who works for his publisher. She faxed it to me in Norwich. Higham's name is there.'

'I see.'

Nobody spoke. They were waiting for me. Knowing that Vinton had trodden this path before me – it sullied it somehow. Just how much did he know? I poured myself another drink, lit a cigarette.

'Harry?'

'OK. If Higham has the notebook we have to get it. Which doesn't mean we'll publish.' I paused. 'I want to know this: did Higham speak to Vinton? Did he *give* him Alison's work?'

'Who can tell?'

'How much does Vinton know?'

'I think it's pretty patchy; he's just scratching the surface.'

'And what about you, Judith? What else do you know that you haven't already told us?'

'All I know is what I surmised from being with her. I don't have any facts. Only what she told me.'

'And what did she tell you?' Helen asked.

'We talked about a lot of things. About children particularly. She told me about her miscarriages, you know? It wasn't something she could easily forget. She remembered her due dates as if they were children's birthdays.'

'What?'

Alison had never told me this.

'I felt so sorry for her,' Judith continued. 'As if real people had died, not just embryos. But she was ambivalent about it.'

'Her mother, right?'

Judith nodded. 'She thought if she had kids she might never write again.'

'She had this theory,' I said, 'that only childless women become great artists. I mean – can you imagine Virginia Woolf changing nappies? Or George Eliot breast-feeding?'

'I guess that's why she admired Plath so much,' Judith said. 'The *Ariel* poems, all written at 4am before the children woke.'

'Plath? You talked about Plath?' I said.

'Given her state of mind, it's inevitable, isn't it?'

'And what else did she say?'

'We didn't dwell on it – it was just in passing.'

'But you can remember?' Helen said.

'Sure. There was a poem she mentioned. The last Plath wrote, by all accounts.'

'I know the one,' I said. 'Yes. "Edge". Is that the one you mean?'

Judith nodded. It was peculiar. I knew that Alison liked the poem, but in the years since her death I hadn't once thought about it. Now the lines spoke to me, as if for the first time. I was reminded of my recurrent dream. The image of Alison's face in death. A perfect smile.

'Christ! Is that how she saw it? Did she think suicide was some kind of great achievement? Didn't she have a mind of her own? Fucking mimicry – is that what it was about?'

'I didn't say that.'

'But we all know it's the case. Didn't she know that there was nothing brave or remarkable about it? What *did* she think? That if she killed herself she could make of herself some kind of tragic heroine?'

'It may well have appealed to her.'

'But there's nothing grandiose about it. It's just an awful mess.'

'That's what I'm trying to say – in my book.'

'Fuck your book. What good are words in this? That's what she wanted, isn't it? Eulogies.'

'I'm not writing a eulogy.'

'What are you writing?'

'You have to calm down, Harry. This is getting you nowhere.'

I knew it. I knew, in truth, Alison's decision could not have been based on such cynicism. But suddenly I was furious at her. That she had left me alone.

'But the idea of it,' I said. 'That she thought death could make her perfect. When she was perfect, near as damn it. In the flesh, she was perfect. For me. She spent her life looking for perfection, never knowing that there was no need. She embodied so much that was good. Yes, good. But she didn't know it. There was this strain of self-hatred. So many years, being judged only by her appearance, it made her question the value of what was within. After she was born, her mother stopped writing, and she blamed herself, always, for that. Isn't that absurd? Maybe she was trying, all her life, to make up for what was lost – to live her mother's life for her.'

'It's not unusual. Freud would say that she was trying to restore what was lost by incorporating it within herself.'

'Spare me!'

'There's nothing wrong with analysis.'

'You can analyse all you like, it won't bring her back,' I said. 'We don't need all that Freudian bullshit. There are other ways of seeing.'

'We're seeing the same thing, just using different language.'

'Inter-textual codswallop! As if I haven't seen enough of it over the years.'

'I'm just looking for answers.'

'But that's just the problem,' I said. 'There are no answers. You won't find them. Not in Freud or Jung, Barthes or Derrida.'

'Harry!'

'And you certainly won't find them in fucking Foucault.'

'Nor am I looking there. What's got into you?'

I said nothing, shamed at my outburst.

'In any case,' Judith said with a smile. 'You might try quoting a few feminist thinkers at me – *then* you might be on to something.'

'Forget it!' I said and downed my drink.

I took a walk in the garden. I was quite drunk but it was cool outside and I could breathe again. 'That fucking woman,' I muttered. 'Who does she think she is? What does she know about this? Fuck!' I kept up this quiet seething for a few minutes but even as I spoke, I knew it wasn't Judith that made me feel this way. It was something within me. It had been crouching, holding back, hiding beneath Harry Bliss. But now it was exposed, it leapt out. Here, at the mercy of the unforgiving sky, nothing could be hidden. It was as if Alison watched me and I could no longer keep up the façade. I was myself again, and I felt the rawness of it, the great, gaping wound. Everything was familiar – the landscape of my dream. The damp, salt air stung me. I was stripped bare, released. And in pain. Christ! Everything seemed large and otherworldly, seemed to loom about me. 'That fucking woman!' The odours of night-flowers overwhelmed me. And the brightness of the sky, the pale and unfamiliar stars. How they stared at me, accused me, probed me. I looked back at the cottage: the open door, yellow and intimate light. I could not return to that table and pretend to be something that I was not. I was no longer the school-teacher who spent his evenings in a tower block, ticking exercise books. When I thought of that room, the low ceiling, the dead furniture, the thick curtains that withheld the night – I felt astonished that I could have borne it for so long.

When I returned to the table, I kept quiet. They looked at me, uneasily. Helen touched my thigh but I flinched and she moved away. At first I refused to be drawn. I simply listened.

'If we can find the notebook, I figure we can come closer to Alison.'

'But didn't she tell you?' Helen asked. 'Didn't she say what she had found out? What had happened to Arabella?'

'No. She talked about Higham, but not what he told her.'

'What did she say about him?'

'She was – how can I put it? – infatuated almost. I'm not talking about anything sexual . . .'

I raised my eyebrows.

'I mean she was entirely taken in. She couldn't see him objectively. She so admired him, which I thought frankly bizarre,' Judith said.

'Why bizarre?'

'He was an old man! I mean, what was she doing spending her time with this hermit? If he were an intellectual I might have understood it, but he was just some wiry creature that ought to have been dead by now. I mean, I'd seen him. A walking skeleton!'

'But he had a story to tell,' I said. 'Isn't that the point? He knew worlds she couldn't have reached without him.'

'Sure. I understand that. But she was so obsessed. Maybe, if we find the notebook, we'll get it.'

'Do you think it'll explain her suicide?' Helen asked.

I shook my head. 'I've been thinking about it. I mean – what are the motives that impel a person to suicide? Can we ever understand it? Whatever Ern Higham tells us, whatever this notebook might reveal. Perhaps that's why her suicide note was so meagre. What could she say? Even when a person writes words on a page, aren't they still hiding something? Is there such a thing as absolute honesty? Absolute self-understanding? We don't see ourselves clearly, that's the problem.'

'I don't see what you mean,' Helen said. 'I thought we were here to find out.'

I paused, realising how my words must disappoint. She had just turned away her father. And for what? The inevitability of failure.

'I'm not saying we'll discover nothing. There's a lot that's still mysterious. I just mean that there are limitations.'

'It's kind of like a labyrinth,' Judith said. 'Don't you think? There's an internal world. We don't see beneath the surface. People keep themselves out of sight, I guess.'

'Nothing makes sense until after the event,' I agreed. 'Even now, we're still guessing.'

Helen shrugged, irritated.

'Sometimes I wonder if it isn't the writing itself that creates the misery,' Judith said.

'We're getting nowhere,' I said. 'Nowhere.'

All this talking seemed suddenly fruitless. We would arrive at no answers this evening.

'Judith, I'm so sorry. I feel immensely tired. Perhaps we should leave this for now.'

'Of course. Sure. I'll get going. And tomorrow?'

'Higham wants to see Helen and me.'

'I see.' She paused. Her lips tightened. It was clear she was not happy to be left out. 'You will be careful?'

'Of course.'

'We'll meet up afterwards, right?'

'Yes. Don't worry. I think I have the measure of him.'

Such nonsense I uttered. I felt that I knew less now about Higham than before I met him. Then, at least, he figured in my imagination. Before I met him, my invention was constricted like that of a painter who knows only realism, who can capture a face at a given moment, watch the play of light, crystallise the image, yet cannot see that it is lacking. Meeting Higham had made me see again. A person cannot be contained by thought, by words, by brush strokes. My conception was inadequate. Now, suddenly, the world had turned Cubist. A kind of explosion. When I thought of him now, I wanted to see everything at once – for past, present and future all to be contained within my vision. I wanted to see the front of his head, the back, the skull, the brain, the memories.

Judith nodded. She hesitated on the doorstep, looked behind to see if Helen was watching. She placed her hand on my wrist. Then she turned and left. I watched her as she got into her car; her headlights cut across the lawn. In the kitchen I could hear Helen, stacking dishes. Even that, the slightest of sounds that she made, had the capacity to arouse me. Yet I felt also distanced from the stirrings of sex. A part of me had gone beyond it, saw it for what it was: a small, fragmented part of me; a sliver; a dream.

# 22

THE NEXT DAY WE woke early. By nine we were on the mud-flats at Blakeney, taking a walk together to screw our courage. It was a precious time. I remember Helen's face, small, almost ghostly against her black dress. She seemed unreal: more muse than mistress. She walked ahead of me a while and there was nothing in my vision beyond Helen, the flats, the sky. I do not believe in omens but if ever I have weakened, if ever I allowed a fatalism to enter my thoughts, it was then. Despite the incipient heat, the sky was blackening, the air was humid. Something was waiting to happen.

Now, when I think of my meetings with Ern Higham, I recall the frustration I experienced. I could never pin him down. Talking to Ern, I thought, was like talking to a reflection in a fairground hall of mirrors. I might believe, however briefly, that I was addressing the man himself, but I was always mistaken. It was a distortion; a trick. Ern would invariably have the last laugh. He was hiding there among his myriad reflections but he was not about to reveal himself. Which was not surprising, I suppose, considering his history.

But on that day, I knew nothing of what had gone before. If I had known more, I might not have pushed him as I did. As it was, I began to see him not only as an enigma but also as an obstacle. Despite his frailty there were times when I felt almost violent towards him; when I wanted nothing more than to swipe at him. It would have been no good of course. I wanted to floor the man himself, to hit flesh and bone, not a glass charade.

Sometimes I think Ern liked to encourage such sentiments. When we arrived at his cottage that morning, we were already agitated. Our expectations had made us edgy. The door was open, which surprised me, but still we knocked. There was no reply and after a second, equally vain attempt, we went in. Helen was clearly intrigued and nervous. But when we entered his room, she cried out.

There, in the armchair where I had left him, Ern lay slumped. His long, withered body had slid a little and his head was on one side at an almost impossible angle. It was a chilling sight. His face was lifeless, without expression. Panic arose within me; a sense of responsibility for this. But it was countered by fury: that he had died without talking.

Then he coughed. Briefly his body was racked with it, but afterwards he sat upright, suddenly animated. He must have caught our expressions because he started to laugh. We just stood there like shop dummies, staring at him.

'What be the matter?' he chuckled. 'Cat got your tongues?'

'We thought . . .' Helen began.

'I'm seeing what you was thinking,' he said. 'Ha! Thought I was done for, did you?'

'What the hell do you think you're doing?' I said. I was convinced this was a deliberate hoax.

'I ain't doing nothing. It's you who are jumping to conclusions, see? There's life in the old fella yet!'

I remembered Judith's words, reminded myself to tread carefully. I wanted to walk out. I couldn't bear Higham's one-upmanship. But then I noticed something. A third chair had been placed by the grate. It was a small thing, but from Higham it seemed almost akin to a welcome. He wanted to talk to us.

'You said you wanted to meet Helen,' I said. I was civil but could not keep the edge from my voice. Ern looked her up and down. She cringed beneath his gaze.

'Is this the best you could do?' he said.

'I'm sorry?'

'She ain't so like her, after all.'

'No. She's not.' I couldn't be bothered to argue, to explain that I didn't bring Helen simply for the purpose of unsettling him.

'So, girl. What brings you here? It ain't a place for a whippet.'

'I'm here to find out what happened to Alison Bliss,' she said.

'It's a simple thing,' he replied. 'She killed herself.'

Helen's expression worried me. She had had enough of being patronised.

'Ern,' I said. 'We've come to hear your story. You told me

yesterday that you would speak to us. If you won't, we might as well leave now.'

'I'll tell you what you're needing to know. You just have to ask the right questions, see? Sit down. You'll be wanting some tea, eh?'

He made his way, slowly, to the corner of the room. He had laid out some tea things on a tray. Next to the tray there was a portable gas stove which he lit to boil water. We waited in silence as he spooned tea into a pot. I could see the concentration on his face, the effort involved in not spilling the leaves. His hand moved from the caddy, and, though it barely shook, it was clear from the tightness of his fingers that this was no easy task. I hesitated, wondering whether I should offer to pour, but something stopped me. I was convinced he would rather burn himself than be pitied.

Helen seemed uneasy. She looked almost prim and I guessed she wanted to impress Higham though I couldn't fathom why. Her eyes darted about the room and she sat forward on her chair, as if she thought she might be contaminated by it. But the chair was not dirty, neither was the room. Simply it had the appearance of an object worn down by time. Everything here was like that – ancient, well-used, decaying. The room smelt of rotten wood, of fish, salt, damp rope and moth-balls. The windows were closed and in this heat the stench intensified. I thought what an existence this man must have led, to have lived here alone and for so long. It was enough, surely, to induce madness.

Ern poured the tea in silence then sat down before us. Now he was looking at Helen, not as he had looked earlier, with cynicism, but with intense interest. The façade he had at first presented seemed to slip.

Helen bore the intrusion well. She pretended not to notice and I admired her for it. Her own gaze fell on Ern's photographs which she scanned as he watched her face obsessively. His distraction gave me leisure to examine him, but I could not decipher a face like that. It had seen too much, lived too long, suffered, perhaps, too much.

'Shall we talk about Alison?' I said.

I wanted to distract Ern from Helen.

'Seems a real fuss is being made about that girl.'

'It's not surprising,' I said, 'considering what happened to her.'

'It ain't always been like that. When it was Bella. No folk made a song and dance about her.'

'Bella? You mean Arabella. You don't remember her suicide, surely?' I said. 'It must have been before you were born.'

'Oh I was born all right. I may be older than you think, see?'

I wondered if he might be telling the truth. I wasn't certain of Ern's exact age. It was just possible he might remember it. But it was highly unlikely. Yet how else to account for his apparent involvement in that story? How else to explain the way he looked at Helen?

'So you're saying it was hushed up? Arabella's suicide?'

'Tha's right. I reckon it were. But your wife – they don't stop asking questions about her.'

'Who do you mean by "they"?' Helen asked.

'People that comes here. City-folk.'

'Have you spoken to anybody?' she asked.

'I keep myself to myself. But my grand-daughter – she tells me. Says the place is fair crawling with those that want to know about the Bliss girl.'

'So you've never spoken to a Paul Vinton?'

Ern did not reply. He leant forward and picked up his teacup. It was too small for his huge, ineffectual hands but he managed to get it to his lips. Suddenly I wondered whether even his decrepitude were an act: a clever delaying tactic.

'Well?' I asked.

Higham took a sip and savoured the brew. Then he smiled.

'That man? He was here all right,' he said.

'And what did you tell him?'

'I sent him away with a herring.'

'What?'

'A red 'un. Sent him scampering off, right happy. He ain't got nothing of no worth.'

'So it's true. You gave him an extract from Alison's notebook?'

'You can rest easy, boy. You think I'd give anything precious to a slimy fella like that?' He chuckled over his teacup. 'Ha! You'd'a thought I'd'a given him the crown jewels to see his face. But it was a trinket – glass beads, see?'

'Glass beads?'

He shook his head.

'A page or two – all nonsense. He thinks tha's all there is.'

'And you have more?'

It was difficult to control my mounting excitement. I had not thought the old man would talk so easily, much less that he would truly have words of Alison's in his possession. I tried to speak calmly but I was wasting my time. Ern was a skilled manipulator. He placed his teacup down, turned to Helen and smiled at her, revealing his over-large teeth that I was now convinced were false.

'A girl like you shouldn't be dressed in black, see? There'll be time enough for that.'

'Mr Higham,' she said, 'we just want to know whether you have a notebook that belonged to Alison Bliss.'

'And if I have, why should I be giving to you what I was keeping from Vinton?'

'Because Paul Vinton wants to publish Alison's words,' she said, 'and we don't.'

It surprised me to hear her say that. I knew we might not keep such a promise. Already Judith's influence had begun to bear. And what would I do, I wondered, if Alison's words should prove me innocent? Would that spur me to go public?

'It's not the only reason,' I said. 'You know I have a right to see those words. You can't hoard them for ever. If you don't give them to us, sooner or later they'll fall into other hands.'

'You mean I'll be fair dead, boy?'

'Exactly. Who will you trust then?'

'Not that gran'daughter of mine, tha's for sure.'

'Sorry?'

His words took me by surprise. Though my own instinct was to distrust Mrs Bobbin, why should he feel the same?

'After what she did? It don't bear thinking on.'

'What did she do?'

'In good time.'

'We may not have time,' I said.

'What? I ain't about to cop it yet.'

'I don't mean that. I don't know what inspired you to speak to Vinton, but you can't remain anonymous now. I don't know how long we have – maybe weeks, maybe days. They'll be on your doorstep, Ern. They'll want to know.'

'Are you threatening me?'

'Just telling the truth.'

'The paper men? Tha's what you're saying?'

'Yes.'

He hesitated. For a split-second he forgot to be defiant. He looked to the window as if he expected to see faces there; as if, already, his time was up.

'Telling you won't stop them coming,' he said.

I considered this. I was genuinely afraid for him. I could not see how I might protect him from the very people that had terrorised me.

'No. It won't.' I paused. 'But it might deflect some of the attention. It's a simple equation. Work it out for yourself.'

'I've no fear. You think I'm a'feared?'

'No.'

'You are the image, the very image of all I've come to hate – you're knowing that, are you?' His words seemed to come from nowhere. 'And she –' he gestured towards Helen. 'She is all that's lovely; all that's good.'

'You're not making sense.'

'She's all that's lost, see? All that's left.'

'No,' Helen said. 'I'm not. What you're saying isn't true.'

'Why do you despise me?' I said. I wanted to draw him out.

'You've the blood of Charles Bliss running in your veins, boy.'

'And what did Charles Bliss do that is so terrible?'

'He made Bella mad. He drove her to it.'

Finally, we were getting somewhere. Still I could not think how the past touched him, but for now this was of no consequence. There was an irrational spirit at play here. There was a part of Ern that could not disassociate me from Charles Bliss. If Charles drove Arabella to her death, why should he not believe that I drove Alison? Unless he knew differently, of course.

'Was Arabella really mad?' I asked.

'Why else do they do it? It has to be a form of madness.'

'I'm not so sure,' I said. 'Perhaps any of us, if we're provoked enough . . .'

He dismissed my words with a huff, leant forward and looked me in the eye.

'Not so,' he said. 'There are some souls more sensitive than most. Folk like you with your city airs, you think yourselves cleverer than us, but there are things we're knowing that you'll never know. You live among your tall buildings, drive about in your motor cars, you wear smart clothes, study in your universities – but what do you see, eh? Nothing. All that smog and dust; concrete and glass. You can't see past it. You can't see the earth, boy, you can't see the earth.' He looked away then towards the window. He seemed to contemplate whether we were worth his breath. There was a self-satisfied air about him but also a kind of despair. After a few seconds he resumed his speech. 'Bliss was the same. He was no country fella. He was from Norwich; a stranger here. And Bella too, she was from the city.'

'You said she was sensitive,' Helen said. 'What did you mean?'

'She weren't hardened to the world like other folk. She didn't belong in the city. She was right delicate, you could see it in her eyes. And his Alison was the same. Not meant for this place.'

'For Glaven?'

'Not meant for the world. Too good for it.'

'How do you know about Arabella?' I asked. I didn't want to be drawn by Ern's views. They were too subjective and simplistic. I was beginning to believe that Ern merely fantasised and I wanted hard facts. 'You must have been, at best, a small boy when she killed herself. You wouldn't remember her eyes.'

'It's not just memory, boy! Nor sight!' He spat the words in derision. His mouth quivered. He stretched out his fingers and jabbed at his chest. 'In here, see? I have her eyes in here!'

There was such vehemence in his voice, such passion, and I was silenced by it. We all were. Nobody moved. The only sound was the rasping of Ern's breath, like the crackling of a long-distance telephone wire, the interference of noise before the connection is cut. Once more the cynic in me was rebuked. I did not know where we could go from here. Then another noise, unexpected, broke the stillness: a light rain on the windows. Ern stood up, leant on his cane. Then, as if he remembered our presence, he straightened his back, thrust his chin forwards and walked stiffly towards a small bureau near the fireplace. We watched him, his slow painful gait as he crossed the room and the movements of his hands which seemed almost to flutter like captured birds as he pulled out first one drawer and then another, searching. Soon he found what he had been looking for and returned to his chair.

'This is what you're wanting, ain't it?' he said. 'Her life and soul's in here, do you think? Do you reckon you'll be finding answers here?'

I shook my head. I knew this was the real thing. Alison always used the same notebooks: she'd bought a batch once and had joked there were enough to see her to the grave. Had she meant it, I wondered? Did she, even then, consider such an end?

Now the notebook was so close I felt oddly restrained. It was enough simply to be aware of its existence. Ern was right, of course. No explanation would be enough. He looked at me, as if daring me to take the book, but I did not. Maybe I wanted to spin it out. Once I had read it, once Ern had told his story, what would be left? Perhaps Richard had been right. When this was over, what would I feel for Helen? What would I feel about anything?

'Harry?'

Helen seemed not to understand my reluctance.

'You may be right,' I said to Ern. I avoided Helen's eye. 'Perhaps there are people who simply can't live in the world.'

'You say fair, lad. You say fair.'

'I think Alison wanted to explore a side of herself that most of us don't face.'

'What do you mean?' Helen said.

'Her own vulnerability, her sense of failure.'

'But she wasn't a failure . . .'

'Are you wanting this book?' Ern asked.

'I want to know how you got hold of it. Did Alison give it to you?'

He flashed me a conspiratorial smile but said nothing. I guessed the book was not his by rights. Had he had stolen it? I stood up and quickly took it. Once he had let go, he seemed to regret it. I turned it over between my fingertips. Now I had it, it seemed to grow in significance. No longer an inanimate object but something else. This worn, blue notebook was light in my hands yet it contained something of weight. I wondered at my previous calmness. It was not, as Ern had predicted, that I imagined I would find her here again, but rather that I would find some part of her, however small, a fragment, and that alone might alter the imbalance that had existed since her death.

'Are you going to open it?' Helen asked.

I shook my head. 'I know it's hers.'

I knew what she wanted: to see the evidence that lay between these pages. Alison's last words, her last message to us perhaps. Yet unlike Helen, I didn't doubt Ern. I wanted to delay things. Helen wouldn't like it, but I wanted to read it alone.

'There'll be time enough for this,' I said. 'But what about Bella's story, Ern?'

'I told it to your wife – for what good it did.'

'What do you mean?'

'That book she was writing. 'Twas in there. Lost now. Burnt to cinders. All those hours we talked – gone.'

'Why do you think she destroyed it? I presume you believe it was her, not me?'

'It couldn't've been you. Not possible, see?'

He could not have guessed, of course, the significance of his words. Nor could I have anticipated my own reaction. It was at once an immense relief – to hear my innocence finally proclaimed by another, one who knew – but oddly, I felt also the huge burden of the knowledge: that it was indeed Alison who had destroyed her work. To imagine that level of despair, a kind of double suicide, destruction of her life and thoughts, an obliteration so complete that it was impossible to enter the depths of it.

I looked at Helen. She was watching me, trying to suppress a smile. I understood her thoughts. Now she knew I had spoken the truth. Though Ern had proffered no evidence, his word was enough. But mine had not been. Despite everything, the coupling among the gravestones, her bending at my knees to suck me dry, despite her defiance of her father, her willingness to leave her life behind – she had never believed me. She had wanted to. Perhaps she had convinced herself that she did. But I saw through it. As if Ern's words were a license to love me. The thought left me cold.

'Why do you think she did it? Why would she destroy a thing that was so close to her?' she said.

'She was afraid of it, lass. It wounded her. She thought it would reveal too many secrets.'

'Did you read the book?'

He shook his head in incomprehension.

'I've no time for reading. Why should I read my own words?'

'But they weren't your words,' Helen said. 'They were hers.'

'Hers? Mine? It's all finished now, girlie.'

He paused again, watching her. Helen was too excited to notice that I had fallen silent.

'I don't think it is finished,' she said. 'It won't ever be finished. Alison made sure of it: that people can't forget her.' She turned to me. 'But I've been thinking about it, Harry. It's not just that she killed herself. Nor the model thing. It's her. Something about *her*.'

'No. It was the idea of her. A beautiful model who became the latest in a long line of literary sacrifices. That's what makes it newsworthy. People don't understand what it is to be a writer. They think writers are somehow different, charmed even, but they're not. They're just people who sit in rooms and put words on paper.'

'You sound so callous.'

'No. I care because I knew her, I loved her. It's not the same for other people.'

'You're saying I'm just like "other people"?'

I spoke as gently as I could but she knew it was exactly what I meant. 'I'm saying that even now it's romanticised. Judith had a point. As if she proved her seriousness by killing herself. I don't know why people respect that but they do.'

Helen said nothing but her lips tightened and the muscles in her neck tensed. She looked at me with distaste and I wanted to touch her and release that tension. But my stubbornness prevailed. If the truth hurt her, then so be it.

Ern watched this exchange with a wry smile. It was an interesting diversion. When we fell silent, it was he who broke it.

'The rain's coming down,' he said.

I didn't know how to reply to such a banality.

'You'll not be walking home in this.'

'We'll manage,' I said. I didn't see the point in mentioning the car.

'Don't be a fool. Time's short, you say?'

'Before the press arrive? I can't say, exactly.'

'You ought to know the truth: what Bliss did to her.'

'To Arabella?'

'I've a great storm, in here,' he said, pointing to his head. 'There's nothing will be stopping it. It's been there since the day she died, and won't pass till I've slipped this world. Who do I blame, boy, eh? You?'

I couldn't tell if he were serious.

'I can't be held responsible. Whatever my ancestor may have done,' I said.

But now he didn't appear to be listening. He was quiet, his eyes fixed on some distant point beyond the window. When he spoke, his voice was different, higher pitched.

'Little boy's to blame. Standing on the carpet. Little boy did it.'

He was speaking nonsense. Or rather he was speaking from elsewhere. He spoke quickly too. What was it? An old man's rambling or an elaborate ploy, a bait?

'There's a stain on the carpet. You've stained it. Sorry, daddy, sorry. Can't speak, though. Can't speak.'

Helen looked at me nervously. I began to wonder whether this whole enterprise weren't doomed. I couldn't imagine that we would ever get to the bottom of this and I was tempted to cut my losses and be content with the notebook. I briefly opened it and saw the loose scrawl that I'd recognise anywhere, the pale blue ink that Alison had always favoured.

It seemed that Ern had retreated to a scene from his boyhood but I could find no connection between his words and anything I knew about Charles Bliss or Arabella. Perhaps I was grasping at straws.

'What are you doing with that book, Ernest? Put it down, lad. Put it down! Too late though. Can't be done.'

It was as if Ern were absent and I felt myself withdrawing also. I had been so engrossed by his words that I had barely paused to think. Now I considered our situation. We were caught in this room with a lunatic old man who had no intention of hurrying to tell his tale. He had no concept of time. I wondered, how did he pass his days when we were not here? Perhaps he spent his hours arranging relics on his shelves, polishing the bird skulls, untangling the nets that lay knotted on the floor. Even the air in this room felt like the air from another time: odours of leather, salt, mildew, lace.

Beyond the window, the rain, falling on the marshland, the flat brown boggy earth that never changed. Ern's existence was alien to me. On the pile of books close to my feet were volumes of natural history, manuals of classification, detailing the lives of insects, birds, snakes. Such creatures would barely evolve in the course of a lifetime. Out there, on the wet earth, beneath it and in the skies above, they crept, burrowed, soared. When Ern was a boy, the land must have looked much as it looked today. Two World Wars and the land bore no visible mark. While London, the landscape that I inhabited, was for ever altered. The reconstruction of the city was relentless. I might be reassured perhaps by the benign presence of St Paul's, knowing that however the skyline might dip and rise, this would probably remain.

But change was expected. Each week the architects dreamed up new constructions, the glass-walled buildings of Ern's imagination. I was convinced that he had not seen these with his own eyes. I began to wonder if he had ever left this village. If he had – if he had served in the forces – he surely did not wish to remember it. He seemed to have no desire to contemplate any former life that was not lived here in Glaven. There was no trace of war in the photographs, nor in the room's paraphernalia: no souvenirs; no shells nor guns; no medals. It struck me that Ern had not simply removed all references to time and date from his life, all connections with a world beyond this cottage: it was more than that. It was as if he had systematically eliminated the modern age. As if the twentieth century had never happened.

Now I saw his present rambling in another light. He continued, uttering nonsensical phrases. 'No son of mine should ever do such a thing. I taught you to read, didn't I? Taught you to see.' Ern had forgotten us. He inhabited the same space but a different time. And an idea struck me. Perhaps Ern could barely differentiate between past and present. Perhaps, when we were not here, he retreated to this place that was at once here and not here. Or else he lived a dual existence, where he might slip between two ages and barely know that he had moved.

'You have his eyes, I see that. And his fingers too – ha, ha! A bloody cripple!'

Helen was pulling faces at me as if to say – 'What shall we do? Get me out of here!' – but I did not know how to act. I did not want to leave, yet I doubted my chances of persuading Ern back. I could not believe he would be lucid now. As it happened, I was wrong. I stood up, walked towards him, ready to touch him, in the hope this might disturb his trance. But before I reached him, something happened. He turned to me and was perfectly composed, his voice his own again.

'Sit down,' he said. 'I'm just at the beginning. Ain't you wanting to know what happens next?'

'Yes. Of course.'

'You've his blood in you. You should know his guilt, boy. And mine. I have it on good authority, see? Don't you be doubting a word I say – nor you girlie. I was there. I remember.'

He was ready, at last, to speak. He was about to let the storm spill from his skull. It had been raging for too long and I could not tell what distortions had been wrought, what damage done by solitude and dreams, by false memories and grand fury. But it was enough that he spoke. His words tumbled out and, as I listened, I thought of Alison. Had she made some connection with this story? The truth had been silenced for so long, obliterated from my family's history, but even as I knew it was a part of me, I was certain it had affected Alison more.

One question above all concerned me: could Ern's words alone have driven her to the act that she committed, or was there something else in the equation that I had not allowed for, something darker, more unfathomable still than this? I imagined her here. I knew the expression she would have worn: one of intense seriousness and concentration, her brow furrowed, leaning towards him to catch each cadence of his voice, each shade of meaning. Though it was nearing midday, the room was darkening and when I closed my eyes I sometimes wished I might slip like Ern to some other time, when Alison still breathed and listened and flexed her fingers and contemplated death.

# 23

E RN SETTLED BACK IN his chair, tilting his chin to the ceiling, and shut his eyes, enclosing himself in memory. He remained still, apart from his fingers, which twitched restlessly, and his eyelids, which flickered as if some strange drama played itself out beneath them. When he spoke, there was a concentration of energy in his voice. He did not hesitate or rush to tell his tale. He spoke firmly, with insistence and all the while his fingers in half-prayer, tapping out some indecipherable and silent melody.

'She wasn't meant for this place,' he said. 'She should never have come. She was too bold by far, too restless.'

'Who? Arabella?'

'Bella, yes.' He responded to me, but rather as if I were simply some guiding force to his imagination, not another presence in the room. His eyes still closed, he talked as if to the air. 'Standing on his doorstep. Thin as a stick, like a waif at a gentleman's funeral. He could barely see her face 'neath that great black bonnet. Great black coat too. I see her. Little arms stretched like elastic with the weight of those suitcases. Blistered hands, but she wouldn't put the cases down. Proud, see?'

'Where was she?' I asked. 'Whose doorstep?'

'Bliss's doorstep. Poor little lips trembling. Little sparrow's face. "Come in then, girl!" Him didn't know how to talk to her.'

'I don't understand. Why was she there?'

'Don't you know anything, boy?' He opened his eyes and addressed me. 'Bella was running riot in London. She wore bloomers, boy! She rode a bicycle!'

I laughed. It seemed impossible – Arabella, a New Woman. It was no wonder that Alison had been drawn in. Who would have thought it from the photographs, from the stiff bustles and thick silks that swathed her?

'Her mother couldn't be dealing with her. And her father had enough with one madwoman in the house, let alone two.'

'Madwoman? Who was mad?'

'Her mother. She might as well have been, though the world didn't see it. She had a grey parrot, went by the name of Dizzy. She told the bird her woes, see? It had to be locked away when visitors came for fear it would shout out her secrets. "All alone, Dizzy! I'm all alone!" '

'How do you know this?' The story amused me but I half feared it might be fiction. 'Who told *you* the story?'

'Don't be doubting me. This is in my bones, lad.' Then, as if he realised that I was unimpressed. 'I tell you – I have it on good authority. But if you have no trust . . .'

'No. Please. Continue.'

Again he retreated, closed his eyes.

'Bliss didn't know what to do with her. Man didn't even want a wife, but George needed a mother.'

'And Arabella was chosen?'

'Father sent her. What kind of man was he, sending his daughter to such a place? She wanted to be a scholar. She had her head in too many books. That ain't good for her, they said.'

'And she obeyed?' Helen said. 'Just like that?'

'What else was a girl to do? But it was like death, see? Bliss couldn't talk to her. His head was full of science, full of anatomy it was, bones and muscles, blood and bile. Or else it was his plants. That glasshouse of his. He could talk to the plants, but not Bella, see?'

'So she had no choice? She had to marry him?' Helen asked.

Ern chuckled quietly. He did not open his eyes and I was free to watch him as Alison had. I knew now what it must have meant to her, being here. Back home she had tortured herself. She had tried so hard to write again, but when she sifted her brain she found a blank. Nothing in her current sphere of existence had seemed large enough to commit to paper. She repeated these mantras. 'My life is so ordinary now, Harry. Nothing happens. I sit here in front of this bloody typewriter and no words come. Why should they? I've seen nothing lately, done nothing. Perhaps I am nothing.' It always wounded me, to hear her talk like that. Earlier, when she was writing *Sweet Susan*, she always told me how much she adored our quiet, simple life. Now she was becoming restless. She couldn't go back to modelling, but she had to find a new passion. I was relieved when she discovered the photograph. It sparked something new. After that, she spent her days engrossed, hermit-like, in her notes. When I returned from school, she would emerge, radiant, as if those hours in a dark room had somehow touched her spirit and altered her.

Now I watched Ern talk. Only his hands and his face were animated as if the life had drained from the rest of his body but his soul was still alive and asserting itself there, at his fingertips, behind his eyes. He was talking to himself, with each word recapturing, almost, something lost. His body was done for: his wasted limbs lolling; the skin loose at his neck; his chest that barely moved. Yet beneath this skeleton, a whole history was concealed. I knew what drew Alison here, how she must have observed him as we did, as the rain fell outside, enfolding her in this room while Ern brought life to the woman who had been nothing but an image, a starting-point. The dull thud of water against the panes, the gas-lamps unlit. Between my palms her notebook was pressed and next to me was Helen, leaning forward to ensure no word was missed. In the dim light it would have been easy to mistake her. I saw her in profile: her sharp nose; small wondering mouth; her bare white throat against the black dress that once graced Alison. She held a silence about her. I was reminded for some reason of Whistler's 'Nocturnes'. Something about her brought those mute blue landscapes to mind: thin mists over rivers; light not yet faded; forms half obscured and, most of all, the sense of anticipation those images could conjure, as if, in waiting for darkness, one was also waiting for something else, something deeper and quite unfathomable.

'Bella had an uncle,' Ern said, 'a Glaven man. Her father too was from these parts but he was leaving as a young man. Him didn't have the strength to stay. Afeared of the very wind, I be guessing.'

'What do you mean?' I said. I took his words with a pinch of salt.

'Some folk are believing anything. They say the wind here swallows your voice. So it does, but there ain't no more to it than that.'

'And what did Bella's father believe?'

'Same as many believed and still do. They say that the wind

carries voices; that you shouldn't speak out of doors. You can't be saying nothing but that the Glaven wind will take your words and blow them about like leaves, carry them to the ears of your worst enemy. The wind betrays a man, they say. They say tha's how Bella was betrayed, but I know differently.'

'What happened to Bella?' Helen asked. 'What do you mean, betrayed?'

'Slow down, girl. Give me time.'

I tried to get Ern back on track.

'What about Bella's uncle?' I said. 'Was she close to him?'

'Aye. John Simms. He was against the marriage, thought it no match for his niece. He tried to persuade his brother against it, but Henry Simms was decided.'

'Simms,' I said. 'Arabella Simms.' It didn't seem right. The name Bliss suited her.

'John was fond of Bella. When she was just a whippet, Bella holidayed on his farm. She knew the land, see? Not like her father. She had no fear. That was afore she lost her voice. Afore the parrot.'

'I don't follow.'

'Bella had no fondness for the parrot. She never spoke in that house but in a whisper, else the bird would fling her words back at her.'

'So she lost her voice?'

'Her words were so soft, you might lose them. You had to come close to hear, but many didn't bother. It drove Bliss to distraction. He never saw her as a lass. On the farm she used to shout so loud it might fair burst her uncle's eardrums. She used to run about chasing hens that had escaped the coop. Else she'd be sitting on a stool with a dead chicken on her lap. She'd pluck a headless chicken and not blink at it, that girl. She'd love to feel the warm flesh. Have you ever plucked a chicken, boy?'

He laughed as his eyes flicked open for no more than a few seconds. I shook my head.

'I'll bet you've never shot a guillemot either? No. You wouldn't know a whimbrel from a sandpiper. Charles Bliss was the same and he lived here half his life.'

'But Bella was different?'

'She might have stood a chance here, if Bliss hadn't been such a fool. It kept her sane, this land. She had a feel for it. Knew that shoreline like the back of her hand.'

'I thought she was a city girl. Cycling through the streets of London, you said.'

'Aye. And she went to the libraries too. Only Henry Simms put an end to it. Girl was scandalous. She was wanting to be a man, he thought. Why else would a lass dress that way or read such books? But she often talked of Glaven, see, and that was why Simms thought of Charles Bliss. Only Bella wasn't thinking of marriage. She was wanting to work on the land, or to go out on the punts with the Gentleman Gunners. She was wanting to be on the muds at dawn, waiting for the first migrants. She wanted to escape that house. A great red house they lived in, all towers and turrets. She went from one prison to another. Bliss wanted nothing of her. Him wanted only his books, his glasshouse.'

'What sort of books? Anatomy you said? Was he a doctor?'

'Once a doctor. Aye.'

I had no idea how Ern knew all this. He appeared immersed in this story as if he were its protagonist.

'But his wife died, see? George's mother. In childbirth. Him couldn't keep his wife alive. After that he weren't a doctor no more. Him wouldn't heal nobody. Nothing could move him to it. A fella might be dying in the village, but Bliss wouldn't go to him. No heart, see? Nothing left.'

'That's awful,' Helen said. 'That poor man.'

'No pity. Remember what he did to Bella. Bella had no-one and Bliss hardly spoke to her. That first day when she arrived, hot from the journey, hungry, bundled up in thick silk dresses and petticoats. Bella was in need of rest and a hot bath but him didn't even show her a room nor offer her tea. Him sat her down and brought sullen little George before her, with his pockets full of beetles. Bliss told her what he expected. Said the boy was troubled and needed a mother and he with his studies had no time for coddling. Said he expected her to be obedient, to care for George, to keep house. He'd make sure she'd not be wanting. Bella was supposed to be grateful. Him hoped she would do, that's what he said. He would treat her kindly and be a husband to her. He'd give her a child, that's what he meant. But him was all dried-up, see? Not a seed of life in the man, though he tried all right – chug, chug, chug – like a steam engine he was and she like the track beneath him, not moving an inch.'

It was absurd, I knew, that Ern should assume such knowledge yet I did not challenge him. I was drawn in and appalled by what he told me. In a sense, it barely mattered if he spoke the truth. He told me the same stories that he had told Alison and perhaps the truth of them was less important than the fact that he believed them true. What mattered was the effect of such words on my wife. 'Bliss was all dried-up'. I could not help but be stung. The man whose name I bore was infertile. It was ridiculous to draw parallels. I was not Charles Bliss. I was not responsible for his inadequacies. My marriage had not been a sham. After all, Alison had twice conceived.

'Did she not rebel?' I asked. 'It seems odd that such a woman should so easily bow to her father's will.'

'There was something keeping her in Glaven. Her uncle. Man's heart was going and Bella might have run home if it weren't for John Simms's heart. Bella was afeared if she didn't marry Bliss, she might not see John Simms again. And something else. Bella knew what had happened to Bliss's first wife. She knew his sorrow and believed it might fade. She thought if she kept quiet and was good to him, she might find the man beneath that sour face. But she didn't reckon on *his* heart, see? It was cold as John Simms's was weak. On their wedding night he told her to expect nothing of him nor ever to talk of love. That was after he had bedded her, mind. After she had given up her jewel.'

'You're exaggerating,' I said. 'You must be.' It was impossible to believe in this man that Ern described. 'They were married for twelve years. Are you saying she endured his heartlessness for so long? What about that photograph on your wall? Isn't she smiling there? Maybe Bliss wasn't the ogre you make him out to be.'

Ern cackled and opened his eyes.

'That photograph!' he said. 'Ha! You want to know why she's smiling?' He pushed himself up from his chair. It was like watching some ancient puppet come to life. Ern took the photograph of Arabella from the wall, studied it briefly, then turned to Helen. 'I'll bet you've never smiled like that, girl.'

Helen said nothing.

'Such a smile comes once in a lifetime, maybe. And some may never reach it.'

'What made her so happy?' I asked.

Ern smirked. His broad lips stretched across his large yellow teeth. Then it seemed as if something hardened in him. His mouth trembled, a brief show of weakness, before his whole body grew tense with derision. His eyes alighted on mine as if he wished to pluck out my innards with a glance.

'Do you know what it is to drown?'

The question came from nowhere and struck me where I was most vulnerable.

'Not a day passes when I don't imagine it.'

'Then you and I are alike. What do you see? In your mind's eye?'

'Why are you doing this, Ern?'

'Answer my question.'

'I see how desperate Alison must have been. I try to understand what motivated her but it's beyond me. I see her naked on the beach, shivering. I wonder why. If you want to drown, you weigh yourself down, put rocks in your pockets.'

'She was following Bella. No easy death.'

'It must have been like ice. And she walked into it. It's not like throwing yourself from a bridge. If you jump, there's no going back. But with each step she could have changed her mind.'

'Sea would have got her pretty soon. North Sea has no pity. That wind blows here from Siberia, crosses the pole before reaching Glaven. She had no chance once she was started on her course. Not at night.'

'But why naked?'

'Left the world as she came into it. Maybe as the girl wanted to freeze. Tha's not the worst of it. Takes seven minutes to drown, were you knowing that? Seven minutes, with the waters thrashing at you, tossing you, in your throat, at your eyes. And the pain of it, to suffocate. Not like the first time, in the mother's waters, no cord to keep you safe, no womb to buffet you. We can't imagine it. It's one place we'll never be. Never so close to the elements as that.'

'Why are you telling me this?' I stood up; wanted to leave; to get as far away from Ern Higham as it was possible to be. 'I don't suppose you told Alison?'

'Seven minutes,' Helen said. 'Is that true?'

'Well? Did you tell her?'

I was yelling. Ern was shaking, looked suddenly fragile like the old man he was, with his trousers above his ankles, his prune-flesh protruding from his shirt-sleeves. His look remained defiant but I saw through it. I approached him and knew that this time he was afraid.

'Christ man, can't you answer a straight question?'

We were face to face. Helen grabbed my arm and pulled me back.

'Harry, don't!'

I turned and left the room. I had been so close to it. I had wanted to see him tumble, to watch those brittle bones smash against the floor. Now I stood in the hallway opposite Ern's case of taxidermy. I controlled myself, stood still, closed my eyes and tried to find some purchase on the present moment. I was still clutching Alison's notebook, clinging to it like a talisman. I would not open it now. I had to get back to the cottage. But I also needed to know I could return. Ern had barely begun his story.

'Are you OK?'

Helen's hand circled my waist. I turned.

'Fine!'

'Sorry I asked.'

She withdrew.

'No. Come back.' I pulled her head to my shoulder, kissed her hair. 'I've had enough of this place.'

'Me too.'

'How is he?'

'You shouldn't have lost your cool.'

'I know.'

'He's restless. Won't speak to me.'

'Let me try.'

Ern had sat down, close to the empty grate. He was mumbling and appeared to be counting his fingers. He did not look up as I approached.

'Fifty-three, fifty-four, fifty-five.'

'Ern?'

'Fifty-six, fifty-seven, fifty-eight, fifty-nine.'

'What are you doing?'

'Sixty. Two minutes. One, two, three.'

Again his voice was childlike. He had regressed and I was reluctant to shake him from his reverie. I simply coughed. He looked up.

'What are you doing here?'

'I've been here for some time. Don't you remember?'

'No. Daddy will find you. Go away.'

'Your Daddy isn't here.'

'Go!'

'What are you frightened of?'

'Dark. It's dark.'

'It's not dark.'

'How many minutes?'

'Two. You got to two minutes.'

'Two.'

'Please Ern, won't you speak to me?'

'One, two, three . . .'

It was useless. Was he playing games or was he truly elsewhere? There were times, no doubt, when he found himself immersed in the past, but I began to wonder whether he also used this as a conscious way of blocking the present.

'What shall we do?' Helen asked.

'I don't know. I don't know if we can leave him like this.'

'What do you think this is about?'

'Haven't a clue. I'm beginning to think we'll never find out.'

I touched his shoulder and he flinched.

'Fourteen, fifteen.'

'Ern – how long are you going to go on counting?'

'An hour. Have to get to an hour.'

'Why?'

Then he turned and this time seemed to see me.

'The rain's stopped, boy. Get thee home.'

His voice was his own again.

'Are you all right?'

'I'm still breathing, ain't I? Leave me be.'

'You're sure?'

He turned away.

'Sixteen, seventeen, eighteen.'

'Come on,' I said to Helen. 'He's fine. Let's go.'

We left him there, counting softly to himself in the darkness.

# 24

I T WAS AN EASY drive from Ern's place. The sun was out and the
damp earth shone. We stopped to pick up a sandwich in the
village and ate it in the car. Helen talked eagerly about the notebook
and I didn't have the heart to tell her of my intention to read it alone.
As it happened, solitude was not going to be easy to find.

By the roadside, adjacent to the cottage, a car pulled up. I saw it,
shortly after I turned into the lane, and pulled over myself.

'What's the matter?' Helen said. 'Why are we stopping here?'

'I just want to see who that is,' I said.

We watched as the car door opened and a man got out. He was
fairly tall, stocky, blond. He locked the car, then disappeared
behind the wall, down the path towards Hope Cottage.

'Do you recognise him?' Helen asked.

'Yes. I think so.'

'Who is it?'

'I think it's Gordon Hake.'

Ever since our arrival in Hope Cottage, I had guessed that he might
come. But I hadn't expected him so soon. Who, after all, could have
informed him that we were here? Once again, I felt a deep dread in
the pit of my stomach. I thought of Alison, in the garden once,
shortly after *Sweet Susan* was published. Hake had tracked her
down while she was out shopping, buying groceries from the deli. I
still don't know exactly what he said to her; she refused to tell me
much. But I remember her, pale and wretched beneath the fading
magnolia, curled up, hugging her knees, and rocking, as if the
action itself might banish him. I came down from my study and
found her there. The petals were dropping from the tree about her
and the rich fragrance near-choked me. At the time, I didn't know
what had happened.

'Make it go away, Harry,' she said. 'Make it go away.'

'What, Allie? What is it?'

'Why can't everything be like it used to be?'

'When? When, my love?'

'All this success, it means nothing at all, does it?' Still she rocked, back and forth, over and again. 'I have everything and nothing. Everything and nothing.'

It was the beginning of her new despair, an emotion which crowded her, frequently, until she discovered the photograph of Arabella.

From the top of the path, I could see him. He had a camera about his neck. I stood, Helen at my side, observing him, as he knocked on the cottage door. I froze. I felt unable to act. It was not his physical self that I feared, but rather what he could do to Helen and me, to Ern. There was so much in Glaven that I was discovering. I was coming close, at last, to understanding the past. I knew I must prevent Hake from discovering Ern's involvement in Alison's story. I had to throw him off-course. But how?

Hake moved from the door to the kitchen window, peering through, as we had done on our first day. He knocked there also and I experienced a rising fury. I thought of the photographs he possessed. Alison, naked. Did he get off on them still, I wondered? How could he still live with himself. She was dead and buried but he did not have the heart to let go of the past. Hake had come, like the vulture of my dream, scratching at her remains. But what, exactly, was he seeking? Did he think that he would find her, if he could only look close enough? Perhaps he should look closer. Perhaps she was still lurking in the crevices of the cottage walls?

'What are we going to do?' Helen said.

'It's up to you, Helen. If we go down, face him, you might regret it.'

'Why?'

'You know what will happen. You'll become a part of this, officially. Your face in the newspapers. I don't want you to be hounded, like I've been.'

'It will happen, sooner or later.'

'Yes,' I said. 'I suppose so.'

Helen seemed animated, excited, which irritated me. I knew this was a great adventure for her, perhaps she was looking forward to the notoriety which would soon be hers. I tried to hide my annoyance. She's young, I said to myself. She doesn't know what it's like.

'Look, Harry. If he doesn't speak to us today, he'll find us tomorrow.'

'We don't have to speak.'

'Really? You think your silence, over the years, has done you any good?'

'Yes,' I said. 'Yes. I'm above them, Helen, can't you see?'

'No. I don't see it.'

'If I'm silent, I lose. If I speak, I lose.'

'All I'm saying is that we have to protect what's really happening here. We have to distract him.'

'Yes.' I relented. 'You're right.'

She took my hand, smiled. I read her idea in her eyes. If we spoke to Hake, he would have a story. Harold Bliss elopes with the daughter of his friend. Harold Bliss, in Alison's cottage, with a lover, near forty years his junior. It might just give us space. It might save Ern.

I don't know what I expected from my actions that afternoon. I had kept silent for so long that perhaps what happened was inevitable. Over the years, people had drawn conclusions from my refusal to speak, but I preferred that to the alternative: that my words would be misinterpreted; that they would make sound-bites of my emotions. But from where had it stemmed, this desire for silence? Now, as Hake turned from the window and saw us looking down at him, a memory broke upon me. It seized me, instantly. I looked him in the eye, but my thoughts were elsewhere.

After Alison's death, in the bleak days, after the funeral, before the inquest, a strange thing happened. I had grown accustomed, then, to Hake's frequent presence, but one morning I awoke, late, relieved that he had not yet called. I went to the window, pulled the curtain aside and looked down to the street, half expecting him to be there. Instead, I saw three women, muffled up against the cold, holding banners with Alison's face upon them. I didn't know what to make of it. I didn't, at the time, recognise these three. They were the women from the group of students who had witnessed Alison's arrival at Glaven beach on the morning of her death. I didn't know why they were there. I could not make out whether their presence was designed to intimidate me, or was, rather, a display of solidarity.

When I was dressed, I left the house, but they said nothing. They let me pass by, without comment, and I, too, couldn't bring myself to speak. They remained there, throughout the day, and the following day there were more of them, around a dozen. After that, there was always a presence outside the house. They remained for nearly a week, even at night, keeping vigil outside, lighting candles to her memory. I would watch them from a darkened room upstairs, remembering a person that they never knew. I began to realise that their presence was benign. When I came out of the house, or returned, they would bow their heads, and I began to realise that, whatever was written by Hake and others like him, these women, at least, were on my side.

Still, I knew I was excluded. I mourned alone, they together. Even when the snow came, several days later, they remained there; obstinate. They donned woollen hats and mittens. When their banners turned soggy they made new ones. When their candles went out, they found glass jars and made lanterns. The amber street lights turned the snow a pale orange. The streets were silent. Across the years I still see them, their pale faces lit from beneath, their eyes like quiet moons staring up at me.

Now I looked down at Hake. I felt oddly powerful. During those days of the silent vigil, many other women had written about me in the press, critical of my role in Alison's life. Perhaps influenced by what I read, I felt, at the time, small, colourless, empty. Alone, in the Clapham house, I came to terms with my loss, but I was also diminished by it. I saw her, everywhere. She was not the woman that Hake remembered, the woman who graced catwalks, wore glittering dresses, posed for his camera. Rather, the woman who came to haunt me was the woman I knew. I saw her in the garden most of all, her sleeves rolled up, clutching a heavy watering-can. True, she was beautiful; stunning. It can't be denied. But I did not love her for this alone. It was her spirit that drew me, a certain radiance, not always visible, often hidden, yet there always, at the heart of her, even in her blackest moments. I always imagined that the silent women outside my house remembered her also in this way, recognised the true woman, acknowledged her. Did their silence, I wonder, pervade me somehow, influence my decision to remain aloof, never to speak about my loss? I could not tell. But I knew, now, that at last I could draw strength from that memory. I took Helen's hand and together we walked towards Hake.

He raised his hand in greeting. What kind of a man was this? I wondered what Helen might make of him. Sometimes, when I looked at Hake, I could not discern whether the malice I saw etched in his features was actually present there, or whether it were merely a thing I invented. There was something genial, almost angelic about those features, but the slight squint in his left eye and the over-thick lenses of his glasses, rather skewed that image. He dressed casually, in chinos and a polo shirt. His thick, blond hair was pushed back from his face and he was tanned and leaner than usual. It must be the eyes, I reasoned, that gave him that air of malignity.

'Well, Harry Bliss!'

'Hake. It's been a while.'

'Too long, Harry. Too long.'

That voice again, smooth, swaggering.

'What are you doing here?' I asked.

He raised his camera in response, snapped Helen and I together, before we could protest. 'I thought I might make the acquaintance of Miss Cregar,' he said. 'Will you introduce us?'

However hard I tried, Hake always seemed one step ahead of me. As he had photographed Helen and I, I felt a dull ache, the certainty that now, at last, she was involved. And how did Hake know Helen's name? I would never get used to these invasions.

'This is Helen,' I said.

'I'm very pleased to meet you, Helen.'

She smiled, frostily.

'So, Harry? What are you doing up here?'

'Taking a holiday.'

'I hear you quit your job.'

'Your sources are impeccable.'

'A peculiar holiday, Harry. Staying in Alison's cottage.' I raised my eyebrows. 'Yes, a very helpful young lady at the estate agency,' he continued. 'She seemed rather surprised when I told her who you were.'

'Really?'

'So, Helen,' he said. 'Are you enjoying your little "holiday"?'

'Very much, thanks.'

'Why so unfriendly?'

She glanced at me anxiously.

'You might as well talk to me, Helen. We don't want a one-sided story, do we?'

'What do you mean,' I said, 'one-sided.'

'I've been having a chat with a friend of Helen's mother. Seems your mother's not too pleased about you being here.'

'What?' Helen said.

'Yes. She's having sleepless nights, you know.'

'What *friend*?'

Had she not guessed, already? My first impressions had been right, after all. Madeleine was no innocent. She was to blame for Hake's presence here. She had betrayed Frances's trust.

'You mean Madeleine,' I said.

Hake did not deny it. Yet I gained no pleasure in being vindicated.

'We've got nothing to hide,' Helen said, but I noticed that she was trembling.

'Then speak to me,' Hake said. 'Tell me, what's the attraction here? You're a beautiful girl. I would have thought you could do better than Harry Bliss.'

'That's enough,' I said. 'Come on, Helen. Let's go inside.'

'Not so fast, Harry.'

I turned, furious. But his expression then, confused me. Anxiety was etched across his face, though it vanished in an instant.

'I've been speaking to Paul Vinton,' Hake said. 'He has a little something you might be interested in.'

'Yes. I know what you're talking about.'

He flinched.

'Really?' He paused, perhaps wondering whether I called his bluff. 'Alison's notebook – you know about it?'

'He has a couple of pages. Yes. I don't imagine it amounts to much. And in any case, I retain the copyright.'

Why was Hake suddenly so nervous? Something was going on beneath those thick lenses of his, a nasty gleam in his eye. Despite this, I began to feel I had the upper hand here. The notebook was secure in my pocket, but he knew nothing of it. What would he give, I wondered, for a glimpse at that?

'Yes,' Hake said, surprising me. 'Of course. But I'm looking for your permission, to print an extract.'

'And why on earth should I give you that?'

He hesitated, as if he were about to say something important, something that he had rehearsed before. Now, all I wanted was to go inside, to get Helen away from this man. I remembered his voice, on the telephone, the day Alison's body was discovered. He didn't even have the grace to wait until I'd heard the news.

'I have something else that you might want,' he said at last. 'I think you know what I'm talking about.'

He stared at me then, his eyes askew, distorted. I could hardly believe that he was doing this. When he had, after all, gained a reputation, however undeserved. For years, he had made no mention of the photographs in his possession, but I had no doubt that he referred to them now. Was he blackmailing me, so that I might permit him to print the notebook extract? It seemed far-fetched. Why would he risk this course of action now, after so long? When he had so much to lose?

'You have a few lousy photographs I believe,' I said, 'which no self-respecting editor would print. I thought your tabloid days were behind you.'

'I work for whoever will pay me, Harry.'

'You wouldn't sell those photographs now. What have you to gain by it? Nothing. Nothing at all.'

I began to think, as I watched Hake, that he was really beginning to lose it. He was trying to appear in control, but I sensed an air of quiet desperation about him, as if his actions no longer made any sense. Perhaps his career didn't matter to him any longer and the idea of a ruined reputation was meaningless in his eyes. If his tactics were revealed at last, he would be finished. I began to wonder whether his obsession with Alison was not a means to an end, but rather an integral part of him, an old ghost that he simply couldn't shake off.

'People like you make me sick,' Helen said, suddenly. 'What have you ever done with your own life? You're just a parasite. You think you can intimidate us with your stupid threats?'

'What do you know about it?' Hake spat. 'You didn't see her, did you? In Milan? In New York? Nor you, Harry. You should have seen her then. Alison Oakley. She was something.'

'She was heading for destruction,' I said, astonished at his outburst. 'A beautiful façade, that's all. She wasn't happy.'

'You think she was happier with you? That's why she ended up in the North Sea, hey Harry?'

'Really?' I said. 'You'd like that, wouldn't you? You'd like it to be my fault. To absolve yourself of any blame.'

'There's more to this than meets the eye,' he said. 'Much more. I'm going to get to the bottom of it.'

'You do that,' I replied.


I made my way, with Helen, to the garden gate. Hake didn't follow.

'How are you?' I asked.

'I'm fine. Bloody Madeleine.'

'Yes. Wreaking her revenge.'

'I can't believe that guy, Harry. What do you think he'll do now?'

'I don't know. I wonder if Vinton has mentioned Ern. We can't have long.'

'No.'

'We'll go back to Higham's tomorrow. I'll take a look at the notebook first. We have to hear his story.'

'You don't seem too phased by all this.'

'It goes with the territory,' I said.

Helen pushed open the gate and I walked behind her. She was wrong. I was affected. As I approached the cottage, the garden seemed to sway about me and I opened the door, hurriedly. We entered the kitchen and I steadied myself at the sink, my head bowed. Alison's notebook was in my pocket and as I leant forward, it pressed against my thighs, digging sharply into my leg. I leant further, wanting it to hurt me, but I did not register it as pain. My flesh was thick and impervious as stone.

# 25

HELEN DIDN'T UNDERSTAND about the notebook. I hadn't expected her to. She couldn't grasp the fact that there were some things I had to face alone. She stood behind me, at the kitchen window and together we watched Hake leave. He walked purposefully, briskly, but as he approached the top of the bank, he turned. I closed the curtains briskly.

I went into the sitting-room and sat down. Helen joined me, leaning her back against my chest.

'I'm tired,' she said.

'Not possible!'

She groaned. 'Can't we just go to bed? I want to forget what just happened.'

I tapped my pocket.

'Things to do.'

She twisted around, nuzzling her thighs against mine.

'Aren't you hot in that coat?'

I took it off, removing the notebook.

'Let me see it.'

I gave it to her reluctantly.

'Don't open it,' I said. 'Later.'

'Aren't you dying to see what's in it?'

She opened the cover a few inches playfully. I was irritated but tried not to show it.

'Please – don't.'

'What's the matter?' She held it above my head, teasing me, then realised that I was not amused.

'I'm sorry. God, I'm an insensitive brat, aren't I?'

I laughed, despite myself. It wasn't often that she was so self aware.

'You're not too bad,' I said.

Still she held the notebook, clearly desperate to read it. Her hands traced the worn edges of the book. They were fine hands with long white fingers and short, neat nails. Not like the hands that filled the notebook. Alison's fingers were rather stubby and she suffered from eczema. I used to think she took a certain pleasure in neglecting her hands, a backlash against the years of careful pampering.

'Do you think Ern Higham has read this?' Helen asked.

'I'm sure he has.'

'That man . . .' she said, 'Hake. Did he really think you'd give permission for Vinton's pages to be printed?'

'No. I don't know what he's after. And mentioning those photographs, after all this time . . . He seemed worried about something – or was I imagining it?'

'I don't think so. But what?'

I had my suspicions, but didn't want to voice them. I prised the notebook gently from Helen's hands.

I needed to play for time, so I made coffee while Helen dozed on the sofa. For some reason, I felt uneasy, perhaps imagining that Hake had not, after all, left us alone. I drew the curtain aside again. What I saw was unexpected. A figure stood at the top of the path, where it met the lane. But it was not Hake. It was a woman, in a light gabardine mac. Mrs Bobbin. She must have seen me at the window, but she did not move or scurry away. She was looking down at me, watching. On instinct, I drew the curtain back once more, feeling nervous and rather horrified. Did Mrs Bobbin know that we had seen Ern? Had she spoken to Hake? I wondered, what was this woman's intention? Simply to unnerve us? Or something else?

'What are you looking at now, Harry?'

Helen had stirred and could see me from where she sat.

'Nothing. I was just checking that Hake had gone.'

'Has he?'

'Yes.'

She made room for me on the sofa and I brought her coffee through. I tried not to think about what I'd seen. Instead, I recalled my earlier thoughts. I had wanted to explain my need to keep the notebook to myself. I didn't want Helen to read it, at least not until I had, and perhaps not even then. It would depend on what I found there. I had a need to keep a part of Alison that was mine alone. The events of the afternoon had only served to intensify this. If Hake was already on to Vinton's extract, how long would it be before he discovered Ern? Then how would our Mrs Bobbin react? I wanted to protect Ern, but didn't know how. All I knew was that I had something here that Hake wanted and I was determined it would remain private.

'That smells good,' Helen said.

I handed her the mug and sat down beside her.

'Do you know how long we've known each other?' I asked.

'For ever.'

'Actually it's nearly a week.'

It didn't seem possible. Her answer seemed far more accurate than mine.

'It's been a long week,' she said.

I paused.

'How are you?'

'What do you mean?'

'You've barely mentioned your family. You must be thinking about them.'

Anything to distract myself from the knowledge of the woman watching beyond the window.

'I can't regret this, Harry.'

'You might change your mind about that one day.'

She shook her head. 'They'll come round,' she said.

'You think so?'

'When they see that we're serious. They'll have to.'

I knew that it was wrong, but the word 'serious' made me edgy. Did she really envisage a future for us? The idea of losing her was not one I could contemplate without pain but I was beginning to see this situation as clearly as Richard did. She could not see beyond this glorious week. Infatuated with its intensity, she did not understand that it would have to end.

'You miss them, don't you?' I said.

'How can I? I saw Dad yesterday.'

She put her cup down and went to kiss my neck. I flinched involuntarily.

'What's wrong?'

I shook my head.

'I thought you were tired,' I joked.

'Not any more.'

'So you don't want to sleep away the afternoon?'

'Not sleep – no.'

'And what did you have in mind?'

I was going through the motions, flirting with her with no intention of following it up. She smiled lazily. I was surprised that I could muster no interest in sex. She looked gorgeous in that black dress and silver ear-rings. On Sunday she had appeared on my doorstep and I had practically dragged her inside and taken her on the carpet. It felt as if months had passed since then. I could remember how I had felt on that occasion but could not force myself to feel it again. Something had happened. I couldn't put my finger on what. Helen placed her hand on my thigh, traced a pattern to my groin which was hard and ready for her. I hadn't even been aware of it. I realised it wasn't my body that was at fault, but my mind. I thought perhaps I could go through with it, without engaging. She kissed me, her tongue probing the roof of my mouth. I responded but was detached. I thought that if I didn't make love, Helen would never accept my desire to read the notebook alone. I could not refuse to make love to her, then deny her access to Alison also. Given the choice, I had to offer myself.

It was almost easy. I knew how to please her. I figured that if I focused on her pleasure rather than my own, I might get away with it. But as I peeled the dress from her shoulders, she became aware of my reluctance. The urgency had gone and she did not touch me with the tenderness that she had initially proffered. I sensed an air of despondency – as if she knew I was retreating and had not the strength to fight it. Again I felt responsible. She had not come here seeking misery. She wanted something large; beyond measure; a love that would drown the dullness of reality. Suddenly I wanted to give her that. This sex mattered. I thought of Arabella, the easiest trick in the book. It worked every time: Arabella in her black coat and bonnet, her boots, her blistered hands. Helen's dress had fallen to her waist but I pulled it up again. 'Keep your dress on,' I said.

I led her to the floor on the woollen rug before the grate. I unloosed my fly, all thoughts of pleasuring her first forgotten. I was inside her, fully clothed. I moved slowly, looking down at her and I saw them all: Helen, Arabella, Alison. I raised her arms above her head, leant on them as I rocked into her. My irritations dissolved.

241

Everything seemed simple. There was the burning of my flesh, the rub of my knees on the rug, her small mouth, exhaling softly. There was the smell of soot, the ache in my arms, the crush of her fingers, the awkwardness of my shoes. There was the woman watching outside. We did not speak. Slow fire burning. Dankness of this cottage; dull light; shadows emerging. And stillness. Unreal. Barely more than a schoolgirl. A girl once rode a bicycle but now in petticoats, tight-laced. Her photograph. Words in a notebook. Pale blue ink. They unfurled before my eyes, across the forehead of the girl I made love to. Written here, now returning. A burning at my fingertips. Her closed face smiling. Dank room. Dull light. Nothing. Nothing burns as if it had substance. And then out. A small, soft extinguishing of a violent flame.

We lie still and the light of the afternoon finds a crack in the curtains and throws a beam across her legs, though her face remains in shadow. A small trail of liquid runs between her thighs but she does not move. I remember the hush. Helen rests but seems to hold, behind closed eyelids, a hoard of bright jewels. I close my eyes, capture her in my mind, wanting to hold her there always. I sleep and in sleep I lose her. I am alone, wandering pale corridors, huge expanses of white, comfortless space. The whiteness is terrifying. It is the whiteness of obliteration, of a world that has burnt itself out. All that remains is blankness. No substance, no shadow. I know that she is here. I think, if I can find her, something might be recovered. In her face I might see traces of a world that came before.

Each corridor is identical. How do I know that I approach her? I follow no map, have no stars to guide me. Perhaps there is a map but it is hidden. Perhaps my body is my map. There may be some logical path that I tread instinctively, something written in my veins, pulsing in my blood. I see the thin, blue-purple paths, the intricate web of fragile vessels. She had a path once. She too had a heart that throbbed, a regular beat of life. I think it was too bright for her; she could not stand the rush of it, the complexity. She wanted numbness: for her colour to be bleached out – like the shell of a cuttlefish; a pale and beautiful relic, polished by the tides, whitened by the sun.

Now I have found her, laid out like an effigy. Like something from a fairy-tale. Snow-White, only she will not be awakened by a kiss. And the illusion is too grim for a children's tale. Despite her beauty, there is something awful about this sight. In her face I see the lost world. A garden where brilliant peacocks throw their jewelled feathers open; the sky arcs above, unblemished blue; lush vegetation thrives; bright rhododendrons burst their buds. Why would the children run? Because this death is more real than any horror story. Fangs, blood, bolts through the neck – the conventions of fear, nothing more. But this – this dead woman and her smile of accomplishment – this is the essence of loss and true horror.

This dream, again. It recurs with astonishing regularity. I had never spoken about it. Perhaps I believed, if I described it, it might not return. A strange contradiction. It terrified me yet I did not want to stop dreaming. It was never exactly the same, this is what interested me most; it was a kind of window on my grief that I had learned to welcome.

I awoke on the rug, shivering. Helen still slept beside me. I felt disturbed and hauled myself up, trying to recall the details of the dream. As they returned, I attempted to understand my mood. Surely it would have been worse to have seen the face I saw in the morgue: fish-bitten skin; rotting flesh? Why did the smile haunt me? Because I had never, in life, seen such satisfaction on her lips. This death was her great achievement. Not *Sweet Susan* nor the Arabella novel. These were merely elaborate bridges that led to the true centre of her genius: her skilful self-annihilation.

I didn't know how long I'd slept. Helen showed no signs of waking and I knew this was my opportunity. I fetched a blanket from upstairs. I looked from the kitchen window. Mrs Bobbin had gone. When I returned to find Helen had not moved, I draped the blanket over her. I might not have long, but I could make a start. The notebook lay on the table. I picked it up, held it to my lips. The room was silent but for the rhythm of Helen's breath. I opened the notebook and began to read.

# 26

T HE NOTEBOOK WAS NOT remarkable to look at. It was a slim, blue canvas-bound volume with a black spine, worn at the edges. It is still in my possession. It sits on my bookshelves beside her earlier journals that have since become objects of almost equally intense interest. Alison always favoured uniformity of design. She was not, by nature, a neat person, but when it came to her writing she liked to maintain an appearance of order. The tidy stack of notebooks on her desk belied the chaotic thoughts that they contained. One simply had to open a book to discover something of the writer's personality. Her journals were the place where she could attempt to make sense of her writing, a comment upon her work that did not require the same discipline as the novels themselves. There was an unselfconsciousness about the journal entries which I had never seen in her fiction. Even the style of her handwriting betrayed this. It was large and loose and sprawled across the page at the same pace as her thoughts. She wrote in a watery ink that always gave one the impression it was about to run out. There was something transitory about the look of these pages. The paper was flimsy, blue-ruled, though she ignored the ruling. Only rarely did she date her entries.

In appearance the last notebook barely differed from the others. In that sense it was familiar. But I could not, at first, connect with it. I attempted several times to make a start but each time I found that I was simply scanning the pages, catching odd words but making nothing of them. The words were signs that betrayed no sense. It took some effort of will to force them to yield meaning. Always her dream-image was before me. Whenever her words expressed disappointment or frustration, I remembered the serenity of the face that I imagined. Knowing her destination – the apparent perfection of death – had the effect of altering my reading. I wondered if she had known where she was heading. She was intent on her journey but her ultimate goal was obscure. Only one thing was clear. I was not really a part of it. At her death, a great chasm of silence opened in my heart. But Alison, in her last notebook, did not pause to contemplate my loss.

# 27

# THE NOTEBOOK

*I*  *t's coming clear now. It's beginning to come clear. Finally there's a shape emerging and I'll sleep tonight, knowing that the form of the book is surfacing. It wasn't possible to see it before. Not enough pieces. But now I have them and they're slotting together. The pattern begins to be revealed: like shifting rock faces. Plates of the earth, sliding against one another. The two stories, each solid, immovable, joined and yet separate. The pieces of the novel must be like this: capable of sliding; never fixed. It was making me sick, not seeing it. But it was the depth that I was missing, what goes on beneath the surface. Things we don't see: fault lines. I thought I could control this story. What, with words? But there's something more essential than my own will. I am so small. Isn't that what held me back? When I used to sit in the garden in Clapham looking at the sky and the trees, I was soothed but also terrified. I was crammed in, a little bundle of flesh quivering beneath the brickwork.*

*Already the novel is moving away from the present, back to that house where I spent my childhood. There's so much stuff there to unearth. I don't want to think about the interim, the substance of Sweet Susan. I want to bury those years at last. But I'm afraid of plunging into the childhood stuff, because who knows what horrors are lurking there? Might it be equally painful? It can't be. Can't be worse than the self-hatred I felt when I was modelling, the terror of being discovered. But if I'm to do this, I must be sure it's for the right reasons. And what about my father? How can I write about real things while he's still living? Can I put him out of my mind and just write for the sheer hell of it, really let go and find a place where I can forget who's staring over my shoulder and who's going to care and what people will say? Why can't I do that? It's why I'm here, why I came to this place and sought this story. I knew it would have resonances but I didn't expect they would be like this.*

*I must begin with the garden scene. What I wrote in London now seems flat and unrealised. Ern spoke about the garden today and I dared to question his story. He gave me such a withering glance. I laughed at him and he laughed back. He's so dear. Our lives reflect; spark off.*

*Arabella stands at the window. A simple, still image. Sensations, layering of experience. Recurring symbols, soaked in meaning. I've been haunted by this for months but now I'm ready to write. It began with this, that first night when I saw the photograph, I imagined it. Arabella. She watches her husband in the garden below. The window is open and she wears nothing but a white cotton chemise. He is unaware of her. Bright moonlight in the garden; darkness in the room. If he looked, he would see her. Light reveals her, pierces the garment. (Can I say pierces? Will I be torn apart for that?) Charles Bliss in a silent ecstasy and she excluded from it.*

*Owls. Winking from the branches of the beech tree. She watches as he buries his head in the centre of a great white lily. Too Lawrentian? What the hell. Call it post-modern. Anyhow, that's how it is. I can't help it if all these penetrative images impose themselves. I have to not care what the critics will say because if I start caring then it will cease to be my book. I don't want to write something politically correct. I have to write from the core.*

*Bliss never sniffs Bella the way he sniffs those lilies. Such subtle scents her body gives off but he doesn't know them. If she wore perfume, he wouldn't go near her. Once she wore rose-water and he slapped her for it. She might have splashed water from a stinking ditch across her shoulders and Bliss would have been fonder of her. Arabella is jealous of that garden. She wants Bliss to love her, else why would she wait nine years before rebelling? She knows about the dead wife and babe and pities her husband. And she envies the purity of his experience. Bliss closes his eyes. He wants this blindness. When the forms of flowers are lost to him, when he can see neither branch nor leaf, the voices of the trees intensify. They whisper an obscure language, more discreet than the sound of human tongues. His senses are keen: he can separate perfumes. There is the sea, of course, the damp, salt air. He grows plants to complement that air. He's not simply nurturing the plants but the air itself. Mint and lavender; lilies; night-scented stocks. Bella stands above in the white chemise, goose-bumps on her bare arms, her hair loosed. She stands in the moon's glare, willing him to see her. Her breasts in silhouette but Bliss sees nothing, only the closed-up roses and the white throats of the lilies. Bliss nurtures his garden while Bella withers. Nature's growth; human decay. A thread of symbolism? I want symbols to work like this: gilded threads, connecting, catching light.*

*This place possesses me. I have been here five days yet I can't imagine ever leaving, returning to London and Harry and the horrible glare of attention. I know I can't hide here. Hake would find me, in the end. But now, if only for a week or two, it's so good to be away from all that. The absence of a telephone!*

*For some reason, I keep thinking of Harry's face when I miscarried. I don't know why these feelings have resurfaced, but I couldn't face him right now. Christ, I should stop this. So pointless. I must think of the work, refuse to look within if I want to avoid going under. But how can I avoid it? My lost embryos are a part of this. And Harry's face. One might have thought they were real bairns the way he looked. Yet they were nothing, barely the size of coffee beans. We walked around as if the world had cracked open and taken our children, our parents, our siblings, but in reality we mourned a few cells, nothing more. A blue line appears on a thin, white stick. I start to vomit each morning. The cells multiply and I am different now. We make plans, pull focus on our world. A child in a high chair, gulping goo from a spoon, smiling: milk-teeth in tender gums. But I won't follow mother. I can write and rock the babe with one foot, can't I? Nothing will stop my pen, not sleepless nights nor domestic numbness.*

*Enough! I'm not creating here, merely torturing myself. Outside, night has the earth in a cold claw-grip. I'm glad to be alone. Nobody to watch me here. Nobody to judge. I want my prose to be like that night: perfect, calm, crystallised. And last night – the stars: a thousand brittle eyes. Rawness. Stillness. Is this how Bliss saw it? Even in winter when the earth is simply a promise? Branches like bones stripped of flesh. Last night, I could not believe the silence. Strip the city bare and it would be the same. Neon glare fools us. A fool's halo above London. Yellow smog. But beyond it this same sky.*

*Could I live in a place like this always? When I was a kid I couldn't wait to get away from the country. Is that why I was attracted by modelling? Did I feel rescued, somehow? I see my child-face at the window. There's nothing outside but trees and cloud – nowhere to run to. Need a torch to get about at night. And mother gone. Father and I in that house at the heart of the valley. I needed streets and lamplights and corner shops and doting aunts and sisters. Instead the four walls of my bedroom hemmed me in. The window opened out on a world so dark that my grief was swallowed by it, sucked out into the night, leaving me hollow. Like in Eliot – remember when Harry first read Eliot to me? 'Shape without form, shade without colour, Paralysed force, gesture without motion.' That pretty much sums it up. And father the same in the study along the corridor. The Hollow Men, he and I. He at his desk with mother's manuscripts before him, reading, annotating, searching for references with barely a clue where to look, only a vague, haunted emptiness of spirit that forces him to attempt the impossible.*

*He's looking in those poems for the woman he lost. I wonder, did he love her more, when she wrote? In all the years when he trotted off to the bank and left her with me – changing nappies, playing mindless games – did he love her equally like that? Or did he miss the poet whom he married? In their wedding photograph, she stands in the church porch looking so dark-eyed and intense despite the costumed frippery. The two photographs. Could I juxtapose them in the novel? Arabella and my mother. Two brides; two deaths. My mother's waist is nipped as Bella's. A bustle. A frothy fifties whirl of a dress. Women crushed by marriage: their very bones. Mother wears a jewelled hair-band, carries a tight posy of yellow roses. She holds father's hand but her eyes appear fixed on another point, beyond the camera, as if, even then, she is composing words to capture her delight.*

*I romanticise, as father did. Yet wasn't it he who encouraged her to stop writing? Suggested it might be too much for her? He thought her frail. Wanted to protect her from her own imaginings, as if poetry itself might unbalance her. But isn't it rather that it is we, the unbalanced, who write it? The only action we can take, to wring meaning from chaos. But what use is it, in the end? Less shallow than my former life, but who does it help? I'd rather do something genuinely useful: heal the sick, aid-work, teaching. But I'm not fit for such selflessness. This is all I can do now.*

*Wherever I look I see parallels. Hidden patterns that repeat. I want to dive into my material; retrieve treasures from the wreck of it. Two stories: rotting wrecks. But what grows there? On rotten timber, bright corals flourish. I want to pluck them out. And where do I stand in this? Are there parasites in those waters? Was I the worm who ate the wood? Mother's poetry, a great ship consumed by a tiny gnawing creature. When I sucked at her breast, did I suck the music from her? I remember when father showed me the poetry, later, when I was in my teens. I hadn't known! I thought of her, always, as one thing and now she was another.*

> *'Little creature runs a dance in my belly.*
> *The dance of the unborn.*
> *Quiet steps that will erupt soon and quieten me.'*

*Every line written in her pregnancy in the knowledge that the poetry would stop at the moment when I burst from between her legs.*

*'And she will be my voice and my words will sing from her throat.'*

*Why? These words I write cannot be hers. If I write to imitate her, I fail. If I try to recreate her in words (and won't this be my purpose?) then will I not fail also? Harry has told me a million times I have to lay her to rest, write in my own voice. He doesn't know I'm writing about her. He thinks I'm writing about him! But how could I write about Harry? It's too close. He was fooled by the photograph of Bliss, their resemblance, but that was merely the starting-point and I've gone beyond it. Ern has laced my brew with stories and each day I drink them, like a woman parched. And my thirst always returns. I write till I'm bone-dry, till every word he offers has been used. Once more the parasite, only this time I don't simply drink and posset up again. I absorb the stories into my blood, my being. When I release them they have already altered. Some transforming power is at work.*

*

*I have just returned from Ern's cottage and the story burns in my brain. I have to get it down; don't want to forget a single detail. Not only the story, but the time we have spent together.*

*Remember the fields as I returned. Barely possible that it is winter here. Light seemed made of pure gold. Fields illumined in pale yellow. Glowing. Long shadows of trees across that gold. I felt a kind of yearning. These moments so rare. When did I last feel it? Something about the brilliance affected me. Gorgeous bursting of colour; the last flourish of day before it fades.*

*In Ern I see a reflection of myself. I saw it when I first met him but I didn't understand it and now, finally, I do. I think of the tricks he played when I arrived. 'Get back to London, girl.' Ordering me away was a sure-fire way of keeping me. Each day he has teased me, insulted me, made me mad at him. But he too must recognise how alike we are. I'm stubborn and bad-tempered as him. And his story is beneath my skin.*

*Until yesterday I was half-convinced that he, like me, was simply spinning fiction. It all seemed too improbable, too Madame Bovary. The way he talks, it's like some character in a book. He spoke as if he were a witness to Arabella's life when in fact, surely, he could barely remember her. He leads me into strange rooms. He layers words thickly like oils. His artistry has more purity than mine. He doesn't pursue success as I do. I am his only audience. His imagination so rich, yet working in a vacuum. Images haunt him; conjured every day of his life for himself alone.*

*Is it possible to find some form that echoes his telling? The chaotic framework of his vision? A scene is drawn, then altered, painted over with colours not quite identical: constant tampering. Dissatisfaction with the texture or the hue. And leaving blank spaces*

251

*within the frame? Get down what he told me today. And yesterday. The richness of it.*

*Arabella had a lover. The fact blew me away. Everything I planned to write about – sterility, frustration, thwarted sexuality – wiped out by one piece of information. I was making assumptions: that she killed herself because her marriage was a kind of death. But it was more complex than that. If the boatman hadn't entered her life, perhaps she would have continued to endure.*

*In a sense, it's strange that they didn't connect sooner. She must have been aware of him. She was always drawn to the punt-gunners, Ern said. Perhaps she thought him some kind of oddity. They were from different worlds.*

*In the early days, he said, practically every male inhabitant carried a gun. But the Gentlemen from the cities came to the punt-gunners. They knew the lay of the land and ferried them to favoured mooring places where good shooting was guaranteed.*

*Should the novel begin here? With these wild-fowlers? On the muds, early. A bluethroat morning, as Ern called it. Before first light and the morning still: a velvet darkness. Water metallic, whispering over the muds. Only sounds are the sucking of clams; skittering of gilly crabs; murmur of sea. And the wading birds. Soft piping and whistling of their voices. Then at first light, pandemonium. First a single shot, rending the silence. A brief hush, then the babble of bird cries and a mad rush of wings. Then more shots. Endless. Bucket-loads of birds fall from the sky. All this in the year that Bella came to Glaven. By the time she met her boatman, the law forbade such indiscriminate shooting. But not before her boatman had been damaged.*

*Could the novel be wound according to the movement of the day? Beginning at first light? (Like* The Waves *I suppose, only tangents of time are crossed also.) This bluethroat morning. Then Arabella at dawn on the morning that she drowns herself. And myself, on the morning that mummy died. Being woken by the telephone. Falling asleep again, not knowing that my world was irretrievably altered. How can I have a form that is chaotic but coherent? It troubles me.*

'In a moment of revelation I may lay hands on it, but now the idea breaks in my hand. Ideas break a thousand times for once that they globe themselves entire.' Can I hope to globe this idea? It is so complex and I'm afraid of that. The recognition I've gained for Sweet Susan, *totally unearned*. Why do they not see the faults? It's overwritten; self-indulgent. Why these prizes when it's so flawed? Because I was once Alison Oakley. I have no faith left in critics. Who then, am I trying to please?

I'm losing it. Don't lose it. Don't think about the self. Only the work; the text.

Long-barrelled guns. Shooting ducks. In winter, people were kept going on duck, Ern said. Fading light and they're heard before they're seen. In the snow, even an expert might make a mistake. Load it through the muzzle. Only the muzzle is choked with snow. The gun bursts. His right hand and wrist are shattered. Half his arm is gone. (Missing limbs. Parts of the body torn away or damaged. Harry's father and his war wound. My mother – the breast that fed me cut clean off.)

So, Bella falls in love with a one-armed wildfowler. His gun was as tall as he, Ern said. A weakling man could barely lift it, let alone take aim. But this boatman could lift the gun to his shoulder with one arm and a stump and his aim was not affected. There is a photograph of him on Ern's wall. He poses on his boat with that gun at his side in his good hand. A huge man. Difficult to make out his face. Dark. Unsmiling. Unkempt. Something wilful in his look.

What was it that drew her to this man? And that other man who she was half in love with also – her uncle. Last night I dreamt of them – Bella and John Simms. My vision so precise and the sense of loss I felt on awakening, as if her loss were also mine.

Austerity of the coastline. Remember this. Bella knows his life is ebbing. She wills herself to remember each detail, to seize the moment in its entirety. Her uncle walks in silence. They are alone on the beach. Sky bears down and wind blasts their ears. They could not talk. A human voice is too small here. It is the realm of birds.

He walks slowly. A short, slightly plump man. His breath heaves. Scarcely any breath left in his body. His legs giving out. She too has trouble moving. Fully corseted, her coat skims her bustle and tiny shoes hinder her steps. She trips on her petticoats. Her bonnet, tied firmly beneath her chin but her face is unprotected from the bitter February wind. They cling to each other, determined to progress. It is certain madness.

Cries of gulls in their ears. Streaming eyes. Ice feet. Near-paralysed by the wind. Yet it was her uncle who suggested the walk. 'Will you join me Bella, for a shore-tramp?' As they reach the sea's edge, she turns anxiously and he signals that they should continue. He summons a smile, exhilarated by the elements. But he is in pain. She searches his face: red-raw and ruddy. Wisps of silver hair stray from beneath his cap. And his eyes! Tiny and grey as the pebbles at their feet. Whites turned milky yellow; bloodshot. He is like her father and also unlike him. The same face, animated by a different spirit.

How is it that the dying man smiles? In a day or two, he'll be gone. Bella too is in pain but it could be nothing compared to his. Her chest is constricted. And the air so cold. She turns towards the sea, hides her face. She is not strong enough! She won't make it! But her pride forces her on. She can't say at what stage it happened, when the tears that pricked her took on a different character. She knows simply that there was a moment when she was in pain and a moment when it was gone, replaced by a sense of intense happiness, which did not diminish as she continued walking.

Her uncle squeezes her hand. Soft, warm living hand. She fixes it. Fixes the exact cry of the gulls, the hue of the sea. Ahead, the coast curves towards Blakeney and at that distant point, pale rays of light break the clouds. Briefly the wind ceases and she catches echoes of laughter. Her uncle is splitting his sides; clutching his chest in agony. He sits on the pebbles, unable to control his mirth.

John Simms is not yet sixty years of age. His small mouth near-cracks with breathless pleasure. And Bella laughs too. She sinks down beside him, faces the furious sea and laughs as foam curdles at their feet and a thin rain begins to fall from the sky.

# 28

I SAW HELEN BEGIN TO stir and closed the notebook quietly as if to stop a child from waking. She let out a soft grunt and it was clear my time was up. I placed the book down and waited. She rubbed her palms against her forehead, rolled over and saw me.

'Oh God, what time is it?'

'Nearly five.'

'How long have I been asleep?'

'An hour or so. Maybe longer.'

She sat up.

'What have you been up to?'

I paused. I couldn't lie. She had guessed that something was wrong.

'Harry? You look terrible.'

I looked down at the notebook and she followed my glance.

'You've read it?'

'Not all of it. Not even a half.'

'While I was asleep?'

I nodded.

'I don't believe it!'

'What's the matter?' I asked.

'I thought we'd read it together.'

'What? That you'd read it over my shoulder?'

'Not exactly. But it would be something we did together. That you'd read some of it aloud.'

'I wanted to read it alone,' I said.

'And now you have.'

I said nothing.

'It's like you've read it behind my back,' she said.

'She was my wife, Helen. Please. I haven't got the energy for this.'

'Then why did you do it? Why didn't you wait until I woke up?'

'I don't think it was unreasonable. I just wanted to read it first. Without interruptions.'

'And I'm expected just to sit back and say "OK"?'

'I don't see that you have a choice,' I said quietly.

'Thanks a lot.'

'Please, Helen.'

I knelt at her side, touched her leg but she withdrew.

'I thought we came here together? To do this together?' she said.

'So we are together.'

'No. Not now.'

'You can read it,' I said. 'Afterwards. Is it such a big thing?'

'Yes. Can you remember what you told me? When we stopped on our way here. For the picnic?'

'I'm sure I said a lot of things.'

'You said, "There's nowhere to hide here." '

'Did I? I don't remember.'

But I was thinking of Alison's words. She knew it too. No hiding in Glaven.

'I thought it was wonderful. But you're hiding now, Harry. You don't want me to get close.'

'That's not true. What's brought this on? Because I read the notebook?'

'Not just that. Something's wrong. I can sense it.'

'Haven't you forgotten something? Before you slept . . .'

'No! I haven't forgotten!'

She was close to tears.

'It was – really something. But it doesn't make everything right.'

I was silent. I couldn't understand what had brought this on. I knew that I should care; that if I didn't act in the right way I would lose her. But so many other thoughts filled my brain that I couldn't focus on her. She looked at me. She wanted something that I couldn't give. I wanted the present moment to dissolve, for Helen to fade into thin air. I wanted to pick up the notebook and immerse myself again in the past.

'Now you won't even talk to me,' she said.

'Yes. Yes, I will talk.'

Words seemed useless, lifeless things.

'So?'

'What do you want to talk about?' I said.

'Anything.'

I did not reply.

'Tell me what you read.'

'I can't.'

She looked at me; pulled her skirt over her knees.

'I'm going to have a wash,' she said. 'I stink.'

What happened next was not planned. I did not pause to think about the consequences of my actions. I did what felt right at the time.

Helen had gone upstairs, no doubt expecting me to follow her. But I had no desire to apologise. Instead I picked up my coat, took the notebook from the table and stuffed it in my pocket. I found my wallet and keys and left the cottage.

I got into the car, feeling mildly exhilarated. The afternoon was over, yet the sky remained bright; such clarity of light that each object seemed perfectly defined. I wanted to drive, nothing more. I knew that I ought to see Ern, speak to him before Hake found him, but I simply couldn't face it. I thought about heading west towards Holkham where I might take a walk on the dunes. I started the engine. I did not look behind.

I entered the village as the shops were closing. As I drove past the bookshop, I caught sight of Phil Bobbin, on the corner, chatting with a couple of friends. It seemed I couldn't avoid that family and I found myself remembering his mother's presence earlier, outside the cottage. How strange, I thought, that she and this young man should be descended from Ern.

As I left the village behind, it occurred to me that, if it were not for Alison, Glaven would be no different from a host of other villages scattered along this coast. A tourist passing through would find it unremarkable. He might stay a night or two, sample the local cuisine, the crab perhaps and the samphire. He might take a walk along the beach at night and watch the flints spark up at his feet. Beyond this, there would be nothing to detain him. He'd soon tire of the tea-shops and the pub. Unless he were an ornithologist, he'd grow bored; feel hemmed in. Once he left the place, he wouldn't think about it again, except perhaps with a vague fondness and a certain relief that he wasn't himself condemned to live here.

I was soon out of it and on the road to Blakeney. I deliberately blocked the thoughts that threatened to overwhelm me. I thought instead of the gap between this place as it appeared in the imagination and the place itself. In Ern's fantasies, in Alison's imaginings, Glaven took on mythic proportions. It became a huge tragic arena, a landscape where great dramas might be played out. But in fact it was a dull little village, a place where creativity might be strangled.

Yet there was something about this landscape. Out here, away from the village, it was impossible not to feel awed. It was a brilliant evening. I opened the window. A slight chill in the air. The scent of sea-lavender wafted into the car and I thought about Alison. Surely it was my reading of the notebook that made me feel as I did now, oddly joyful. I couldn't understand why I'd had such a reaction. Much of what I'd read had disturbed me – the passages about her miscarriages and her mother. Yet nothing she wrote had truly surprised me. Rather, the notebook brought her back, closer than she'd been in years. As I'd read, I'd almost forgotten that these were the thoughts of a dead woman. The voice was so familiar, the words so new, that it seemed she spoke afresh. Perhaps it was this sense of engagement that left me now so optimistic. She had been working well. She was struggling to find a form but the struggle clearly invigorated her. I had expected something darker still.

Now I had begun, I couldn't stop thinking about Alison. I wondered why the dream continued to disturb me. I realised now that I had imagined her, as she perhaps had imagined herself. I had been haunted by her smile. It was a more cunning image, more haunting than the real face of the drowned woman. I could not let it go.

This was the same road that Alison had taken on her frequent journeys to Ern's place; these fields the same fields that had so impressed her on the particular evening that she wrote about. The revelations about Bella had startled me as they must have startled her. Yet there was still no hint in her journal of why she had followed in Bella's footsteps. It didn't seem like the journal of a would-be suicide.

Still intent on my journey to Holkham, I kept heading west away from Blakeney. I was thinking again about the lost manuscript. If Alison had been able to open the door on her childhood, the result might have been astonishing. She did not speak often, even to me, of those early days. I saw her childhood as a secret part of her; an essential part. But I could not see how she might connect her story with Ern's. He was dealing with ghosts, after all, people he could barely have known.

I was coming close to his place. The cottage was visible from the roadside. I remembered how we had left him that morning, counting softly to himself. I tried not to think about him, or Helen. All I wanted was to be alone on the dunes. I had visited Holkham years ago and still remembered the hush of the pine forest and the bare expanse of the sands. Surely Helen must understand this need for solitude? If she could not, there was no future for us.

Ern's place was behind me now. I was driving back towards the coast. The sun was low and dazzled me. I slowed down and for some reason looked over my shoulder. I don't know what I expected: some sign that he was there and alive, the twitching of a curtain perhaps. But I could not have predicted what I saw. It was too unlikely.

I saw a figure: a tall, black silhouette; a bony shadow hobbling towards the estuary. I could make out no details, only the thin bent shape against the sky. Within seconds I'd stopped the car and stood at the roadside watching. Was it possible that this was Ern? I couldn't be sure. Ern usually stood tall and this figure was crouched. He was pulling something: a large object trailed behind him. So surely it could not be him. Yet the more I looked, the more convinced I became that it was. His shape was unmistakable. It was the weight of the object which so bent his body. How was this possible? I'd heard he barely left the cottage and now he was hauling some huge bulk across the fields.

I hovered awhile, but could make no sense of it. Lunatic thoughts occurred: he's getting rid of something – before the press come. What? A dead body? I dismissed such lurid imaginings but remained intrigued. What possessed him, a man in his nineties, to make such a prodigious effort? What was this object? I wanted not to care; told myself I shouldn't alter my plans. But it was useless. I could not ignore this.

Back in the car, I headed for the cottage. Sometimes Ern went out of sight, obscured by a hedgerow or trees but mainly I kept him in view. Then I took a turn in the road and lost him for a few minutes. When I saw him again, I was astonished at how far he was from the cottage. He must have walked half a mile or so and was nearing a small inland river. I parked and made after him.

The air was warm, the sky bright. Near the estuary, a few cows chewed the cud, oblivious to all else. Above, a flock of swallows. I had almost caught up with Ern when he stopped, balancing on his cane. I saw that his other hand had a rope about it, which trailed across his shoulder. I approached him. Now I could make out what he was pulling. It was a large rowing boat.

He had not seen me. I said nothing; watched him. He began to pull the boat again and I tried to imagine his motives but could find none. His progress was immensely slow but it was dogged. He inched along, bowed by the boat's weight. Having seen his difficulty in crossing a room, I could not believe that he had come so far.

I caught up with Ern and began to walk by his side. I slowed my pace to meet his but said nothing and he stubbornly ignored me. I looked right in his face but still he did not speak. He kept his eyes on the ground as if looking for a stone that might trip him. He was breathless; bared his teeth and panted hard. His hand clutched the cane as if his life depended on it. I did nothing. Several minutes passed, the two of us keeping silent. Ern seemed to need every ounce of his strength simply to keep moving. I looked at his hand which circled the rope. It was raw. I wanted to stop this madness.

Behind him, the boat lumbered, forming a gully in the earth. It was an ancient thing, yet appeared well-preserved and possibly sea-worthy. I hung back to take a closer look. I had already noticed the oars which lay across the narrow seats, but now I saw what was beneath them: a gun. A polished, long-barrelled gun.

Suddenly Ern stopped, exhausted. His legs trembled. He was fighting for each breath. Slowly he uncurled his back and stood up to face me.

'What be you doing here, lad?'

I shook my head.

'I was driving past. I saw you; wondered what you were doing.'

His chest heaved. He found his breath and spoke haltingly.

'Taking the boat out. What does it look like?'

'Isn't it rather late?' I said pathetically. I couldn't bring myself to voice my real doubts.

'There's still some daylight left, ain't there?'

'By the time you reach the river . . .'

'That's the Blakeney Channel.'

'Whatever. You'll be returning in the dark.'

'And what if I will, boy?'

'The boat – it's very heavy. Perhaps you'll make it to the Channel. But back again?'

He snorted. 'I can tether the boat and fetch it in the morn.'

'Do you want some help?'

I figured I might as well go along with him if I wanted to discover his motives.

'Aye,' he said, unexpectedly. 'You can take the boat if that's your fancy. But don't think I couldn't do it myself, see? I've made it thus far. I ain't dead yet.'

'No. I didn't say you were.'

The boat's weight took me by surprise. There was blood about the rope and as I began to pull, I asked myself it I weren't mad as the old man, to assist him in this apparently purposeless task. I wondered whether, like Sisyphus and his rock, I might be condemned to pull this boat for ever, a punishment for my uncertain sin. It was an absurd undertaking. I was complicit in Ern's game but did not know its object.

Again we fell silent, my energy focused on the task in hand. Ern walked ahead, chuckling to himself. Within minutes, I was short of breath. We were slow as one another, he hindered by his frailty, I by the boat. It was another fifteen minutes before we reached the Channel. At first I thought I wouldn't make it but after a while I was buoyed by my own exhaustion; jubilant.

When we reached the Channel, we stopped on the mud-banks. There were no moorings here, but the water was not so shallow that our boat could not be used. I looked at Ern expectantly. His breath heaved and his legs were trembling. Suddenly they buckled and he fell hard on the bank.

Immediately I panicked. I went to his aid but even before I was at his side he was finding his feet again.

'Hang on,' I said. 'Put your arm around my shoulder.'

'I'm no pansy-boy. I don't need help.'

'Yes you do. Take it easy.'

'I'm fine.'

But he allowed me to help him. With one hand I supported his weight and with the other I overturned the boat.

'Are you hurt? Have you broken anything?' I said.

'My bones ain't never been broken and they ain't about to be breaking now.'

'Come on. Perch yourself here.'

I helped him to sit on the base of the boat.

'Are you in pain?'

'What are you boy, a doctor? Like Bliss?'

'No. I'm not a doctor.'

'What then?'

'A teacher. School-teacher.'

'Clever fellow, eh? Might've guessed.'

'You're sure you're all right?'

'Takes more than a little stroll to knock the life out of me. Now, what do you think of this, lad?'

'Of what?'

But already I realised his meaning. He was referring to the landscape. Before us, the waters twisted away, caught the late rays of the sun. The earth soaked up the light, the streams reflected it.

'Listen,' he said.

In the silence, the birds held sway. Their cries echoed in the empty air.

'Silver rivers. That's what we call them.'

'Yes. It's beautiful.'

'Where's my gun?'

'It must be beneath the boat. Why?'

'Why do you think, lad?'

'You can't want to shoot the birds.'

'Who else might I be shooting?'

'Aren't they protected nowadays?'

'Do you see a warden?'

'Surely that's not the point. It's the law.'

Ern laughed.

'Shooting is my life. I ain't going to be stopping because of some city-fella's law. I ain't a criminal, see? Now where's that gun?'

I tried to stall him. I didn't know what might happen if he got his hands on that trigger and I didn't want to find out. He was talking in the present tense as if these shooting expeditions were a regular thing, but I didn't believe it. Something had brought him out here today and I wanted to find out what.

'Did you bring Alison here?' I asked.

'Aye. Girl had to see it for herself. Wanted to see how it used to be for the old wildfowlers. But it ain't the same now. The heart's gone from it. City-folk come here and perch up on those pebbles gazing out to sea through their eye-glasses. All they want is to spy the birds but what good is spying them, eh? Hoping to catch a glimpse of the storm petrel or a rare visit from the black guillemot. As soon as they've focused those lenses the bird has gone. That ain't the way of the land.'

'And what would be your way, Ern?'

'Shoot the little buggers. Have some sport of it.'

'Shoot them till there's none left? Why do you think these birds are protected?'

'Ways of the city. You people have no respect for our ways.'

'I wonder what Alison thought of your views?'

'We didn't talk about such things. She was only interested in Bella, see? Bella was a fine hand with the gun.'

'Bella? Shooting?'

'Aye.'

'Who taught her to shoot? Her wildfowler?'

Ern smiled.

'You didn't tell me she had a lover,' I said. 'Who was he, this wildfowler? What did he mean to her?'

'So many questions.'

It was getting chilly and I fastened my coat. Ern did not seem to notice the cold. He continued talking in a low voice that has since permeated my memory. As he spoke, I noticed no hint of affectation or game-playing. His words were like the rivulets that stretched out to sea, twisting silently away, never still, catching light.

' "What's hit is history, what's missed is mystery." That's what they used to say. "Shoot first, check after." Killed anything that moved, they did, in the hope it might be a rare'un. Half the time the buckets were full of common migrants – your robins and redstarts. But it were worth it to bag the odd gem, that's what he said.'

'Who? Who said that?'

'When I was a lad, I used to wander the fields. And my father a learned man, shut in his study with his books. I couldn't've been more than five years old. And the books weren't for me, see? I was out in the fields, picking up what treasures I could muster: a little whitened skull-bone of a stoat; a live lizard; a piece of lace from a petticoat. I used to walk the tides, picking up mussels and crabs. Birds too. Shore-birds on the shingly spit of the creek. Do you know how that feels, boy? To hold a warm bird in your hands? Feel the blood on your palms. Life draining even as you watch?'

I shook my head but he didn't notice.

'So many birds. No matter if a few got shot. In spring, thousands of swallows over the salt-marshes. From Africa.'

I was growing impatient. I wanted to know about Bella's lover.

'Charles Bliss – he wasn't close to the land, am I right?'

'Never been more right. He and that garden – a fool's paradise: kept the wilderness outside. Him was so drawn to cultivating his plants, him didn't notice what grew wild in the fields.'

'It must have been difficult for Arabella.'

'Aye. And once him got going with the orchids, it were worse.'

'Orchids?'

'Him acquired a little hot-house. Following in Mr Darwin's footsteps.'

'What was the point of it?'

'Fiddling with nature, that was the point. Not letting it go its course.'

'And how did that affect Bella?'

'Him was always out there, tampering with his stamens and his pollen: playing God. Wanted to make something beautiful with his bare hands.'

'And Bella?'

'Bella had George. Made that child her own, though he was undeserving. Bella hoped she might fall herself, but Bliss was all dried-up. It was her burden, see?'

'How did she survive those years? Before she met her lover?'

He laughed. Still he did not turn to me, as if he did not wish the sight of me to distract him. He wanted to remember, perhaps. Yet these were not his memories. Whose then? Who had told him these stories and why did he speak as if he were a part of them? Something that Alison wrote suggested that she believed him. He had convinced her of his truthfulness but I did not know how.

'What could she do but survive? What can any of us do? Seems to me we have a choice: stick it out or jack it in. Most of us are cowards at heart.'

'Is that what you really believe?'

Ern laughed.

'I ain't believing a word of it. Open your eyes. What man could take his life who lives in a place like this? This is paradise. I ain't going nowhere.'

It struck me, as he spoke, that the truth was more complex. Neither his first assertion nor his second was quite true. It seemed he did not want me to take him entirely seriously. He turned and looked at me. There was something about his eyes, the clarity of his gaze. I tried to imagine him as a young man, before the eyes turned bloodshot, before the skin about them had crumpled. I imagined those grey eyes in a younger face but it was barely possible. Both the young man and the boy were lost. The man that remained had lived too long and the child had receded into some distant space, a place that only Ern could reach.

'It must be an odd life for you,' I said. 'Out here alone.'

'Each day is much the same. It's only the sky that changes. The birds too. Their comings and goings. But what's in my mind don't change.'

'You must have had a wife once,' I said.

'Aye. And a son. He married a city girl. But the girl was soon regretting it.'

'Why?'

'Don't waste my time, lad.'

'But they had a daughter. Your grand-daughter. Does she visit?'

'Aye, she comes here. But she takes after her mother. She's one of them, see? With her airs and graces. She does what she must, but I ain't never forgiven her.'

'Forgiven her for what?'

'What she did weren't right.'

'I don't understand.'

'No. Not yet.'

'You're talking in riddles,' I said.

'May be as I don't know any other way.'

He smiled, gently, to himself.

'Tell me what happened to Bella,' I said.

'Have you not read the book I gave you?'

'I haven't finished it.'

He shook his head.

'Something happened to Bella. Aye. Something happened.'

'What?'

'She used to keep away from the wildfowlers, see? She was a curious lass, but she knew what people was thinking.'

'What did they think?'

'She was the wife of Charles Bliss – the doctor who wouldn't tend the sick. They couldn't forgive him for that. Not even after what happened. It weren't right to mourn so long. Shutting himself up in his glasshouse. It was no wonder his new wife was half mad.'

'But she wasn't mad?'

'No. Headstrong. She had no time for village life. She hated the folk here. Or leastways, her own type of folk. She'd wander about alone, walk the beach, pick flowers in the lane. The lass always had a book under her arm and they didn't like that neither.'

'So what brought them together, Ern? Bella and her wildfowler?'

'First George went away to the University. Him didn't need Bella no more. Perhaps him didn't even like her.'

'She wasn't his mother,' I said. 'It couldn't have been easy.'

'Easy or not, him was a spiteful lad.'

I shrugged. I knew nothing about my grandfather. What concerned me was Alison. This story was nothing but a way of reaching her.

'After George went, Bella started watching the shoot. Nobody stopped her. Some said she was a kind of attraction for the Gentlemen. They came from all over – there was good sport to be had. She was here most days, watching. She'd be on the muds early. See that spot there? Behind the reeds. The raised land.'

'Yes.'

'I see her, don't you?'

'I can imagine her, yes.'

'But you see nothing?'

'A ghost? Is that your meaning?'

'A presence. Always her presence.'

'I have no sixth sense, I'm afraid.'

He tutted as if I hadn't understood.

'The wildfowler felt her watching him.'

'Was it not purely fantasy? At that distance?'

'Fantasy or no, he had her in the end.'

'But how?'

'She followed him. Back to his cottage. After the shoot, in midsummer. The Gentlemen had returned to the inn. They'd bagged enough birds to keep 'em happy and were worn out with the heat. Bella used to leave before the shoot was over but this time she stayed. She watched the boatmen as they cleared the muds. She must have followed him because when he got home, he looked from his window and there she was, in his garden.'

'What did he do?'

'What would any man do?'

'He made love to her?'

Ern chuckled.

'A blue dress, she wore, and a white bonnet. Didn't move. Garden gathered about her. Little insects buzzing. And the heat – girl could barely stand. Air was thick with pollen. Garden running wild. But she stood and waited. And he not knowing what to do. He sorting through his bag of birds with his one good hand. Bag of birds on the table: goldcrests; firecrests; red-breasted flycatchers. Him half wanted her to go; kept his mind on the birds: bluethroats; whitethroats. But she was still there, see? He thought she might faint. She had been watching him for so long, don't forget that. He had dreamed of her, see? But her hadn't seemed real until that day.

'In the end him went outside leaving the little birds all in a pile. Ripe for stuffing they were, but him forgot about that when he saw Bella. Didn't ask questions. Him knew what to do. Crushed her mouth, as if to squeeze the life from her. Now, boy, where's that gun?'

'I told you. Under the boat.'

'Let's get it out then.'

'But you haven't finished . . .'

Ern had already picked up his cane and was levering himself up from the upturned boat. I was furious. It was typical, that he should stop at this point. He knew exactly what he was doing: spinning the story out; making me wait. I stood up.

'What are you going to do, Ern?'

'We're going to turn this boat and take it up the Channel. Boat needs using, if it ain't going to rot.'

'Isn't it a bit late?'

'There's light in the sky.'

'Are you sure it won't spring a leak?'

He ignored me.

'Come on. Get it turned.'

Reluctantly I did as he asked. I knew that having come thus far, there was to be no returning. It seemed, as I stood in the fading light, that I had left my old life entirely behind. For some reason I thought of the dinner party at Richard's; the falseness and pretension of it. I remembered it as if it were a scene from a play. I remembered the room: the mirrors and chandeliers, the candles, the vase of lilies. I remembered Madeleine with her strained smile, her nervous laughter, the pearls at her neck. Everything about that woman was bound in; contained. Her neatness had irritated me – as if she ordered her appearance to fend off impending chaos. But what was she afraid of? What were any of them afraid of? Would they be kept safe, I wondered, by the painted walls that surrounded them? Would the objects they so revered act as charms to protect them?

Perhaps I was merely bitter. Perhaps I was the mad one and they the sane. What was I doing out here after all, being ordered around by this old man, acting against reason? My shoes had begun to leak and my socks were sodden. Crabs were creeping at my feet and I crushed one accidentally as I turned the boat. I saw, as I turned it, that the oars were half sunk in the mud but the gun rested on them and remained clean. I lifted it, then began to unbury the oars.

What was Richard doing now I wondered? Christ! What about poor Helen? She had been right, after all. She ought to have been here, with me, listening to Ern's voice, helping me make some sense of this. Or else she should have been home, enclosed by the walls of her father's house, being normal, being young. Alone in Hope Cottage, what would she do?

I pushed it to the back of my mind; told myself I could make it up to her later. Now I had to think of Alison. And of myself.

'What are you doing, lad? Where's your strength?'

I was heaving the boat along the flats.

'Do you want to do it?'

'Aye. If you're not up to it.'

'Forget it.'

The boat kept sticking but eventually I got it to the water.

'Are you getting in?' I asked.

The whole enterprise was absurd. But I held the boat steady while Ern clambered in, then jumped in myself and pushed off. Within seconds we were free of the banks. The boat was adrift.

The sky was fading now; a shade of greyish lilac. The sun muted behind a bank of cloud close to the horizon. A thin mist diffused the light, lending the scene a certain unreality. Yet which of my existences, I wondered, was the most unreal? This, being present here, on the river at dusk? Or the dinner table at Richard's? The shining glasses, the starched table-cloth, the napkins? I knew which Alison would have preferred.

'When you knew my wife,' I said to Ern, 'did she talk about her work?'

'Her scribbling?'

'If that's what you want to call it.'

'When she weren't asking questions, she spoke of little else.'

'Did it make any sense to you?'

'Girl was struggling. I was knowing that much. She kept asking about Bella, but it weren't Bella she was wanting to write about. Girl had demons enough of her own.'

'What are you saying?'

'What you well know.'

'No. I don't.'

'Then you's a fool. Your Alison had no mother. Nor no child. All the world had adored that girl, but it weren't enough, see? Even that, it weren't enough. Girl thought she could take a pen and write that misery out. But misery ain't so easy to get rid of. Not if it runs deep.'

I wanted to tell him it wasn't so simple as that, but I refrained. It wasn't just the mother thing that got to her, nor her childlessness, though these contributed to her state of mind. It wasn't simply her fame that crushed her either, nor the memories of her illness. I wanted to explain Alison's ambition; her desire for greatness; perfection in her work. How she felt herself inadequate. But this would mean nothing to Ern. He had seen a woman whose connections to her past were cut off, whose links with any future were denied. I guessed, if she had only been able to make sense of her childhood through her work, she might have been saved. Maybe she came to Glaven looking to be saved, but something went wrong.

I supposed she felt her work wasn't up to it; didn't explain what she needed to explain.

'Fix those oars, lad,' Ern said, when it was clear I would offer no response to his wisdom. 'Boat's drifting.'

I did as he asked and began to row.

'Did Alison tell you that she wanted a child?' I asked.

'Her wanted to write about Bella. How Bella had no child. Her asked, "Is that why Bella killed herself?" I told her, she had it wrong.'

'Because there was more to it?'

'Aye. I told her about the wildfowler. Folk knew about it but there weren't a soul who'd tell Charles Bliss what his wife were up to.'

'What sort of a man was her lover?'

But Ern did not reply. He had closed his eyes. When, eventually, he did speak, he mumbled quickly, in the boyish voice again.

'Let me out. Let me out. I'll be a good boy.'

'Ern?'

'I'll not be touching them any more.'

I shook him. I didn't want him to retreat. His past didn't concern me.

'Ern!'

'What?'

He was back, as if nothing had happened. I was relieved.

'The wildfowler. What was he like?'

'Him knew how to hold a gun. Like this.'

He picked up his weapon and made to stand, leaving his stick lying, using the gun to balance. His unsteadiness rocked the boat and I thought we might capsize. Ern stumbled, but recovered and leant on the barrel of the gun.

'Ern – sit down!'

He merely laughed.

'Give me my stick!' he said.

'I don't think that's a good idea.'

'Never mind what you think. Get it for me.'

I did as he asked. He took the stick and jammed it between the planks at the base of the boat. Despite the swaying of the vessel, he balanced by leaning his elbow on the stick keeping his left hand free to manipulate the rifle.

'Is that thing loaded?'

' 'Course it is,' he said. 'What do you take me for?'

He tapped his pocket.

'Enough in here to bag a few waders.'

'Look. Don't you think . . .'

'Your job ain't to think. It's you that followed me, boy. You just watch.'

Ern was lurching about desperately in his attempt to avoid falling. Eventually he stood upright. He left his stick behind and aimed the gun at a flock of geese overhead. For a few seconds he stood still. He had gained his balance and gave the appearance, however briefly, of a much younger man. I watched him, astonished. The moment seemed to extend. It was long enough to form an impression, to forge a memory. It seemed that he used every ounce of his energy to hold that gun aloft. Each muscle, each sinew was tight. His whole body seemed contracted as if into some impossible contortion. I remained seated and he appeared, in that instant, huge, like a great Colossus of a man. His face was screwed to a ball of concentration. Then, at the shock of the explosion, that expression became one of bewilderment. The blast reverberated, punctuated by the terrified cries of birds. There was a thud as a goose hit the bank, and a second as Ern collapsed at my side. Immediately I feared the worst. He lay face-down, his face crushed against the planks. At first I did nothing. I was petrified and thought only of myself. If he was dead, how would it look? I half thought I saw the cameras flashing, waiting for me onshore, as if the whole thing had been an elaborate set-up, designed to maximise my disgrace.

Then he moved. First his elbow, then his arm and his torso. He turned over and pushed himself up. A trickle of blood ran down his face from a deep cut on his cheek. He was laughing.

'Did I bag him? Where is the little blighter?'

'Yes, you got him.'

'Nothing better than a good bit of roast goose, eh?'

His mirth was apparent.

'Are you all right?'

'I'm right as rain. Righter.'

'We should be getting back,' I said.

'We're just beginning.'

'Beginning what? You said yesterday that you would talk to me. So far I know only half the story. We don't have much time. There's a journalist in Glaven already. Here –' I offered him a handkerchief from my pocket. 'You've cut yourself.'

He took the handkerchief and dabbed at his face.

'No. The other side.'

I couldn't believe he didn't feel such a wound. He looked at me suspiciously.

'You want to know what happened to Bella. Is that it?'

The blood seeped through the cotton.

'I think I've made that clear,' I said. Then I leant over and pressed the handkerchief to his face. 'Hold it tight. Like that.'

'Just a little cut.'

But the handkerchief was soaked.

'Here,' I said. I pulled my shirt from my trousers and tore a strip of cotton. 'Use this.'

Reluctantly he took it, discarding the handkerchief in the water, the river marbling with his blood.

'What happened to Bella, is this,' he said. 'Her blood dried up.'

'What are you talking about?'

'She thought she was ill. Didn't tell a soul. Every month, when she expected blood, there was none. She wasn't eating. She had made herself ill. The blood dried up. She thought it was a punishment for what she was doing. But she didn't stop. She couldn't keep away.'

'She was wasting away then?' I said. 'Even before she killed herself.'

Suddenly the attraction for Alison became clear. Bella stopped eating. Her periods stopped. She had a form of anorexia. So Alison was exploring the same ground once again.

'First she grew thin. You could see her skeleton. But something wasn't right. Her belly. One day she felt it flutter. Like something jumped inside of her.'

'My God!'

'Aye. Bella was with child. She was a bag of bones with a great big swollen belly. Little babe was growing, even as she shrunk away.'

'And that was why she committed suicide? Christ. Because she was pregnant with her lover's child?'

'Don't go jumping to conclusions,' Ern said. 'She weren't pregnant when she drowned.'

'She lost it then?' I paused. A worse thought struck me. 'Or she killed it?'

Ern seemed to enjoy my confusion. He still pressed the rag to his cheek. The blood was running slower, trickled across his hand. I thought of Alison. Of the morning when she woke wanting to vomit, staggered to the bathroom, reeling as if drunk. She didn't know where she was. After she'd thrown up, she sat on the toilet, clutching the wall. She peed as I watched and when she wiped herself she saw it. 'I'm bleeding. Shit. It's happening again.' I helped her to the bedroom. She lay on the bed and suddenly clutched her stomach. She was screaming. 'I'm losing it. Harry – I'm losing it.' Curled up like a foetus herself, she was crying, pressing her abdomen into my back. 'God, it hurts.' Now I imagined Bella, hitting her stomach, wanting the loss, unable to face the shame.

'Bella weren't a murderer,' Ern said. 'You're slow, I'll say.'

'I don't see what else . . .'

'Bella grew big. She had the child.'

'But you said it was her burden – to be without . . .'

'She thought of it as her burden. She never thought she'd fall.'

'Then what happened to the child? And what about Charles?'

Ern looked at me. He didn't need to speak. I knew the answer.

'Christ.'

He smiled.

'It's you, right?'

'Got it in one, boy.'

'But how? Wait a minute . . . Your father . . . Didn't you say he'd shut himself up with his books? And the wildfowler . . .'

Though it made sense, I couldn't quite accept it. I was trying to rewrite the story in my mind. It was too much to take in all at once. Yet when I thought of Ern – how he had stood with that gun at his shoulder: he had seemed a natural. As his father would have stood, though he had but one arm to hold the gun.

'The man I thought was my father – he had the books. Bliss.'

'Bliss brought you up? As his own? He forgave her? Then why do you hate him? That must have taken some doing.'

'Him didn't forgive her, lad. Him didn't know. At first, him thought I was his son.'

'I had the impression they never . . .'

'Bliss hadn't stopped having her, boy, if that's your meaning.'

'Then how was she sure of the father?'

'In nine years Bliss hadn't gotten her with child . . .'

'Yes,' I said. 'Yes.'

Yet this whole thing made less sense to me now than ever. I felt as if this revelation ought to act as some kind of closure, yet instead it merely opened doors.

It was getting cold. The cut on Ern's forehead had dried; he was shivering. The day languished, the sun reluctant to give up its hold, but the sky at the horizon was dim violet and the mist thickened. I turned the boat. We did not converse but Ern began to mutter under his breath. He seemed to be counting again, unaware of me. While I was still taking it in. With each stroke of the oars, I felt more aware of my ignorance. The water beneath me gave way to the boat yet I knew the river had more force than I and my apparent mastery of it was a mere illusion. I had come closer to some truth, yet I felt more excluded than ever. In the head of this old man lingered a story that Alison had wanted to prise out, shape, make her own. But his story was not the same as hers. I could know nothing until I had opened her notebook again and read her version of events. It was still there, in my pocket, potent symbol of the gulf that had opened between Helen and myself. Briefly I took my hand from the oar and touched it. Then I continued rowing, making my way towards the shore.

# 29

I TETHERED THE BOAT ON the remains of an old jetty and helped Ern to climb out. He was unsteady on his feet and I was worried about him. Though I felt guilty about the state he was in, I knew it might have been worse if I had not arrived when I did. I didn't know what had prompted this excursion and in a sense it didn't matter. What mattered was that the story was coming clear. Finally I understood Ern's connection to it and his obsession. When he was no more than a babe, his mother had committed suicide. For the first time, I felt sympathy for him.

My curiosity was enormous. But to push Ern any further would have been foolish. He needed rest. No doubt he also needed a doctor. After a fall like that, it would be wise to have him examined. In the meantime, I had to get him home. I strapped the gun across my shoulder. Ern kept his stick. With my help, eventually, we made it.

When we reached the door, he was weak; almost too tired to speak. I thought I should settle him in; get him into bed. But he wouldn't let me in.

'I can look after myself,' he said.

'I'll call a doctor. That's quite a gash.'

'I'm not wanting no doctor.'

'I'll call one from the village.'

'Do as you will,' he said.

'All right. I'll go now.'

'Aye. Go.'

'Just one question. Was this your father's cottage?'

'Aye.'

'And this the garden, where Arabella stood, on the day she followed him?'

'You said one question.'

'The same question.'

'Then you need no answer.'

'What was his name?'

'Robert. Robert Higham. Now leave me.'

He took the gun and closed the door without another word.

I didn't know what to do, where to go. I knew I ought to go back to Helen, but I couldn't. What had happened would make matters worse. I had taken off on my own and had the experience that she craved. She would have loved to have been out on the muds with the old man; to hear the birds; to watch the goose fall from the sky; to hear the story from his lips. I could not give the evening back to her and so I could not face her.

Instead I headed to the mill. I stopped en route at the village phone booth and called Directory Enquiries then the surgery, which was closed but I got through to a locum. He wanted to know the circumstances of Ern's fall but I gave nothing away. In the end he agreed to come out and I hung up.

I parked at the mill. It was dusk and the memory of my first arrival there lurked in my mind. I came here as all that I had clung to crumbled about me. I had never realised how I relied on Alison; how our daily existence – our chatter, our meals, our rows, our love-making – how these things formed me. On my first night in Glaven, I realised the horror of absence. That she would never be home. That her not being there was permanent. I would never speak to her again, nor touch her arm nor her face. She would not be able to moan about writer's block and I would not be able to sympathise. She had blocked her voice for good.

This was what Hake's photographer captured. That blank face was the face of a man entering a new life, which he did not yet understand. After that night, I was a different person. Hake reinvented me. Harold Bliss, notorious widower, twisted man who drove a beautiful artist to her death and destroyed her final work of genius. It seemed the world, also, was ready to condemn me and I had only one course of action: to construct defences. But while I succeeded in keeping the enemy out, I forgot to look to the enemy within – the worm in the bud, as they say. I realised now, it had been eating me all along.

Now, outside in semi-darkness, I listened to the whisper of the reeds. There were no photographers. The mill was closed. I had to bang on the door to get the proprietor to open up.

He was clearly shocked to see me. I remembered him from years ago, a compact, bearded man with a large mole on his right cheek. Since my first visit the beard had greyed somewhat, though his hair remained dark. Our relations before had been cordial. Now he seemed faintly hostile.

'I've come to visit a friend. Judith Frazer.'

'The Professor?' he said. 'Yes. I think she's in. She was here for dinner.' He paused. 'Harold Bliss, isn't it?'

'Yes.'

'I wasn't expecting to see you here.'

'No.'

'What brings you back – if you don't mind my asking?'

'Actually, I do. I'd like to see my friend?'

He shrugged. 'She's on the first floor. The Grain Room.'

'Yes. I know.'

'Digging up the past, is she?' he said. 'There's been a lot of that in recent years.'

'I'm sure. Now, if you don't mind?'


Judith came to her door, pen in hand. She didn't seem surprised to see me but looked behind me as if expecting Helen at my heels.

'Can I come in?'

'Sure.'

She stepped aside and followed me into the room.

'Something the matter?' she said.

I nodded. She took off her glasses and placed them on her desk.

'You two had a row?'

'Something like that.'

'You're shivering.'

'Am I?'

'You're covered in mud!'

'Can I sit down?'

'You'd better take your shoes off first.'

'Of course.'

'Brandy?'

'I think I'd better.'

Judith fetched the drinks while I removed my shoes. The bottom half of my trousers were sodden. I was cold and confused. Whereas

Judith, as usual, appeared composed, even relaxed. She was wearing black slacks and a mauve T-shirt; smelt clean, as if she'd recently showered.

'You can dry those trousers on the radiator if you like. I'll get a blanket for your legs.'

I nodded.

'I won't look!' she joked. She fetched a blanket and threw it in my direction. 'Catch!'

She turned her back as I removed my trousers, then wrapped the blanket about me. I cupped the brandy between my palms.

'Now are you going to tell me what's happened?' she asked.

It seemed so much had happened in the space of a day that I could scarcely believe that so little time had passed. I began with the obvious. How Ern had given us Alison's notebook. Hake's appearance. And afterwards, Mrs Bobbin. I explained that I'd begun reading while Helen slept. That she'd been upset and we'd argued. I told her how I'd walked out and visited Ern again. I told her about the boat and the gun. I added that Ern had told me something important, though I held back on that, made her wait. But I mentioned his regressions, and filled her in on the beginnings of Bella's story. I was talking quickly and frequently Judith stopped me and asked me to expand. What was in the notebook, she asked? Did I mean to say that I had Alison's notes for her final novel? Did I realise the significance of this? What was that, about a wildfowler? A lover? The questions were incessant. Jesus, Hake was here? Already? What did he say? I spoke about the notebook also. There were only two things that I withheld. I did not yet tell her about Bella's pregnancy, nor, in my account of the day, did I mention my love-making with Helen.

'Do you want a top-up, Harry?'

I nodded. The second glass sustained me. I was loose-tongued; buoyed by adrenaline. Something about Judith that evening meant I could not be angry with her. I began to think she was on my side; one of 'us'.

'I can't believe this,' she said. 'You have a complete notebook. In your coat pocket? It's better than I hoped.'

'You want to use it?'

'Of course. It'll be invaluable.'

I laughed.

'You presume, Judith!' I said. 'How you presume!'

'You can't keep it to yourself!' She paused. 'Unless you're afraid of something?'

'There's nothing for me to be afraid of.'

'Don't you think she would have wanted it? For her thoughts to see light of day?'

'If she'd wanted that, she wouldn't have burnt the novel.'

'I'm not sure she knew what she was doing.'

'You do believe me, don't you – that it was her? We've come that far?'

Judith nodded. She drew her legs up, tucked her toes beneath her thighs.

'I'm just not sure that she meant to burn it. I accept it couldn't have been you. But . . . she wanted to be remembered. It seemed to me she wanted nothing more than that. But for her work, not her looks, nor her dumb suicide.'

'Are you saying you knew she was suicidal?'

She shook her head.

'No. If I'd known, I wouldn't have left Glaven when I did – the day before it happened. At the time, I didn't put two and two together.' She paused. 'Afterwards – well it made sense.'

'What do you mean?'

'She talked about the future. About her reputation. As if it would be something solid; fixed. If you intend to live, you think of reputation as something fluid, don't you? Something that changes with each work?'

'So why do you think she did it? What's your theory?'

I shivered, pulled the blanket closer.

'It must have been a fit of anger,' she said. 'A moment of despair. She was so excited about the book. Though she said it frightened her. So much talk about darkness. The darkness of memory. But she also said that the act of writing could cure her. That only by plunging into darkness could she find light – that's what she said. Don't you think the work was too important for her to have intended to destroy it?'

I said nothing. Judith stood up to refill her glass, leant over and filled mine again. I felt uneasy, her being so close. I could smell her, some perfume of deep vanilla. Her nipples stood out beneath her T-shirt. I couldn't help but notice. She flopped down at the other end of the sofa.

'I've never spoken about this, Harry. I've kept pretty stumm, you know?'

I nodded.

'She had this astonishing energy about her, didn't she?' Judith said.

'It could go either way. She had a ferocious temper.'

'Really?' She paused. 'Yes. I can imagine it.'

'Mainly in connection with her writing. "I can't fucking do it, Harry. I can't fucking do it." I wanted to say, "Well don't. No-one's making you." But that would have made her worse. She was driven to it. There was this demon. It wasn't easy, being with her.'

'No. I can see that. She was so hard on herself. I couldn't understand it. She'd talk about her work with such intelligence – and passion. Then later she'd pull it apart. Like she was two people. Like sometimes she was this self-assured artist and then something happened, something kicked in, some bitch of a critic who thought her work was junk.'

'Who do you remember most, Judith? Artist or critic?'

'Neither. Some other person. A face she barely wanted to show but you couldn't help seeing it. In her dreams most of all. Or rather, not in the dreams themselves, but in her desire to have them. She was haunted by Bella. She made some connection between Bella and her mother.'

'What kind of connection?'

Judith shook her head. 'I remember one of her dreams. She was alone at night in a woodland, in Suffolk, I think, close to where she grew up, only now she was adult. She was searching for her mother but couldn't find her. She knew her mother was dead but she kept searching. In the end she starts scrabbling in the dirt, and she cuts her knee on a stone. Then the stones and the earth dissolve into water. She's kneeling at the edge of a pool and Bella's upturned face floats to the surface.'

'Why didn't you tell me this?'

I couldn't believe she had kept quiet about it. At once I was making connections. Both Alison and Ern lost their mothers; bereaved children both.

'It didn't seem important. I don't see what it tells us.'

I paused. I too had been less than honest.

'What Ern told me – tonight – I'll tell it straight. Before she killed herself, Bella got pregnant.'

'What?' Judith's composure, for once, was ruffled.

'So she was pregnant when she . . .'

'No. She had the child. Before.'

'Hang on . . .'

'It's Ern. Ern Higham is Bella's son.'

'What?'

'Exactly.'

'By her lover?'

'Yes. Robert Higham. A local boatman.'

'Now who's been keeping secrets?'

'Actually, I haven't even told Helen yet. She'll be furious I've told you first.'

'Helen is just a child, Harry.'

'What's that got to do with it?'

'Nothing. It's just . . . Really. It's none of my business.'

I looked at her; tried to decipher her expression. Something about her face compelled me to look: the largeness of the features, heavy-lidded eyes, beak nose, huge lips.

'No – tell me. What do you think of my little liaison?'

'Isn't it obvious?'

I shrugged.

'I've told you. She's just a baby. You're both playing games. Having your little fantasy. Well, make the most of it.'

'I intend to.'

'Good. Now can we talk about the interesting stuff?'

She was changing the subject; trying to get away from the fact that she'd revealed something of herself.

'So Ern is the living remnant of Arabella's love affair?'

'Spot on.'

'Jesus.'

'How will that sit in your little book?'

'Cut it out, Harry. Tell me – what happened?'

'She had the child and passed it off as Bliss's.'

'But he doesn't take Bliss's name?'

'No. There's a lot he's not telling. I don't think he knows how.'

'Too painful?'

'Or so repressed it's half forgotten.'

'We must talk to him some more. Can we go back? Tomorrow?'

'We?'

'I have to meet him again, don't you think? I mean, especially now Hake's here. We have to protect Ern from Hake.'

'I know. I know.'

'How much do you think he knows about Ern?'

'I'm not sure. Whatever he's heard from Vinton, I suppose.'

'The man is a crook! Why do you put up with it?'

'Because the alternative is worse,' I said. 'I don't want to speak about it in public.'

She looked despairing of me. 'In my book, I'll redress the balance. Show the little shit for what he is.'

'Really?' I smiled, ironically.

'And I have to speak with Higham. The book won't be whole without it.'

'Is that all you think about? Your book?'

'No. But I thought . . .'

I was losing patience.

'I don't care what you thought.'

'OK fine. I'll forget about the book.'

'What are you talking about?'

'Maybe I should forget the whole damned project.' She shook her head. 'It's not easy, Harry.'

'What?'

'I have a lot invested in this book. And I'm not talking about money. I have something to say.'

'Nothing that hasn't been said before.'

'That's not fair. Alison's death has affected me in ways I couldn't have imagined.'

'You barely knew her.'

'I knew her at a crucial time.'

'A time when I was absent.'

'I didn't say that.'

'But you implied it.'

'No. I was her last friend, that's all. Her last girlfriend in any case. But I couldn't stop her. There was a momentum building and I didn't see it.'

'Even if you'd known, you could have done precisely nothing.'

'I know. That's why I need to write. To find some objectivity. I've come too close to this. I need to stop looking to myself and start looking to her. The more I learn about Alison, the more I discover my own innocence. Do you see?'

I nodded. I knew her meaning well.

'What you've told me tonight, about Ern. It fits. If hearing his story made her think of her own mother, it could have sparked the whole thing. It's pretty common, you know, among suicides – the death of a parent in childhood.'

'Spare me the psycho-babble.'

'But all I said . . .'

'I'm sick of theories of any kind.'

'What you're doing is no different. You're looking for reasons,' she said.

'Yes, you're right. We have a choice, I suppose. Blame ourselves, blame someone else, blame circumstances. Or leave it alone. Perhaps I was wrong, coming here.'

'If anyone is to search for truth it should be you. You have the notebook now.'

'And you'd like access to it.'

'Of course.'

'Do you ever question your need to write this book?'

She hesitated. She had moved closer as we spoke and now she leant her head against my shoulder, her gaze directed at the ceiling. It seemed a natural enough move, but I was uneasy. I wondered if she were simply playing games, in an attempt to gain my co-operation.

'Yes. I question it every waking minute.'

'And have you reconciled yourself?'

'No. There's a fundamental contradiction. By writing the book I'll be fuelling the very industry I'm trying to expose. There's no getting away from it.'

'The industry?'

She raised her head, twisted in her seat.

'They'll make millions at the box office. By glamorising her death. And each time such deaths are glamorised there'll be more victims, more women lining up to write literature as a prelude to self-slaughter.'

'So you admit your involvement?'

'I'm not on their side, but yes, I've become part of the money-machine. As you have. There's something parasitic about my work. I'll admit it. But there's a purpose as well.'

'Which is?'

'To try and stop the madness.'

'You talk as if it's an epidemic.'

'Like Werther, eh Harry?'

'Exactly. All those young men blowing their brains out because someone in a book made it fashionable. It's hardly come to that.'

'You'd be surprised,' she said. 'I've found a few cases.'

'You're not serious?'

'Absolutely.'

'Young women? As a result of Alison's death?'

'There's no definite proof, of course.'

Immediately I thought of Helen. I knew it was crazy, but once the idea was planted . . .

'I have to go.'

'What? What's the hurry? I wanted to ask you about . . .'

'Really. I have to get back. Can you get my trousers?'

She fetched them from the radiator.'

'Harry – Helen will be fine.'

'I shouldn't have left her alone.'

'She'll be fine.'

She reassured me as I dressed.

'You can't drive,' Judith said. 'You're over the limit.'

'Tough.'

'You ought to walk. Or stay here.'

'It's a quiet village. Nothing will happen.'

'I'd drive you myself . . .'

'Only you're pissed too, right?'

She didn't reply, merely frowned. She followed me to the door. I fastened my shoes, then unhooked my coat, feeling instinctively for the notebook. For a moment we remained silent, each watching the other. I fumbled for my keys and turned to go. Judith stopped me, touched my wrist.

'Take care, huh?'

I nodded. But I was no longer thinking of myself.

# 30

OUTSIDE THERE WAS nothing. The mist had thickened to a dense fog and the sky held no light. The salt air was sharp, seared my throat as I breathed. The air went to my head that night. I couldn't think or see straight. Nothing was permanent, and every dark space seemed capable of shifting.

I took tentative steps towards the marsh-path, guided by a rickety banister. The stink of the sea rushed at me, odours of shrivelled fish, fresh weed and dog-roses. Perhaps I merely imagined the roses. My remaining thoughts so grim, the shades of obscurity merely echoed me. Such blackness, emptiness, and I a part of it, my own hollowness seeping out, blurring the distinction between my skin and the air about me. Somewhere in all this was a bad dream but I could not locate it. From where did these terrors originate and where had they lodged? Were they born here, in my own heart, or were they marsh-creatures, primordial forms that multiplied in the bogs and crept out, infected, insidious, unseen?

I don't know how I made it to the car. I was not so drunk that I could not walk but I had lost my grip. The car, when I found it, seemed too solid: its very tangibility an aberration. I got in, found ignition, seat belt, lights. Lights threw their beam across the marshes and I was struck by the innocence of that sight. The beam revealed nothing, no nightmare visions. Only the reeds, unsettled by the wind. They had been present even in darkness, when no eye was there to watch.

It was not far to the cottage. I avoided the main village, passing only a few small dwellings where the lights were already extinguished. I barely remember the journey, except that I had to swerve to avoid an errant cow who stood in the road, directly in my path. If I hadn't been drunk, the event might have seemed stranger. As it was, the cow's sudden appearance was only fitting. What might have been surreal was merely ordinary. That bovine face which had appeared from nowhere, startled, uncomprehending, was a necessary omen. I looked at that cow as in a mirror, and while my hands and feet acted to avoid collision, my eyes stared at the space on the windscreen where the cow had been. I saw it still, the blank face that barely knew the disaster that approached. The image persisted, as if burnt upon my retina. While I sped up the lane, I imagined the cow, unmoving, still standing in the centre of the road.

I turned on to the drive. The house was in darkness. My fear was not new. I entered, stumbling on the step.

'Helen?'

My voice resonated in silence. I made my way through the cottage, switching on lights, hoping that she would be revealed, curled in a ball, sleeping, crying, anything so long as unharmed. In the sitting-room, nothing, nor the bathroom. I ascended the stairs, sent up a silent unbeliever's prayer. The spare room was empty, the door to the other room closed. I turned the handle and the light from the landing spread across the unmade, empty bed. The overhead light failed and I fumbled for the lamp but the room had not been touched since we had left it that morning. Helen was absent.

I remember kneeling at the bedside, distraught. I knew I ought to refuse to dwell in self-pity, but I could not. I imagined the worst: Helen at the water's edge, ready to cement my awful future. If I could only stand up, get back in the car, drive to the beach, stop her. I did not understand my inaction, my inability to wrench myself from the depths of my exhaustion. Was it my own dread certainty that disaster could not be avoided?

Then, downstairs, a clicking sound, as if someone had entered the cottage. I lifted my head and waited. I was about to ignore it when I heard something else. This time I stood up and went downstairs. I didn't know what to expect. There was nobody in the sitting room. I opened the kitchen door and she was there, at the table. She didn't turn as I entered. Her eyes were fixed but on nothing.

'Helen?'

Her face didn't even flicker. No suggestion that she even noticed my presence. She was like a shadow, her face pale, her hair tangled. She sat huddled in Alison's black coat, shivering. I came closer. Her eyes were reddened. She glimpsed up at me and then away, giving no hint of emotion.

I crouched at her side, took her hand but she pulled away. She smelt of nicotine.

'Thank God you're OK.'

She let out a grunt of contempt, raising her eyes to the ceiling.

'I thought . . .' But I couldn't finish my sentence. Still she didn't speak. 'Where have you been, love?'

'I might ask you the same question.'

Her voice was cold. She too had been drinking.

'Helen, I'm so sorry.'

'Yeah.'

'Really. I was wrong to walk out like that.'

'Forget it. Just forget it.'

'Please. Helen, I was so afraid – when you weren't here.'

'Sure.'

'You don't believe me?'

'I don't care.'

'About the notebook – I was wrong. You must read it.'

'What's the point?'

'I want you to be a part of my life. I just didn't realise . . .'

'You're talking crap, Harry.'

'No. I'm not. Please, look at me.'

Now she turned. It pained me to see her face.

'Where have you been, love?'

'To the pub, of course.'

'But you don't know anyone . . .'

'You don't bloody rule my life, you know.'

'No. I know. It's just . . .'

'It's just that you walked out on me and expected me to stay at home like a good little girl. Well I'm not a good little girl, Harry. You should know that. Anyway – three guesses where you were tonight?'

'What do you mean?'

'As if one fuck in a day isn't enough.'

'What?'

'Oh come on. She has her charms, doesn't she, the Professor?'

'What's the matter? You know that's not true.'

As I spoke, and watched her, so furious and hurt, I was struck by a memory of her, only three days previously, when we had stopped to picnic in the fields. So much had changed since then, since we had lain in the shade of the horse chestnut tree, since I had traced my finger down her spine and there had been no trace of animosity between us. Hope had sustained us then and innocence. Now, already, we were stuck in the mire. There was no path that could lead us back.

'I'm going to bed,' she said.

'Not yet. Please. I'd like to talk.'

'Tomorrow.'

'I was with Ern Higham this evening. He told me something important.'

'With Ern?' There was a flicker of interest, of that old desire to know. But her dark mood prevailed. 'Save it. I'm too pissed.'

'I can make coffee.'

She shook her head.

'I'll make it up to you, Helen. Believe me.' She simply looked. 'Don't leave, will you?'

She stood up, left me in the kitchen, contemplating my failures. She didn't belong here, of course, in the middle of nowhere, with a man so haunted by his past that he could not consider a future without it. The radiant creature that I had brought to his place deserved something better, brighter. I wondered, if I kept her here, what would become of her. Was it possible that we might mend the damage? And were my earlier fears merely paranoia or something more? It might be better, perhaps, to accept my loss, for the alternative might be worse. It would be easy enough to drive her away. To do so would be to destroy myself, yet she would gain a life, recover her self. I tried to see her in the future, in the arms of a young man, lying beneath the same tree. But it seemed impossible. Surely our lives now were too entwined; surely once separated, neither of us could thrive. It would be better, I figured, to see this thing through, to involve her. I didn't know where the events of the past few days were leading and I felt certain there would be no conclusion that would satisfy us. Still the notebook remained in my coat pocket and Ern had not finished his story. We were not yet through and I wanted to get it over with.

A half hour later, I ventured upstairs. Helen was sleeping; tranquil. The sheets were rumpled about her legs and she wore only a thin chemise. Her arms and her neck were bare. I leant over her, pulled the sheet across her chest. She stirred, murmured something. Quietly I bent down and picked up my coat where I had left it. I had decided to read the notebook. In such circumstances I needed, more than ever, to hear Alison's voice. Whether inspired or dispirited, her presence was necessary to me. When I had finished I would return and lay the notebook by Helen's side. I knew it might not be enough, that the gesture was doubtless too small and too late, but if I had not the courage to let her go, then I knew I must continue to entice. Helen needed, most of all, to know the necessity of her presence here. I had to convince her that she could not abandon me now. It seemed, as I gently closed the bedroom door, that without her I too would sink. I needed her to stay. Until the thing was through.

# 31

# THE NOTEBOOK

*I*'m ransacking my memories; sifting my past, wondering if there's a shape to the apparent chaos that is my life. If I'm to make fiction of it, I must find some pattern, but I can't get a grasp on my experience. When I write, I'm appalled by the randomness of my thoughts, my phrases, my choice of words. Why, when the resonances are all about me? It scares me. That it must be I who orders these events, attempts to wrest some meaning from them. Ern throws out threads and they attach themselves to me. I labour within a framework of his creation.

*Those shadows today in the open fields. Sometimes the threads are so thin they're near-invisible. Was it possible that I was reminded of Marsden? It wasn't a conscious connection. When I wrote about Bella's uncle, was I actually recreating that other myth? Yet I was only five. How can that day resurface now, so bright and polished as if the light that broke across the fields this afternoon now breaks across memory and makes it fresh and present?*

*We went to the sea-stacks. Mummy and I. On holiday without Daddy. Marsden Rock on the cold north-east coast of England. It rises over a hundred feet from the beach, like an eruption from the earth. I thought I had stepped into some giant's lair. Those huge rocks, sole remnants of eroded land, gave the place the air of a fairy-tale.*

*A cold day; the wind high, tide out. Cloud hung low in the sky but the sun spilled through, illumining the beach; long afternoon shadows. I danced, thrilled by the magnification of my self. I played on the long dunes, uncowed by thoughts of giants, and* squatted down beneath the rock's arch, clutching my bucket, filling it with small creatures which I prised from the base of the rock: anemones, mussels, starfish, crabs. I liked to watch them writhing: the crab-claws grasping the air; the shivering spines of the starfish. I decided their fate. They would be free, but only if I willed it. Later, I showed them to Mummy, as I flung them into the water. She watched with apparent interest. It was the focus of my day, my rescue of the shellfish and crustaceans. I saw only this small beautiful perspective, all the world crystallised to fit a simple vision. But something else was happening that day. Years later, I read the fragments of poetry she wrote after that visit, unpublished scribblings, among the few attempts she made at writing after my birth.

> Strata of rock, worlds unfathomed.
> Countless deaths compressed in coloured stone.
> What matter one more, when birds still will roost
> And rock not rot despite my passing?

There were no references to me, nor my childish games. Her cancer had just been diagnosed. She thought she would die. Instead, she lost a breast. She lived for three more years before it began again in the breast that remained.

I wonder, if I coerce my brain, might I recapture her as she was on that day? Or will memory deceive me? Will I see her, as in a photograph, not the real woman but the frozen image that has become her? I must get beyond that. If I'm to plunge into this work, I must shed surfaces, unpeel veneers. Yet when I think of her now, I see only the stilled image. I see her grey eyes screwed up against the light; her thick lips; fleshy cheeks. Return to that day and see something else, beyond the child's vision, the woman contemplating her own mortality. How is she now? Wan face, ghost-eyes, gaze fixed on sea and shadows and on the rock. Her fear of death is alien to me. But then I have no child. She must have looked on me that day and imagined me motherless. I can't think about it: a time when the world might be perceived through her eyes. After her death, there was a great alteration. The world continued to exist but she did not. I looked at objects differently. A tree was not the same tree; a cup not the same cup. Because *they could not be seen by her, their identity had changed irretrievably.*

*Think of the striations of the rock at Marsden. No longer shifting or subterranean, the rock now solid; made permanent. The sea's erosion has revealed the layering of time; the pattern beneath the surface. So my imagination must erode the past. The form of the art-work has simply to be revealed.*

*Ern's story and my own must meet in this novel; the tales somehow combine. Two women face the sea and death; one chooses death, one rages against it. Both leave a child to exist and grow without the being who gave them life. I was bowled over today by Ern's revelation. I see now why I was drawn to him: we are alike; our lives run parallel. Though his refuge was in solitude, mine in the camera's glare, we are, essentially, of the same stuff.*

*Words will not make our mothers flesh again. But I'm certain of the necessity of my work. Still I fear. How can I make fiction when fact itself so overwhelms? At first I didn't believe Ern's tales, believing they were half-truths, garnered from gossip. I speculated: how can he speak with such certainty, as if he were there, in Arabella's head and heart? The knowledge that he learned this from his father does not explain the depth of his understanding. 'Over and over, see? I've heard these tales more times than you might imagine girlie.' But when he speaks, it's as if the words are his. He's taken the tale, unravelled and rewoven it: a transformation, as if, when he speaks, he has entered her heart, as if he has burrowed there in the blood-warmth and panic of the place. I must attempt it too. To move beyond my own loneliness and inhabit the space that Bella once occupied.*

\*

*I am barely sleeping here. This great fat pen won't let me sleep — torturous thing. My body is exhausted but my brain so full it bursts. Rather than break my skull it channels thought to my fingertips. Excess thought spills out as blue marks on the page.*

Soon I'll return to London. I'm afraid that when I leave, the story won't burn as it does now. I live so intensely here; I can't bear to think of going back, lest it should be like before. Those long days. Harry at school and me staring at a blank screen willing words to come from a void. The sterility; lack of purpose. A few literary parties, calls from journalists, hardly enough to break the monotony. How will it be possible, in a Clapham terrace, to recreate my obsessions? When I see Ern daily, I can enter his world. Thinking of Bella, I forget my self. Listening to Ern, I'm so close to the past that I can touch it as I touched the rock at Marsden. So close that I can pick the barnacles.

Take this moment then. Before the return to the cold room and the grey London light and the absence of ghosts. While they dance in my brain, seize them and make them step to the rhythm that I set.

To write of that final night. If I can enter her mind, surely the novel will sing? Otherwise it will bomb: too depressing to read. Just what the critics have been waiting for. Time to shoot me down at last. Like before, they're waiting to find me out. I remember the photographs they published, shortly after I left hospital. At six and a half stone, I was considered semi-cured. But I'm sure people relished seeing me like that, no longer beautiful. Now they want proof that I can't, after all, write terribly well. Is it worth the effort, I wonder, that I'll put into this book, knowing it might be ripped apart by strangers? Don't believe it. Never believe that. This book must have a heart or I might as well go back to the catwalk. Sell my body rather than my soul.

Ern has told me his version of events but I must create it anew. First George. Without George, Harry's grandfather, none of this would have happened.

I barely considered George before I came here. Remember when Harry mentioned him, in the Tate café? I didn't want to know. Yet George is at the heart of this. He too lost his mother. He remembers her when her belly was swollen with child. He was going to have a brother. He remembers being removed to a neighbour's house. His mother was pacing her room, making strange grunts like a sick cow.

*He was told, when he returned there would be a new baby. Instead there was a baby's corpse, wrapped in a winding sheet, and his mother on her death-bed, crying for the lifeless thing beside her that only a few hours previously had kicked her innards, so that she had wailed for its release. They told George the baby had been a girl. A baby girl had killed his mother. A boy would not have done such a thing.*

*Bella did not stand a chance. By the time she arrived, George's character was formed. Four years since his mother had died and the boy trusted no-one. He is the very agent of this tragedy, yet I feel only sympathy for him. I know his abandonment too well and the effects of a father's grief. Like my father, Bliss sought solace in books. My father retreated into poetry, Bliss into medicine and natural history. The outcome was the same: a child so alone and angry that he does not know the meaning of connection; a huge hole in the child's world, and a desperate longing that the father fill it. In each case, the child can do nothing but copy the remaining parent. So I too took to books, as did George. I read poetry, crammed my head full of obscure words, wrestled with adult griefs compressed in verse. But what could the torments of the poets mean to me? I remember reading Donne, 'A Nocturnal upon St Lucy's Day', and trying desperately to understand it. The words seemed to echo my anguish yet the sentences were too contorted to yield meaning to me.*

> *If I an ordinary nothing were,*
> *As shadow, a light, and body must be here.*
> *But I am none; nor will my sun renew.*

*Years later, I finally understood what I had felt when first I read it: the sense that the death of a loved one removes one's very being. One is nothing. No, less than nothing. One has no substance at all.*

*I wonder, did George feel this too? When first faced with his father's library, did he feel, as I have felt, invisible? What was it that led him to the book which stirred his imagination? I see him, small, dark-haired thing, feeble in limb yet climbing the ladder to trail his finger along high shelves. Ern told me today about the boy's*

*fixation and still it chills me. His father at least chose flowers, the
orchids that his wife had once so admired. But George found a
different consolation. His finger rested on a canvas-bound tome
which he levered from the shelf. It sits before me now, courtesy of
Ern, a work of scholarship penned, ironically, by a woman.
Perhaps it's not such a strange interest for a boy of his age, but
that does not make me like it any more: the child was obsessed by
snakes.* This book, Curiosities and Wonders of Serpent Life *by
Catherine C. Hopley, was his starting point.*

*I try to imagine what a boy in mourning would make of such a
book. The illustrations are plain and uninspiring, so it must have
been the text that George pored over, the anatomy lesson. The book
is intelligent, witty even, but ghoulish too; bursting with hellish
anecdotes. The snake can be severed, the author writes, but its body
still will move, coil and spring and its head may bite, its tongue dart.
The serpent, she confides, has a partiality for milk and there are
tales of snakes being found upon the breasts of women in the tropics
where nursing mothers lie exposed. It makes my blood run cold, yet
George admired the beast. It could, after all, 'outclimb the monkey,
outswim the fish . . . outwrestle the athlete . . . The serpent uplifts
its crushed prey, and presents it grasped in its death-like coil, as in a
hand, to its gaping mouth.' Thank God I had John Donne!*

*I wonder, how could Bella connect with this small boy? She too had
a love of the natural world, so perhaps that was it. Yet her labour of
love was wasted. She brought him up as a son; he was the focus of
her life. It is no coincidence perhaps, that it was shortly after his
departure that she first made love to her boatman. There was a
space to fill and Robert Higham filled it.*

*Higham, it seems, commanded respect in this village. Even later,
after the suicide, people protected him, while Bliss became an
outcast. Bliss had the care of the babe, but that was all. He knew
now it was not his son, but he would not relinquish him. Ernest was
his prize. His last remaining triumph.*

*Robert Higham. A huge, ambiguous man. Why is it I can't yet fully
imagine him? All I have is an image and Ern's idealising. It's so easy*

to make a caricature of such a person, to make a Heathcliff or a Mellors of him, a bit of rough for a lady, a wild creature who awakens her lust and makes her defy the conventions of her class! But this was a real man, a private man. I look at the photograph. That is simply the shell of him. I see from his dress that he is poor. I note the missing limb, sole imperfection, for he is tall, broad-shouldered and lean. Easy to define, the handsome hero of the tale, but not easy to penetrate. Something about his face, some clue there perhaps? Cynical and knowing. His face in shadow but the gaze is direct. His lips half-smile, half-sneer, difficult to be certain beneath the moustache. There is nothing exotic about his face. Rather, he has a sturdy English look, the look of a working man. His appeal lies chiefly in his stature and his expression, eyes almost soulful yet countered by the set of his lips which give the impression that he mocks the person that he looks on.

Go beyond this appearance and what do I know, what can I surmise? Robert Higham lived alone. His income was gained from shooting and fishing. He supplied birds, Ern told me, to the local taxidermist, who paid a fine price for a rare specimen. He would be up early to lead the shooting parties. In the evening he would be out in his boat with other men, watching for shoals of mackerel to approach the shore.

When I think of Robert Higham, I think of him first alone, at night in his room as he undresses, and myself, hiding in the mirror, watching him. I see what Bella saw: the naked torso; maimed arm. The room is plain: a wooden floor, a simple bed, a chest. Ern's place without the clutter of years. Nets across the floor, dead birds in bags, the stink of fish, guns against the wall.

I want to see these lovers together, to see beyond their differences. Arabella, who once wore bloomers and cycled the streets of London. She opened books in the British Library and was scowled upon for her sex. Now, as she hovers on the brink of adultery, her step-son is there, beneath the pale blue dome, opening books that he till then had only dreamed on, books where coloured serpents are illustrated large and clear, in brilliant oils, as if they might leap from the page and devour the scholar at his desk. Bella had known the *pleasure of pages beneath her fingertips: the crackle of paper, scent of leather. But the only man she had known was Bliss. 'Chug, chug, chug!' Isn't that what Ern said? Hard for me to think of Bliss and Bella. I see his face and I can think only of Harry. But it could not have been like loving Harry. When Bliss was inside her, he saw the face of the wife he had lost. No more than a physical necessity perhaps; his bearded face brushing hers with barely a kiss. Perhaps he found her faintly repulsive, blamed her for his animal instinct.*

*Whereas Robert Higham was like a book she had never read. If Charles was a dry, dusty volume that demanded no attention, her boatman was bound in calf-skin and beckoned to be opened. His pages were of paper so smooth that she might have spent days running her fingers across them, forgetting even that there were words upon the page. Later, much later, she would read them, and find there a plain-written tale, shielding depths she could not fathom. Yet the words alone would never satisfy. It was not the words but the echoes they cast out, afterwards, when she was alone. Those words, like nets. When Robert spoke, whispering in her ear, she was already drowning. It was the quiet insistence of his voice, coarse dialect from a jewelled throat. Sense had no sense. Nothing had meaning beyond his breath and then, to follow, the fingers of his one hand at the nape of her neck, unbuttoning the silk garments, the like of which she had worn for nine years to preserve her husband's reputation.*

*If I look for the connection, it is not in the mind that I should seek it. Nor was it bodies alone that first met on that small white bed. Physicality can go beyond the body. She has come to him but she will not act. She stands in the garden and waits. And when he has kissed her, led her inside, to his bedroom, she continues to wait. Despite her longing. Once she had a will but her will has shrunk in this place. Enough is defied simply by her presence.*

*Where does it lie then, the force of this union? Nothing more erotic than this coupling: that is how it must be. The knowledge of Bliss's violence lies beneath it; the risk she takes. For there is a violence in Bliss. I see him – as Bella stands in the shade of the bedroom, faint with the heat, the sweat still glistening on her forehead – I see him in* his glasshouse, bending over his orchids, a pair of tweezers in his hands, his face in rapt concentration. What is it in that face that so alarms me? He has never raised a finger to her and yet she has never erred.

How to convey the eroticism? How to wrest the images from my head? That room, the shadow cast across the bed, the dinginess of it and the appeal of this. She is wilting, her white garments near-soaked-through. Smell of his sweat and hers, like over-ripe fruit. Her clothes fall to the ground, the gloves, the dress, the petticoat, till she stands in her stays and the bones of her skirt. He cannot negotiate these with one hand. Like a second skeleton; a carapace. The contraption is unfamiliar. She removes it deftly and, when it is gone, he places his index finger on her shoulder and begins to circle her, to trace a spiral across her shoulder blades, beneath her breasts, to the small of her back. Without the carapace she is vulnerable; soft flesh, easily crushed. His fingers know nets and ropes. The ribbons of her stays speak a different language. Still he unravels her. She is wrapped like a present, so many layers of tissue and paper that his appetite is whetted by the unwrapping. He can barely believe that this delicate creature has presented herself. What will she make of him, he wonders, when she sees the stump of twisted skin and bone, the silver-blue scar tissue? He cannot bear to look on it. Sometimes he forgets that he has lost an arm. He reaches for an object but where his hand should be, there is nothing. It is odd, this absence. His arm is buried in the garden, the flesh decomposed, but the bones are out there, his arm, his hand, beneath the earth.

Something else lies with those bones. Some shred of self was blown away with the arm. Before the accident, Higham was no different from the other young men of the village. His expertise with the gun gave him a certain authority but the future he envisaged was ordinary: to make a living; to have a wife; children. He should never have taken the gun out in the snow. Dazzling whiteness distracted him. The mud flats frozen and the snow settling. Early morning and the boat slides to the river, not yet ice. Snow in the air; landscape hidden beneath this coat of white. He hears the ducks, their cry, the sound of wings beating the air. He could not allow his parents to go hungry.

*Long muzzle raised. He stands on the bank, inhales ice air, listens to the vast muffled land. There is no sound beyond that made by his prey. He has not checked the muzzle since the snow began again. The world then was stilled; contained. A perfect correlation between his concentrated mind and the motionless beauty that surrounded him: heavy yellow sky; black, iced silhouettes of trees; frozen marshland. And his arm, his strong left arm supporting the barrel, dirty fingernails, calloused tips, red knuckles. He pulls the trigger. Impossible to differentiate between the noise and the pain. One arm has killed the other. He stumbles, remembers only the sight of blood, marring the whiteness, and the duck overhead, untouched by the bullet's intention.*

*Bella sees the remainder of his arm. Where there was strong brown flesh, now is a tangled knot of gristle. When Robert thinks of his body, this is all he sees: the stump; the gnarled tree-root where a branch should grow. What woman would touch such a deformity? He has learned to shoot again, better than any man in the village. It is not enough. He feels the invasive stare at the loose sleeve pinned to his chest. He has become a freak; a marvel. He never speaks of his self-pity but it eats him. He has lost his humour. He might joke with the other gunners but his laughter is false. He is sick with envy at their good arms. When people look at him, he thinks they see the stump. He forgets that the monstrosity is hidden. When a woman smiles, he thinks of the marks left by the surgeon's clumsy stitches. He looks away.*

*Why, then, is it different with Bella? It is several years since the accident. His parents have passed away; he has inherited the cottage. Perhaps it is her very persistence that wears down his self-disgust. At first he despises her for staring, yet, unlike others, she is not put off by his indifference. He barely looks at her but she returns daily to watch him. He knows who she is: the wife of Charles Bliss, the doctor who attended his own birth. They said that she was unbalanced; that she walked the marsh path alone at all hours. She spoke to serpents, some said, though he didn't believe such superstitions. Nor did he believe that she was mad. He had caught glimpses of her. She was too beautiful to be mad.*

*Arabella Bliss was not looking for a husband. Rather, she was fleeing one. Even Robert Higham was not such a fool that he could not see her desire. He tried, for several weeks, to find some other explanation, but the harder he looked, the plainer her intention. Her face began to haunt him. But he would never have approached her, if she had not followed him that day and stood in his garden, waiting. If he had not gone to her then, she would surely have been burnt by the sun.*

*Enough. That's enough of them. Let her wait in the sun. I'm so tired and somehow I have to summon energy to start again, to return to an earlier point in the story, to work on the novel itself. Christ, it's so slow. I can whiz through the bare bones in an hour or so, but that won't make them come alive. I have to give them voices, make them speak. And to find my own place in this text. This must be a place where other losses are unwrapped: the arm; the breast; the life; the mothers; the embryos. We all have losses. They can't be restored, except perhaps through art. Why then am I so terrified of this? I'm afraid to sleep because I can't sleep, recently, without nightmares. I sleep for no more than two or three hours because I can't bear to close my eyes. My mind is in overdrive, terrified of failure. It's as if they all depend on me: Bella; Robert; Ern; Mother. And Harry too. I try to forget what I'm putting him through but it's hardly possible. It's as if I'm pretending he doesn't exist, as if, while I can't see him, I can't bring him anguish. But I know that's not true. He worries about me every minute. I know that, yet I won't contact him. We discussed it, didn't we? No interruptions of the flow.*

*The trouble with Harry is that he tries too hard. He wants to mend me. What a crazy enterprise! Perhaps I too believed it possible, once. When he first found me, in the National Gallery, it was as if I'd been waiting for him, willing him to come. I was so damn ignorant then, my head so full of crap. All I could think of was food and trying to be normal about it, trying to believe that it was acceptable to eat. I was starting to write then, of course, my saving grace, but I had no models. I needed Harry to come along and show me the way. Seeing the Piero was a turning point. A purity there, that I'd hardly ever known, not since the early days when Mummy was alive. Those gorgeous, calm blues, ochres, ivories. The serenity of the Christ figure. It was right that Harry should be there. Such sweets he offered me.*

*But he should never have married me, of course. I'm the wrong woman. I know that now, but how can I break it to him? He thinks, if I would just open myself to it, his love would obliterate every other pain, every loss. But nothing will remove those dark days with my father, nor the years of emptiness when all the world adored me and I learned to despise myself. Nothing can take away the fear that Gordon Hake inspired. Nor compensate for my two dead embryos. I know this now. Harry's love won't invent the poems that were stopped at my birth. All it can do is dull the hurt.*

*Yet I miss him. At night I miss the hulk of him against me; the give of his belly; scent of wine on his breath. I miss that Viking face. Shabby bear of a man! He is too patient; too kind; too tolerant. I know I disappoint him. What he wants is the woman he first met, the woman that I appeared to be: cultured; intelligent; attractive; creative. And happy – don't forget happy. I used to admire women like that. I worked so hard at imitating them. If I appeared to be balanced, I thought, I might achieve balance. Only I went further. I wanted more than stability. I wanted brilliance too. I didn't know, when I painted that picture of myself, that the cracks would soon appear. Nor that the man who married the woman in the portrait would soon discover the underpainting. On the surface, a Leonardo, a small, secretive smile. But nobody told him it was a fake. The artist was merely joking. As the palimpsest begins to flake, another face is revealed, a grotesque, split mask, one of Picasso's grimacing whores.*

*The truth is, Harry can't hack the vileness of my anger. When we make love, perhaps then he touches it and makes sense of it and uses it in some creative way that leaves me drained of it. Afterwards, when I'm calmed, he thinks that's the real me, the me that he has rescued. He is so wrong. He wants life to be ordered and serene. He thinks London streets will shelter him, that culture is the new religion. He is pleased by book-talk; delighted at good food; overwhelmed by a smile. He is capable of happiness, and for that I admire him. He concentrates his mind on his own pleasure. But for me, that's impossible. Pleasure does not make disaster vanish.*

*Can I find a place within my novel for the blackness of my thoughts, the terrors of my nightmares? Who will read it in the end? Not people like me, with a death wish, half a longing for some great full stop. No. Rather those who are curious, who look astonished on, as at a side-show. There is, in the end, no horror in the reading of it, only in the living.*

# 32

THE ROOM WAS GLOOMY and full of shadows. No sound now from beyond the window; even the marsh-birds that earlier had screamed their mating-calls now had fallen silent. Nearly an hour had passed since I sat down with the notebook. I had lingered, trying to discern meanings from randomly scribbled words. Yet now, despite my desire to read on, despite my intense love for the author and my immense involvement and curiosity, my eyes and my body failed me. I could not continue. I was smarting at the sting of Alison's words; bitter at her death wish and her belief that I wanted her to be other than what she was.

My eyelids seemed lead-weighted. Perhaps my body protected me. Unlike Alison, I had defences and now they were raised; a wall of tiredness to keep out this flood of feeling. Doubtless it was too late. In Bella's day there had been no bank of pebbles to contain the sea. The bulldozers had not yet come and the waters must have rushed inland whenever the tide ran high. Still I retained enough energy to fulfil my earlier promise. I closed the notebook, turned out the lamp and went to the bathroom. Then I climbed the stairs. Helen was still sleeping when I placed the notebook by her side. It was her right to read it. I had forgone my privacy and perhaps even Alison's, when I had brought her here. It was not enough, this token, yet I clung to a shred of hope that she might find a way of forgiving me.

I leant over Helen to kiss her and, as I did so, something brushed my hand. I started, thinking it was an insect, but it was no such thing. It lay on the bed, close to her hand. She must have been clutching it as she fell asleep: a wilted daisy chain. I picked it up, took it to the door to examine it. It was fairly fresh and long enough to encircle her wrist. One of the stems was broken. I couldn't understand why she had made it, still less why she had taken it to bed. Was it meant as a peace-offering, I wondered? Or was it nothing to do with me? Woven out of boredom and frustration?

Quietly I replaced it across her hand. I watched her, lying there, her hair near-transparent against the pillow-case. I caught a trace of some scent; fresh-cut grass. Then my eyes returned to her wrist, so thin and delicate and the small wilting chain across it. She looked like a kind of spirit child and I could barely imagine her awakening then. I began to remember her words, which she spoke out in the fields, before we even arrived here. I remembered the sky. 'Tell me a story, Harry.' We couldn't have guessed – impossible – where our journey would lead. What about our story, I thought. Should I tell you that? Would even that compel you to stay?

I left the room and as I did so a phrase came to mind, a line of poetry. Perhaps Alison's words had sparked it. It was from Donne. *A bracelet of bright hair about the bone.* The phrase seemed to come from nowhere. A lover, gone to the grave, her flesh rotted away but a love token intact upon her wrist.

It was inevitable, I suppose, after reading the notebook, that my thoughts should be so dark. I entered the spare room, knowing that I'd be unwelcome in Helen's bed. I stripped to my shorts and lay down.

The room was bare and bright. The moon shone through curtain-less windows, a chill, intrusive gaze. The pink walls irritated me. Like sleeping in a cold womb. Too many thoughts rushed through my mind and sleep eluded me. I was in awe at Alison's ambition, the complexity of her project. But mostly, I was hugely saddened at the despair I sensed in the notebook. I was trying to square it, the burgeoning creativity and the drive towards self-annihilation. True, there were no definite signs in the notebook that its author was suicidal. But the clues were there: the exhaustion; her fear of returning to London; her linking of home-life with lack of creativity; her conviction that she had let me down. As I lay shivering, I began to think that Alison had wanted to control her life the way she controlled the crustaceans in her child's bucket. This was at the heart of it, I thought, the struggle for control over a world that would not yield to it. What she could not take, I reasoned, was the everyday chaos. She was ready to address her fears but not to face them. She was in possession of eloquence but not strength. I had read, in the passage on Robert Higham's self-pity, something essential about herself. *He forgets that the monstrosity is hidden.* His stump, hidden beneath his sleeve, the Picasso beneath the Leonardo. I saw now what I had always missed. She was right. I had thought that I could deflect her terrors, that love was enough, but all I did was to encourage the veneer. The emptiness that she wrote of was unimaginable for me. I remembered making love to her, unpeeling the tissues of deception, discovering the anger inherent in her passion. I thought of Arabella, in her stays, before the carapace was removed. Semi-undressed, but something demure about it, still the façade. And afterwards she would spread her legs, the glaring red cunt, the chaos of sex where it all began.

Eventually I slept, a deep sleep; undisturbed. I heard nothing that night, not the flicker of a light switch in the adjacent room, nor Helen's footfall on the stairs, as she went to make herself tea. That was later, around four. Apparently she had looked in at me and closed the door. She was up until first light, reading the notebook. Then, glutted with Alison's words, she lay down again, and slept, but fitfully.

The next morning I was woken, again, by the sound of knocking. I was disorientated and cold; painfully aware of Helen's absence. I could hear voices too and engines running. I heard Helen stir, but leapt out of bed to stop her. I put my head around the door.

'Who is it, Harry?'

'I don't know. Don't worry. I'll sort it out. Stay in bed. You OK?'

She nodded, half-heartedly.

I returned to the spare room and looked out of the window. Finally they were here. I had always known it would happen. The press had caught up with us.

There was a whole posse of them. A group of men and one woman, clutching tape-recorders, microphones, cameras. Hake, however, was absent. I couldn't make out how they had all arrived at once but that was the least of my worries. My immediate reaction was anger, not that they were here – for I'd known, as soon as Hake arrived, that the rest, in turn, would follow – but that they had arrived before I was ready for them, before the tale was complete. I knew that I had to get to Ern before they did. I had to hear the rest of his story, not only about Bella but Alison too. There was still much I didn't know and I was damned if these bastards were going to stop me now. I had to outwit them. I had to keep a clear head.

'There he is!'

Their heads tilted up to the window. I was naked apart from my shorts but I didn't budge. I looked down at them disdainfully. One of the photographers seized the opportunity and zoomed in. I retreated into Helen's room, scrabbling in the wardrobe for some clothes.

'What's happening?' she said.

'The press. They're here. Seven or eight of them this time.'

'What do they want?'

'I don't know. Just stay here, love. It'll be all right.'

'I don't think so.'

'Really. I can handle them.'

I went downstairs, took a couple of deep breaths and prepared to face them. I needed to get them off my back for a few hours. I would have to throw them off track.

In the kitchen, I paused. I made them wait. Something about their presence reminded me that all this would soon be over. What was next was anybody's guess. Like Alison, I began to fear normality, the return to London. Unlike her, I envisaged a future, but I knew it would be a precarious one and I knew that no experience could rival my past with Alison, nor my present, here with Helen.

I closed my eyes. They had all been here, in this room, at this table: Charles, Bella, George, Alison. They seemed more real to me than the small crowd beyond the door. They had become a part of me. Whereas the people outside seemed mere phantoms. They had less substance, in my eyes, than those already dead. Our stories had kept the dead alive, given them form and depth. Outside I envisaged a mere rabble, a pack of hounds. I tried to remind myself that they too were human. They too had families, histories. But I could not truly see it. I could not justify their actions.

I opened the door. Nothing unexpected. Microphones beneath my nose, tape-recorders thrust in my face. Voices, impossible to differentiate.

'Mr Bliss, have you heard about this morning's events in Blakeney?'

'We understand that you've had dealings with the old man?'

'Have you heard what's happened, Harry?'

I recognised several of the reporters, but though they claimed intimacy, there was none. What I had not expected was their references to Ern. I was worried. I had been a fool to leave him.

'Look,' I said. 'I don't know what you're talking about.'

'But you do know the old man?'

'You mean Ern.'

'Ern, yes. The old hermit. His great-grandson says you've been visiting him.'

'Phil Bobbin?'

'Yes. You have met Ern?'

'Look – what's happened?'

'Did you know that he kept a gun?'

'Jesus. Just spit it out. Is he dead?'

'Him? No. He's a crazy man!'

'Has he threatened one of you?'

'Worse, Harry. A few of us were over there this morning. Gordon Hake was with us. He tried to talk to Ern. Ern came out with a rifle.' I could barely believe what I was hearing. 'There was a confrontation. The old man was acting like a lunatic. He shot Hake in the shoulder.'

'So he's alive?'

'He's in hospital. In a bad way. But he'll pull through, apparently.'

'Thank God.'

It was difficult to get a grasp on this. Peculiar to be relieved that Hake lived. For a moment I had believed the worst. But the truth was bad enough. Why had I left Ern alone the previous evening? I should have known he would do something stupid. I felt, as I continued to talk, a strange distance from these events, as if I watched myself from afar. Something surreal about the skewed justice of this.

'Where is Ern now?'

'He's barricaded himself in.'

'The police are there,' said another.

'Christ! I have to get over there.'

'He's a dangerous man, Harry.'

'He's harmless.'

'He was raving like a lunatic! He tried to kill Gordon Hake!'

'If he'd wanted to kill him, he would have done it,' I said.

I shut the door in their faces, furious. Helen was downstairs now. She'd clearly heard every word. She touched my arm.

'I'm to blame for this,' I said.

'No.'

'Ern was petrified of the press. I shouldn't have come here.'

'They would have found him anyway, Harry. Vinton's material would have been leaked whether you were here or not.'

'We've got to get over there.'

'We?'

'You do want to come?'

She nodded. For the time being there was a truce. It had seemed only natural that she would come, but even as I suggested it, I began to doubt the idea. After all, there was more than one story. The press knew about our relationship. Why else would they have been here this morning? They had clearly come seeking more information about Helen, about Vinton's notebook extract. But they had got more than they bargained for.

'I don't care, Harry – about the reporters. It's out in the open now. Hake made sure of that.'

'You know what it means?'

'I'll be infamous as you, right?'

'Something like that.'

'Fuck it. I don't care.'

'Last night . . .'

'I don't want to talk about it,' she said.

'If you say so.'

'Poor Ern.'


We left together, close but not touching. I had brought the notebook, for fear it might be stolen. I'd warned Helen how to behave – walk quickly; don't make eye-contact; don't betray emotion; don't speak. It was difficult for her. The photographers hung back, but their zooms were on her face. The reporters came closer.

'Do you have any comment to make about the shooting, Harry?'

'Are you aware of the papers in Paul Vinton's possession? I've heard the old man was involved.'

'Why are you staying in Alison's cottage?'

They gave us no space. The woman, in particular, kept close to

Helen. She was well-groomed, conventionally attractive with soft blonde hair and flawless make-up.

'Look,' she said, 'don't feel you have to say anything to these people.'

I couldn't see what she was getting at. The others were firing questions, but she talked in an almost pally voice. As we reached the car, the others gave up, but she remained with Helen. I was on the driver's side and we were briefly parted.

'The thing is, Helen,' she said, 'it's easier to talk one to one.'

'Why should I talk to you?'

I gestured to Helen to get in the car, but for some reason she hesitated.

'We're talking a substantial amount of money for an exclusive. You might want to consider it. There's no need to decide now. Here's my card. It's got my mobile number. The public are going to want to know your side of things.'

'Get lost.'

'Like I said, think it over.'

But the intrusion was too much. Helen's face crumpled and a photographer caught her despair.

'I mean what do they want me to say?' she said. 'Shall I tell them that we had sex in the graveyard? Maybe that's what they want.'

I started the car. 'I'm so sorry.' She didn't reply. 'Perhaps you wish you'd never come?'

'No! I just wish you'd involved me.'

'I know. I know that.'

'You're worried about Ern, aren't you?' she said.

I nodded. 'I think we'll be too late.'

After that, we fell silent. Both of us were fretting: about Ern; about Hake; about 'us' and the story that was about to be cut short. I didn't know then that Helen had read the notebook. But I knew that something had changed. There was no trust remaining. Helen told me, later, that she was thinking about Judith, imagining I'd been with her the previous evening. I was equally suspicious. What had happened in the pub? Who had she seen or spoken to?

As we approached the cottage, I told Helen about my evening with Ern. I told her about the boat, about his fall and what he had revealed about Bella. She seemed almost uninterested. I imagined that she was in shock at the shooting. But I also thought that the story no longer mattered to her, when in truth it mattered immensely. Simply, she was one step ahead of me. She had finished reading the notebook. The news about Bella was no news and she didn't have the energy to pretend that it was.

The flashing lights were visible from the roadside. It was still early. The mist over the landscape had not yet dispersed and the blue lights seemed unreal. There was something of the film-set about the scene; a hint at closure. Finally the outside world had broken in upon the idyll. The air was cold, the light hazy, the police cars oddly silent. I could barely believe that this was happening, that Ern had become a criminal. It seemed, as I approached, as if everything had been stilled. There were brief moments, between flashes, when one might believe that nothing had changed, that the house was simply sleeping. But then the flash again. And again, gone.

I got out of the car. Helen remained inside. There were two police cars and an ambulance. A couple of officers were hanging around, speaking into walkie-talkies. One of them held a loud-hailer which hung limply at his wrist. A few reporters were also lingering and those that had visited the cottage pulled up behind us. I approached a young officer, a new recruit perhaps, who seemed at a loss.

'What's with the ambulance? Isn't Hake in hospital already?'

He glimpsed at me and nodded.

'Is the old man all right?' I asked.

'You're that Bliss fella, right?'

Clearly he was a local man.

'Yes.'

'I'd keep well back if I were you, sir. There's no telling what he'll do.'

'He's still in there then? Alive?'

'There ain't been no accidents yet. But you'd better be keeping back.'

'I don't think I'm in any danger.'

'Tha's what they thought this morning.'

'I've heard. What are you going to do?'

'They be going in shortly. He ain't been listening to a word they've been saying.'

'Has he responded at all?'

'Nothing. Absolutely nothing.'

'Why the hesitation?'

'This wouldn't have happened if that scum hadn't come here in the first place.' He gestured to the reporters, but I guessed that I was also implicated. 'There ain't none of these fellas that want to arrest Ern Higham. Even them as don't know him. He's an honest Norfolk man.'

'Is that the official view?'

The young officer grimaced.

'We have to do our job, see? But we don't want no mistakes.'

'Mistakes?'

'Who knows what a mad old fella like that might do?'

'I see.' I paused. 'Perhaps I can help.'

'I don't see how.'

'I'm a friend. Of sorts. He might let me in.'

He shook his head.

'I don't think so.'

'No. Really. Let me try.'

The officer remained sceptical but agreed to put my idea to his superiors. I suspected that I'd be refused, but I was wrong. Several of the officers knew of Ern and they were convinced he had only acted from extreme provocation. Nobody, it seemed, was keen to make a forced entry. They would not, naturally, agree to Helen coming with me. When I told her, she leapt out of the car and made her way to the officer in charge, pursued by several reporters.

'What do you mean I can't go in? Are you going to physically stop me?'

'If necessary, Miss.'

'You'll let him in, but not me, right?'

'Please, Miss. I'd advise you to calm down. You're obstructing our business.'

'Harry?'

Her look demanded action, but I didn't know what I could do. I could hardly believe that they were letting me in. What mattered most was that I should speak to Ern.

'I don't know why you brought me here,' Helen said. She turned to the journalists. 'Look, piss off, will you?' But none of them budged and again she addressed me. 'My face will be plastered all over the papers tomorrow. And what's the point? You don't want me to be a part of this.'

I took her aside. The officers seemed embarrassed. Even the reporters appeared reluctant to follow, though the photographer didn't miss the opportunity. I took her hand but she pulled back.

'Please,' I said. 'There's nothing I can do about this. What choice do I have?'

'You could walk away. Forget it. We could go back to London. Together.'

'Is that what you want?'

She shook her head.

'Just go. Just go, Harry.'


The garden was still damp; the dew had not yet evaporated. It must have been around dawn when Hake had knocked on Ern's door. The 'paper-men' had finally come for him, disturbing his sleep. Now they were being kept back by the police and I was alone. I bent at the letter box and shouted.

'Ern? Are you there? It's Harry.'

There was no reply.

'Ern? Please. Let me in. Are you all right?'

Again nothing. I decided to take a look around the back. One of the officers followed me at a distance.

I banged on the window and continued to call. The curtains were closed but I saw a slight movement behind them and I approached. When his face appeared, I was shocked. He looked so pale and wasted, a yellow pallor. It seemed as if his flesh had shrunk, clung tighter to his bones, so that his face was less real, more mask-like. The fresh scab on his right cheek stood out. It seemed impossible that such a face could bleed.

Suddenly, he withdrew. I banged again on the glass but before long heard the creak of a second window, further along. Another curtain was pulled aside. He spoke to me through the gap.

'What are you wanting, boy?'

Something about his voice didn't seem right.

'Are you going to let me in? We have to talk.'

'What good's talk?'

'There are still things I don't know.'

'A man learns to accept it, see?'

'You can't stay in there on your own for long.'

'I've been alone long before you came along, lad.'

'Have you looked outside your front door?'

'Aye. The coppers. They won't touch me.'

'They'll have no choice.'

'Pah!'

'Please. Will you unlock the door?'

'Climb in the window if you must. I ain't unlocking that door for no man.'

'OK,' I said. 'Fine.'

The opening was narrow, but I managed to clamber through. The officer watched me. Soon I was inside. In my panic I had almost forgotten what it was like here. I understood now why Ern felt so inviolable. The room was like a capsule; detached from the outside world. With the curtains drawn and gas lamps burning, it was impossible to believe the scene outside. The only natural light came from the window but within seconds Ern tugged it shut and fastened a bolt. He drew the curtain and we were enclosed.

'Sit down. I ain't moved your chair,' he barked.

I did as he asked. I felt a strange relief, being here. I drew comfort from Ern's presence and the objects about me: the books, the nets, the crockery, even the guns. Briefly I forgot my purpose; indulged myself. I glanced at the photographs on his wall and knew I was in the company of familiars.

Ern sat down opposite me. He sat straight in his chair, chin thrust forwards. But he could not fool me. Now I could not look at him without thinking of the child he was: Bella's son. I couldn't get it out of my mind. She killed herself when he was just a baby. Before he could speak or move alone.

'Well? What are you wanting?'

'I want to help you out of this situation.'

'Don't prattle. There's no use trying to save me.'

'What do you mean?'

He merely laughed then said, 'What is it you're really after?'

'Why did you do it, Ern? Why did you shoot the man?'

'I saw him off, didn't I? Man had it coming to him. You know that.'

'You can't justify what you did.'

'Say what you came to say, boy. It's not the shooting that concerns you.'

'I told the police I'd talk to you. Get you to open the door.'

'You had to tell them something. Now stop wasting my time.'

'Do you want me to go?'

'No, lad. I want you to speak your heart.'

I huffed. It wasn't like him to be sentimental. Nor was I certain I could speak truths to him. But he was right. I wanted more from him, even now.

'I still want to know what happened to Alison; why she followed Bella.'

'Ain't you read the book I gave you? That man I shot. He wanted to see it all right. He knows I've found him out.'

'What are you talking about? I haven't finished reading it.'

'Hah! And he claims he loves the woman.'

'Loved,' I said. 'How can one love the dead?'

'If it ain't a thing you know already . . .'

'If you won't tell me about Alison, tell me about George.'

Ern shook his head. 'He was no brother of mine, that's for sure.'

'But you were told he was your brother?'

'Aye. But what brother would put a serpent in a babe's bed, boy, tell me that?'

'Jesus Christ.'

'He was glad my mother died. He willed it.'

'Wait – you're serious about the serpent? A live snake?'

'He'd just returned from the University. He put an adder in my crib. It was after Bella had gone. She weren't there to watch over me.'

'Did it bite you?'

'No, boy. It slept beside me. When Bliss came into the room, he found me stroking it.'

'A lucky escape.'

'Not *so* lucky, boy.'

I ignored his comment, perhaps not wanting to analyse it.

'What did you mean before? You said George willed Bella's death.'

'Bella and my father in this cottage, see? In this room, stripped naked.'

I thought that he was rambling, wished that he would come to the point.

'I was here too; wrapped in swaddling, in a basket. And they coupling. Aye. I remember.'

'You can't possibly.'

'George saw it, though. George followed my mother.'

'He saw them together?'

'He had heard talk; wanted to know if it were true. Him stood watching at the window. Something dark and strange, boy. A secret thing, a dark bloom. Only George saw nothing but the bodies, the bare flesh.'

'What did he do?'

'He walked home. It were a hot day, my father said. The land were parched. But George walked back across the marshes. He had seen what he came to see and was glad of it.'

'Glad?'

'For years my mother nurtured him, but he could not love her. Now he had his reason. She weren't worthy of his father. He saw the plain sin afore his eyes.'

'And when she returned home, what happened?'

'She carried me home in a bundle. She sheltered my head beneath a shade, and stopped to rest on a stile while she fed me from her breast. When she got home, she wanted nothing more than a cup of water. She was weak, see, not just from the heat. She was thinking of my father; could still feel his hand on her. She wanted to lie alone in a cool room; wanted her babe to sleep so that she could recall him: his hand, his skin.'

'But George? What did George do?'

'George waited for her, in the porch. She knew, when she saw him, something was wrong. He blocked her path and looked strangely. "George," she said, "Whatever is the matter? Has something happened?" First he said nothing. Couldn't bring himself to say the words. "What is it?" He made her wait a little longer, wanted to prolong her suffering. Then he spoke: "You are a whore, Mother," he said. He had been taught to call her Mother though he never forgot that she was no kin. That was your grandfather, boy. Are you not ashamed? He called my mother a whore when it were Charles Bliss that drove her to it, when her only sin was to love a man.'

'I can't help my blood. I can't be responsible for his actions.'

'He was evil. He left the mark of his hand across her cheek, though she held her babe in her arms. She fell hard, cracking her hip against the path. Her elbow jammed the earth, boy, as she cradled my head to protect me. "It's not true," she cried. "What they say, it's not true." He kicked her in the ribs. "I saw you with that boatman! Naked in his arms!" '

'How do you know this, Ern?'

'My father heard it from her lips, what he did to her. She begged him – lain there on the path, clutching me, a screaming infant. "Do not tell your father this. I pray you. It will injure him." "What? To know he has provided for your bastard." "I swear it is his son." "Liar!" "George, I cannot believe that you so hate me. Why have you no pity? Your father does not love me. He loves only the memory of your mother. Yet I have tried to be a mother to you." "But you have failed," he said. "I cannot call you 'Mother' now." '

'Where was Charles Bliss, Ern? While this took place?'

I believed his tale; was still reeling from its impact, yet I knew some details must be invented. It was as if, in remembering the tales that his father had told him, he had embellished them and made them whole. He had imagined the scene so many times, perhaps, that now he had forgotten what was fact and what fiction.

'Bliss?' he said. 'He was in his glasshouse, tending orchids.'

'Did he not come to her aid?'

'He heard nothing. George walked into the garden and she called after him. "Tell me, George, what will you do?" He turned. "I won't tell him today," he said. "Perhaps tomorrow? I can't say." '

'My father told me none of this,' I said. 'Perhaps he didn't know.'

'No doubt George told him falsehoods. What man would tell his son he drove a woman to her death?'

At this we were interrupted by a loud noise, a heavy knocking. 'Shit.'

'Leave'm be, boy. They won't break that door.'

'It's not a good idea. I'll have to tell them something.'

'Are you afraid?'

'No. But I want to stall them.'

'Be it as you will.'

I left the room and walked along the corridor. Ern had somehow managed to push a wooden chest in front of the door. I tried to shift it, but it wouldn't budge. It didn't seem possible. It would take a colossal effort for me to move that chest, but somehow Ern had done it. True, I ought not to have been surprised. Had I not witnessed him, only the previous evening, doggedly dragging a row-boat across the marshes?

The knocking did not abate.

'What do you want?' I shouted.

'Mr Bliss?'

'Yes.'

'Will you open this door?'

The officer, also, was shouting to be heard. It was a ridiculous way to hold a conversation.

'I can't.'

'Why not?'

'There's a huge chest blocking it. I can't shift it.'

'Can't be so heavy if the old man put it there.'

'Look – give me a chance. Ern's not ready.'

'Are you getting anywhere?'

'Yes.' I hesitated.

'So you'll be bringing him out shortly?'

'Please. Be patient. It's tricky. You'll have to wait a bit longer.'

'We can't wait all day.'

'It won't take all day. I have it under control.'

'You're sure?'

My voice was tired from shouting. I was afraid, if I said the wrong thing, they might indeed lose patience. I had to convince them to remain put.

'Look, as you know, the man has a gun. He's not threatening me, but if you come in at the wrong time, I can't be held responsible for his actions. Give me more time. He's coming round. He knows there's no way out.'

There was a brief pause. Then the voice again.

'All right. You win. Half an hour. We can't wait longer than that.'

As I walked back along the corridor, I envisaged the scene that would soon take place. I wouldn't be able to stall again. Eventually they'd force their way in. I imagined Ern, handcuffed, bundled in the back of a police car. I could see his face already, the grim hopelessness of it, staring out at me as the car pulled away. I imagined his hand, touching the glass. I guessed he would go quietly. He would be broken by this. I saw him turn and watch me as the car vanished. Did I feel accused? Was I responsible for this?

I was anxious to hear the rest of Ern's story. I wanted to press him again about Alison. I could not believe that all I needed to know was contained within the final pages of her notebook. And what did he mean, about finding Hake out? I could barely believe my own failure the previous night to continue reading. Had I been so dog-tired that I could not even flick ahead to discover the secret I had waited for so long to be revealed? Possibly there was a part of me that didn't want to know the truth. Perhaps I was aware that once I was in possession of it, there would be no place else for me to go.

What I had told the police officer, about the gun, had been pure fabrication. But now, as I re-entered the room, I started. Ern had a gun wedged between his legs. The barrel touched his forehead, just above his right eye. He was fiddling with the trigger. I stopped, terrified. My instinct was to shout but I held back, realising that the shock of it might cause him to shoot. I don't know how long I stood there, probably no more than a few seconds, thought it seemed as if time was extended, as if the moment were of infinite length. Then Ern turned and smiled. There was something about him; some ill intent.

'Ern?'

'It were merely a book. That were all.'

He spat the words out.

'What are you talking about? The notebook you gave me?'

'I gave you nothing.'

'Alison's notebook.'

'I did not deserve that punishment,' he said.

'I don't understand.'

'What you did to me!'

'I've done nothing to you.'

'You know what you did! Why do you deny it?'

I could not believe my ill fortune. I had a half hour left before the police would burst in, a half hour in which to pick his brain, uncover his remaining secrets. Afterwards, there would be only this, the memory of this room, his presence. I had thought that he would tell a rounded tale, that in realising the urgency of our situation, he would reveal all. Instead, he talked apparent nonsense.

'Please,' I said. 'Ern, put that gun down.'

'It has a faulty trigger,' he said.

'All the more reason to put it down.'

'I'm not a child, see?'

'No. I'm aware of that.'

'But you remember what you did?'

'No. I remember nothing.'

'You locked me away! You have not forgotten.'

'Who do you think I am, Ern? Your father?'

Again, time had slipped through his fingers. He did not know who I was, nor Alison.

'You were no father to me.'

I took a calculated risk. 'Why not? What did I do?'

'You found out you were not my father, yet you kept me with you. After my mother's death, you would not let me go.'

'Do you know why I kept you?'

'Hah! You admit it!' he said. 'You kept me as a trophy.'

'A trophy?'

'Aye. To punish my mother for her sins, her fornication.'

'How could I punish her by keeping you?'

'You knew what she would have desired. That I be with my real father. That I be happy.'

'But you were not happy.'

'You know I was not.'

'But why?'

'You did not know the land! I had the land in my blood but you denied it. Your garden was your child. Those orchids! Blasted orchids! There was nothing real about 'em. They might have been made of wax! Outside, in the lanes, beneath the hedgerows – did you not see the wildflowers? The celandine? Anemones?'

'I could not help my interests.'

'No. But you did not involve me.'

'Did you want to be involved?'

'Aye. Why else did I take the book?'

'Which book?'

'You deny you know?'

'My memory fails me.'

'The book in which your head was always buried. Mr Darwin's book! About the orchids!'

'Ah, yes. I remember now.'

'Stain on the carpet.'

'What? What stain?'

'You were ashamed of me. You locked me up.'

'Why? For stealing the book?'

'I did not steal the book. I wanted to look at it, see? But I never even got to open it. I climbed down the ladder, clutching it, but you were behind me, as if you had been waiting for such a sin. That look were enough. I had never been so afeared. You had a scattering of pollen in your hair. A bee was circling your head; you kept flicking it away. "How did that bee get into the library?" I said nothing. "Because you left the door open, Ernest. You left the door open!" '

'So it was for that that I punished you? The open door?'

Ern laughed.

'You know it was not that!'

'What then?'

'For the book. And because of what I did. You said I was filthy.'

'Filthy?'

'I pissed myself, didn't I? Little Ernest pissed himself. On the Turkey carpet! A bed of roses at my feet. Roses were sodden now. They might never recover, you said. Did I know the cost of a Turkey carpet? As for the book, you snatched it. "That is a first edition, Ernest! Do you know what that is?" You called for the maid, ordered her to clean the carpet at once.'

'And then?'

'You dragged me by the collar across the hallway – flung me in the broom cupboard. "Don't move from there, boy. Now Sissy," he said to the maid, "take what you need for your task. This cupboard will not be opened until an hour has passed. Let him stew in his urine! Perhaps he will not be so eager in future to enter my library. And perhaps he will learn to hold his bladder!" Then you found a piece of string, tied my wrists to a beam so I could not bang upon the door. Only you left my fingers free, see? So I could count. It were more than an hour you left me there. I counted sixty times sixty but still you did not come.'

'How long did I leave you?'

'Longer than three hours and I in blackness. I thought you might let me die there. But though I were visited by demons, I did not stop counting.'

Briefly, I fell silent. What could I say to this? Nothing could compensate Ern for his disastrous childhood. If he needed someone to blame, perhaps that was all to the good. Though I was innocent of his accusations, still I felt the weight of them. He believed me culpable and his belief was almost infectious. I couldn't see how the mood might be broken; how I might pull him back to the present. But this was my desire. The past was too bleak; the tragedy too potent. In the end, I went for the direct approach.

'Ern – for how long did you remain with Charles Bliss? How did you come to inherit your father's cottage?'

'Until his death, boy. I stayed with Bliss until his death.'

I could hardly believe it had been so simple. On ceasing my role-play, he quickly slipped back to the present. I challenged him.

'Who am I, Ern?'

He laughed.

'Do you not know that?'

I said nothing.

'You are Harold Bliss, a poor soul who cannot help his history.'

'A few moments ago, you believed I was my ancestor; your step-father.'

'You are he too, see? Just as I am Ern and Ernest. And Alison was Bella too.'

'Alison? You remember my wife?'

'Your wife. My mother.'

His voice now seemed weaker than ever, as if he had lost the will to disguise his lack of strength.

'But she was not your mother. And I am not Charles Bliss.'

'I could swear you said you were,' Ern said.

'I humoured you. That's all.'

'And I you, lad. I, you.'

His admission stunned me. Yet was it true? Was he suggesting that there was not a shred of madness in him? That in fact he was saner than I, and, far from being a rambling old man, he was instead the brilliant trickster I had at first suspected him to be?

I wondered where we might go from here. Throughout our

321

conversation, Ern had continued to fiddle with the gun, but I had grown used to it. We were short of time. Was it too late to act correctly? To encourage Ern to hand himself in? True, two tales remained unfinished, but was it possible now that they might be concluded? My conscience was torn between my own desire and what was best for Ern. The shock of an invasion might do him harm. This room ought not to be violated. Perhaps I should let go. I would always be wanting more. In that respect, I was no different from the reporters who lingered outside. We were hungry beasts, all of us. Nothing would satisfy our greed.

'Maybe you should put that gun down,' I said.

He laughed, a small, defeated laughter.

'I shot him down, didn't I?' he said. 'I'd do it again. Shoot those paper-men down like birds. They're fair prey, I reckon. Only the carcasses would have no worth, see? Too tough to eat; too ugly to stuff.'

'They're only human, Ern. People doing a job.'

But I knew, already, that I spoke a half-truth. The pursuit of Alison had been more than a job for Hake. It had gone beyond that, long ago.

'What kind of job is that?' Ern said. 'It ain't no honest job. What do you reckon? Should I open my doors to the lot of them? Loose my ghosts?'

'I didn't say that. But your gun is no solution.'

'Ha! If you had the spirit you'd shoot 'em down yourself.'

'You think so?'

Already, I regretted agitating him. His voice worried me. Something had gone from it. His strength was clearly failing him. The voice was hoarse. Some crackling tone about it, like a scratched gramophone recording. As if he couldn't pretend any longer.

'Aye. You see them for what they are, lad. A string of paper dolls, see? All the same.'

'If they were paper dolls, you wouldn't be so afraid.'

He snorted.

'Look,' I said. 'I'm on your side. But you're wrong to think I'd take a gun to them.'

'A city boy to the last, eh?'

I smiled grimly.

'Those people destroyed you,' he said.

'What would you know of that?'

At this he stood up, using the rifle as support. It was an awesome sight, yet achingly pathetic, to see this thin ghoul of a man rise up and cross the room. He reached to a shelf above his desk where a row of keys were hanging and took one which hung alone on the far right and a second which he pocketed. I caught my breath. I watched as he unlocked a desk drawer, followed him so that I could peer over his shoulder. He opened it, and immediately I caught sight of myself. It was a newspaper clipping, one I didn't recognise. He handed it to me, but I barely looked at it. Instead I was looking at what lay beneath. Reams and reams of cuttings.

'What is this?' I said.

'Take a look.'

I lay down the piece he'd given me and flicked through the top of his pile. It was a familiar collection. I had an identical one at home.

'These are about me. And Alison.'

'Aye. I know what they did to you, boy. That Hake in particular. And to her.'

I was flabbergasted. My perceptions of Ern were shattered. I had thought he was removed from society; set apart. But here was evidence that he scanned newspapers as I did, read each word that was written about my life. Perhaps he knew more of the world beyond his cottage than I imagined.

'Who brings you these?' I asked.

Now I dug down to the bottom of the pile, pulled out a few from underneath. These also were the first in my collection, beginning with the discovery of Alison's body. He had been at it for years.

'Ellen gets 'em.'

'Ellen?'

'Aye. My granddaughter.'

'Mrs Bobbin.'

'Aye, she married that Bobbin fellow.'

'Does she bring you the cuttings?'

He laughed inaudibly.

'I wouldn't be trusting her with that, the vixen. No, she brings me the papers, with my groceries, and I cut 'em, see? I read 'em and see what's in store for me.'

'You've been waiting for them then? Your "paper-men"?'

'I been waiting and now they've come.'

'Why don't you trust her?'

'It's her fault. All of this.'

He picked up a handful of clippings, ran them through his fingers.

'What are you getting at?'

He shook his head, turned and headed for the door. This is it, I thought: he's giving himself up. He was heaving for breath and I figured that he needed a doctor. I followed him into the hallway past the case of taxidermy. But then he stopped. He dug in his pocket and found the other key. There was a door to his left. He unlocked it.

'Something to show you,' he said.

I went before him, uncertain what to expect. As he opened the door, I clutched the frame, needing some tangible reassurance. This room, also, was full of collectibles, objects grouped according to type. I scanned the room, taking it in. Here was the proof of passing time. These objects, reminders of mortality. Ern pushed me in the small of the back, urging me to enter. He came behind me and closed the door.

'Best kept out of sight, eh?' he said.

There, at the far wall, on rows of shelves and tables, were at least thirty clocks, each of them stilled, stopped dead at various times. There was a huge grandfather with a rusting pendulum; several wall-mounted ornamental clocks, adorned with birds and foliage; a cuckoo clock with the cuckoo poised mid-air. There was a carriage clock; a couple of modern alarm clocks; a heavy faced mantel-clock. At the centre of the arrangement was a large hour-glass, laden with dust. It was a plain contraption made of dark wood, yet what was striking was the fact that this too appeared to show a hiatus in time. The pearl-blue sand that should have rested in the bottom glass was stuck in the funnel. Half the sand had run through, the other half remained above. It was a wonderful *coup de théâtre*.

These time-pieces occupied only a small section of the room. On other shelves and tables were further proofs of Ern's obsession. I had thought that he tried to obliterate the passing of time, but it was not so simple. Rather, he shut it away, kept it separate. As if he sometimes liked to remind himself of the passing years. As if each object had some personal significance, could return him to a certain point in his existence. Also in this room were calendars of various descriptions and there was a table to my left where watches were displayed: a brass fob-watch; a gold-braceleted lady's; a leather-strapped man's, half-covered with mud.

I traversed the room in a daze, trying hopelessly to take it all in. I have not yet mentioned the radios: a gorgeous beech forties model; several transistors; remarkably, even a Walkman. 'The wirelesses,' Ern muttered. 'Phil brought me that one.' Still I have not done justice to the contents of that room, nor the effect it had on me. There were the chairs, of course, reminders perhaps that other visitors once graced this cottage. In the far corner were cardboard boxes, overflowing with yellowing newspapers. These were not so striking, however, nor so imposing as those which littered the floor. It was near-impossible to move in the room because piles of newspapers dominated, tumbling into the pathways which Ern had attempted to create. It appeared that he had not destroyed a single one since he had begun taking cuttings after Alison's death, though I must surely have been mistaken on that point, else we would not have been able to move at all. The world and its faces leered up at me. Ern's face, too, was unavoidable.

Here, in this room, he had also grouped his mirrors. They adorned the walls: mirrors of all tastes, sizes and descriptions. Wherever I looked I saw Ern reflected, his jubilant, almost childish rhapsody. Beside it, bewildered, exhausted, I saw myself: doubled; echoed; fragmented. I saw the back of my head several times over. I saw my face, as Alison must have seen hers here, broken, distorted. Like a Picasso, I thought. This is what she meant. Yes, *Les Demoiselles*. Now I recalled Ern's words: 'You are Harold Bliss, a poor soul who cannot help his history.' Was it really so simple? Which of these reflections, if any, were true? How to find the line that divided the images from my self? If it was difficult for me, who had always felt himself to be an ordinary fellow, how must it have been for Alison, who knew the extent of her own complexity, who knew her gift and how it set her apart? Suddenly, perhaps in an attempt to distract myself, I found myself thinking of Picasso's collaboration with Braque, their endless montages: guitars, bottles, newspapers, the same objects portrayed over and again. I was thinking about the necks of the guitars, the keys, the strings. I had always dismissed the images, yet now they seemed incredibly potent. I remembered an argument with Richard, when I owned up to my lack of connection to these paintings. Now I understood his admiration. I saw two faces, Ern's and my own, like hallucinations. Yet they were distractions from the main object: the gun. Ern swung it like a toy, cackling like an old goat. The neck of the gun, not solid; broken. And the muzzle, the barrel, the trigger.

'What do you make of it, boy?' Ern asked.

His every face spoke to me.

'I think you're a cunning devil.'

'Time kept under lock and key, eh? Ha ha!'

'But why?'

'See that hour-glass? That sand stopped dead on the morning my mother killed herself.'

I was hugely irritated by this. I didn't want to hear such myths. I wanted truths, plain truths.

'Hold that gun still,' I said. 'Don't wave it about!'

His voice suggested his profound exhaustion; he winced with each sharp turn. But he would not be still.

'She had unravelled it all,' he said.

'What are you talking about?'

'But Ellen ruined it. Ellen ruined our little plan.'

'Your plan?'

'The book, see? Alison's book.'

'The notebook?'

'No. The other one.'

'The novel?'

'Aye.'

Now I was interested.

'What about it?'

'So many hours we spent. I told it all.' He paused. 'See this?' He stabbed his chest with his index finger. 'This is what I gave her. My heart, see? She too had lost a mother. She knew the absence. But it was for nothing that I spoke to her.'

'Because of what she did?'

'No. I ain't speaking of her death, lad. The book. The book should have spoken.'

'Exactly. That's what I meant. Because she burnt it. But why? It still doesn't make sense to me. It makes her suicide all the blacker because the story that led her to it has also been obliterated. And by her own hand.'

Once more, he laughed, a wild, despairing laughter. I thought that he had finally lost it. Why else would he laugh at the greatest tragedy of all?

'It was not her hand that did it!' he said.

I was immediately defensive.

'Hang on! I thought we were in agreement? You said that you believed me; that you knew it wasn't me?'

'Aye. Not you neither.'

Then it dawned on me.

'You? You burnt the manuscript? You said she did it.'

He shook his head. Such a look crossed his features, of fury and bitterness. His face and throat contracted, his lips pursed as if he could hardly bear to say the words. When he did speak, it was near-inaudible.

'Ellen, boy. Ellen.'

If any words might stop clocks, these surely were them. A silence descended. I did not at first take it in. Ellen? Mrs Bobbin. It made no sense. What motive did she have for this? I could make no connection between the woman and her act. I turned to Ern, about to speak. But something was not right. Some sound had broken the silence; a ghastly rattling. I looked behind me, before I realised it came from Ern's throat. His mouth appeared to droop; his face had turned the colour of putty. I watched as he went limp and keeled over. The gun dropped to the floor, his arm flailed briefly as he tried to grab some purchase. But there was none. His head smashed against the corner of a table, dislodging the hour-glass which hit the ground just before his head. The glass split open. The blue sand spilled with a quiet hiss, a skittering. Then his head smashed on the bare stone. The grey unyielding face; grains of sand; speckles of glass. I remember these and the thin trail of blood that was released from his skull. I had no need to approach him. It was a dead man's face.

I picked up the gun. I did not think. I hauled it above my head and brought it down hard upon the nearest mirror which shattered to smithereens. Then I repeated the action, watching my face dissolve into a million pieces. I lurched from the room, trying to clutch some hint of sanity, but in the dark hallway, all I could see was the case of taxidermy, those blasted dead birds. I stumbled towards them, cursing, and broke the glass case. I poked the birds with the muzzle, clobbered them, dislodged them. I managed to impale the heron and then I dropped the gun. But I was still in there with my bare hands, pulling the bastards out, the ducks, the song-birds, the gulls. I smashed them against the floor. Then I heard a thud. And a voice.

'This is the last time. We're coming in.'

Another thud. They were ramming the door. I came to my senses.

'Hang on,' I said. 'I didn't hear you.'

Now the chest moved easily. My aggression was channelled into shifting it. I felt like the man who lifts a car after a road accident. The chest slid from the door as if on castors.

'About bloody time!' the officer said.

He was a thick-set, bearded man, shorter than me, something of the Neanderthal about him: the hunched shoulders, jutting chin.

'It's too late,' I said.

He barged past me. Then he halted.

'What the hell . . .?

He had seen the carnage; smelt it. Now I was aware of it too. It was under my fingernails: the dank, mouldering odour, something surgical about it, but underneath an earthy scent; the visceral stink of ancient plumage.

'What's been going on in here?'

A couple of side-kicks elbowed their way in: the younger man whom I'd spoken to earlier and a third, smirking, with a military meanness about his eyes.

'He's in there,' I gestured. 'He just collapsed.'

Already I was distracted from them. I turned. Beyond the door, beyond the red-and-white tape which now cordoned off the cottage, standing alone, was Helen. She was some distance away but I was drawn to her. The reporters and photographers, and a few local observers were closer, shuffling forward to get the best view. Only Helen stood back, apart, on a raised grass verge. She was wearing a white dress of Alison's that skimmed her ankles. A slight, lonely figure, the morning sun behind her. She simply looked at me and did not move.

'He's dead! Christ Almighty, look at this!'

The words seemed to come from some distant place, somewhere I couldn't reach. I stood in the corridor, motionless as Helen. There was something comforting in this shade. It numbed me. The sun outside was too bright, too insistent. I could not bear such brilliance now. Everything seemed unfamiliar, even the figure who now approached Helen and placed his hand on her shoulder. If I were to go outside, I felt I might be pierced by the light. Surely it was best to avoid it. Wearily I closed my eyes.

# 33

W HAT HAPPENED NEXT IS a vague jumble of events. It is not something I can easily piece together or make much sense of; a time that seems somehow removed, a kind of aberration. The memories I have are intense but much is forgotten and I hesitate to order what happened because I was hardly aware of the world about me. What I know is an amalgam of memory and written fact, though when I read the newspapers from that time, I admit I barely recognise myself, or the others who played their parts alongside me. In the eyes of the world, we were mere ciphers, ripe for the projection of others' dreams.

This is what I know. I was removed from the house by an officer. Ern remained where he fell, awaiting the coroner. I was accompanied to a police car, required to answer questions at the station. The light outside remained brilliant; the people waiting, still unreal: flat and insubstantial. I squinted, half wishing the apparitions would vanish. Their bleached-out forms crowded in on me.

As I emerged from the house, I had seen Helen. The figure at her side appeared to embrace her, but she pulled away and ran in my direction. A tall, thin man. Richard? It didn't look like Richard. Now, as the journalists pressed about me, I heard her call, but I couldn't see her; she couldn't reach me. There were others, also, who held back from the fray. I saw them watching from the middle-distance. Judith was there. And one other. Ellen Bobbin. They were in conversation. I tried to pull away; wanted to get my hands on that woman. If the reports are to be believed, I began to shout obscenities, but I don't remember that. I remember my murderous thoughts but not my actions. And all the while, Helen's voice, calling.

I saw that woman's face as the car drew away. She looked at me, a cool blank stare, as if nothing lay behind it, no shred of remorse nor pity. Her grandfather was dead and perhaps she blamed me. But I saw the fault etched on her face, knew that her actions had culminated in this moment.

After that, the picture is more hazy. Removed from the scene, I was removed also from myself. I did not speak in the car, nor was I required to. I was not under arrest. Perhaps it seemed pretty clear to them. Ern had gone on some mad, destructive rampage and the effort involved had killed him. Except, perhaps, there were some lingering doubts. There must be a chance it had happened otherwise: that in admitting me to Ern's presence, they had unwittingly delivered his early death.

The Neanderthal had remained behind, to admit the coroner and the forensics. Until their report was in, my guilt was in the balance. I barely cared. I held in my pocket all that I now required: Alison's notebook. With Ern dead, what other enlightenment might I find?

When I think back to that time, I realise now it is the external happenings that escape me. The substance of my thoughts is clearer, though I confess, even there, certain moments seem to have vanished entirely, even the workings of my own mind are lost to me. I remember barely anything about the police station. There was a lot of waiting, and, inevitably, a statement was taken. I confessed to the destruction of property. It occurred to me to lie, crossed my mind that my fingerprints on the rifle might be explained by a tussle to remove it, but something about such a lie irked me. The day's events had left me reeling and I couldn't stop thinking about Ern. There was a great thudding honesty about the man, despite his trickery. It was in his bones. This remains with me above all. The sudden knowledge of what Ern was: a man who adhered to his own truth, who followed the stirrings of his heart and mind, even to the brink of madness.

I don't know how long I was kept waiting at the station, only that I did wait and it seemed interminable. I remember pressing the notebook between my fingers, so hard that the indentations are still visible. But I could not bring myself, then, to confront Alison's last thoughts. I had witnessed one death already that day and was not ready to remember another.

After the questioning I was released, on the understanding that I might be called back should further complications arise. There was the question of criminal damage, but that would depend upon charges being pressed. Later, when the coroner's report arrived, my innocence in his death was established. Ern had suffered a massive stroke. It was unusual, the press later reported, that it had killed him instantly. This led to suspicious articles hypothesising about what actually took place within that cottage. The scandal surrounding Hake's wounding and Ern's death could not easily be left alone. Nor was the later revelation of Ellen Bobbin's guilt with regard to the manuscript particularly pleasing to those who had reviled me for so long.

These are the facts of the case. For the press, the story was pretty much concluded, at least until the event of Vinton's book. For me, however, the story was not over. I had to return to the cottage, to face people. Still I felt I lacked understanding; what happened to Alison remained obscure.

It was Judith who took me back to Glaven. She picked me up at the station. I sat silently in the car and she made no demands. I felt myself small; diminished. I watched the clear green fields, the yellow acres of rape, and the clouds above, so high and still it seemed they were knotted to the zenith. There was indeed a numbness, a sense of my own nothingness. What lay beyond the glass was surely beautiful but I did not feel it. I was separate. It reflected no part of me.

As for the reporters, their presence does not stick in my memory. They were there, of course, but my mind was elsewhere and for the first time I felt able to elude them simply by my own indifference. There was a tussle, I believe, when we reached the cottage, but once we were inside they seemed to lose interest. No doubt they went to the pub to swap stories about the case.

Judith made tea. Helen was not there. I felt her absence keenly. It was strange, this silence, as if, by avoiding conversation, I could contain everything. All that had happened, the hugeness of it, was crammed into my brain. I was struggling to make sense of the day's events, to see them as some kind of conclusion. But it was not possible. I was glad to have Judith around. Her quiet, efficient presence was deeply comforting.

We had been back near an hour before I spoke. I can't be sure of the time lapse but when I went to drink my tea it was cold. The question had been on my mind ever since we arrived, but as I believed I knew the answer, it had hardly been urgent. Still, it was the first thing I articulated.

'Helen?' I said. It seemed an enormous effort, simply to pronounce this single word, heavy in my mouth, as if a stone lay on my tongue.

Judith paused. She was sitting opposite me, looking for once pretty ruffled and tired. She was pale, as if, after I'd left her the previous evening, she'd barely slept. When she spoke it was reluctantly.

'She's gone, Harry.'

I took it in. I knew, of course.

'You mean, she's left me.'

'I don't know. Maybe she just doesn't want to face you right now.'

'Who can blame her?' I said. 'Her father?' I paused. 'He's here, right? Or have they left already?'

'I haven't seen her father.'

'He was there this morning, wasn't he? Didn't I see him with her?'

She shook her head; appeared nervous.

'What? What aren't you telling me?'

She stood up, crossed the room, sat next to me. She bit her lip. I smelt that perfume again, faint vanilla.

'I thought I saw him. She was with a man. I wasn't sure but . . .'

'That was Phil Bobbin,' she said. She spoke sharply, as if she wanted to get this out of the way. 'She was with Phil Bobbin this morning.'

'What?' It didn't make sense.

'Ellen Bobbin's son.'

'Yes. I know who he is.'

But I still didn't understand.

'Last night, Harry. When you were with me . . .'

'Yes?' And then I realised her meaning. Helen had been at the pub last night. She wasn't the type to drink alone. And something else. I remembered the daisy chain that I had found in the bed.

'What happened last night?' I asked.

Judith said nothing but her expression was clear.

'Perhaps I should be hearing this from her, right?'

'Right.' Judith nodded.

'So there's something between them?'

'They've only just met.'

'Where is she now?'

'Look, don't be angry with her.'

'What do you know about this?'

'I know that she's very young.'

'What actually happened?' I asked.

'How the hell do I know? I wasn't there, remember? I was with you!'

She was right, of course, to be angry. How could I blame Helen? Last night I left her alone. I had been with Judith.

'Look,' I said. 'Don't pity me. I'm just want the truth.'

'OK. But she didn't say much. I don't really know what's going on. He had his arm around her. They kissed. Hey, do you want this?'

I nodded.

'I think she's confused; doesn't know what she wants. She's there now. She'll be staying there tonight.'

'Where? The Bobbins' place? She can't be.'

'I'm sorry, Harry.'

'But that woman!'

How could she think of being in the same house as Mrs Bobbin? She must be feeling pretty desperate. Else this lad was really something.

'Why staying there?'

'Afraid to come back here, I guess. And of going home to her parents'.

'Afraid of me?'

'She thinks you're cutting her out. That's what she said this morning. She's pretty bitter, Harry. She's got this crazy idea that you're after me. And now, after Ern's death . . . It's too much for her. She's just a kid.'

'As you keep reminding me.'

'Because it's true. You might want her to be the repository of your dreams, but she's a young girl. She doesn't know what she wants yet. What's happened . . .'

'Do you think he's handsome?'

'What?'

She was incredulous. She reached out, briefly, and touched my hand and I laughed, despite myself.

'You heard.'

'You've seen him, haven't you? How Ern must have looked, seventy years ago!'

'You think there's a resemblance?'

'Absolutely.'

But even as she spoke, a thought struck me. I remembered how familiar the boatman had appeared, in the photograph on Ern's wall.

'Like the boatman,' I said. 'Bella's wildfowler.'

Now I watched Judith's face, those great hooded eyes, staring at me. How lucky she was to be outside this, to be simply the biographer, the person who observed. I knew there was nothing strange in these events. I brought Helen here. She happened to meet Phil Bobbin, not such a coincidence, given the circumstances. Still, the resonances choked me. Arabella left Charles Bliss for her boatman. Helen left me for his great-grandson. Doppelgängers, all three of us. It was as if Alison's death had somehow precipitated this repetition; her death a catalyst. Or was it rather me? Had I, in my refusal to let the past rest, caused it to partially repeat itself?

Poetic justice, however, did nothing to reduce the sting of this double loss. Ern dead. Helen gone. Was it possible that it had come to nothing? That my future lay elsewhere? I couldn't stop myself from thinking of Charles Bliss and his loss of Arabella. I remembered the painting, the seascape. It was dated 1901, the year of Bella's suicide. This was his second loss. Whatever his sins, what man deserved such a thing? Now his painting made utter sense to me. Before I had made only a partial connection, had felt the draw of it, but had not fathomed the depths of my ancestor's grief. To endure a double loss was to force a man to look into his soul. If Bliss was to blame for Bella's desertion, was not I equally accountable for Helen's?

In my analysis of the past, I had made one vital mistake. I had forgotten Bliss's first wife. His obsession with her, so huge and all-consuming, had dulled his heart and prevented him from enjoying a second love. I had not learnt from his mistake. However I had loved Helen, my love for Alison remained unrivalled. Now, unsurprisingly, she had deserted me. But where did this knowledge leave me? Where was it possible I might go from here?

I looked at Judith Frazer. I saw the large intelligence of her eyes, the frown that belied her concern. Something appealing, after all, about that preppy look; some hint of beauty in the line of her body, the sharp boniness of her physique. She had such a smooth appearance, that glossy aubergine-coloured hair, the creamy skin, the neat long-fingered hands. Surely, I thought, I might find something here. What else could I do but risk it? I leant towards her, rested my forehead on hers, then found her lips. She responded briefly. There was a moment, as I encircled her back, and breathed that deep and gorgeous scent, when I believed this was an answer. It was an odd beginning; not a passion, but rather a necessary union. She opened her mouth; a bright warmth enclosed me. Then she pulled away.

'What's the matter?' I said.

She said nothing.

'You didn't want me to do that, right? OK. It was pretty stupid of me.'

She shook her head. 'Not so stupid, Harry.'

'Bad timing, huh?'

'It would never be a good time.'

'No?'

'No.'

'Look,' I said. 'You think this is just a reaction. Maybe it is. I can't tell. Only last night . . . I mean, you can't pretend that nothing was going on?'

'Going on?'

'Come on. We were flirting.'

'Sure. But it was safe. Absolutely safe.'

'Because of Helen, you mean?'

'Exactly.'

'And now I'm jumping the gun. I'm sorry. For a moment, I thought . . .'

'It wouldn't work, Harry.'

'Are you certain?'

She nodded; looked pretty resigned. I knew, already, that I was simply saving face. It had been a stupid move by all accounts. At once I guessed what the problem was.

'You have a partner, right?'

I don't know why it hadn't occurred to me before. She nodded.

'Only you didn't mention him,' I said.

She laughed. 'Not "him", actually.'

The revelation startled me, though I tried not to show it. It hadn't occurred to me that she might be gay.

'Right.'

I didn't know what to say. Here was I, ready to invite her into my life, when in truth she was a stranger; she had a whole existence about which I knew nothing. It seemed that over the previous days, Judith Frazer had come close to knowing all there was to know about me. That was her job, after all. I had been fooled by those intimate little chats we'd shared.

Out of the blue, a vile thought occurred to me. What if all this intimacy had been a sham? What if she were simply here, now, like Madeleine, because she wanted to get close to my story; because her readers would enjoy the extra titillation that her closeness could afford? And something else. If she were gay, why had she flirted with me? Surely I had not simply imagined it. But such musings, of course, were boorish. Already I rejected them. I had to trust Judith. Perhaps she guessed my thoughts.

'I'm sorry if I gave you the wrong idea.'

I shrugged.

'I shouldn't have,' she said.

'What? Pretended to feel something you didn't?'

'Wrong. I do find you attractive.'

'Of course.'

'Cut it out!'

'Look. It doesn't matter,' I said. In a sense it didn't. I had made a mistake. I was still mourning Helen. I was confused.

'I think it does,' she said. 'Why don't you believe me?'

'You have a girlfriend, remember?'

'I do like men, you know. I used to be married to one.'

'You're serious?'

'Yes. In fact . . .'

'Yes?'

She hesitated. 'This isn't the time for you to hear my life story.'

'I'm not asking for the full story. Just a glimpse,' I said. 'I barely know anything about you.'

'Please, Harry . . .'

Clearly she regretted her openness. For the moment, I let it go. But I wasn't about to give up altogether.

'So you didn't have any children?' I asked. I thought this might be a point of connection. But I was wrong. She smiled, ruefully.

'Oh yes. A boy. He's fourteen.'

I was taken aback. My assumptions were all wrong. I knew nothing.

'Where is he now?'

'He lives with his father. He doesn't approve.'

'Approve?' Then I got her meaning. 'Christ. I thought kids today were supposed to be open-minded!'

'Not my son. He "tolerates" me. But he can't stand Liz.'

'Your girlfriend?'

She nodded. I tried to imagine her situation. To have a child but to be alienated from him. I had always thought of children as echoes of oneself, the foolish, romantic view that only the childless might hold.

'That's a shame,' I said.

'I'm used to it. We get by.'

'I don't know how you do it. I mean, coming here. Becoming involved in all this – in Alison's story. I know it's your job, but . . .' I didn't need to say more. A thought crossed my mind, quite suddenly, a passing shadow. It seemed obvious. Yet I didn't want it to be true. 'Unless . . .' I began. 'You and Alison,' I said. 'Did you . . .'

She shook her head.

'But it would have been nice,' she said.

'Did you make a pass at her?'

'Hardly. I flirted. It was clear she wasn't interested.'

For the first time I understood what she was doing here. If her desire to write about Alison were not purely financial, there must be some other motivation. And here it was.

'Was that it?' I asked. 'A flirtation?'

Judith winced. Something about her expression: too much anguish was registered there. She had only known Alison for a week. It didn't make sense.

'So there was something sexual, right?'

I told myself, if it were true, then I must bear it.

'No.'

'So what aren't you telling me?'

She paused.

'I fell for her, Harry. Hook, line and sinker. I knew she wasn't interested but it didn't stop me. I was still married at the time.'

'But you knew . . . that you were attracted to women, I mean?'

'Sure. But it was something I tried to suppress. Until I met her.'

'Jesus.'

'After she killed herself . . . Well . . .' She grimaced. 'I couldn't look my husband in the eye. I didn't want to be with him, right? Couldn't stand to be touched by him. All I could think about was Alison. Even though she was dead.'

'You're saying it destroyed your marriage?'

'Not right away. But pretty soon, yes. I mean, things hadn't been great before. But after that . . .' She paused; laughed. 'I left my husband for a phantom. Now that's crazy, huh?'

I laughed with her. What else could we do? A kind of hysteria was creeping in. We barely knew if we were laughing or crying. Both of us had reached that stage where we couldn't take much more grief. Something had to give. If we hadn't laughed, we would have gone right under.

When the laughter subsided, I stood up, announced that I'd get us a drink. I went into the kitchen and opened a bottle of red. I poured a couple of glasses and hunched over the sink before the window. It was early evening, around six. The sun was veiled by a great reef of herring-bone cloud, but its brightness shone through, swathing the land in a kind of violet shimmer. The silence of those fields moved me somehow.

'Look, Harry . . .' Judith stood in the doorway. 'Perhaps I should leave you for a while?'

'I've just poured the drinks.'

I offered her one and she took it.

'What's the problem?' I said.

'I just thought maybe you'd like some time alone.'

'Running away?'

'No.'

'Then stay. I could do with the company. Only . . .'

'Yes?'

'Actually there is something I have to do.' I went to the door and fetched my coat, extracting the notebook from the pocket.

'Is that it? Her notebook?'

I nodded. 'I haven't finished reading it. Perhaps it's time I did.' I paused. 'I haven't told you the half of it; what happened this morning. I'm surprised you haven't asked.'

'I've been biting my tongue. I figured you'd had enough intrusions. Actually, I wanted to be with you today. I figured if I asked too many questions you might lose patience.'

I smiled.

'Why don't I go home and get changed,' she said. 'You read the notebooks. I'll come back later and we can get the hell out of here – drive over to Wells for dinner.'

'And you can tell me the rest of your secret history,' I said.

'Not much left to tell,' she replied.

But all the same she raised her glass and chinked it with mine. Then she downed what remained in one. I followed suit, hardly relishing the task ahead. Even so, a certain excitement was building. In my hand, the final point of connection with all that had obsessed me. I couldn't think beyond the reading of it. Even the idea of dinner hardly registered.

For now, I had simply to blank the day's events from my memory. There would be time enough, later, to shoulder the burden. I had been waiting for six years for the answer to a single question. Why? Could a new death, a further abandonment, be allowed to stall me now? No! Here in my hands lay all that I required. I would go upstairs, open the window on to the garden. What matter if I were observed or photographed? I would sit at the window and read. The light was still sufficient. Beneath the shifting clouds, I would find her again and all that had happened since might surely dissolve as the cloud itself, watery vapours, still shielding the glare of the sun. Judith smiled, touched my hand and left. These words must be enough. The night would draw in and I would be a wiser man. There was no reason now to delay. I was at last alone.

# 34

# THE NOTEBOOK

Several days have passed since I've written a word here. I've been working on the novel itself, but tonight I can't face it. I'm circling the central problem – how to write about the night of her death – and afraid of getting it wrong. Frankly, I feel like death. Writing at all hours – ghastly this sleeplessness – my being washed away by the process of the work. It's there. My substance is there on the pages, but my self? Gone, I think. Really, I feel completely done in.

Something unexpected has happened. A woman. I met her a couple of days ago in the village. She's an Eng. Lit. professor, originally from New York. The point is, she's interested in my work. No. That's only the half of it. She's interested in me. I mean sexually. She hasn't said as much, but the way she looks! It's strange. I mean, she's married, has a son. But we've had a couple of drinks together and I swear I'm right. I don't know how to handle it. The problem is, I do like her. Being in the pub together, it's such a relief. To have a couple of hours each day when I don't feel the usual intensity – to feel normal again; the next best thing to having Harry here. Or rather, better, because there's no pressure, no need to pretend to be more cheerful than I am. Seems I can be black as hell with Judith (that's her name) and she'll not chastise me for it.

Am I myself with her? No, only when alone. With others, we're always projecting something. Even with Ern. 'Not meant for this world,' he said. It's not true. The world pains me often, more than I can stand, but if not for the world, then for where was I intended? He sees one side of me: the irrational, instinctive, non-intellectual. I revel in it. So indulgent, to be that way: exposed. It's like sex, *perhaps. Everything touches me; as if my skin were stripped away and my bare flesh smarting. With him, I forget my other self; the would-be academic. The part of me that chats to Judith in the pub and finds a voice to make a mockery of this.*

*But alone? Where is the true self? I live here in a state of perpetual excitement, experiencing such extremes of emotion. Yet I try, also, to make sense of it. I was thinking, earlier, of one of Turner's paintings,* The Evening of the Deluge. *It moved me immensely when I first saw it and now connects with my thoughts about Bella's death. Such depths of blackness, yet above, such luminosity. I imagine the sea, the nightmarish tug of black water, but the light also, the serenity. To merge with the elements – to transcend fear? Here, in this state of perpetual exhaustion, I am at once sinking and rising up. By crawling back into the child's fear, I am also liberated.*

*Harry, of course, would have a fit if he saw me. He can't stand my agitation. He'd wrap me up in blankets, bring me tea, make me laugh. Anything to rouse me from this intensity. And maybe, for a while, I'd thank him. Perhaps, when I return, he'll make me feel secure and loved, but all the creative energy would be sapped; the poetry would be sucked out of me. I don't write well when I'm comfortable. What do comfortable people write? Anodyne stories about middle-class love affairs! Do I mean an artist has to suffer? That's a crude analysis and not what I mean at all. But surely an artist has to at least confront suffering. Else what is there to write about? Even comedy has misery at its source.*

*Last night, I was reading Camus on suicide. He urges the reader 'to live and to create, in the very midst of the desert'. Later, when I couldn't sleep, I lay listening to the wind. The shutters were slamming against the windows downstairs but I couldn't rouse myself. Those words kept banging about in my skull.*

*So I have to face the act of creation, to write the pivotal scene. The novel will buckle if I get it wrong. But how to forge the facts into a work of art? How to parallel Ern's loss with mine? The stories must connect if the book is to have a centre. But God, I'm so tired. I can't do this. I can't. Yet I must. I want to write the bulk of a draft here in*

*Glaven. What does it matter if I'm consumed by it? There will be time, later, to recover. Let me become a wreck. I'll be brittle and weak and wasted, but for what end! Dying is an art, after all. Can I not, also, rise up again when it is done?*

*Write then. What point in sleeping when it brings only nightmares? When I've left here, the muse may flee and I'll perish in a different way, a slow, silent suffocation. I must use the nightmares, make them work.*

*The corridors. The dream I used to have, as a child. It recurred in the days before I came here. I remember telling Harry about it on the morning that I left, though I'm not sure he was listening: he was too distracted at my departing. Only last night it was different; much worse. The ghastly brightness of that place was nothing now, compared to what followed. The corridor was lined with doors, but I had never looked beyond them. I always fixed my eyes on the walls. But last night some errant spirit goaded me. I no longer liked the monotony, the blankness of the place. I wanted to know what lay beyond it. So I opened a door, a small, neat door. How could I, even I, in a world of dream, have prepared myself for what I saw? Where, in the dimmest recesses of my mind, could such ideas have lurked? As I touched the inner surface of the door, I recoiled, my hand across my mouth to stop me vomiting. Its outer surface had been a mere façade but the inside revealed its true nature. It was made of flesh: a bleeding door, sponge-soft. Blood across my fingers, my face. I stumbled back. I felt I had committed a crime but didn't know what it was. In desperation I opened a further door. There I found what I desired. This door was made of water and as I opened it, a whole sea began to pour.*

*On waking, I knew my crime too well. My own body's crime against my self. My own blood that left my body, twice, escaped my womb when it should have held fast, thickened, nourished my embryos. Now I have one child only. I give my mother-love to the page; this novel my infant.*

*I hold now a photograph of Bella, taken, Ern said, by a gentleman* punt-gunner, an amateur photographer. In it, Bella seems un-leashed. I see a vibrancy that I had not imagined her face could wear. Even her body speaks a different language. Though her legs are hidden beneath those ludicrous skirts, she appears to move as if she is no longer encumbered by them. She remembers, perhaps, wearing bloomers; visiting the British Library; or a childhood on her uncle's farm, clutching a warm chicken between her knees.

What is this but the flush of sex? She had known only Charles Bliss: his cold loins; stiff botanist's hands, holding her at arm's length. Robert Higham has but one hand yet she has felt its impact. His palm has pressed the small of her back, his fingernails trailed her spine; the whorls of his fingertips have traced the contours of her face; his wrist has brushed her lips. Dare I mention the other places that this hand has lingered? When writing of the Victorians, should one do as they did and invent a code that conceals more than it reveals? I couldn't contemplate such a betrayal. Sex is what animates Bella here. The illicit thrill of what she has done; the sting of youth. There's another code, however, that inhibits me now; a modern code which assumes that even sex must remain within the bounds of a certain correctness. But I must be true to my imagination; work within the bounds of my own knowledge. She has enjoyed passivity; abandonment. Being fucked senseless – isn't that what I mean? But not just by anybody. By the object of her desire.

I see her, lain on her side on that bare white bed, Higham behind her, his good hand clutching her hip, jamming into her. The repetition of the act has moved her. Yet to watch would convey nothing. Unless one were to watch her face: cool, almost expres-sionless, not through lack of pleasure but because what she feels is too much, it overwhelms. To understand, one has to be there, inside her head, her body. One has to feel her pleasure at each point where his body touches hers. It comes again and again and again. Any man could not do this to her, but Higham can. It is his body, his skin. Her gaze is fixed on something outside, beyond the window: the moon perhaps, its dalliance in the morning sky. She is emptied, briefly, of her self. The physicality remains a part of this, the ache between her legs, the hollowness. But it is not simply her body that *has been moved. Something sweeter has been released and flies up there, astonished, with the moon.*

\*

*Glaven, today, has left me grim and depleted. I've been trying to fight it, to reach into my fiction to relieve this anguish, but no, I can't seem to shift it. What has happened, I wonder? This morning, even before I opened the curtains, I felt it. The room in near-darkness yet it was already eight. Ern's bastard clouds again. Last week I laughed at his stories, his stupid predictions that I'd be driven away. I knew he wanted me to stay. But, true to his prediction, the clouds did get to me today. Or rather not the clouds themselves, but the lack of light. I felt oppressed.*

*This afternoon, I took a walk across the marshes. The village, in such weather, has a small-town, dingy feel, and I wanted to get out. It felt like a dying place and suddenly I found myself longing for London, for lights and noise. It seemed so far away, impossible to reach. Even the marshes could not lift my spirits. I felt dull and flat and empty, like the land itself. In the bleak, bare landscape, I saw an echo of my own being. Is this what I was seeking when I came here? An environment to correspond with my own hopelessness? As I walked, I felt that I could hardly breathe, as if the air were congealing. Dark skies bore down on me. I walked on the marsh-side of the pebble-bank and the view was grim; nothing but dull-eyed cows grazing and acres of bogs. I couldn't remember my reasons for coming here. How was it possible that Bella had loved this place and for so long? I wanted nothing more than to be with Harry, to curl in a sofa in front of the TV, to eat pizza and ice-cream. I wanted comfort and there was none.*

*When I returned to the cottage, I tried to distract myself with some research: those books about Glaven's history that I've been meaning to read for weeks. I thought that I might be buoyed by this, that to read of the village in Bliss's day might inspire me. But no. Seems it was dying even then. Apparently, at one time Glaven was one of England's busiest ports. I can hardly imagine it, but it makes sense. Look at the church, for instance – too huge for this tiny village.*

Now I learn the village was once a town, extremely prosperous from the thirteenth to the sixteenth century. The real decline, however, began in the nineteenth century. At a time when ships were growing ever larger, Blakeney Channel was beginning to silt up, making it impossible to negotiate. Business soon moved to King's Lynn, and then, in 1884, the railway came to Holt. That was the end of the trading ships, the end of prosperity.

This then, was the world that Charles and Arabella inhabited: a place in its death-throes. Amazingly, it's survived till now, though nobody young lives here now. They leave for the cities as soon as they're able. There's no future for Glaven, except as a resort. Only the ornithologists and the tourists keep it going. Which only begs a single question. What the hell am I doing here? Me? Alison Oakley? (Why did I ever take Harry's name?) And did I really reject the world I knew before – Milan? Paris? I'm burying myself alive like this, with this man who lives in the past.

*

But my refuge is the story, the past. When I attempt to think of a future, I falter. In Ern's room, time does not exist and his tales occupy me. I write most of the night. I can barely stop my pen, as if the story has grasped my spirit and will not let it rest. I feel weak; light-headed. I let myself be taken. This novel will prove me at last.

I do this for my mother. What she lost, I will return to her. I have been waiting so long for this. Yet I find the cost is steep. Sometimes I think that I should like to be ordinary. I should like to find pleasure in simple things. But I can't. I feel I'm losing my place in the world; there's no place where I can rest. Here I can write but could not live. In London I can live but cannot write. And what is my life without writing?

This afternoon I visited the church again. I was intrigued by yesterday's conversation with Ern. 'Find the imp, see?' he said. 'Sit yourself on the north side of the aisle – the second pew, in the middle. Then look to the chancel and you'll see him. Crafty little fella. He has a glass eye, see? But there ain't no-one in that church

346

*will think it at all peculiar, except the folk in the middle of that second pew. That was where Bella sat. After George Bliss knocked her down, she carried me to the church. She had wanted solace, but she sat beneath the glare of the imp. That were an omen, she thought.' Naturally, I was curious.*

*I didn't stop to eat, just drove until I reached the church. Even before I arrived, I knew my intention. I didn't immediately enter the church, but began wandering in the graveyard. I couldn't help myself. I hadn't expected it to get to me, but it did. To be the only living soul there. Memorials crumbling or covered in lichen, angels crouching beneath an unlistening heaven. We live, I thought, with the knowledge of death. What choice do we have? Something banal about such questions, yet I couldn't avoid them. What is the purpose of living? Is art enough? Or love? Something that Camus wrote: 'killing yourself amounts to confessing. It is confessing that life is too much for you or that you do not understand it.'*

*Eventually I found what I was looking for. It was a double tomb: grand, pompous and neglected. A single angel blew a trumpet, but its bell had broken clean off. There, silent, I paused. The wind was rising and my hair cut across my eyes. I tried to make out the inscription but it was damaged, the stone pitted with large holes. The names however remained. It was as I had suspected. Charles Bliss was buried here, but not Arabella. He was buried with his first wife, one Catherine Bliss. And Bella? A pauper's grave, no doubt, for a suicide. On her last day, she had visited this church, seeking guidance. But in death she was cast out.*

*I saw the imp before I reached the pew: a ghastly little creature. But how had it affected Arabella? For some time, I have been trying to place myself in her position, to imagine her state of mind. As I walked that aisle, however, something slotted into place. For years she had endured a marriage with Charles Bliss, an existence which should have suffocated her, yet she survived it. How so, unless, somehow, within that intolerable relationship, she had carved out a space for herself, a mind space, a part of her that neither he nor George might reach. On her solitary walks, she must surely have retreated to that place and found some consolation there. But on*

347

*the day she walked down this aisle, the space had gone. It had begun with the physical. Robert Higham claimed her sex and Bliss too. She might have coped with that, had there not been this baby to suckle. No. Even that was tolerable. But when George Bliss struck her across the face, his physical battering preceded the spiritual.*

*She feels still the ache between her legs from the morning's love-making; she feels the milk swelling in her breasts, beginning to leak through her dress as the babe Ernest starts to cry. Now she feels the sting of George's hand upon her cheek. The fall bruised her hip and she is limping. Surely her sense of self has begun to dissolve? What room is there for the self when there are so many claims upon it? The space within her has shrunk to nothing.*

*Feeling that zero, I also walked, my eyes averted from the imp, squeezing between the pews until I reached the place that Ern had specified. I sat down. Briefly I closed my eyes. Like her, I am afraid, seeing no direction which I might safely take. She knows that George will betray her. When he does, her whole existence will be shattered, her marriage over, her child a known bastard. She is beyond reason now. There is no space within her where rational thought might take place. Perhaps she wanted peace but the child would give her none. The young Ernest opened his lungs and wailed; he threw his head back, his face beetroot-red, his cry loud, violent. As his voice assaults her ears, she looks up and by chance she sees the imp. She was not forewarned; the spectacle imposed itself. She had heard of this creature but never before now had she seen it do its worst.*

*An optical illusion. Nothing more. But it is a fiendish face: bulging eyes, thick-lipped cavernous mouth, truly one of Satan's familiars. I too was startled. From the middle of the pew, the creature's eye appears to catch light and flickers at the beholder. Something deeply unsettling about it, a feeling of being observed by an instrument of evil. Even I was unnerved. One can't help but shift in one's seat, though shifting achieves nothing, the imp continues to glower.*

*So it was there, beneath the gaze of the imp, that Bella decided.*

*Perhaps she felt that God did not pity her. He was against her; like George, he thought her a sinner, a whore. But when she watched the babe's mouth, pulling on her breast, she could not believe that it was born in sin. Nor did she believe her love-making was evil: it was the purest thing that had ever happened to her. So she stood, turned from her accuser and left the church to visit her lover for the last time.*

*Bella had no space left within her. I have too much space. Physically, she felt assaulted, there was no part of her body she could call her own. I am too much myself. I feel nun-like. I have left Harry behind me; I refuse Judith's attentions; my womb is hollow; my skin unbruised. Didn't the poet Hopkins once demand that God should 'batter' his heart? Sitting in that church, I felt I needed such an assault. The spaces within me were too huge. I felt that the imp mocked me, for while his glittering eye drove Bella to despair, for me it was not enough. I wanted something larger, more dramatic, to echo my own nothingness, for every idol and gargoyle to splinter and fall, for the bright windows to shatter. But there was only calm and silence and vacancy. God would not batter me because there was no God and this place nothing but a conceited shell, the vast spaces above me designed to inspire awe for a figment of the human imagination.*

*Bella left the church, returned to Hope Cottage and later, while Charles Bliss played God with orchids, she put her babe Ernest to bed. How did she say good-night to her little one that evening, as he fell into the sleep from which she would not see him wake? How will I, ignorant of mother-love, write of such a moment? Will she simply turn and walk away? Or will she stand, watching? I see his tiny face in shadow, small curls clustered about his forehead, little eyelids flickering in dream. In sleep, his mouth would suck the air in remembrance of the warm breast he has so recently known and expects to find again come morning. There is a murmur. She starts, afraid that he will wake, perhaps desiring it. Instead he simply turns, his face in light now, a warm blue light thrown by the moon. It is the same moon his mother had gazed on while making love that morning: indifferent, blind and quite uncomprehending.*

*How many times, I wonder, has Ern imagined the scene? When he lies in bed each night, does he pull his shrivelled limbs to his chest in unconscious remembrance of that moment? How does he live with the knowledge that she left despite his helplessness? He lives, perhaps, as I do. In dreams and grand resentment. Like me, he fills himself with stories. And he desires that his own be known.*

*

*In Blakeney last night, drinking with Judith. I must have got pretty plastered; it was the first night since I've been here that I've really slept. I turned up late and pale-faced at Ern's this morning for which he mightily scolded me. I told him I hadn't written and he made a point of punishing me. He wouldn't tell me a damned thing about the past nor did he take me out again on his boat as promised. Damn him.*

*Last night began well but ended weirdly. The afternoon had been fine, the sky a great swathe of blue, only a few high white clouds. Judith called for me around seven, and as we stepped outside, I instinctively looked up at the stars. The sky, wide and unfathomable, but pierced by such points of brilliance that I could only stand there like a lunatic to admire them.*

*We drove to a pub close to the harbour. We sat outside – it was hardly cold – and talked incessantly about all manner of things – the perils of academia, limitations of marriage, the need for higher goals, the purpose of poetry – and later, when I'd had a few, I told her about the novel and about Ern. I guess I rather went on, but it gave me a real buzz, the intensity of our talk. She seemed happy – really happy – and I guess I felt connected. Even when I began to talk about suicide, she didn't seem phased. I told her how Ern's descriptions of Bella's death had got to me; my ghastly dreams; how I felt possessed by it. She started spouting on about the high Roman ideals, the nobility of the act; about Stoicism. She was pretty far gone herself and began listing notable suicides from the ancient world: Socrates, Seneca, Hannibal, Boadicea. It all seemed so distant and inappropriate. I don't know why but all this theorising made me furious and I told her so. I said she didn't know what I was talking about, that the problem with academics was that they knew nothing of real life, they were too busy being analytic. At this she burst out laughing, kind of hysterically I'd say. I asked her what was the matter. And she blurted it out. About her father. How he'd killed himself a couple of years back. It had been completely unexpected; no explanation. She hadn't seen him for a few years but that had only made it worse – her own alienation, sense of guilt.*

*The worst thing about it was the fact that I was pissed. I couldn't deal with it. She's so bloody hard, that's the problem. After that burst of laughter, she seemed to pull herself together and she spoke with a kind of venom, so that any sympathy I might have expressed would have seemed misplaced. I knew she wanted to prove a point: that I was selfish, made easy assumptions, had no right to criticise her. All of which, of course, was true.*

*Somehow we got through it. We didn't change the subject exactly but continued to talk around it. We circled it like moths about a flame. We leant our heads together, eyes lingered too long, hands brushed across the table. If truth be told, I can't get what happened out of my head, the sweetness of that talk, the depth of it. Even when we argued, I didn't mind. How could I in such a place, with the night pressing in on me? She accused me of much: said that I was clearly drawn to suffering. That it wasn't modelling or writing that was the problem, but something within me instead. I said I couldn't help my nature. She argued that one's life doesn't have to be dictated by external events, that I had to shake off childhood angst. I told her it wasn't that simple; that I couldn't just drop what I found here; it corresponded with a part of me. The truth is, I live now in a world of such intensity that I feel certain I can't return to London. My art is stimulated here as it has never been. It seems impossible – the volume I've written already – but astonishing what one can manage when one barely sleeps.*

*I know I have been affected by the talk with Judith. It has created a strange alteration in my thoughts, but I can't contemplate it right now. It began on the walk home. We left the car outside the pub and set out, buoyed by the chill air and the infinite black spaces about us. The alcohol had loosed our tongues and as we swayed*

351

*along the open lanes, arm in arm, suicide was still on our lips. I had
forgotten my earlier inhibitions. If she had made a move, no doubt I
would have responded. Perhaps I wanted her to make a pass,
wanted to lose myself, fend off the dim terrors that surrounded me.
Instead, we decided to go to the beach at Glaven, to kick up a few
sparks. Actually, I had a hidden agenda – I was thinking of Bella's
final night, needed to be on that beach to imagine it. But I let Judith
believe I was just in it for laughs.*

*Something about that beach at night; it struck a terror in me. Such
blackness. A void, broken only by the white lines of breakers, which
cut across the darkness like trails of blazing coals. We had no
energy to tramp the pebbles; we collapsed in a heap, giggling like
schoolgirls. But I think she felt the terror too. She began speaking
about her father, quickly, as if she'd held back for too long. Before
his death, she'd virtually lost touch with him; had felt no sense of
connection. But afterwards, she realised she'd been wrong. She
hadn't tried to connect: there were a million questions she ought to
have asked. Now she talked about the loss; the impossibility of
recovering a part of herself. I nodded dumbly. I felt ill. The stars
bore down on me: their brilliance seemed to gouge my flesh. Again,
I was thinking of Bella, At once, I knew what I must write.*

\*

*At night, for his own pleasure, he takes the boat out. Along the
Blakeney Channel, he lets slip the mooring, and glides into the
darkness. Out there, on the black waters, he feels at ease. He
experiences no fear. The emptiness, and capacity of the night calm
his spirit, elate him. He forgets about the snow, the maiming. He
closes his eyes, breathes, listens. His lungs thrill at the first inhala-
tion of damp air. His ears are precision instruments. He knows the
cries of individual birds, can tell a bluethroat's warble from a
whitethroat's.*

*Since he has known Bella, he goes out at night more frequently. It is
difficult to sleep in the empty bed; he can still smell her on the
sheets. Cold night breeze can still his beating heart, calms the ache
in his ribcage. It is better like this. To watch the open sky, feel*

*himself dwindle beneath it. He is a large and handsome man but his deformity has crushed his spirit. Sometimes he wants the air to swallow him.*

*That night, as he pushes away from the muds, he sees a figure approaching. He thinks it is a figment of his imagination and is astonished at his ability to so conjure the object of his desire. Her pale dress appears blue in the moonlight; she moves quickly; with urgency. Do ghosts move in such a fashion? He turns, ready to dismiss the apparition. Then he hears the voice. 'Robert! Robert!' Why is he so afraid when he realises it is really her? Does he think some disaster has struck? Why else would she leave her husband's bed, take the one risk they had agreed was not worth taking?*

*Yet he lifts her into the boat, attempting to raise her skirts clear of the mud (which is useless – her petticoats are ruined). He does not ask a single question, nor even enquire about the well-being of their child. How can he question her, when she is so distressed? His instinct is to act. ('Oh,' she says, ' – my shoes', for the shoes are soaked through). Her fear is nothing to do with petticoats or shoes, but still he arranges her skirt, removes her shoes and tells her they will come clean. It is, indeed, too much for him. Her proximity pains him. He is not eloquent but he knows she wants him to speak. He finds it impossible. There are no words to encompass his emotion. Does she expect words at such a time? She is trembling, her face expresses such agitation. He is struck dumb. He shivers slightly. He wants to explain the burning within his chest, the abstract beauty of his reaction. It is at once pain and pleasure; it is white hot; it has damaged him. The moon above is so separate, its stare indifferent. He wishes also for such separation but it is no longer possible. 'I cannot return to him,' Bella says at last. This he knows already. She is absent from Bliss's bed. He cannot envisage the future.*

*All night, Ern told me. They stayed together out on waters. How can I write of such a night? No doubt they didn't sleep. But of the rest? A numbness; a fear. It could hardly have been comfortable. Yet they would have been safe there, the night cradling them, the silence broken only by bird-cries and the quiet lapping of water* against the boat. And the strangest thing? That it really happened. It is not the stuff of fiction, though I will make a fiction of it. Already I imagine them as in a painting: by G.F. Watts or Burne-Jones. The former would make them aetherial, she a spirit fading on the wind. And Burne-Jones? I fear that he would ruin it. His vision is too bright and too precise; he would make an allegory of it. I can see it now, hanging in a gallery, with the words of Rossetti's sister at its side:

> Remember me when I am gone away,
> Gone far away into the silent land;
> When you can no more hold me by the hand,
> Nor I half turn to go yet turning stay.

Can I, who have not half the talent of these artists, make art from this loss? Can I capture her face, the still vacancy of her stare, like one who lies in a final rhapsody but already has half left the world? The night was too soon over. The search party she had expected did not arrive. Charles Bliss did not discover the empty bed until the following morning. He too had been up by moonlight, engaged in his orchid-house, such a delicate art this cross-breeding; he wanted to create the perfect bloom, in form, in colour, in scent. He would call it Catherine, after his first wife. It would surely win horticultural prizes.

First light came too quickly. She had hoped for a miracle: that the sun might fail to rise. But she did not regret her actions. When she was with him, she knew she would risk anything for this, could endure torture now that she had spent one whole night in his presence. It was her body, however, and not her eyes, that first told her it was morning. The milk began to leak from her breasts; they were sore and swollen and heavy. Soon afterwards, at the horizon, the sky began to pale.

They were approaching Blakeney Point, beyond which a small boat might not proceed. She determined to cross the strip of land, to reach Glaven beach alone. They must not be seen together. He thought she appeared oddly elated; there was an unfamiliar brightness about her. He was afraid for her, yet he let her go. She stepped out on to the pebbles, barefoot. He found her shoes and gave them to her. 'Don't forget to clean 'em,' he said. Then, without a kiss, he turned and pushed away. The darkness began to fade. The wind was rising and gulls began to swoop. She did not touch the shoes. Bella crossed the marsh-paths barefoot and, when she reached Glaven beach, she discarded her dress and petticoats also. The whale-bone corsets also were removed and left to rot, as if the poor creature had been stranded there and now only his skeleton was remaining. It was, of course, a selfish act. Walking into those waters, chest-deep now, her milk seeped away unseen. The babe Ernest stirred in his crib, opened his mouth and howled.

*

Ern today – speaking about his father. I prompted it, of course. I have fathers on the brain. It began with Judith, and what she told me on the beach: the alteration in my thoughts that I mentioned. Something has happened that I never expected. I thought I had dealt with it, but here it is, like a fresh wound, the most awful thing. What if I got it wrong? That's what I've been thinking. What if I've made a huge mistake: spent my life mourning the dead, when I should have concentrated on the living?

I'm shaken up. Judith's regrets have led me here but it is barren, unknown territory. I do not know my father. I have lost him. I can't brush it aside. The thought has rocked the foundations on which I stand. Nothing is steady now; everything shifting. And the novel, a rushed draft nearing completion, but it's made a nonsense of by this. It is blown apart. I should try to forget it. If I follow this path, I must not only revise my life, but my work also. Something I thought was solid but now it shatters.

I felt envious when Ern talked about his father. After the death of Charles Bliss, he was brought up by Robert Higham. He had, at least, one parent. Whereas I had no such thing. Yet it was not my fault! So I have told myself over the years. My father neglected me – it's only right that I've become estranged from him. Why, then, do I suddenly desire to see him? Why do I want to understand?

355

*Perhaps this is the end point of my journey? Perhaps I have been waiting for this revelation all along? It seems so obvious now. Who else might understand my loss if not my father? He is the only one who was there, with me, who experienced the void created by her death. How is it possible then that I let him go?*

*I last saw my father on my wedding day. A civil service, with him a 'witness', an apt description, for it was all his role amounted to. One who watched and yet was not involved. I was irritated that he should even be a part of it. But Harry was insistent. In time, he said, I might forgive him. I should wipe the slate clean, start again. He soon realised, of course, that it wasn't possible. Still, I always suspected that Harry rather liked my father; that he pitied him where I could not.*

*What did I think of my father on that day? Nothing. My thoughts were dulled by the memories that weighed on me. He kept trying to catch my eye, but I refused to look at him. I tried to blank him out. If I had allowed myself to feel a single thing, the day would have been ruined. So I pretended he was not there and perhaps my actions have been eating me ever since. Because I thought I did not see him; that I had mastered my grief; or rather felt none. But if I did not see him, and felt no grief, how is it that I think of him now?*

*I see him, tall and distracted and desperate. He parades a kind of elegance: a raffish look, cream linen and Panama hat. But his manner does not fit with his attire. Whenever I noticed him, engaged in some conversation, it seemed clear to me that he was not listening. I knew, perhaps, that he could think only of me, but I would not come close to him nor give him the opportunity to talk. I remained, on my wedding day, the stubborn child that I had always been. I believed that I was missing one person only, that my mother would have made the day complete. I did not know that I was missing my father also. How could I? Is it possible to miss a person that one has never known?*

\*

*Something terrible. Hake is here. I thought, like a fool, if I could only obliterate that part of my life, refuse to write about it in these journals, then it might vanish; cease to be. Will that man never leave me alone? What will it take to make him forget me? I simply do not understand it.*

*I had just returned from the village. Thinking of Eliot, I had bought hyacinths. Only a few minutes after my arrival, there was a knocking at the door. I answered it and there he was, like a bad dream, grinning in the doorway. He said he simply wanted to talk about Sweet Susan, but I knew it was more than that. It's never the story he wants, never. If only it were so simple. I see those eyes, squinting at me still. The fullness of his presence, his insistency. Go away, I told him. Please. For once, just leave me. What do you want from me, Gordon? Blood? He said he wanted to know about my new novel. What was it about? Why was I here? Just thinking of him makes me nauseous. I feel hemmed in. Trapped, even here. I'm beginning to feel that there is no place on this earth where I can truly rest and be alone. Wherever I go, always, I will be followed. And those photographs of his. Sometimes I wish he'd just go ahead and print them. I told him so tonight. Print your fucking photographs, I said. What are they, after all, just celluloid! I wish he'd do it. Really. I'd rather the whole world saw them and he knows that. The worst thing is the idea of him, believing he possesses something of me. I feel myself shrinking, knowing that he's here. I'm losing purchase on my self.*

*

*I can't hear the sea tonight. Why is that, I wonder? Perhaps it has never been audible from this distance and I have simply imagined that I heard it. Or else, what has happened this evening has dulled my senses. I am hollow; my imagination all snuffed out. I can't work on the book; can't conjure a single ennobling thought.*

*I have made a mistake. What did I expect, after all? I should have left it well alone. Christ, I feel enclosed tonight. Solitude has never oppressed me as it oppresses me now. And I hear nothing. The walls deaden sound. For so long I have been communing with the dead and now they are absent. There is nobody here but myself and I am choking on my own regrets.*

357

*Even the novel is all wrong. It circles about a half-truth. Ern pressed me to read aloud from it this morning; he wants to hear how I have interpreted his past and is terribly impatient. But I can't read something that is so imperfect, so far from the thing that I had wanted it to be.*

*I don't know what possessed me to do what I did. Hake's visit perhaps. It had shaken me. I had decided to call Harry, but when I got to the telephone box I couldn't do it. We had a deal, didn't we? I made the rules myself: no communication for a fortnight. My pride prevented me from dialling, but something else too. I was afraid of the consequences. I was looking for comfort, but knew that the very thing I craved might destroy my ability to work. I feared that if I spoke to Harry, all that has happened here, all that I have become, might dissolve. If I allowed the façade to crack, my self to spill out, then the urgency of my work might be lost. I'd relapse into pathetic whingeing; I'd lose my self-respect. Also, I might be disappointed. I envisaged, at first, an ideal Harry, a person who instinctively would understand. But as I picked up the receiver, I knew that if I spoke to him, we would speak across a precipice. Everything that I have lived for these last weeks is alien to him. He knows nothing of Bella or Robert. Though Charles Bliss is his ancestor, and George too, at present they are simply names and nothing more.*

*I acted on an impulse. I dialled my father's number.*

*What was I hoping for? I can't say. I stood, alone in the telephone box, breathing the scent of stale urine. I heard the ringing tone and wanted to leave, but didn't. Outside it was dark. I could see nothing. There was the light above my head, myself, the telephone. As I was waiting, a car passed by. The headlights flooded the fields ahead and then, as quickly, shrunk away. A voice answered. 'Hello?' I couldn't speak. 'Hello? Who's there?' The shock of hearing that voice. It was at once strange and familiar. I wanted to speak but my throat had seized up. Perhaps I made a noise because he stayed on the line. 'Who is this?' It wasn't a good line; he sounded so distant. But I knew it was him. Somewhere, in that house of my childhood, where every dream had turned sour, my father still paced the empty rooms. I wanted to say, 'Daddy, it's me,* it's Allie.' The words were close, they would surely come. But before I could speak, there was a pause, a pregnant silence, and I thought he knew that it was me; as if we both knew and in that silence there was acknowledgment. Then the line went dead. My father had hung up.

I stood, clutching the receiver, motionless, gasping like a fish. At the other end of the line, I imagined my father walking quietly from the room. I saw him at the foot of the stairs, hesitating, running a hand across his forehead. I did not know this man; I saw only a figure, a stranger. And he walked away from me. He didn't even have the grace to turn. I was nothing; a silence at the other end of a telephone wire; a hoax-caller. I let the receiver drop, opened the door and went outside. A slight wind had risen and, looking up, I saw a great swathe of cloud, a vibrant gauze, racing across the black sky. Something so purposeful about that cloud, its urgent motion, clarity of form. I watched it, mesmerised, uneasy, but not certain why. Then it was clear to me. Such lightness; I have never known such lightness. As if the one thing I should have known all along had eluded me and now I faced it and the release was instant. 'Then is it sin, to rush into the secret house of death, ere death dare come to us?'

# 35

THE ACT OF REMEMBRANCE is a task fraught with difficulty and contradictions. At no point in my story have I been more aware of this than now, when I attempt to throw light on that evening when I reached the end of Alison's notebook. The truth is, my confidence falters here. In a sense, one might say that nothing happened. A man sat before a window and read a journal. Occasionally he could be seen to wipe a tear from his eye but he did not at any point give in to his grief. Afterwards, he placed the journal down and gazed vacantly ahead. He did not move for a long time. Even when there was a loud rapping at the door, he failed to hear a thing.

Alternatively, one might try to go further: to look inside the man's head and trace the patterns of his thought. Yet while the first method reveals too little, the second approaches chaos. What goes on in his head is too huge, too various, too random. Any attempt at ordering the man's reactions is sure to diminish them. There is perhaps a falsity in order. Indeed, it occurs to me that the very act of creation is actually a kind of faking it. What chance do we have of approaching authenticity? Reality, unmediated, is anarchic. And this fact, perhaps, in the end, destroyed my wife.

She could not face the chaos. Often, in relating her story, I have hit upon the writer's dilemma: the desire to express oneself, coupled with the infinite means of so doing. The existence of choice is a truly terrifying thing. To face a blank page daily, wrestling with thoughts and images that crowd the teeming brain. I think of Ern's cottage, how he could not throw anything away but preferred, rather, to order his possessions, to make a display of their variousness; to hide those objects that he could not face, but never to discard them.

What remains of this story shrinks away from me, resists being told. Yet it has such life and intensity. The end, in a sense, is simply the beginning; both arrival and departure. So, if I wish to move on, I must also return to that evening, before the window, the moment when I placed the notebook down.

First, it was too beautiful an evening. What was I supposed to make of that, immersed as I was in such spiritual gloom? Ern's clouds had withdrawn. Perhaps it was only appropriate: his parting gift. It was the bluest sky; an astonishing, clear light. Without it, I might have gone under.

Most of all, I was struck once again by my loss; the waste; the life we might have had. I had been reminded of Alison's intensity. It had always drawn me. 'Such lightness', she wrote. Yes, it seemed appropriate. That she found lightness in the idea of death, for in life she had found lightness impossible.

It was difficult, naturally, to read the passages that concerned myself with any degree of objectivity. True, it was now clear, beyond a shadow of doubt, that it was not I who had destroyed her. Yet I felt no sense of triumph. How could I? What was more difficult to bear was the view she clearly had of me: that I was her comforter but not her muse. She needed me, loved me even, but not with the passion I felt for her. 'Limitations of marriage.' She wanted something larger than I could offer. Perhaps she imagined that Bella found it with Robert Higham. Perhaps I found it here, with Helen. What happened in the graveyard: love-making of such intensity that one loses sense of self. For Alison that intensity came only with her work, her memories. If the windows of Glaven church would not fall on her, then she needed something else. In the end, it seemed only death could offer it.

As I watched the sky grow pale above the fields, I realised that my assumptions about Alison had been all wrong. I was thinking about my dream, the recurrent one, which has not returned of late. When I first had the dream, I made no connection between mine and hers. I had somehow forgotten her recounting of the dream, yet it must have entered my subconscious and eventually I made it my own. I embellished it; made it yield meaning. I remember how vivid it was: that image of her perfection. But now I realised how the image of her smile had fooled me. Did I truly believe that she had killed herself out of vanity? To secure a place in literary history? Did I believe that death was her accomplishment, not life, when nothing could be further from the truth? If the journals are to be believed, she died in a state of enormous uncertainty. She had urged herself to live and to create but in the end she simply could not find the strength to do so. There was nothing grand in the manner of her self-destruction, nor is there comfort in the fact of her current status. No post-humous fame can justify such a ghastly death. Nor did I find answers in her notebook. I could not even blame Hake, though at last I had an explanation for his recent behaviour. No doubt he feared that Alison might have written about that final encounter. No doubt he thought himself culpable for her death. But in the end, he was only a part of it. In fact, her decision to give in seemed sudden and arbitrary. Nothing of vanity about it, just a mistaken belief that it was the only path that remained open to her.

I did not hear Judith knocking at the door. In the end she went into the garden and attracted my attention by shouting. I could have done without it, but I waved, stood up and went down-stairs. Actually, I should have been more grateful, since it was her actions that had kept the press away while I read the journals. I later discovered that Judith had joined them in The Ship, just as a couple of them were about to seek me out. In a sudden act of self-sacrifice, she'd held an impromptu press conference, agreeing to be interviewed on the understanding that I would be left alone until at least the following day. The idea of such a sure-fire scoop secured their agreement. While one might be cynical and interpret Judith's behaviour as self-serving – mere publicity for her forth-coming book – I chose not to be. I have few enough friends, after all.

She was all dressed-up, in a clingy black dress. She had painted her lips. It didn't seem 'her', but I was hardly going to complain.

'Jesus, Harry,' she said, when she saw me. I must have looked pretty grim.

'Sorry. I lost track of time.'

'No. I'm sorry. Dinner was a dumb idea.'

I shook my head but without conviction.

'I can get changed,' I said.

'No. Let's forget it. You're in no state . . .'

But the idea of getting out seemed suddenly appealing.

'Yes. I am. I'll be ready in fifteen minutes.'

I left her waiting downstairs and appeared a quarter of an hour later, clean, fresh and groomed. I had made a resolution, though I was reluctant to spring it on Judith. Still, I wasn't about to be swayed.

'You look fine, Harry.'

'Good. I'm feeling better.'

'The journal, right?'

'Let's just say it's not exactly light reading.'

'I should have thought.'

'Not at all. I'm in need of a good dinner.'

'If you're sure . . .'

I nodded.

'I know a great place. Tucked away.'

'Sounds good. Only . . .'

'Yes?'

'There's something else I have to do first.'

She looked disappointed.

'I have to see somebody. Something I haven't told you . . .'

'You want to see Helen, right?'

'No. Mrs Bobbin.'

'You are kidding?'

I shook my head.

'What's the deal, Harry?'

'OK. Let me explain. I'm getting out of here, back to London. Tomorrow preferably. I've had enough.'

'So you want to hand in the notice on your tenancy?'

'No. Or rather, that's not all.'

'I don't get it.'

'I have to see that woman before I go. Look, I don't know how to put this . . .' I paused. 'She started it all. That's the bottom line. She's to blame.'

'What do you mean?'

'The manuscript. Ern told me. Alison's novel. It was she who burnt it.'

'What?'

'Mrs Bobbin.'

'What are you saying?'

'Yes. The old man was pretty cut up about it.'

'She burnt the novel? Jesus.'

'I have to confront her before I leave.'

It was nearly nine when Judith parked the car outside Mrs Bobbin's cottage and I sensed she was uneasy about the time, thought we'd miss the restaurant. The cottage was situated on the road to Salthouse and even in the fading light I could see how smart it was, a detached property with a neat-laid lawn and colour co-ordinated flower-beds, with the Land-rover in the drive outside. Judith raised an eyebrow. Clearly she didn't agree with my rashness. No doubt she thought my frame of mind rather delicate and wasn't in the mood to pick up the pieces.

'I have to do this,' I said.

She shrugged nonchalantly.

'Don't you see?'

'It's all ego, Harry. You want to barge in there and show her who's boss.'

'That's utter crap.'

'I can't think of a single woman who'd behave as you're about to.'

'What are you talking about? Have I missed something?'

She turned away and I got out of the car. I didn't want a disagreement, but neither was I about to let this matter go. I was serious about leaving and I couldn't go without seeing my landlady.

I knocked and there was a pause before anybody answered, long enough for me to wonder whether Helen was inside, to briefly doubt my presence here. Again, I noticed how well-kept the place was: the paint looked fresh; the brickwork had been repointed; the curtains were perfectly draped. It couldn't have been more different from Hope Cottage.

A face appeared briefly from behind those curtains, then vanished. Soon afterwards the door was opened by Phil. Oddly, I was unaffected to see him again.

'What do you want?' he said.

'Not what you think.'

'You should have called first. We've had the journos here all afternoon. Anyway, Helen doesn't want to see you.'

'No. I imagined not.'

Already I was comparing him to Ern. He had the same build and something about the lips was familiar, the way he pressed them together in a kind of sneer.

'Then what do you want?' he said. 'You've got a nerve, coming here.'

'Have I?'

'Yes. Haven't you forgotten something?'

'Your great-grandfather. He died this morning.'

'Might have still been here if he hadn't been so wound-up.'

'He was in his nineties.'

'What's that supposed to prove?' he said.

Already I was impatient. I was relieved when Mrs Bobbin appeared behind him.

'It's all right, Phil,' she said. 'You go upstairs. I can deal with this.'

He did as he was asked. Helen deserved better, I thought.

'Come in, Mr Bliss.'

I entered the hallway: gold-framed prints on the walls; a vase of fresh flowers; an umbrella stand. I thought of Ern's place – the bare stone floors, the clutter. How did she come to be this way?

'Take no notice of Phil,' she said. 'He's rather jealous.'

'I thought I was supposed to be the jealous one.'

She smiled, in a superior way, but I was surprised that she appeared less hostile than before.

'Is Helen here?' I asked.

I had neither expected nor intended to ask that question.

'Yes. She's upstairs. I don't think it's a good idea . . .'

'No. I didn't come to see her. I wanted to let you know that I'm leaving Glaven. Tomorrow. I thought you ought to know.'

She nodded. Clearly she sensed there was something else.

'Would you like to come through to the lounge?'

I followed her into the next room, all plush brocade and tasteful antiques. She gestured that I should sit.

'Would you like a glass of sherry? I think we can be civilised?'

'No. Thank-you. I have a friend waiting outside.'

I could barely believe the woman's duplicity.

'I'll pour a glass for myself.'

'It can't be easy,' I said. 'Your grandfather . . .'

I was holding out; wanted her to believe she was safe.

'No,' she replied. Her voice was brittle. As ever, I was thrown by that blank face, the weird waxen look about it. 'Your presence has not been easy for my family, Mr Bliss.'

Nor yours for mine, I thought.

'I think your grandfather rather enjoyed my company,' I said.

'He would have been better off without you. And that Vinton chap.'

'Vinton? What's he got to do with it?'

'He harassed my grandfather, as you have. He was the last tenant of Hope Cottage.'

'What? The "nice young man" you spoke of?'

'Exactly. How was I to know?'

I was thrown by this knowledge; felt furious. Why wasn't I aware of this?

'I did not harass your grandfather,' I said.

'He was a delicate man.'

'I've never met anybody less delicate in my life!'

'You didn't know him,' she said. She spoke in a tight-lipped manner, barely concealing her dislike of me. 'He put on a brave face.'

'Actually I think I did know him. He certainly felt able to talk to me.'

She shifted in her chair.

'Of course,' she said. 'Hope Cottage will remain in the family.'

'I'm sorry?'

Didn't she mean Ern's cottage? What did ours have to do with this?

'It belonged to my grandfather. I simply managed it for him.'

'How so?'

It had never crossed my mind to question the ownership of the cottage where we stayed. Suddenly I saw the irony of this. If Hope Cottage had been passed down through generations, it would by rights have become mine. Indeed, as such, it might have become Alison's second home.

'I thought you were aware? It was a bone of contention between our families. When Charles Bliss died, he left the cottage to my grandfather and not to George. A kind of atonement, I think.'

'You mean he regretted his treatment of Arabella?'

'If that painting is anything to go by . . .'

'Ha!'

What could I do but laugh? Mrs Bobbin seemed triumphant, no doubt expecting me to take the side of Charles Bliss. Yet to me it was only fitting that he should have suffered pangs of conscience.

'Whatever happened to the glass-house?' I asked. I was killing time; procrastinating.

'Ah – the orchid-house. My grandfather had it dismantled. It was the first thing he did once the cottage became his. He couldn't bear to see it. Did he mention the night of Bella's death?'

'Of course.'

'He blamed Bliss for remaining in the orchid-house. If he'd returned to his bed, he would have discovered her missing. She might have been saved.'

'She would have found another way,' I said.

It was an involuntary thought, perhaps inspired more by thoughts of Alison than of Bella. Perhaps I had given up laying blame.

'Well,' Mrs Bobbin said, draining her glass, 'it has been a very long day. I hope you are satisfied, Mr Bliss.'

'Satisfied?'

'My grandfather's wounding of that dreadful man. His death. That too might have been averted. It was inevitable, of course, when you appeared on the scene.'

'Yet you accepted me as a tenant,' I said, bitterly.

'Yes. A mistake.'

'What is your problem, exactly?' I was tired of being polite; sick of her accusations and patronising manner.

'We had protected him thus far,' she said. 'But you should have kept away. And your wife too. If she had never come here . . .'

'But she did. And she's dead as well. I think she's paid dearly enough, don't you? I mean you're hardly innocent yourself in this.'

'What are you talking about?'

She was clearly rattled. I had never seen her quite so imperious.

'The manuscript,' I said. She didn't flinch. 'Ern told me that it was you.'

'What are you implying?'

'I'm merely stating a fact. You burned the manuscript of my

wife's last novel. Had it been in existence, the press interest would have been reduced. That's the best part of the story, don't you see? *I am the story. Me. Harold Bliss. The bitter husband who destroyed a great work of literature. Do you follow or need I go on?'

'You have no proof of what you say.'

'No. But you and I know the truth.'

She paused, appeared to be weighing up the situation. I laughed. I couldn't help myself. Then a movement caught my eye. I turned and was shocked to see Helen standing behind me, near the door. I didn't know how long she'd been there, but I felt relief in her presence.

She stepped into the room; approached us.

'Is it true?' she asked.

Mrs Bobbin laughed, a peculiar, slightly manic laughter.

'Helen, dear,' she said. 'There are many things you don't understand.'

'Such as?'

'You met my grandfather. Can you imagine how publication of that novel would have affected him?'

'So you're admitting it. You did it?'

'It was for the best.'

Helen gasped, turned to me, clearly distraught.

'I *knew* Alison didn't do it,' she said. 'I knew it.'

'My family were quite content before Alison Bliss came here,' Mrs Bobbin said. 'You have no idea how she upset my grandfather. Digging up the past like that. Things best forgotten.'

'I don't think he had forgotten it,' I said. 'He wanted that novel to be published.'

'Nonsense.'

'So why did he keep her notebook?'

'What?'

'A notebook. Her journals.'

'You mean the pages he gave Vinton?'

'No. A whole notebook.'

Clearly she knew nothing about this.

'I don't think so,' she said.

I wanted to take it from my pocket and wave it gloatingly before her nose. But I thought better of such juvenile actions. After all, it wouldn't do to let her come too close to it.

368

'He's not lying,' Helen said. 'I've read them too.'

I thought she was bluffing. It wasn't until later that I found out she spoke the truth.

'You people,' said Mrs Bobbin, 'you have no idea.'

'Of what?'

'Of how you damage lives.'

'I can't believe you're saying that,' Helen said. 'I mean, I'm just taking this in, that it was you. Do you have any idea what you've done to Harry? Letting him take the blame?' Mrs Bobbin merely huffed and Helen continued. 'You're an evil woman. Evil. To destroy an artist's work! You're such a philistine. What do you know about literature? You don't have a single decent book in your house. Alison Bliss died knowing that her work would speak for her. But you've taken that away.'

Even I was astonished at the outburst. Mrs Bobbin was clearly shaken. She turned away, sat down, trembling. When she spoke it was in a quiet, strained voice.

'I may not read books,' she said, 'but that does not make me any less human.'

'You could have fooled me,' Helen said.

'My father was taken into a mental institution last year.' She turned to me. 'I don't suppose my grandfather mentioned his son?' She paused and I said nothing. 'No. I didn't think so. Can you imagine what it was like for him, to be brought up by my grand-father in that demented house? To have a father who lived in the past, who drummed his obsessions into his son's young mind? Let us say it hardly makes for stability. It didn't show at first, of course. Why else would my mother have married him? It was quite a scandal at the time, that a woman of her class should marry a Higham. But his behaviour drove her to madness too, in the end. And who was left to care for my father, my grandfather? Do you think I want to speak about this? Do you think I have ever wanted it?'

Her face wore a wild, almost rhapsodic expression. Now, for the first time, the façade had dropped.

'You see, Mr Bliss, I have spent half my adult life caring for two old men: the daily grind of it, the washing, the cooking, the bed-pans in my father's case. I've had to listen to their grim stories over and again. Whereas your wife heard the story just once. She stuck

369

her nose into our business. Soon, every last filthy scrap of my family's history, my history, will be public knowledge. And why did your Alison do it, tell me that? To make money from our misery.'

'That's ridiculous,' I said, though I was not unaffected by her speech. 'Alison had no interest in financial gain. She was filthy rich already.'

'She wanted to make a Romance of my grandfather's life, when it was a blighted, twisted life.'

'He wanted it too,' I replied.

Mrs Bobbin shook her head. I had the impression that every ounce of her energy was channelled into recovering some sense of decorum, so that her tense, bitter face might no longer reveal the slightest suggestion of weakness.

'I think I should go,' I said. 'Are you staying, Helen?'

She glanced at Mrs Bobbin and shook her head. 'I'll get my stuff,' she said.

Strangely, I felt some pity then for the woman who sat before me. I looked about me at the pristine, ordered room. Everything she had done was to preserve this. To preserve not merely her privacy, but her fragile sense of self. All along, even in her burning of the manuscript, she had feared this revelation of her past. She was the antithesis of her grandfather, whose authenticity, like Alison's, might never be doubted. I was reminded of myself, in my Oxford days, donning a façade, as if there were some sin in being normal, being human. Truly, I pitied her, though I could not bring myself to forgive her.

'I'll wait in the car,' I said.

I expected some final words from Mrs Bobbin, but it seemed that she had said enough. I turned and left her there, holding the empty sherry glass, quietly mourning the death of her grandfather.

# 36

I SHOULD HAVE EXPERIENCED some relief as I walked out of that house. It was finished now; nothing left to be revealed. Instead, as I left the neat garden behind me, I felt only a kind of mute sorrow, a numbness. I had thought, when I first came to Glaven, that if I could only find out why my wife had killed herself and the truth about the manuscript, then it might be possible to conceive of a way forwards. I had imagined, naïvely, that such release might be instant but I had been unprepared for ambiguity.

I opened the car door. Judith looked up, grim-faced. I told her that Helen was coming and she nodded, as if she had expected it. I climbed in beside her.

'The woman admitted it,' I said. 'Can you believe it?'

'Well, well. I guess you're happy now?'

'What do you mean? I'm happy?'

'Do you feel better?'

I shook my head, irritated. Why should Judith be so smug? She was supposed to be on our side but right now she seemed to be claiming some kind of moral high ground, which was absurd.

'What are you implying?' I asked. 'That Mrs Bobbin didn't deserve this?'

'Sure she did.'

'Then what is your problem?'

'I've just had enough, that's all. Give me a break, Harry.'

'Why? You're not giving me one.'

'Wrong. This afternoon, actually. I spoke to some reporters – to keep them out of your hair, you know? And it wasn't easy, OK? I thought I could do it, but I just kept remembering Alison.'

'What about her?'

'There was one evening – I haven't mentioned it before – when we got pretty blotto. It was kind of tender. No. Nothing happened. But I told her some things about myself and it was like . . . Oh, she was so damned beautiful, Harry, you know that, so fucking alive and gorgeous. And two days later, that was it. On a slab. And I thought, how can I be doing this? Telling the world . . .'

I guessed that she was talking about the evening Alison had recounted in her journals. I pitied Judith but I remained bitter.

'And now you're blaming me?' I said.

'No. I'm just sore.'

'Stop being sore. It gets in the way of your job.'

'Well thanks.'

'Look – if you've had enough, why don't you just let go?'

'Will *you* ever let go, Harry?'

'I don't know.'

'I have to make sense of it, that's all. But you're right about getting out of here. I don't know what else can be achieved by staying on. Only there is one thing . . .'

'Yes?'

'This probably isn't the right moment.'

I had already guessed her purpose.

'You want to see the journals, right?'

She nodded, cautiously. 'I need to know if you're with me on this.'

'You mean, will I collaborate?'

'Answer my questions. Let me quote you.'

I smiled, rather wryly perhaps, still unable to answer her. Since reading the journal, I'd begun to ascribe reasons to Judith's need to write this book, not least the suicide of her father. But I wasn't ready to mention that. She looked over my shoulder in the direction of the cottage and, as we watched, a lamp was switched on and the front curtains were drawn.

At the door, Helen appeared. She walked up the path, pausing at the gate to look up at the sky. I too looked up. High amber clouds; the heavens paling. Unexpectedly, Richard came to mind. What would he have made of that sky? It was changing so quickly as the light waned. What would he have told the boys? They'd be gathered at the gate, sitting on the damp grass with sketch-pads across their knees and chalk pastels. He'd crouch beside them, saying, 'Work quickly now, don't even think about it,' and his confidence would spur those lazy young minds into action. He'd have shown them slides beforehand – Pissarro, Monet, Sisley – and as they worked, these images would come to mind, and for a time at least, they'd believe themselves to be geniuses. Some hope, some vision would grab them and they'd do as Richard asked and work so unselfconsciously that something rather marvellous would result.

His daughter, my lover, approached me. I got out of the car, wondering what it must be like to have such a daughter. If she was precious to me, how much more so to him, who had made her, watched her grow. I could not imagine the immensity of his love. It was surely immeasurable. I remembered Helen in tears in the graveyard, after she'd spoken to her father, and how sex had distracted her, seemed more important for a while. Beside me was Judith, staring through the windscreen, seeing nothing, unless, perhaps, her father's face stared back at her. Then there was Alison, alone in the telephone box, listening to a stranger's voice, knowing that the stranger might have been her father, if things had worked out differently.

Helen placed her suitcase down. She had changed her clothes, wore her own white dress and denim jacket. She looked nervous, as if she expected me to bark at her.

'I'm really sorry, Harry.'

'No. I'm sorry.'

'Why? I walked out on you.'

'Perfectly understandable.'

'I'm not coming back.'

'I know that.'

'But if I could just kip . . .'

'I'll take the spare room. That's understood.'

She nodded. I opened the door. Judith, to her credit, switched on the charm.

'So,' she said, 'where to?'

'Were you going out?' Helen asked.

'To Wells,' Judith said. 'But we can forget it.'

'No.' Helen spoke firmly. 'Drop me off and you two go out.'

It must have taken some guts to say that. I knew that she was jealous of Judith and me.

'We've left it too late, I think,' Judith said. 'And we can't leave you at the cottage. The place is crawling with journalists.'

'We'll all go back,' I agreed. 'Hole up for the night. I can cook noodles.'

We barely spoke in the car. Perhaps none of us knew where to begin. When Helen announced that she'd eaten and needed to sleep, I felt relieved. There was a definite tension between the three of us. And I'd been looking forward to talking with Judith. I'd speak with Helen in the morning.

We were photographed as we left the car, but beyond that we weren't bothered that evening. We kept the curtains closed and, as I cooked, Judith sat at the table and began to read the journals. I had decided, in the car, that she should see them. I realised, finally, that I trusted her. It was a step forward, a small achievement.

She said nothing as she read, but her presence was comforting. I chopped and sliced and threw everything in the pan. I opened a bottle of wine. It must have been adrenaline that kept me going or else the trauma of the day had been such that I couldn't rest, however I desired it. Fixated, I turned events over in my mind. Hake lay wounded in hospital. Ern dead. I couldn't get what had happened out of my head. I kept remembering his face as he fell, his arm flailing hopelessly. It seemed absurd that I should be there in Hope Cottage, cooking a meal, when earlier I had been waving a gun about, battering a case full of stuffed birds. I put the noodles on the table with a ladle and two bowls.

'Ready to take a break?' I said.

Judith looked up as if she'd forgotten me. She shook her head in astonishment at what she'd been reading.

'I didn't expect anything like this,' she said.

'No. Neither did I.'

'How did Ern get hold of it?'

'Haven't a clue. I don't suppose it matters really. They've survived. That's what counts.'

'This stuff about Bella's uncle. It's so revealing.'

'What exactly?'

' "How is it that the dying man smiles?" Remember that? They're laughing in the face of death, Harry. And the way she writes, it's like it's another person. Still something girlish and naïve about it, but so much stronger than *Sweet Susan*. I mean, the way she describes herself. "To be less than a shadow." Where is it? Here.

"To live and yet to have no substance." Can you imagine that level of despair?'

'I've known despair, but not quite like that. You're right. She writes as if only annihilation was enough. But she wasn't always like that.'

'That's the weirdest thing, I guess. The way she writes about Bella and Robert – there's such involvement. It doesn't seem possible that a person who felt like that could write with such objectivity.'

'You should know, I suppose.'

'What do you mean?'

'I mean you're the expert.'

I began to ladle the noodles into bowls, but Judith wasn't fooled by the friendliness of the gesture.

'You should make up your mind, Harry.'

'Hmmm?'

'Whether I'm friend or foe.'

'Ah.'

'What will it be then?'

I gave a wry smile.

'I'll think about it,' I said.

But as we ate, I began, slowly, to talk to her. We talked, first, about the shooting. I could not imagine how it might affect Hake. I tried not to think about it. I found myself filling Judith in on details of the story that she didn't know, recounting fully my latest visits to Ern. I knew that, by talking, I was going against everything I'd ever believed. As biographer, Judith ought, indeed, to have been the enemy. But it wasn't quite so simple. If such a book were to be written by anyone, I figured it should be her.

I told Judith particularly what had happened that morning. How Ern had forced me to climb through the window and the look of his face: yellow, mask-like, the fresh scab on his cheek. I told her about George and the serpents, revealed how my own grandfather had threatened to betray Bella to her husband and how this had been the catalyst that had driven her to suicide. Judith was fascinated. She was on good form that evening, looking good, enjoying herself. Between mouthfuls, she'd ask me questions, and even when she was shocked, she appeared high-spirited. I didn't blame her for this, because I needed to talk and I saw, in her fascination, something of Alison's.

Upstairs, Helen probably lay awake, feeling herself excluded. We'd had a few glasses by now but that did not alter our seriousness. I wanted Judith to know everything, how I'd felt when Ern held the gun to his forehead, and the strangeness of his subsequent behaviour when he took me to be Charles Bliss. I told her about Ern's childhood and the incident with Mr Darwin's book. I took my time. I went on to describe the room where he died and explained how it was there that I saw myself divided, fragmented in Ern's mirrors. I spoke about the hour-glass and how it cracked on the floor, seconds before his head. Naturally, she refused to believe me. She said she wouldn't put that in her book if I paid her to. At this, the implications of my talking really hit home. I had a moment of panic, when I wanted to take back every word, but of course it was too late.

'It's OK,' Judith said, without prompting. 'I'm not one of them.'

'Sorry?'

'Not one of Ern's "paper-men".'

'We draw a distinction, I know. But I wonder whether any writing about Alison isn't in some way amoral?'

'I've thought about that too, but it's not true. What I want to do is analytic.'

'Whatever. I've always believed that we shouldn't expose her any further.'

'I don't want to expose. I want to approach understanding. Don't forget, what you've just told me is no part of my story. It's anecdotal. Interesting, but not relevant. Ern's story and Bella's – they're only important for my book in so far as they influenced Alison. What matters more to me is Alison's psyche and the society that helped to create it.'

'I don't know . . .'

'I want to change people's perceptions, Harry. Ambitious, yes. But I want to make it clear that there are more valuable things a woman can do with her pen than writing extended suicide notes.'

'Is that what you imagine Alison's novel to be?'

'I never saw it, so I can't be sure. But it's my hunch, yes. Why else did she leave such a short note to you? Because she believed that the novel would speak for her; she knew Ern had the notebooks. Oh, she was too self-absorbed, Harry, you know that.' For once I had to agree. 'Her intelligence could have been put to better use.'

'Will you try to explain her suicide,' I asked, 'in your biography?'

'Can *you* explain it?'

I shook my head. 'I can tell you some of the contributing factors. But the thing itself? No. Loneliness isn't enough. Nor fame. Nor self-doubt.'

'Something Camus wrote . . .'

'Camus? Did you get that far – in the journals?'

'No? Does she mention him?'

I nodded.

'Well, I remember she was reading his work. We talked about it.'

'Ah.' I paused. 'Moths about a flame.'

Judith looked quizzical.

'That's how she described the two of you. When you talked about suicide.'

'Nice.' She paused as if remembering something. 'What else did she reveal that I've yet to read?'

'She writes about your father. That he committed suicide. Though she doesn't say how.'

She paused, taken aback.

'You don't want to know how, Harry.'

I didn't know what to say.

'So what did Camus write?' I asked.

She seemed pleased of the distraction.

'I found it this morning. I half remembered it. Then I looked it up: "An act like this is prepared within the silence of the heart as is a great work of art." '

'A work of art?' I considered it. 'I'm not so sure. Though I suppose, in the end, her suicide is practically all we have. The real work of art is lost.'

'Only she didn't intend it that way.'

'No. But something artful in the way she copied Bella.'

'Sure. But what interests me', she said, 'is the other phrase – "the silence of the heart". That's just it, isn't it? We'll never really know. It might as well read, "the silence of the grave".'

'Very catchy,' I said. 'Make a good title for your book!'

'Come on. Don't mock. I mean silence is all we have left. All we do is conjecture and imagine. We can't get inside her body. We weren't there.'

'No,' I said. 'You're right. It's hidden. Some devious plan. Maybe it began before I ever met her.'

'She suggests as much. When she writes about "going back to that house"; unearthing the past. And she's so worried about what her father might think. I mean, I never heard her say a good word about that man.'

'I don't think she knew how to,' I said.

I was thinking again about her final night. The image of her, alone in the telephone box. It was as if I watched her from a distance, or perhaps I was the driver that passed by, illumining the fields with my headlights but not stopping to save her. I saw the darkness of that night and her in the kiosk beneath fluorescent light, clutching the receiver, listening to the disembodied voice of her father. She must have known, in those moments, what I knew now. That the kiosk could not protect her. It was fragile; man-made; a mere membrane that sheltered her. In leaving London, perhaps she had been looking for such exposure. She had felt hemmed in by brick terraces and smog. Here there was only the clear air; the night. It was no wonder she felt a certain lightness. Yet perhaps she realised, also, the terror of this, of our essential solitude. She looked that night for a connection but there was none.

'What is it, Harry?'

Judith began gathering the plates of half-eaten food.

'Nothing,' I said. 'It won't do to fall apart.'

'What will you do? In London?'

'Face the future. What else?'

'We'll speak on the phone, right?'

'Of course. The question of the book.'

'Not just the book.'

I nodded; smiled.

'No. But I imagine your biography will dominate our conversation for some time.'

Now it was her turn to smile, only she stifled her pleasure somewhat.

'Thanks, Harry.'

'Don't mention it,' I said. 'I shall need some diversion, I think.'

The truth was that, despite everything, I was beginning to feel a peculiar optimism. Perhaps, having sunk so low, I could only imagine that things must now get better. I had spent so long in the pursuit of answers that now, when I realised their absence, I felt oddly liberated.

'You must come up and stay sometime. I'd like you to meet Liz.'

'Yes. I might just do that.'

I knew that she pitied me. But I had never been afraid of solitude and already I had plans. Not just the old plans – India, Mexico – though these still beckoned – but something else I had to do. For Alison.

When Judith said good-bye that evening, I kissed her on both cheeks and the two of us hesitated slightly on the door-step.

'We'll be in touch, OK?' she said.

'I'll get these journals copied and sent to you pronto. I trust you to do a good job and knock Paul Vinton's book off the shelves.'

She must have known what it took for me to say that, but she chose not to acknowledge it.

'It's not what I meant.'

'No,' I said, 'I know. Now go, woman!'

She shook her head, smiling in mock desperation. Then she turned and walked up the path. I closed the door and stood there for a moment, still warmed by her presence. Then I left the kitchen, switched off the light and made my way to the bathroom.

# 37

I AWOKE EARLY, BEFORE Helen. It had hardly been a comfortable night and it had taken me several hours to get to sleep but I found myself now, unexpectedly, in buoyant spirits. I opened the curtains on a fine, dry day and smiled to see the fields stretching away to meet the salt marshes; the sea beyond.

Doubtless I was glad to have made it thus far. A gaggle of reporters were approaching the cottage, but I'd already resolved not to let them get to me. I wasn't sure how Judith would play Mrs Bobbin's book-burning incident, but I guessed the truth would come out and I would finally be absolved of guilt. In the meantime, I was content to ignore them. I had more important things to consider.

Helen seemed surprised at my good humour. I took her tea in bed and she appeared embarrassed, perhaps even suspicious, believing – wrongly – that my intention was to win her back. True, when I saw her, with only a sheet wrapped about her for modesty, I felt a deep pang of desire; an immense longing that I knew I would carry with me always. It is possible that I tortured myself that morning, perched on her bed, watching her sip tea and smile knowingly. There was a moment when I believed I would lean over and touch her. How could I not imagine it? She wore a slightly pained expression but, in a sense, she had never looked so beautiful. Perhaps it was the light. From where I sat, I could see nothing beyond the window but the sky, the vast, pale profusion of it, and it seemed to me that all the light of that sky was here in this room, illumining her hair, her face, her skin. Or was it, rather, that she held the light within her? That she had, at the heart of her, a brilliance that only the young may possess. She did not know – how could she? – the effect of her presence. She smiled, and I took the empty cup from her hand. Our fingers brushed together, so briefly, and I hesitated, thinking – now, now is the moment. I believed, perhaps, it was at least possible that she might respond.

'You're being so sweet, Harry,' she said.

'Why shouldn't I be?'

'I've been rotten.'

'Not at all. I rather deserved it, I imagine.'

The sheet had fallen from her leg. I wanted to bend down and caress it; to kiss the small hollow behind her knee, to catch the scent of her. She looked at me – such a lack of guile, such openness in those eyes. Her hair fell across her face and she brushed it away, not knowing that so simple an action was enough to make me weep. I stood up, moved to the window. Out there, in the distance, sea met sky. Blue met blue, no line, merely a dissolving of matter. I wanted to be out there, in that gauzy no-man's-land. But it was out of reach. When I turned, again, to Helen, it was with the knowledge that we would never again be alone like this. We would leave this house, this moment, behind us. We would move on.

'Look, Harry, about Phil . . .'

I shook my head. I needed no explanation.

'It was nothing. I was just angry.'

'I know. I know.'

Still, I tried not to picture them together.

'His mother was awful, wasn't she?'

'I'm rather biased about that woman,' I said.

She laughed and paused then, as if she had something important to say. She looked away, then back again, with such anguish that it was difficult to bear.

'I've had the best time, Harry.'

I thought, hearing that, that I might at last crack; that I was wrong to give her up. I would do something, anything, to get her back; seduce her again with words.

'Yes. So have I,' I said. 'I shan't ever forget it.'

I leant over and touched her hand. I gave her a fatherly kiss on the forehead. Then I went to the door. 'I'll get us breakfast,' I said and left the room.

Over toast and cereal, we talked about our plans. There was something false about our chat now, as if neither of us could bear too much honesty. We were interrupted several times by a knocking at the door, but knowing it to be reporters, we ignored it.

'We'll be on the road soon,' I said. 'It's a good day for the drive.'

I was remembering the other drive, just five days previously, when we had stopped to picnic in the fields, full of hope and expectation.

'Yes,' she said. 'I'm glad it's not too hot.'

'Your father will be pleased to see you.'

'Will he?' Her voice was flat and dull. 'I don't know what I'll say to him.'

'Say you're sorry.'

She looked towards the window and closed her eyes.

'Helen?'

She did not reply. Now she was shutting herself in. I couldn't reach her. I went to stand, thinking I should leave her alone but the movement seemed to rouse her and she spoke.

'But I'm not sorry,' she said. 'I'm not sure I even want to see him.'

I hardly knew what to tell her. I was glad that she was not sorry, that she found it perhaps impossible to regret the days we had spent together. But her second comment distressed me. I couldn't help but think of Alison. It had occurred to me that the telephone box which she had visited on her final night, was the same box where Helen had also called her father, to tell him of our affair. Afterwards, I had chosen to ignore her anguish. I had put my own desires before her attachment to her father and his to her. Even when he had visited me, and I had seen him, pale, broken, I had refused to give in. Worse, Helen had been ready to leave, but I had used my last remaining weapon to keep her: the word 'love'. If I had not used it when I did she would have gone back with him, but in desperation I had let it slip, when nothing else would do. And was it love? Might I say, at least, that I did not lie to keep her? Or was it rather true that I have only ever loved one woman and her name was Alison Bliss?

I had not forgotten Richard's words on that day. 'Don't get my daughter involved in your stupid attempts at self-redemption.' Maybe he was right. I had believed, foolishly, that my own experience here was more important than his loss. Now I did not believe it. I had seen too many broken connections, human beings divided, to think my own little quest of much importance. True, the notebook was now in my possession and I felt calmer, clearer than I had done for years. But who else had gained from this? Would Judith's book make any difference to her life or that of others? Was Mrs Bobbin right and could Ern's death be traced directly to our presence? Certainly, if Judith or Vinton had never spilled the beans, he might still be there, living in his self-imposed exile from the outside world.

The more I thought about these issues, the more confused I became. When I arrived in Glaven, I had wanted answers but I had discovered, finally, that there were none. Now, remorseful with regard to Richard yet unable to fully regret my actions, I could only conclude that life is complicated and all we can do is make the best of it.

'Why don't you want to see him?' I said at last.

'He'll never forgive me.'

'He won't forgive *me*, Helen. But you? He might be grouchy for a while, but you can't truly doubt that he wants you back?'

'Things won't be the same.'

'No,' I said. 'You've grown up somewhat.'

It didn't take long to pack. We had brought the bare minimum. I had a short while alone downstairs while Helen got ready and I wandered about the place, taking it in for the last time. Oddly I felt no nostalgia, only a dull regret that I didn't like to analyse. Already I was eager to get going. I was glad when Helen came downstairs and handed me a small bundle.

'Her clothes,' she said, and I nodded.

As we left, half a dozen reporters crowded us, thrust their microphones, shouted questions, about Ern in particular, about Hake. Helen was clearly rattled and we barged through them, determined not to speak. It was clear, from our suitcases, that we were leaving. What more did they need to know? At last, we approached the car. As I went to open the door, however, one of the journalists came closer, placed a thick envelope in my hand. He spoke quietly, insistently.

'I've seen Gordon,' he said, 'in the hospital. He asked me to give you this.'

I wanted to ask how Hake was, but the others crowded in. Clutching the envelope, I got into the car. The journalist smiled, grimly, and waved. I started the engine and drove off, leaving Hope

Cottage and the garden behind us. It was not until we were out of the village, driving east towards Salthouse again, that I stopped in a lay-by.

'What do you think it is?' Helen said.

She wound down her window and we each of us paused to look out, across the reeds, to the distant, shimmering horizon. Slowly, I peeled the tape that sealed the envelope. I had guessed, already, what I would find. Now, in the palm of my hand, I held a pile of photographs. The negatives slipped to the floor as I turned them over, one by one. There, at last, she was again. Naked. But not as I had expected. There was nothing crude or distasteful about these images. Alison lay on a crumpled bed, sleeping. There was a tenderness here, which even I could not deny: her face in repose; her bare limbs relaxed. There was an intimacy; a startling innocence. Alison had so feared the existence of these photographs that I had imagined they would be vulgar, even pornographic. Instead, here, she was untouched, like a sleeping child. A note slid from the envelope, in Hake's hand. 'Something the old man said, Harry: "The living have no hold on the dead. It's the dead that have a hold on the living." '

I could hardly believe it. That Hake should relent at last. A small noise rasped from my throat. I did not know what it was at first, until there it was again; laughter. I laughed louder, riotously, uproariously. I climbed out of the car, gasping for breath, barely knowing how or why I was laughing. I could not explain it. I only knew that this great whoop of joy was for real. It was a large, human laughter. Even the wind, I thought, could not swallow such a sound.

# Epilogue

I WROTE THE LETTER the day after my return to London. I acted quickly, while my resolve was fresh, and I suppose I had a need to write it. It gave me a sense of purpose at a time when I might otherwise have been at a loss. I don't know what I expected from it. Certainly I did not want to delve further into the past, though my actions might be read that way. Rather, I was looking for resolution; a way forward. It was not possible to remedy what had gone before, but I wanted something positive to emerge from the mire.

The idea occurred soon after I had read the journal. Sitting at the window, before Judith arrived to rouse me, I had imagined it all: the letter; the response; the meeting. It seemed clear that in her final days, Alison had been shaken by the knowledge that she had failed to know her father. I did not count this the sole reason for her suicide, but it played a large enough role for me to take it seriously. After all, I'd suffered the same fate, never knowing the cripple at the card-table, the son of George Bliss: my own father.

But it was not my father that I was thinking of now. He was dead and buried and I'd come to terms long ago with the inevitability of that failed relationship. I could not have helped his drinking nor his distance from me, any more than I could have made him see that he had not lost his son simply because his son had gained an education.

Rather it was Alison's father that intrigued me. I wondered, was he still the dapper fellow I had met before, the vague but somewhat charming man who barely ever met my eye? I knew so little about him. At the funeral, he was so choked up he didn't speak. He left after the service and, when he shook my hand, I had believed he was about to say something but clearly he thought better of it and managed only a brave half-smile. As for Alison's version of her father, it was surely partial. She realised it herself in the end. The man who sat alone in his study, reading poetry, mourning the death of his wife – these just a collection of facts, revealing little. What of the man himself? How had he learned to live with his double tragedy?

A couple of weeks went by, if I remember rightly, and I'd almost given up hope. I got by, somehow, with rather a lot of help from Judith and some inspiration from a few travel brochures and guide books. In truth, I was desperate to get away again. London seemed a hollow place now. I missed school and I missed Richard. Helen phoned me a couple of times, never from home, but I knew that I should keep away from her, at least for a while. Often, at night, in the yellow, incomplete darkness of the City, I'd lie in bed and remember how it felt to have her beside me. I could almost see her, stretched out on her belly, her face turned in repose. Sometimes the memory was too much and I'd rise weeping. I would stand before the bathroom mirror, clutching the sink, wondering who this man was before me, why he wept, what he had lost.

Then, one morning, I received a response to my letter. Alison's father had moved to Wales, he explained, and my letter had not been immediately forwarded. He was immensely apologetic, as if the mix-up had been his fault. His note was short, polite, enthusiastic. Yes, he would be delighted to meet me. He had always regretted not knowing Alison's husband. By chance he would be in London the following week to visit friends. Might I suggest a convenient meeting-place?

We spoke briefly on the phone to fix it up. Even his voice confounded my expectations. He spoke slowly, with long pauses, choosing his words carefully. It was a more resonant voice than I remembered; a serious voice. We agreed to meet in the White Swan for lunch and he asked if I knew any good second-hand bookshops in the area. He always enjoyed browsing in London bookshops, he said. Perhaps I could accompany him?

We fixed the meeting for the following Tuesday. When the day arrived, I began to wish I'd chosen some other meeting-place but it was too late to make changes now. Later, as I made my way through the little maze of streets that led to the pub, I began to feel more comfortable. It was a fine afternoon, and there was a buzz about the place that is only experienced in London at the height of summer. Something about the shedding of clothes, I imagine, that makes people more congenial. I'd almost forgotten how I liked that area. It was so different from the rest of the City, more lived-in; the red-brick buildings less imposing, the roads narrower and quiet. I even remembered to look up that afternoon at the small patch of blue sky above, the ornamentation on the eaves, the unexpected profusion of window-boxes.

I entered the cul-de-sac which led to the pub. There were a few benches left outside in the courtyard. No sign yet of Alison's father. Inside, I ordered the beers and as I brought them out again, I struggled to erase memories of my last time here, when Richard had invited me to dinner and unwittingly sealed the end of our friendship. As I sat down, I asked myself if I would have had it differently. Given the chance, would I have resisted my attraction to Helen and preserved the status quo? Before I could answer, I was distracted by the sight of a man who turned into the street, looking rather lost, squinting up at the street names on the corner. I recognised him immediately. He was tall, somewhat broader than I remembered, dressed in a creased linen suit. As he came closer, I saw his face, a tight exuberance about it that I had not expected. I stood up and waved to him. When I caught his eye, he seemed to laugh as if in relief. He walked towards me and when he shook my hand, I was surprised by the warmth of it.

# A NOTE ON THE AUTHOR

Jacqui Lofthouse was born in 1965. She studied Drama and English at Bristol University and has an M.A. in Creative Writing from the University of East Anglia. She has worked as a script-reader, radio producer, actress and teacher. Her first novel, *The Temple of Hymen* was published in 1995. Jacqui Lofthouse lives in London.

## A NOTE ON THE TYPE

The text of this book is set in Linotype Sabon,
named after the type founder, Jacques Sabon. It
was designed by Jan Tschichold and jointly
developed by Linotype, Monotype and Stempel,
in response to a need for a typeface to be
available in identical form for mechanical hot
metal composition and hand composition using
foundry type.

Tschichold based his design for Sabon roman on
a fount engraved by Garamond, and Sabon italic
on a fount by Granjon. It was first used in 1966
and has proved an enduring modern classic.